THE BOOK OF THOTH

Carya Gish

arcane
publishing

ISBN: 978-0-9573572-1-1

Cover artwork, design and typesetting:
Matt ArtPix
(www.mattartpix.com)

Back cover dragonfly by
Lelong Designs
(www.lelongdesigns.com)

Printed and bound in the UK
by Bell & Bain Ltd,
Glasgow

In memory of
Raymonde Pons
and
Jane Mage

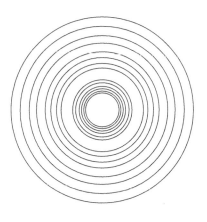

Special thanks to Corinne Cox
and of course to Matt Cox whose
support has made everything possible.

Cast of Characters

Adam Tuckfield, private tutor

Dimitri Chronos, future adventurer and explorer

Lord Vangelis Chronos, scholar, scientist, alchemist; Dimitri's stepfather

Saturnin Bloom, Lord Chronos's assistant and secretary

Lady Sophia Chronos, former stage actress, Dimitri's mother

Maeve Hayward, jazz journalist, Lord Chronos's niece

Lady Amunet 'Amy' Whitemoor, Egyptian princess and high priestess

Elliott Mills, head gardener

Mrs Abbott, cook

Gabby Ramsey, socialite

Gilbert Ramsey, journalist and dandy

Gladys, maid

Ginny, Lady's maid

Mr Simms, head butler

Mr Suleman, estate manager

Paul, kitchen boy/porter

Rose, kitchen maid

Ethel Taylor, dressmaker

Brother Thomas, member of 'The Family'

Sister Angelina, member of 'The Family'

Will Reynolds, injured WW1 soldier and Elliott Mills's friend

Prayer to Thoth

Oh thou, majesty of the godhead, wisdom-crowned Tahuti,
Lord of the gates of the universe.

Thee, thee I invoke.

Oh thou of the ibis head. Thee, thee I invoke.

Thou who wieldest the wand of double power. Thee, thee I invoke.

Thou who bearest in thy left hand the rose and cross of light and life.
Thee, thee I invoke.

Thou whose head is as an emerald, and thy nemyss as the night sky blue.
Thee, thee I invoke.

Thou whose skin is a flaming orange as though it burned in a furnace.
Thee, thee I invoke.

Behold, I am yesterday, today, and the brother of tomorrow. I am born
again and again. Mine is the unseen force whereof the gods are sprung,
which is as life unto the dwellers in the Watchtowers of the Universe.

Invocation of Thoth - Esoteric Order of the Golden Dawn

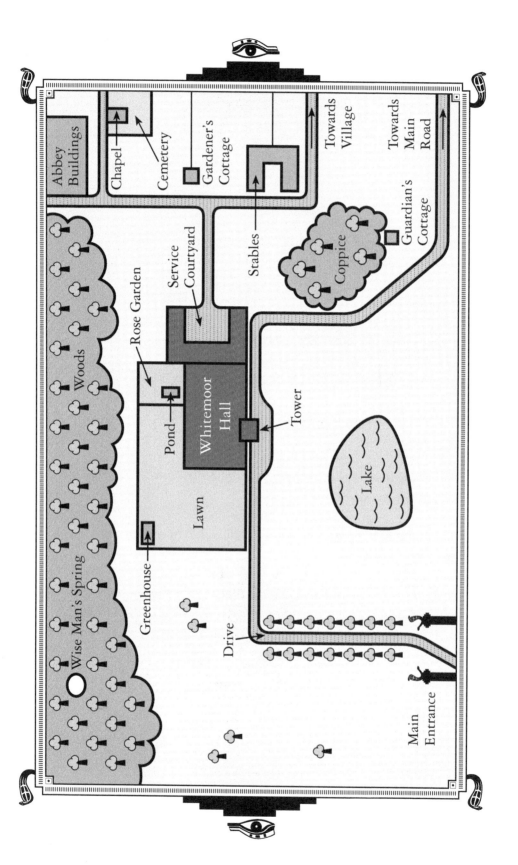

Abbey Buildings

Chapel

Cemetery

Gardener's Cottage

Towards Village

Towards Main Road

Stables

Service Courtyard

Coppice

Guardian's Cottage

Rose Garden

Woods

Greenhouse

Pond

Whitemoor Hall

Wise Man's Spring

Lawn

Tower

Drive

Lake

Main Entrance

PART I

At the Wise Man's Spring
September 1925

ONE

Here goes my summer!' thought Dimitri with a heavy heart as the storm raged outside. It had already lasted two days and didn't show any signs of weakening.

The boy was being kept inside like a sad little prisoner and was spending most of his time with his forehead pressed against the cool, smooth glass surface of the tall study room window with his knees resting on the embroidered cushions of the window seat. He was studying the screaming, cataclysmic rage of the sky with a mixture of apprehension and excitement; he had always marvelled at the power of Nature.

The summer had been unusually splendid and Dimitri had happily carried on his endless exploration of the Whitemoor estate, barely noticing the passing of time. But now it was September, and the boy could feel that his beloved freedom was running out. Soon enough, he would be forced indoors for hours on end; he dreaded the long, gloomy winter evenings.

The battering winds, the rain pouring out of the sky and the thunder had as much of a destructive effect inside the house as it had outside: it had sent Dimitri's mother into one of her angry, despairing fits and he had heard her scream and throw things around her large bedroom upstairs. As usual, he hadn't been allowed in the immediate vicinity but had hung around long enough to see Ginny, his mother's maid, come out of her mistress's rooms bleeding from a large scratch to the cheek. Then at some point, Vangelis and Mr Bloom had gone in and administered whatever drug they had to calm his mother down. Afterwards, she had kept to her room – under close supervision – for the remainder of the storm.

Sophia Chronos – Sophia Augarde at the time – had given birth to her son eleven years earlier on a warm, sticky stormy night, with the wind and lightning relentlessly assaulting her gloomy Covent Garden lodgings. The pain had been unbearable, the blood loss terrifying; her tormented flesh had been ripped apart and for several days, she had barely been alive. Miraculously, and to her doctor's astonishment, she had survived; but she had been scarred forever, physically and psychologically. Since then, Sophia had been a mere shadow, if an impossibly graceful one. The ordeal didn't seem to have ruined her beauty; if anything, it had made her more otherworldly, poignantly fragile. But it had also reduced her promising acting career to mere ashes.

The storm had brought everything back from that night in 1914 and Sophia had lost her mind: she had rolled around on the thick rug, hitting her belly, scratching it until it bled, tearing at her clothes, at her hair. Her milky, flawless skin had been badly bruised; she had bitten her lovely lips, cried until her beautiful dark brown eyes had gone all red and puffy and howled until her vocal chords couldn't take it anymore.

Dimitri had remained ignorant of the role he had been playing in his mother's daily misery. All he knew was that she was a quiet, ethereal person whom he shouldn't upset and who ought to be left alone. He had grown used to her erratic behaviour: she could be attentively reading one of her books one moment and then suddenly stand up and take her place by a window, her eyes glazed over, and stay thus for several hours: immobile, looking at something or nothing out there in the garden or on the horizon. The boy couldn't make any demands on her, and he had learnt to be increasingly self-reliant – especially since the departure of his latest governess – spending so much time on his own that he had grown almost wary of the sound of his own voice.

TWO

At last, the wind and the rain receded. When Dimitri woke up to a silent house on the morning of the third day, he threw away the thick blanket, jumped out of bed and ran to the window to have a peek outside.

The sky was still tormented by some grey and uninviting clouds, but they were high enough for him to know that it probably wouldn't rain that day, or only lightly. The gravel on the terrace, the vast lawn as well as the water in the pond were covered in leaves and broken branches. Further away, on the edges of the woods, the tree tops looked funny, all lopsided and ruffled up. Everything appeared soaked and ready to dissolve on the spot like lumps of sugar in water.

Elliott the gardener was going to be mightily cross, thought Dimitri. He quite liked Elliott. Like him, the gardener was a quiet, thoughtful type. But contrary to the boy, who was slight and small, Elliott Mills was tall and powerfully built, and his eyes of steel dominated a strong-featured face. Dimitri envied him a little. That's how he wanted to be when he grew up, full of confidence, honour, bravery and strength; and much like the gardener, he wanted to work close to Nature, get his hands dirty and feel the earth under his fingers, smell the flowers and the plants all day long and, most importantly, avoid talking to anyone.

Dimitri wasn't so sure he would be able to be like Elliott. He knew that he was fair like his mother, that he was painfully shy, introverted, fearful and generally ignorant of the world outside the gates of the house. Not that he knew much more of what was going on *inside* those finely crafted cast iron gates…

He encouraged and dared himself. He regularly set himself some challenges, because no one else did, and he thought it would help him grow stronger. He sometimes worried that his efforts would not lead to anything, and he most certainly didn't receive any encouragement from the people around him. He knew that they didn't really like him and saw him more like a hindrance than anything else. Vangelis and Mr Bloom were busy with their research and their studies, the staff behaved like automatons and performed their tasks without thinking about anything much, their eyes empty and vague; they were just *there*. Maybe their vows prevented them from interacting too much with people from outside their community. Nobody had explained to him what was going on there at the abbey, not really. He had tried to discover more about them, but he had never managed to catch a glimpse of what was going on inside the old, weathered walls.

Vangelis, his stepfather, had explained to him once that the people at the abbey had suffered terribly because of the war and that the community had been a refuge for them. But the scholar had never gone into much detail, because he never had enough time and would invariably interrupt himself, turn round and trot back to his study, his long coat floating around him and his white beard trembling with scholarly anticipation. Vangelis would sometimes disappear for days on end, somewhere in the belly of the house. Everybody knew His Work was important.

Yet, if his stepfather didn't find time for him, he would manage to spare some of it for Sophia. Dimitri had always been stunned by the adoration Vangelis had for his much younger wife: he literally revered her, absolutely, completely. The boy would sometimes observe the couple discreetly, not entirely understanding the patient, attentive courtship performed by his stepfather, who was invariably met with a cold, barely polite behaviour on his wife's part. Even the boy could see the one-sidedness of this love. He didn't really comprehend the funny ways of adults. He probably would, one day, but he wasn't in any hurry.

* * *

It was with great relief that Dimitri sat at the little round table in the deserted morning room. His mother would probably not appear before the evening, he predicted. He had been told that Vangelis and Mr Bloom were working on a complex piece of research and hadn't gone to bed at all for several days. How could people not sleep at night, he wondered. Dimitri loved sleeping; sometimes, it was so much simpler than being awake. His bed was also wide and comfortable, the pillows bouncy and the bedcovers all soft. It provided him with the kind of physical warmth and tenderness he couldn't find anywhere else. Yes, sleeping was one of Dimitri's favourite activities, together with reading and exploring the house and grounds.

His *least* favourite thing was eating, hence the joy of finding himself on his own for his breakfast on that post-storm morning. Nobody would be staring at him as he fiddled with the food, no one would make acerbic comments about him being so strange a child, so ungrateful, so very beastly for upsetting his mother and Cook. Sophia herself didn't eat much either, but she was getting away with it because she was 'a Lady'; Dimitri was a young boy and it was considered odd that he wouldn't like his food. When he still had a governess, most meals would turn into a psychological battleground. This routine had been going on for as long as Dimitri could remember, and they had been going through the motions at almost every single mealtime.

Nowadays, everyone felt awkward when he happened to like something that was on the table and didn't 'make a terrible fuss', as Sophia always reproached him. He was not being fussy; he just didn't like eating. He found it vaguely unnatural and off-putting; when people chewed, they looked very similar to the placid cows and the nervously disposed sheep he saw in the fields. Pronounced tastes were too strong a shock to his system and all the cooking smells would turn his delicate stomach. And he couldn't, just *couldn't*, eat any dead animal.

Gladys, the maid, soon entered carrying a tray burdened with various plates, one cup and saucer, bits of crockery, a couple of dishes and a pot-bellied teapot.

'It's just you this morning, Master Dimitri. Ginny said Madam needed to rest again today.'

Gladys had recited her usual line without a smile on her freckled face; there had been no intonation in her flat voice. The girl silently positioned the various objects on the flowery tablecloth and poured some tea in the cup, then stood next to the table, waiting awkwardly.

'Thank you, Gladys. I'll ring when I've finished,' said Dimitri.

He was relieved when she was out of the room. A plain, unhappy girl of about 15, Gladys was a shifty grey presence gliding along the walls and corridors of the house. But Dimitri knew there was a little bit more to her; he could feel, sometimes *see* her pervading sadness, the subtle aura that surrounded her, and it made him uncomfortable. He was glad to be sitting on his own to drink his tea, without anybody's emotional energy putting him off. He lifted the silver lid of the dish: the smell of hot, buttery scrambled eggs made him wrinkle his nose and he slammed the top back on. Two pieces of dry toast would probably do, that morning. He ignored the butter and jam and concentrated instead on his beverage; he had his tea black, with a little sugar.

The sound of something rolling over the gravel outside attracted him to the window: he stood there for a while, sucking on his toast, observing Elliott Mills who was getting ready to clear up the mess left by the storm. The gardener was on his own; his two young apprentices hadn't yet arrived from the village or were busy doing something else in another part of the estate. There was so much to do at Whitemoor Hall, and the grounds were so vast that the boy had always wondered how Elliott could do it all with only two assistants. Some people from the abbey would give him a hand from time to time when necessary, but Elliott didn't seem to like the community and made sure he avoided its members as much as possible. His two apprentices had been recruited by him at the nearest village, and he had always been adamant about not allowing the abbey community to interfere with his work.

Dimitri managed to tear himself away from the window and gulped down the rest of his tea standing up. All he wanted now was to get out of the house and feel the fresh morning air on his cheeks. He pulled the rope to ring for Gladys to come and collect the tray but didn't wait for her, and instead made his way downstairs to the cloakroom at the back of the service quarters. He hadn't passed anyone on his way along the corridors, but now he could hear the clutter of activity coming from the kitchen. The service quarters had always felt more alive than the rest of the house – even though the staff were certainly quiet compared to that of any other country house. In truth, the whole domestic set up at Whitemoor Hall was unusual and only loosely structured.

Dimitri looked for one of his coats for quite a while before getting his hands on an oversized woollen jacket. He opened and closed the door as silently as possible: he hoped to slip out unnoticed.

THREE

As soon as he was out, Dimitri turned his back on the manor house and headed straight to the woods. He thought about going round the building and stopping by Elliott's wheelbarrow to have a chat with him, but he wasn't sure the gardener would appreciate the diversion from his work. The boy's leather boots were sinking into the saturated ground with squelching noises. He would have to be careful not to slip over the leaves or slippery roots in the woods. Everything looked off-kilter, as if the storm had vigorously shaken the countryside and put it back not exactly in the right order. The birds were incredibly noisy and their chatter resonated across the sky, filling the whole horizon. He shivered… The storm had definitely put an end to the mildness.

At last, he reached one of the paths that criss-crossed the estate beyond the lawn and entered the wood. The ground was strewn with leaves and broken twigs; the trees were still shaking off their extra moisture, and the boy got bombarded with cold drops of water that splattered his face. He could even feel the ones falling on his head as in his hurry, he hadn't taken any hat. He mischievously thought about Mr Bloom's shaven, shiny cranium. What would it feel like having the water from the trees fall on *his* head? Would it be very cold? Would it tickle? The thought made him smile to himself, especially as he reminisced about the glum Mr Bloom's non-existent sense of humour.

Under the trees, everything was glistening and dripping, and the air smelt of moss, decaying leaves, mushrooms and drenched wood. Dimitri liked it very much. It was the smell of, well, of *life*, of the ever changing nature of the countryside. He preferred those raw, natural fragrances to the ones he would perceive around the house: the waxed but lifeless wood of the furniture, the vaguely dusty whiff emanating from the carpets and rugs, the choking heaviness of the smoke coming out of Vangelis's beloved pipe, Mr Bloom's strangely fragrant cigarettes, his mother's feminine but artificial flowery scent. He inhaled deeply: his lungs were gladly clearing up the air accumulated during the two whole days he had spent inside.

After about ten minutes, he arrived at The Cross, thus named after the worn out, moss-covered old stone cross that stood on the spot where the three main paths split. Without hesitation, Dimitri took the smaller track to the left.

In his head, he had already decided on the day's route: he would spend some time at the Wise Man's Spring, where he would make sure that the flow of water hadn't been blocked off by leaves and branches. He would then walk across the woodland to the south and along the footpath sandwiched between the edge of the wood and the outer wall of the abbey. He could have a look at the angels in the graveyard; who knows, he might even see Nutty, the resident red squirrel! Then he would walk up Greenside Hill where Elliott's cottage was located. And finally, if he had time, he could finish off his day at the small lake and watch the ducks and swans paddle around the smooth water.

He had remembered to slip his notepad and pencil in the large inside pocket of the coat and would take some notes on his walk. He liked writing things down; it gave him a purpose. Also, as soon as he had started being aware of Them, he had felt compelled to record the date, time and place of his encounters. He knew he shouldn't have been seeing Them. He didn't dare talking to anyone about it. One day, maybe, he would be able to understand what or who They were, and why he could see Them.

He wrote about those 'beings' he had been seeing, those feelings and emotions he had been sensing, those auras he had been perceiving. He now had a stack of small brown notebooks hidden away in his secret place. They were his diaries in a way, even though they were more random, irregular notes. He scribbled liberally, sometimes not even making full sentences, just tracing words on the paper and sketching.

He thought that if he kept a written track of the apparitions, then later on he would be able to talk about them and someone would come to him with an explanation. Maybe he would write a book about it! Why not? His stepfather had written *loads* of books: serious, mysterious, labyrinthine volumes full of strange letterings, formulas, abstract symbols and convoluted illustrations. The boy had seen a few of them and had been fascinated. Most were in English, but still, they were full of strange sentences and words for which he didn't have any meaning.

Yes, he was proud of his stash of carefully dissimulated notepads, they were his treasure, and the one he had taken with him on his walk would one day go and join the others.

FOUR

To reach the Wise Man's Spring, Dimitri had to take a small track departing to the right of the main footpath. It went along the side of a small rock formation – some kind of geological oddity – a mini-mountain in the middle of the woods called The Green Rock. And it was there, at the heart of this protrusion that gushed forth the clear, pure water of the Wise Man's Spring.

When he reached the spring, Dimitri started feeling rather hot with exertion. He stopped on the edge of the small pool and the air instantly cooled down. It was always the case at the Wise Man's Spring, and for that very reason, it was particularly delicious to take refuge there on warm, uncomfortable summer days.

He saw it immediately, as soon as he reached the mossy side of the pool: on the opposite bank, its explosive colours clashing with the brownish-grey tones of the rough rocks, was the strangest flower Dimitri had ever seen. It was a solitary, single flower perched on its long, graceful stem emerging from the water amongst the rounded floating leaves. It had long, pointy petals, going from bright blue at the tips to pale bluish-white closer to the yellow centre.

Dimitri stayed there for ages, incapable of moving, his arms dangling on each side of his body, his mouth half-opened with surprise and awe.

Everywhere around him, autumn had firmly taken hold of nature, muting the colours, revealing the twisted branches of the trees, the shrubs and the bushes, stripping the earth of its lush summer coat. Even the last roses in his mother's beloved rose garden had now faded and decayed, a few dry brown petals still hanging onto their prickly branches. Autumn was not the right time for flowers to bloom, especially those like this one. The boy had never seen it before, there in the pool or anywhere else. It looked somewhat exotic, alien. He felt compelled to try and see it closer; he was desperately attracted to it, hypnotised by its radiant, vibrant colours. He wished he could somehow pick it up and plant it back into the pond in the rose garden, where he would be able to see it from his bedroom window. It would cheer him up no end, and maybe it would his mother? Sophia adored flowers; sometimes, Dimitri thought that they were her only consolation and comfort in life. During the winter, she would spend hours making artificial flowers and exhibited her work all round the house. He wondered what she would think of this peculiar one? What kind of material would she use to make her own immortal version of it?

Now... How was he going to reach it? The pool was in a half-moon shape, surrounded by an irregular wall of rock about twelve feet high; in its centre was a narrow crack from which spurted out the spring water; it fell into the pool below among bubbles and raised a misty veil; it was just like a mini-waterfall. The flower was growing on the right-hand side of the spring, literally against the rocky edge as if using it for support. Just there, some kind of hollow in the rock could provide a boy the size of Dimitri with just enough space to crouch and inspect the flower.

He had to cross over the small stream at the end of the pool; once on the other side, he would have to climb over the rocks that blocked the access to the hollow space. He would have to be careful not to wet his boots as the water would inevitably get inside and soak his woollen socks. Thinking about wet wool made him wince. He knew that his health was relatively fragile and that a cold would take ages to get rid of and could turn into something far nastier if he were not careful.

He therefore decided against risking getting his feet wet and instead opted for walking around the pool over the wall of rock and onto the other side. It didn't take him very long, even though it meant getting stuck in brambles along the way. Soon, he found himself looking over the 'roof' of the hollow, just above the flower.

Carefully, he stepped over the slippery rocks blocking the access to the edge of the pool. He had to be extremely careful as the surface, covered in some form of moss, was treacherous. At last, he managed to find a stable enough spot just in front of the hollow space under the rock, and crouched there to have a closer look at the flower.

It really was a wonderful thing: at the same time delicate and strong, smooth and sharp. The stem looked slightly bent, the head of the flower turning towards the dark recesses of the hollow, as if it were trying to look at something there, like a sunflower turning towards the sun.

Dimitri was not in a very comfortable position and somehow managed to lose his balance; he fell back on his bottom and ended up with his head against the back of the cavity, propped up on both elbows. It smelt of dampness and mildew, in there. He was about to sit up and get back to his flower observation when his eyes caught a corner of the rock wall at eye level. There seemed to be some sort of compartment carved into the rock and clumsily concealed with a loose flat stone propped up vertically against the hole. He hadn't seen it before, for it was located at the deepest end of the hollow in the rock. He spotted two strands of string sticking out from behind the stone, together with a fragment of a dark brown, soft material. The boy awkwardly changed position. His fingers found the flat stone, which he was able to dislodge without encountering any resistance. There *was* a nook in there, and something had been pushed back inside it.

Curiosity got the better of the child and he pulled the strings. A bundle slipped out of the recess, bringing with it some dirt that had accumulated around it. It was surprisingly heavy and Dimitri had to place his second hand underneath to prevent it from hitting the rock. It was some kind of average-sized, soft leather pouch, tightly shut and fastened with two solid leather drawstrings. Dimitri felt the leather. There were some objects inside: something that could have been a book, and another one, bigger, more like a box.

Forgetting about the chilliness of the air and the wetness of the ground, the boy sat cross-legged on the rock and placed the bundle on his lap. He then spent close to twenty minutes trying to undo the knot, tugging at the strings with his fingers, his too short nails and his teeth. After a while though, he started to despair of ever being able to open the bag. Why didn't he have his pocketknife with him? He rarely went out without it and today of all days, he was not carrying it with him! He could have cried with frustration, then. Looking around in desperation, he spotted a long, sharp fragment of stone lying on the floor of the hollow. He picked it up and began sawing at the strings with it. The sharp edge started to bite into the tender leather and soon, the drawstrings loosened their grip. Dimitri's heart made a jolt. Just as he was about to discover the nature of his 'treasure', the all too familiar feeling started creeping over him. *Oh no! Not now!*

He stopped moving, the open bag still on his lap. The boy's head was bent towards his find, but he could now feel that he was being observed. The strange numbness of the body, the drowsiness of the mind... The feeling that all of a sudden, he had been transported into a world where everything was in slow motion: movements, noises... One of Them was here at the spring with him. Even after all those years, it still brought tears to his eyes. He didn't dare look up, afraid of *what* or *whom* he might see. The cheerful sounds of the spring and the flowing water were now distorted into an ugly kind of echo; he couldn't hear the birds anymore. He finally looked up...

The world around him seemed to have frozen and the man was standing next to him. He had one foot on the ground and the other visibly above the water, as there was not enough space for two people in front of the hollow rock. Dimitri knew that the man was not human, at least not anymore. As they always did, the uncomfortable feelings receded, now that the boy had acknowledged the apparition.

The man was dark of skin and thin of face, with very black, intense but sad eyes. His hair too was jet-black and cut below the ears. He was tall and lean underneath the white and layered tunic that covered his entire body; he looked serious, almost solemn. Like all the other apparitions witnessed by Dimitri, the man had this strange quality to him, some kind of transparency or immateriality, as if he existed between this world and another.

The man and the boy looked at each other in silence for a few seconds. Then the newcomer gestured towards the pouch Dimitri had left on his lap and the child noticed his long, elegant fingers.

'I see you have found it, at last.' The voice was otherworldly, as if not coming from the man himself, but from some mysterious, mythical entity within him.

To Dimitri's surprise, the eyes of this graceful, proud individual filled up with the glistening of tears. The apparition bent over and placed his hand on the boy's shoulder in a warm, sincere gesture of recognition. He simply said 'Thank you', while slightly squeezing the boy's shoulder.

He then slowly turned round towards the spring and started walking – no, floating rather – towards it, until his body came into contact with the wall of rock and *entered it*, dematerialising as he did so, as if melting into the surface.

There was a moment when the whole wood seemed to miss a beat and take a deep breath, and then everything went back to being seemingly normal. The birds started tweeting even louder than before, the trees resumed shaking the water off their remaining leaves, the debris from the storm began floating around the pool again, as if the apparition had been enough to stop the flow of the natural world.

Only Dimitri, still sitting on the cold rocky ground, hadn't moved. He was waiting for his heart to stop beating so quickly and for his body to cease shaking so much. It was always the same each time he encountered one of Them: he would feel exhausted for a good fifteen minutes afterwards.

This time around though, it took the boy a little bit longer than usual to recover. Maybe it was because he hadn't seen one for quite a while. When had it been? In June maybe, near the stables? This young soldier who had only wanted to be around horses because he had taken care of them during the war and had died with them in France... Yes, it had been as far back as June.

In the absence of ghosts, his attention would turn to the living. He kept seeing or sensing people's auras all the time, but he had noticed that the longer he was around someone the less he managed to feel them after a while. Gladys and Ginny, the two young women who worked as maids at the house, were still relatively new, and their auras were still quite potent. The other ones had been around for longer and he was more comfortable around them, now.

His mother's case was something else altogether: layer upon layer of icy blue cold energy surrounded her all the time, freezing him to the bone if he got too close. He had learnt to deal with it over the years.

*   *   *

When he felt better, Dimitri plunged one hand inside the leather pouch and emptied it of its contents. There were only two objects in there: a leather notebook and the prettiest box he had ever seen. It was chest-shaped and looked exotic and mysterious. The boy guessed that it was made of wood, but the object was so ornamented that he couldn't say for certain: it was resplendent with its blue, red and green mosaics and its gold paint. The long sides showed what looked like two stylised human figures standing in the middle of a temple of some sort, symbolised by four solid pillars.

The two other sides were decorated with flowers very similar to the blue one that had guided Dimitri towards his 'treasure'. He glanced at the flower in the pond: yes, it was the same indeed. Strangely enough, the boy wasn't that surprised; there must have been a connection between the flower that had grown in the pond, the man who had appeared to Dimitri earlier and the objects he had found in the recess.

The most impressive aspect of the box though was the very life-like plump scarab that adorned its top. Its marbled, sheer black and green shell was perfectly smooth. Dimitri couldn't resist touching it, half-expecting the creature to start moving as he did so.

He then picked up the box and gently shook it: from inside came some jangling and clinking noises, as if it were full of metallic items. Would there be coins or precious stones? Feverishly, Dimitri turned the box round and round, again and again, examining it in every possible angle, looking for some sort of lock, a lid, a button, a latch, anything that would give him access to the marvels that had been locked within. But he couldn't find anything at all and decided to come back to it later, before turning his attention to the leather bound notebook.

He found himself flicking through the yellowed pages of what looked like some kind of diary full of a strange language: there were pages after pages of a fluid, curvaceous, impregnable handwritten dialect. Dimitri bit his lip with despair at his ignorance. How he would have liked to have been able to understand what had been written in this notebook! He was certain that this was an important find, chronicling some exceptional events or tales. He was feeling incredibly frustrated: there was no way he could open the box, and he couldn't decipher the text on the ancient pages of the notebook. What a treasure, indeed!

Despite his disappointment, he took his pad and pen out of his pocket and wrote down what had happened to him so far: the blue flower seemingly showing him the location of the recess at the back of the rocky hollow, the way the bundle had been concealed from preening eyes, the apparition and what the man had looked like, the very few words he had uttered. He decided that he would add some illustrations on the very same evening, in the safety of his own bedroom; for now that the excitement of the discovery had passed, Dimitri found that he was growing increasingly cold. He placed both the notebook and the box back inside the pouch and tightened the drawstrings.

His enthusiasm for a long walk had disappeared and he had no wish to spend the whole day outside carrying the bundle around with him. He would have to go back to the house and then try and smuggle in the leather bag. He didn't want anyone to see his treasure; maybe he could use the small service door on the corner of the South Wing, and take the abandoned staircase and corridor there to reach his bedroom safely. It was the only way really, for lunchtime was approaching and everyone would now be going about their business in the service block and courtyard. Mr Bloom and Vangelis might even be around, driven from their lair by the rumblings of their stomachs, and he wanted to avoid their suspicious questioning.

The boy resolutely took the path out of the wood, looking back a last time at the bright blue flower he was leaving behind. Weather permitting, he would come back the following day to try and get it out of the pool, then replant it in the rose garden water feature where it could be admired by all.

Thankfully, the service door was still unlocked. It creaked dreadfully when Dimitri opened it and he paused for a few seconds, expecting to hear some hurrying footsteps. Inside, it was horrendously dark. This door opened directly onto the small wooden staircase leading to the floors upstairs. There wasn't any entrance towards the service block nearby or any window. The boy cautiously climbed up the stairs, holding his precious bundle tightly. In the first floor main corridor, some daylight peeked through some small dust-encrusted stained-glass windows.

He quickly walked towards the door he knew would lead to the East Wing where his own quarters were located. He glanced in passing at the silent closed doors aligned along the wood-panelled passage; he didn't stop because he knew they were all locked. No exploration was allowed around there, sadly; whole sections of the house were off-limits.

Once in the safety of his bedroom, the boy turned the key inside the lock as a precaution against unexpected intruders. He knew that no one would come and enquire about him. He climbed on his large bed and deposited his 'treasure' in front of him. He then opened his pad and painstakingly illustrated his adventures of the morning. He was particularly proud of his detailed reproduction of the impenetrable box, complete with bright colours – thanks to the fabulous box of colouring crayons from the Cumberland pencil company that Vangelis had bought him for his 11th birthday.

Dimitri spent the whole afternoon absorbed in his new-found possessions. He tried again to open the small colourful chest but to no avail; he tired his eyes looking through the pages of the leather notebook in detail, looking for clues. He scored a few points by discovering some rare words written in English. For example, he spotted the name of the estate itself, 'Whitemoor Hall', several times. Another name that he had been able to read was 'Lord Whitemoor'.

He also found a strange symbol scribbled on several pages, like a signature:

He thought he recognised it from somewhere but couldn't remember where he had seen it. It looked like the mysterious icons that peppered the pages of Vangelis's books.

That's when the boy realised that the only person who could help him open the box and solve the mystery of the journal was his stepfather. Nevertheless, the thought of having to go and disturb Vangelis Chronos filled the child with horror. Even after all these years, he was a little scared of the man who had married his mother when he was a tiny baby of only four months: Vangelis was – to his eyes at least – ancient, eccentric and more often than not too preoccupied with his work or Sophia's state of mind to show any real concern for his stepson. However, he seemed to have been taking more notice of the child over the past six months and had begun to encourage the boy's interest in writing, reading and drawing. Dimitri proudly thought that it might be a sign of his growing up and turning into a fine young man. Maybe Vangelis hadn't been interested in him as long as he had remained a silly little child. Now that he was – admittedly slowly – developing a personality, his stepfather might consider him more worthy of his attention. This very fact bolstered his courage.

Several times in the days following the discovery of the bundle, Dimitri prepared himself to go to his stepfather and tell him about the objects he had found at the Wise Man's Spring. But his excitement and apprehension would make him hot and feverish; he would stand behind his bedroom door with the bag in his hands, repeating in his head the very words he would utter when standing in front of Vangelis. His heart beating so very fast, he would put his hand on the door knob... Unfortunately, he had never managed to go beyond the landing outside his bedroom.

Again and again, he had found an excuse not to pursue his mission: the sound of his mother's voice rising from the floor above, the sight of Gladys or Ginny coming out of a room, their arms full of laundry or cleaning products. Or Vangelis had appeared in a bad mood the last time he had seen him, and so on and so forth. Dimitri deplored his own lack of audacity.

FIVE

At last, on a quiet Sunday afternoon, after five days of procrastination, Dimitri was able to face his stepfather and present the 'treasure' to him.

The boy had once again decided to go and find Vangelis and had picked up the leather pouch containing the box and the notebook. He knew that the house would be as quiet as can be: his recovering mother would be having an afternoon nap and the staff always had the Sunday afternoon off from 12pm to 5pm; they would all be at the abbey by then.

He didn't have a clue whether his stepfather would be in his study or if he would be in the 'lab' – he didn't know where the fabled laboratory was located and wasn't sure that trying to find it would be a very good idea. Dimitri opened the door, and as he was getting out of the room, collided with Vangelis himself. Both cried out in unison; the boy almost dropped his precious bundle and his stepfather nearly lost his velvet hat. The two of them had to catch their breath first.

'Are you alright, young man?' enquired the scientist.

'I am, sir, thank you, sir. I apologise, sir.'

Vangelis looked at the boy, who had never stopped calling him 'sir', despite the scholar's insisting on his stepson using his first name, 'Vangelis', which he did from time to time. But on that day, the situation was just too downright embarrassing. Dimitri felt his cheeks grow red with confusion and mortification. The last person he had expected to be up there on the first floor of the East Wing was Vangelis Chronos. He certainly hadn't foreseen any physical collision. How awful he felt! Was Vangelis about to berate him for his distraction?

The scholar looked at the child who was now shaking like a leaf, his eyes on the floor; he was holding his bundle close to his chest as if it were his most treasured possession.

'Don't apologise, Dimitri. It's my fault, entirely! I carry on thinking while I walk, and I am not aware of my surroundings. Your dear mother has told me a hundred times that I'd be coming to some harm one day… Absent-mindedness is a dangerous thing, my boy!'

The scholar sighed at his own weakness.

'I wasn't expecting you around here, sir,' remarked Dimitri in a smaller than normal voice. He had rarely found himself face to face with his stepfather on his own, and he now felt extremely shy and awkward. To the boy's surprise, Vangelis put his hand on his shoulder just like the dark-skinned man had done a few days previously at the Wise Man's Spring.

'Of course, you didn't my boy.' He said this reassuringly, before raising his voice: 'I've spent the past twenty minutes trying to find someone in this house who could help me!' He impatiently waved an arm in front of him, and Dimitri noticed for the first time that Vangelis's right hand was wrapped in a bloody piece of cloth.

'Oh!' he exclaimed.

'Please do not worry yourself, it's nothing serious, just superficial cuts that refuse to stop bleeding! I was manipulating an empty bottle, thankfully! It could have been much worse if it had been full… I only need someone to help me clean and bandage the hand.'

'What about Mr Bloom? Wasn't he with you?'

Vangelis made an exasperated face; his beard trembled.

'Oh, no! Mr Bloom has some urgent business away today, and so of course, he was not with me when the bottle exploded. On top of that, nobody is answering the service bells. I just cannot find a soul in this house! Do you know that even the kitchen is empty?' Vangelis's voice was rising with his increasing indignation.

'It is Sunday afternoon, sir,' ventured Dimitri, 'the staff always have the afternoon off on Sundays.'

Vangelis paused, taken aback, then roared.

'Ha! Sunday afternoon off! What a brilliant idea! Just to be able to spend a few hours doing their idiotic rituals? Why do they have to do it on a Sunday anyway, they're not even Christian! Utterly ridiculous.'

The scholar paused to catch his breath. He had been close to shouting and his voice had been echoing along a corridor more used to silence. Even the walls seemed to have recoiled in fear. He felt slightly ashamed of himself and cleared his throat before carrying on: 'We should review the way the schedules are organised. I don't think it a good idea to leave the estate like that every week without anyone to attend an emergency. There should always be some people at hand. What with the dangerosity of some of my work, and your poor mother's condition. At least, before, we had Miss Finch.'

Vangelis stopped once again to think, then looked at the boy with worried eyes.

'Your mother, Dimitri... Where is your mother?'

'She is having her afternoon rest, sir. As usual.'

'Is she, now?' The old man frowned, as if realising once again that he had either forgotten or never been entirely *au fait* of his wife's daily habits. He then focused his attention on his stepson. 'This means that it's just you and me, my dear boy.'

'Y... Yes, sir,' blurted Dimitri anxiously.

'Now, do you have any idea of where I could find something to clean my wound and bandage my hand?'

Dimitri suddenly understood what was now required of him. He had to show his stepfather to the medical cupboard in the small bathroom at the end of the corridor, and bandage his hand. This was a big responsibility and it might even be a marvellous opportunity to talk to him about his finds. His face lit up.

'Yes, sir! The medical cupboard in the bathroom! I know how to make bandages! Miss Finch showed me before she left! I'll do it all for you!'

He momentarily feared he had appeared far too eager.

'That sounds very good indeed,' replied the scholar. 'Let's not waste time and go there straight away. I need to go back to my work as soon as possible.'

Vangelis and Dimitri were now in the boy's room, where the scientist had never previously set foot. It felt odd, and his presence filled the space and made everything look small and insignificant. In order to fetch the necessary medical attire, Dimitri had had to leave his bundle on the floor by the door. The boy had picked it up immediately when he had come back to the bedroom and had deposited it on the bedcover. While he finished off fixing the bandage on his stepfather's hand, the latter turned his attention to the 'treasure'.

'Tell, me, my boy, what is this leather bag you are so keen on keeping within your sight? You seem to be quite preoccupied by it.'

Dimitri had just finished attaching the bandage and let his hands fall back onto his lap. He felt a little bit flustered, but now was the moment.

'Well, I found it. I was bringing it to you so you could help me find out what it was, when we collided on the landing...'

'What a strange coincidence!' the scholar remarked pensively.

Dimitri stood up and went to fetch the pouch. He carefully took out the notebook and the box before placing them on the small table. They both turned their chairs around to get a better look at the objects on display. Vangelis scrutinised them with genuine interest and curiosity. The boy even thought he had spotted a recognition of some kind in his stepfather's eyes, especially as the scientist started flicking through the notebook. Dimitri told him how he had come across the blue flower at the Wise Man's Spring, and how he had discovered the recess within the rocky hollow next to it. The boy left out the apparition of the man dressed in white; he always left out apparitions, because he knew people wouldn't believe him or worse, would mock him or berate him for uttering such childish nonsense.

'And is this blue flower still there?' queried Vangelis.

'No, sir, I have managed to pick it up and to plant it back into our pond in the rose garden. It's a surprise for Mother, for when she feels better and can go for her walks again.'

'This is very generous of you, young man. I thank you for thinking about your mother in this way!' Vangelis let Dimitri show his pride. Nothing was too good for his beloved wife. He stayed silent for a while, his brow deeply furrowed, his injured hand brushing his beard in a repetitive, automatic gesture of reflection. 'And you are saying that you couldn't find any way of getting to the contents of this box at all?'

'No, sir.'

'I wonder...' Yet another brushing of the beard. 'You see, Dimitri, the flower you describe is a very important Egyptian flower, a sacred one: a Blue lotus. How such a thing has managed to grow in one of our English woods in September, I have no idea. I will most certainly go and have a look at it myself this afternoon while no one is around. Now...' Vangelis opened the notebook and showed the handwriting to the boy. 'See this? If I am not mistaken, this is Egyptian arabic. This has been written by someone who knows a thing or two about our research and this estate. I can see some familiar names and some symbols that I know well. Unfortunately, I am not the person who will translate it for you and make sense of those texts. Mr Bloom will.' As Dimitri looked startled, Vangelis explained: 'Mr Bloom is a language specialist and has spent many years in Egypt. I did too, but my knowledge of the language is limited. I am myself more acquainted with ancient hieroglyphics. Therefore, I suggest you should be a little patient. I will ask Mr Bloom for his opinion on this. I am sure he will help you to discover what you've got your hands on here.'

Vangelis had replaced the journal on the table, and did his best to appear light-hearted and playful about it. But somewhere within his scholarly brain, a light went off. Even though he couldn't read the language, he had seen enough in those short minutes to make him think that the boy had come across something important, if not sinister. He would have to bring the notebook to Saturnin Bloom as soon as his assistant returned to Whitemoor Hall. But for all his worry, he also felt an incredible trepidation.

'Now, then, let's have a look at this box...'

Vangelis picked up the ornate object and, much like Dimitri had done so many times, started turning it around in his hands, while uttering exclamations of appreciation.

'Beautiful... Fabulous... Wonderful craftsmanship... You see, my boy, yet another Egyptian artefact! These here obviously represent a temple, and these greenish figures here are priests or worshippers. Now, on the sides here, you can recognise your blue lotus flower, can't you?' When he had stopped looking at every detail, he put the box on his lap and then pointed at the scarab. 'Amazing creature, isn't it? It looks almost real! A perfect shape!' Vangelis put his uninjured hand on top of the sculpted insect, his palm covering the whole body.

'It exactly fits in my palm, doesn't it?' he remarked, smiling and looking at the boy.

They heard a sonorous 'click' coming from inside the box and the lid of the chest was loosened. At the same time, Dimitri uttered a 'Ah!' and he and his stepfather looked at each other; Vangelis lifted the lid.

A vague musky smell reached them, and the contents of the box revealed themselves: the chest was full of the most handsome Victorian insect jewellery! Everything was mixed up and interlocked: rings, brooches, chains and pendants, all tied up in knots with chains of silver and gold. It was a bizarre bestiary of shiny, precious arthropods: spiders and bees, scarabs and flies in various sizes, set in every stone possible. So great was Dimitri's and Vangelis's surprise that they didn't dare touching the pieces. They looked like a strange nest of gleaming insects, all crawling and heaving on top of each other, entwined in the glistening of the silver and gold chains as if caught on a gigantic spider web.

'It is a *real* treasure, isn't it?' murmured Dimitri, his nose almost touching the big mother-of-pearl scarab brooch on top of the pile.

'It is indeed. What a find, my boy!'

'Whose jewellery could this be?'

'I do not know any more than you do. But something tells me that we might find the answer in there somewhere.' Vangelis tapped the leather cover of the notebook. The scientist was silent again for a few minutes, leaving Dimitri to shift uncomfortably in his chair, unable to take his eyes off the content of the box. Then he suddenly stood up, having made a decision.

'Dimitri, you have made an intriguing discovery indeed. I will now have to examine these objects with care and try and discover who has hidden them at the spring and why. Now,' he looked at his stepson gravely, intently, 'I want you to promise me the following: you will not mention these two objects to anyone, do you understand? Not to the staff, especially not to your mother. It would worry her unnecessarily, and I would like to surprise her with our findings at a later date. Do not mention them to Mr Bloom if you happen to see him. Is that clear? You do not tell *anyone* about the journal or about the box. Out of your head it goes!' He snapped his fingers near the boy's right ear. 'It is very, very important. And mentioning them to someone without my consent could have very grave consequences. Egyptian artefacts are not to be taken lightly. Think of Tutankhamun!'

Having uttered this warning with his index finger raised in the air like a prophet of doom, Vangelis picked up the box, the notebook and the leather pouch and left the room, once again called by something greater than life. The vision of his long coat and his cap seemingly floating on his white hair stayed imprinted on Dimitri's retina for a long time after his stepfather had left. He felt sad to have parted with his treasures so rapidly. The notebook and the box were no longer in his possession; they were now objects of study and were out of his reach...

*   *   *

Vangelis mumbled to himself all the way down to his study, located in the north-east corner of the house on the ground floor, as far away as possible from the hustle and bustle of the house. The artefacts were burning his hands, so to speak. He knew, *he just knew* that they were so much more than mere objects.

He had made a decision though, as soon as he had seen the jewels: he wouldn't say a word about them to Saturnin Bloom. He would show him the notebook and together, they would work out what it was all about. But the jewels were to remain hidden until a particularly special day... For a moment, Vangelis Chronos, scholar, forgot about his precious studies and lost himself in his thoughts. Things could have been so different. *If only...* To console himself, he went back to his research, annoyingly handicapped by his bandaged right hand.

PART
II

The interview
September 2014

ONE

At 27, Adam Tuckfield was contemplating the smouldering ruins of his life. He had spent the best part of the last year as if absent from his own existence; he seemed to have vacated the premises, leaving behind an empty and battered shell. The only thing that had stood between him and complete oblivion had been his friend Jimmy. Without him, who knows what would have happened? If Adam hadn't been living at Jimmy's when Dolly had dropped the bomb and all hell had broken loose, then he probably would have ended up under a bridge or something similar...

He was still feeling groggy and dazed by the rapidity with which his life had unravelled. Maybe he should have spotted the warning signs earlier and acted there and then, instead of careering forward in his chosen path ignoring them. It would have prevented the downward spiral from unfolding, and preserved his pride.

The meeting he had just had with his tutor at the City and Guilds had been a gloomy affair and had had a definite sense of finality. He wouldn't be able to complete the Postgraduate Diploma in Conservation on which he had embarked on the previous year. Now that he had lost his teaching position at Belford High School, he wouldn't be able to finance the course. Moreover, Richard Clunes, his mentor, didn't think that Adam was in 'the right state of mind' that would allow him to succeed in his studies. He wouldn't be offered a second chance, at least not in the near future. Adam had been three months into his new course when things had kicked off, and today had been the first time he had set foot in the building since 'the incident'. Adam had almost lost his temper when faced with a patronising and hardly sympathetic Clunes.

He was now standing in front of the City and Guilds entrance, blinking in the September sun, with the vague impression that he had now severed the only remaining link to his previous life. He was racked with regret: this course had meant so much to him... But he knew he just couldn't handle it, either financially or emotionally. He had to let it go, that and all his hopes for the future.

He hesitated before going down the stairs and then started the short walk along Kennington Park Road to the Tube station. He was already dreading the journey back on the Underground. He hoped the trains wouldn't be too busy, as the agoraphobia and claustrophobia he had been suffering from for a while hadn't completely cleared up. He had postponed the meeting with his tutor for as long as he could until he no longer had the choice but to drag his weary self to South London and sort out the issue.

His journey down hadn't been too bad; he had sat down at the end of a row against the glass panel, his eyes fixed on the pages of a book he hadn't been able to read, as he had been trying to concentrate on controlling his breathing. When the train had finally stopped at Kennington station, Adam had been turning the pages at regular intervals without reading more than one line on each page. In order to keep calm, he had been picking up one sentence per page and had read it over and over again until his brain had focused entirely on it, stopping on every word. The tiny letters had started dancing on the smooth paper in front of him until it had been time to turn the page. His eyes would then choose another line and the process would be repeated. He had been trying purposely not to look at the other people sitting or standing around him; he hadn't wanted to see them for fear of finding the eyes of one of them set on him. He hadn't looked at them, but he had heard them and even smelled them. From time to time, the muffled sound of music or bribes of conversation between two fellow passengers had reached his ears. Images of what the people would look like according to their voice and conversation had come into his mind, but he had never lifted his head to check.

Sometimes, it had been the strong fragrances of a costly aftershave, or the flowery tones of a feminine perfume. At other times, it had been a not so pleasant body odour. All these had found their way to him, but he had stubbornly kept his eyes on his book. He had been incredibly relieved when the train had reached the station and when he had stepped out onto the street without having suffered any major panic attack. He had taken a deep breath and congratulated himself for having managed his first Tube journey in a year.

Now the time had come to make the reverse journey, and Adam was not exactly looking forward to it. Luckily, the lift that took him to the level of the platform was empty apart from an elegant elderly lady with a small pooch. The little dog observed the stranger with its round, wet brown eyes; Adam thought that maybe he should be getting a pet, for company. Jimmy was away on a project thousands of miles away and wouldn't return for a good six months. He had been alone in the flat for so long. He was dreading and craving companionship all at the same time.

He smiled at the old lady, who sweetly – and surprisingly in those paranoid times – smiled back at the pleasant young man sharing the lift with her. But they didn't have time to strike any conversation as the lift had reached its destination and the automatic doors opened with a strident, grimace-inducing sound. He reached the platform at the same time as the next northbound train.

Adam took a seat on an empty carriage and opened his book where he had left it. He tried to concentrate but found it difficult to ignore the reminiscing of the depressing and tense conversation he'd just had with Richard Clunes, and what it would mean. He couldn't overlook the strange sensations that had been flowing through his body and mind since he had left the flat a few hours earlier. He hadn't ventured voluntarily any further than the street corner for such a long time; now he was back amongst the melee of the thriving metropolis. He should have felt elated; he should have been congratulating himself for vanquishing his fear and weakness at last, but he couldn't. What was he going to do, now? He didn't have any direction.

Dolly was gone, he couldn't face going back to teaching in any school after what had happened, he had lost his place on the course, his so-called 'friends' had ran away at the first whiff of a problem. And as far as his parents were concerned, well... The only one left was Jimmy, who was busy with his research at the other end of the world. People in general had been a disappointment; yet, the biggest disappointment of all had been himself. He hadn't been able to manage things properly. He had been too meek, too weak, maybe. He had fallen prey to his instincts and emotions without evaluating the repercussions of it all.

He could sense the pang of panic deep within him and started worrying about getting visibly agitated in public. He felt terribly self-conscious. The train was filling up more and more as it approached Central London. Adam could feel the sweat forming on his back; he was hot and uncomfortable. He was also aware that the person next to him, a woman, was reading over his shoulder, and he had to fight the urge to shove the book in her face. He suddenly wished he hadn't boarded the train. Maybe he should just get off, anywhere, and walk for a while. No, he wouldn't... All he wanted to do was get home as quickly as possible, close the door and find himself within the reassuring environment of the flat. He needed to be alone with his thoughts and think seriously about his future. He had to build up his confidence again and find a way of repaying Jimmy's generosity.

The train stopped at yet another station. Adam couldn't work out which one it was, he had lost count by then. It felt as if he had been on that carriage for ever. Little by little, a strange feeling crept over him: his eyes still on the book, Adam could sense a slight change in the temperature and light of the carriage, as if he had been outside in the sun and some clouds had come over and passed between him and the star. Maybe he was about to have a fit? A pleasant smell of warm vanilla reached him and he felt an overwhelming urge to lift his eyes from his book and look at the person who had just sat opposite him. It was irresistible and he couldn't fight it. He looked up.

She was reading a newspaper, he wasn't sure which one. She looked like she had been transported from another dimension, as if she wasn't made of the same flesh and blood as all the other human beings in the carriage. Adam was rather shocked by the vision – because it *was* a vision, wasn't it? He closed his eyes for a few seconds and reopened them. She was still there, looking as if she were floating on the edge of her seat, all poise and perfect pose. Her gloved hands were firmly holding the folded newspaper and she was concentrating on what was on the page. She wore a little cloche hat perched on her short dark bob and what appeared to be a vintage, dark grey dress ornamented with black lace. Her heart-shaped face, with its high cheekbones, drawn on black eyebrows and fiercely red mouth was uncommon, unique: a mixture of calm, confidence, femininity and elegance.

Then her long black lashes fluttered for half a second and she looked at him; it is then that he realised that there was much more to her than just a faintly old-fashioned loveliness: in her big, dark green eyes, he saw drama, fire, passion and steely intelligence. He was able to see it like that, just in the few seconds their eyes met in the overheated Tube carriage. She never smiled at him but held his gaze for a while; she didn't look surprised or even flustered by his insistent interest. Her face was immobile and grave. Her eyes seemed to say to him: *At last, you've decided to acknowledge me. Now we've connected, and that's all I wanted.*

Adam was transfixed, as if hypnotised. No one else seemed to have noticed either the change of atmosphere or the bizarre face to face that was taking place at one end of the carriage. People were still flicking through their free papers, fiddling with their phones, fixing an undefined area somewhere on the opposite wall – anywhere but on the person sitting opposite them. Adam and the stranger were acting out some kind of scene playing out in a different universe, as if all of a sudden they were the only people in a carriage running on a parallel track.

The train slowed down and stopped, the automatic doors sliding open to disgorge their flow of urban passengers. The spell was instantly broken: Adam found himself confronted by the wall of impatient bodies queuing to exit the carriage. The young woman was among them; she was now part of the anonymous herd that moved along the stifling corridors of the Tube station, and was walking out of Adam's life.

When the train started once again, the carriage was half empty. Adam had been so confounded that he hadn't found the time to react at all. His eyes were still fixed on the empty seat opposite him. The quality of the light had shifted back to normal. The dreamy atmosphere had dissolved, as if the stranger had taken it with her as she had alighted from the train. Everything looked once again dreary and bland. The vision had gone and left Adam filled with an odd sense of loss. He then realised that the woman had left her newspaper behind. He sprung forward and picked it up before anyone else could. It was neatly folded so as to show some job advertisements. In the middle of the page, among the dozen ads, was a particular one that had been circled in red pen. It read:

LIVE-IN TUTOR REQUIRED FOR HOME-EDUCATED 11-YEAR-OLD BOY

We are looking for a young, artistic and well-educated male teacher with a minimum of one year experience to teach English, art, history and geography. The position is located in a beautiful country estate in Somerset. Hours will be flexible, plenty of free time. Would suit an open-minded, reliable person looking for an unusual new challenge. Very generous pay, own spacious en-suite room. Interviews will take place as soon as possible in London. Please send CV and letter to...

Adam looked at the address: the name 'Whitemoor Hall' stood out, and his mind immediately started imagining what life must have been like at the estate. He loved manor houses and old estates; they were so evocative, so heavy with history, so creaky with old age and the passing of time... He stared at the advert for a while, the black letters imprisoned by the red, curly felt tip oval that screamed for attention.

He frowned. This was a job he could have done if... This was a job he *could* do... This was something he *wanted* to do... This was what he needed! He fitted the candidate profile; better even, he had more than one year experience teaching art and English literature. He badly wanted a new challenge, a reason to get out of the torpor he had been drowning in for the past year. He needed a place to stay, far away from London and from his old life; he needed somewhere new, someplace where he could forget everything, shake off those dreadful months, explore, lose himself, observe and find a new source of strength and vitality.

The prospect of getting himself attached to some posh family somewhere in the middle of nowhere would have literally terrified him only a year ago. Now, he was ready for *anything*. Anything was better than the stagnation, the dread and the questioning. He read and re-read the advert about a dozen time and missed his stop.

TWO

Adam's initial excitement receded as he approached the house; by the time he had put the key inside the front door lock, it had given way to a gnawing self-doubt. Once inside Jimmy's familiar and spacious flat, Adam had decided that there was something positively wrong about the whole thing. But what was it?

The air in the apartment was still infused with the smell of the morning's coffee, and Adam couldn't resist the urge for a fresh cup and a shot of caffeine. He walked into the bright kitchen with the newspaper still in his hand and threw it on the breakfast table before busying himself with the cafetière and kettle.

While waiting for the water to boil, he looked at the advert once again; he thought about the young woman who had left her paper behind. He could still see her face, and he just couldn't forget the luminescent quality of her skin and the intensity of her stare. There had been something else, though, something he simply couldn't grasp. He couldn't ignore the discomfort, the annoying tugging at his brain; something was bothering him.

His eyes caught the red felt tip circle around the advert: it looked somewhat impetuous, determined. Had the young woman circled the text herself? In that case, why would she have been interested in the position, as it specifically called for a *male* tutor? Maybe she thought that she could still try her luck… Then he remembered the knowing way the stranger had looked at him and sustained his gaze with a terrifying, almost haughty aplomb. She had seemed to have known him then, as if she had been waiting for him to look at her. She had…

Something clicked inside Adam's mind. He came to a realisation that made him go cold in half a second: *what if…* What if the woman on the Tube had purposely left the paper behind, with this specific advert circled in red just for him to see? Had she somehow known that he would pick up the paper, read the circled ad and apply for the job? Adam shivered. That would be bloody sinister. It couldn't be. It must have been his imagination going into overdrive… But then, it was all a very strange coincidence, wasn't it?

He could feel goose bumps spread all over his body; his heart rate had increased slightly and he sensed a childish wave of excitement and trepidation rise within him. The paranoia he had developed over the past year was sending him warning signals, but he chose to ignore them and concentrate on the unexpected opportunity offered to him. If he applied, maybe there would be a slight chance that he would see the woman again? If she was in any way involved with all this, then yes, there *might* be a chance. It would be worth it, only for that reason. Sipping his coffee, he felt almost dizzy with feverish expectation. He would need to get to work straight away. He couldn't lose any minute, any second!

Adam picked up the newspaper, the cafetière and his mug, and went straight to his bedroom, taking care of not dropping anything halfway down the corridor. He was feeling odd... Elated, focused... His purgatory had come to an end, and he felt capable of taking his future into his own hands once more.

The sudden change within him made Adam see his surroundings with brand new eyes: he stopped on the threshold of his bedroom, glanced around the messy dark space and winced. He had always prided himself on his tidiness and cleanliness; obviously, the events of the past twelve months had turned him into a lazy, self-loathing good-for-nothing wreck. Well, he wasn't one anymore. Today, he had completed the slow recovery he had always known would be awaiting him at the other end of the tunnel. He had to prove himself once more: to others, but mainly to himself. He was not finished yet, he knew this now, and he simply needed to reinvent 'Adam Tuckfield', to find a new version of him. But he would do so whilst remaining true to himself, even more so than before, because he was on his own, now.

He had seen too many people go through a 'reinvention' phase that had led them to betray who they really were. The worst offender had been Dolly... Dolly, the free-thinking, feisty girl with the multi-coloured hair he had fallen for; Dolly, with her love of loud bands and psychedelic art. She had been his partner in crime all through their university years, but then, afterwards, she had slowly turned into a corporate nightmare. A PR demon had risen within her and had proceeded in killing off every single thing he had loved about her, and this methodically, one by one, until she had finally committed the ultimate betrayal to her former self and to him. For a long time, he had thought that he would be able to retrieve the Dolly he had loved from within the corrupted unconscious of that woman he didn't recognise anymore; needless to say, all in vain. She had been that far gone.

Adam sat down at the end of the unmade bed and, still holding the mug and the cafetière, started crying. But this time around, he could sense that those were tears of relief, of release; they would be the last ones he would be shedding over Dolly and his past. He was expunging his previous life before embarking upon a new journey. The path in front of him was uncertain and littered with unknowns, but he was gladly embracing it, even if it meant facing failure and rejection. He had had so much of both already... He felt that he was now immune to their poisonous bites.

Putting his CV together was easy enough, but composing the covering letter proved to be a rather excruciating exercise. He began by sounding pathetically self-apologising. Then his second attempt read as too cocky and arrogant. Thereafter, he found himself with a dilemma: how was he going to justify his leaving his last position? He also wanted to show his worth and say something about having been taken on at the City and Guilds for a postgraduate diploma. That would play to his advantage. But then, how would he explain the interruption of his studies without appearing too weak and lacking in resourcefulness?

Adam sweated over it for a good three hours. He had to get it right and then give himself the best chance. He *had* to be called in for an interview, because then he would be able to show how much he wanted the position. He was worried about it, but for some reason, he was also convinced that he *would* be offered the job and would be allowed his chance to start afresh. If the whole thing had been a set-up, if the mysterious young woman had indeed attracted his attention on purpose and if the advert had indeed been composed so as to fit his profile, then... *then what?* Did he really want to know what this was all about? He would learn early enough...

Maybe he should have been more reasonable and not answered the ad. Maybe he shouldn't have pulled the string that had been so obviously laid out in front of him. He still couldn't explain what had happened on that Tube carriage. He could have sworn that the light and the temperature had changed with the arrival of the woman. He could still remember the strange, out-of-this-world quality of her whole person. Had it all been a prank? Did he really care either way? Maybe he was just going mad, finally...

That night, he found it hard to fall asleep. Not that it was at all unusual, but contrary to his other regular bouts of insomnia, it was not anguish that was keeping him awake, it was excitement. Even though he had only sent his application, he couldn't help trying to figure out what it would be like to work and live on a venerable estate in the middle of the English countryside. Adam was a Londoner, an urban child whose idea of greenery had been shaped by afternoons spent on Hampstead Heath and by excursions to Richmond Park, Hyde Park and other London green spaces. His father lived to work, and had never bothered to take his family on holidays anywhere. Adam had grown up in a nice and leafy street, but his parents' house had been located bang on in the middle of a row of terraced houses, and therefore he had never really known anything other than life within a limited space. Even their little back garden had felt slightly cramped. And that was nothing compared to the shared accommodation he had lived in until Jimmy had taken him in almost two years previously.

Adam was lying there in the perfect darkness, his eyes blindingly searching the invisible ceiling above. The immobile air and blackness were all-encompassing. He could only imagine the painted white walls, anonymous and mute; their smooth surface had witnessed his worst moments: the excruciating lows, the desperate hours, the long days of stunned silence and prostrate isolation; Jimmy's pleas for him to get better… Those walls were full of the two friends' whispered conversations. Jimmy, bless him, had really tried to help Adam like a true, proper friend, when everybody else had given up without even trying. Jimmy himself had lost quite a few acquaintances in the process, so outraged he had been at the behaviour of the so-called friends who had played along with Dolly's unspeakable plans. Now, with a bit of luck, he would soon be saying goodbye to the room. He would be glad to finally put it all behind… He knew it would be emotional for him to leave Jimmy's place, but he had to regain his independence and move forward.

I am thinking too much, he decided. *I'm never going to fall asleep if I let my thoughts run wild like that.* He needed to try and empty his head. In order to achieve this, he ought to close his eyes instead of attempting to find something to look at beyond the darkness of the room. *Close your eyes and stop thinking. Don't think about anything. Nothing matters at this very moment.* He closed his eyes, shifted his body to his left side, his head lying on his folded arm. Soon, he felt the pleasant heaviness of sleep spread all over his body; his muscles relaxed, and he let himself be pulled into the sweet unconsciousness of slumber.

It was the smell that woke him: it was a sweet, creamy scent, good enough to be eaten; it had reached his nose before he had even opened his eyes. When he finally opened them, fear rushed in: the room was no longer plunged in complete darkness but bathed in the soft orangey glow of the small lamp resting on top of the chest of drawers. He felt a presence and propped himself up on both elbows.

She was standing there, at the end of the bed, her hands behind her back like a studious, attentive little girl. She was looking at him with her big and serious eyes. Even in the low light, her skin retained the same ethereal quality that had so struck Adam on the Tube carriage; only here, in the bedroom, the contrast between light and shadow was accentuating the gracious bone structure of her face. She was bare-headed and her short dark locks were reflecting the light from the lamp. She was wearing a thin, silky nightgown that revealed only her white, elegant neck and her tiny waist. She didn't say a word and walked slowly to the side of the bed, her eyes never leaving his face.

Adam hadn't moved; he was transfixed, paralyzed with fear, shock, lust... He wouldn't have been able to say which. He didn't manage to take his eyes off the young woman, who climbed onto the bed and lay down next to him. Adam's skin grew in turn hot and cold and his t-shirt began to feel itchy and uncomfortable.

The stranger's face was suddenly very near his own, her right hand resting lightly on his stomach. He immediately found himself wrapped in a cloud of face powder, milky vanilla and something similar to almond. The last things he saw before their lips touched and he closed his eyes was the red bow of her mouth.

He abandoned himself to her kiss while she drew closer; now, she was on top of him, the silk of her nightgown brushing his neck. Her hand slowly felt its way up his right arm and her fingers began lifting the sleeve of his t-shirt. She then sunk her lacquered nails into the skin of his forearm. She suddenly felt heavier and Adam, due to both pain and surprise, opened his eyes to find that the mysterious stranger had been replaced with an altogether different creature.

The woman who now straddled him looked formidable: her skin was of a tight and shiny texture and was the colour of the highest quality dark chocolate; she had an incredibly structured, angular face with a long aquiline nose, a large and sensual mouth and stupendous violet eyes circled with kohl.

Her thick black hair was loose and fell in abundant locks all over her white tunic. She wore wide, ornamented pieces of golden jewellery around her neck, wrists and ankles; she was barefoot. Adam's expression was now of intense disbelief and horror... She was much more imposing than the young woman in the silky nightgown: her athletic, full body was all tight muscles and raw power; Adam could feel himself close to suffocating. The woman laughed a deep, raucous, terrifying roar that fitted well with her predatory appearance.

Something glistened in her hand and Adam realised that she was holding an exotic-looking golden dagger. She violently thrust her hand over Adam's nose and mouth to stop him from screaming: her patchouli-scented skin now prevented him from breathing; her nails cut the side of his jaw. Her arm moved, and Adam, filled with horror, saw the dagger cut through the skin of his arm where his small tattoo was etched. The sight of blood seemed to excite her and her frenzied eyes stopped on Adam's face for a moment, a grin fixed on her beautiful but cruel mouth. She then resumed the cutting; her white tunic was by then smeared with his splattered blood. The realisation of what she was doing hit Adam like a train at full speed. *She is carving out my tattoo!*

Until then, he hadn't had time to feel the pain. From deep within him, stifled by the incredibly hard hand that dug into the skin of his mouth and jaw, came a desperate, tormented cry of agony. It filled the whole room and resonated in the pitch-black space like a thousand thunders.

Adam fell to the floor. In the dark, panicking, scrambling around to find his bearings, he felt his wet t-shit and reached for the skin underneath the short sleeve: intact. He crawled towards the chest of drawers and blindly searched for the switch. The light threw its orange gleam around the room. He stayed sprawled on the floor, soaked in his own sweat, dazed yet awake. He then lifted his body up and managed to get onto a crouching position; he glanced warily towards the bed: no blood, no gold dagger, no alluring murderous woman nor amorous brunette in a silk nightgown. He was alone, and in one piece. He could feel a slight throb on his arm where the small tattoo was still in place. The skin of his jaw felt slightly sore, but after close inspection in the mirror, Adam couldn't see anything wrong with it, not a scratch. It had felt so real, ridiculously so.

He started laughing, a strange, bitter laugh of relief and maybe, just maybe, of disappointment.

THREE

The autumn weather had suddenly deteriorated and it had rained for four consecutive days, playing in Adam's favour and handing him on a plate a ready-made excuse for not venturing out of the flat. Jimmy had called earlier on from his scientific camp somewhere in the Pacific Ocean; he had been delighted when he had heard of his friend's new-found energy. It had been nice to hear someone who cared.

Adam had also started sorting out the mess that had taken over his bedroom. The space was crammed with boxes of CDs and books, hundreds of them. These were his only possessions. He had never bothered with furniture beyond a few sets of shelves. He had been glad he and Dolly had never moved in together; it would have been a complete disaster and would have added to the pain. When they had split up – when Dolly had dumped him, she had simply walked out the front door and slammed it shut behind her. She had never left any of her belongings at his place, ever; not even a toothbrush. Adam had since guessed that she had been planning her exit all along and had only been lying in wait for the right moment.

He knew that he shouldn't have been so optimistic about the job. He was behaving as if he had already succeeded; he dreamt of forests, fields and lakes, of dark-panelled rooms with high ceilings and tapestries. He had been wondering about this young boy growing up on his own in a remote and unfriendly place. He could see him, silent and shy, surrounded by strange adults who didn't pay attention to him and who nevertheless thought him somehow too precious to be sent to a normal school, where he would have been able to interact with people his own age.

Adam had often wished he had been home-schooled, having never enjoyed the company of the often boorish, shallow youths at his school. He had never really bonded with anyone, enjoying a kind of gentle, non-committal popularity brought on by his bookish but edgy good looks. He had never really cared for anyone there, not really.

He wondered whether the boy was spending his waking hours left to his own devices, exploring the maze of corridors and staircases criss-crossing the structure of the building. Did he go to sleep in a four-poster bed that was far too big for him, shaking with fear whilst thinking about the rows of terrifying portraits aligned along the walls outside his door? Did he imagine those people, all of them long dead and buried, suddenly coming back to life and stepping out of their ornamental frames to wander around the building in search of a soul to vampirise? This had made him smile... He couldn't believe his head was full of such clichés! He didn't know then how close to the truth he was...

*   *   *

The letter arrived five days after Adam had dropped his application through the red letterbox round the corner. The envelope was of a cream-coloured, sturdy paper, with his name and address neatly written at the front with black ink in an elegant, precious and old-fashioned hand. When he turned it over, he was surprised to see that it had been sealed with a red chunk of wax. He felt like an actor in a costume drama, about to learn about his fate by breaking a red, waxy seal at the back of a fateful missive.

Adam stood in the entrance hall staring at the red seal that showed the imprint of a sundial, of the kind found within the grounds of a manor house or castle. Very fitting indeed. And of course, it came from Whitemoor Hall, Somerset. *This is it!* he thought, his heart pounding in his ears. He was bracing himself for rejection. He wouldn't have the slightest chance of seeing the young woman again...

'Fuck it!' he exclaimed out loud, finally breaking the seal with his impatient fingers. He unfolded the letter. He hadn't made any mistake: the pattern on the red wax was repeated at the top of the piece of paper as letterhead, and represented a dial that had been split in two: one half for the sun and the other for the moon, both encircled with a 'magic ring' featuring various esoteric symbols. Adam's curiosity was picked; he started reading the short letter, once again written in black ink and in the same overly elegant, scholarly handwriting.

Dear Mr Tuckfield,
Thank you for the interest you have shown in the position of live-in tutor at our house. We were very impressed indeed with your covering letter and Curriculum Vitae. We wish to meet with you face to face in order to further discuss your background and the position of tutor at Whitemoor Hall.

Would you be available on Monday 15th September at 11am? Please reply by return of post with an alternative date and time if the ones offered are not appropriate. If the dates are convenient, then please let us know with a short note as soon as possible.

The interview will take place in London at the address below. We are looking forward to meeting you.

Yours Faithfully,

Saturnin Bloom

On Behalf of Lord Vangelis Chronos

He had made it to the interview! He felt relieved, and yet, just like after his encounter with the woman on the Tube, something felt not quite right.

Adam read the letter several times, taking in the myriad of odd little details contained within the missive: the thick, smooth, formal paper; the strangely esoteric letterhead; the evocative address of the manor house, the impressive Central London address, the aristocratic handwriting and the painstakingly traditional methods of communication: no telephone, no fax, no email address. Then there were the names: 'Saturnin Bloom'? 'Lord Vangelis Chronos'? What kind of elaborate prank was this?

Yet, Adam was not ready to dismiss the whole thing altogether. The strangeness of it all was one of the reasons he had decided to hang onto this one opportunity to get out of the horrendous rut he was finding himself in. Since he had set his eyes on the extraordinary young woman on the glum Tube carriage, his life seemed to have taken a much more interesting turn. His mood had lifted, his energy levels had risen. Moreover, he had always been attracted to unusual things. The circumstances surrounding the tutor position had been unconventional enough for his imagination to start running amok. Nothing felt completely real, and it was a welcome distraction from the grimness of reality. But it had to be real enough for him to be able to move on.

FOUR

aybe he shouldn't have drunk that second cup of coffee. Adam could feel the liquid at the pit of his stomach, and it was not very pleasant. He unbuttoned the collar of his shirt and loosened his tie. He felt incredibly conspicuous in his suit, convinced that people could guess how nervous he was just by looking at him.

The day of the interview had arrived and until now, Adam had been pretty confident; then he had gone to bed the previous night slightly anxious, and had woken up that morning positively wretched. He was now walking down a rather anonymous if slightly grand Central London street in the vicinity of Baker Street. The tall Georgian townhouses looked dirty under the light drizzle. There were very few people around.

He reached a small, continental-style café that was surprisingly bustling on this gloomy late morning. Office workers were coming in and out, making the most of the takeaway service on offer. Some more people were huddled around the wooden tables, cupping their mugs with their cold hands and munching on homemade cakes and sandwiches. Quite a few were busy discussing work, gesturing over humming laptops, colourful smartphones, diaries and folders. A group of trendy young men had been brave enough to settle for the tables and chairs outside underneath the awning. They were sucking furiously on their cigarettes whilst talking loudly on their mobiles all at the same time, letting their hot beverages go cold. This place seemed to be the only hub of any kind of visible activity in the whole street.

Adam felt self-conscious whilst walking towards what could be a life-changing interview. He found himself very lonely and gauche, and had to stifle the urge to take refuge within the odorous walls of the café. He bravely fought his instincts and decided to reward himself afterwards with a hot, comforting drink when the interview was over.

The address he was looking for stood just next to the noisy café. He pressed the only buzzer, as indicated in the letter. There were a series of electrical crackles and a disembodied voice came out of the slightly rusty entryphone.

'Yes?'

'Good morning. It's Adam Tuckfield here. I have an appointment with Mr Saturnin Bloom.' Adam had to concentrate in order to ignore the conversations reaching him from the café next door. He almost shouted his reply. There was a pause. He thought he could hear some heavy breathing, just for a very few seconds. He dismissed it as a trick of his imagination. The voice, deep and perfectly calm, finally replied:

'Mr Tuckfield! Wonderful! Please do come in. At the end of the corridor, go up three flights of stairs. Go through the double door on the landing, then walk straight until you reach the red door. I'll see you soon.'

The entryphone screeched once more and went dead, immediately followed by a buzzing noise at the door. Adam pushed the surprisingly heavy and thick entrance door which closed behind him with a sinister 'click'. The entrance hall and the corridor leading from it were deafeningly silent. The urban sounds of the street were completely prevented from penetrating the building, as if it had been placed inside a large cocoon. Adam paused for a moment before starting towards the stairs he could just make out at the other end of the corridor.

The place had seen better days and time seemed to have stood still; it looked like the premises hadn't been inhabited for decades. The corridor was dark, with the original wallpaper, floorboards and ceiling still in place. The interior was entirely devoid of any furniture; Adam could see into the succession of still, empty rooms that were lined up on either side of the hallway. His footsteps echoed across the ground floor, bouncing off bare walls, going up cold and empty fireplaces and losing themselves among the dusty folds of the drawn curtains that obstructed the windows. This was definitely an unusual place for a job interview to take place. Were they trying to test him and see how he liked it walking around an old, creaky house?

He climbed up the stairs slowly to avoid making too much noise. Every sound was amplified tenfold in this place, much like inside a cathedral. He guessed that each landing would open on yet some more vacant, silent rooms. He finally reached the third floor and pushed his way through the double glass door.

Adam found himself on the threshold of a large and bare room that had the same half-decrepit, forgotten-by-time feel as the rest of the house. At the other end, straight in front of him, was an open door leading to yet another similar room, and then to another one; it looked endless. What had the voice in the entryphone said again? 'Walk straight ahead until you reach the red door.' He was about to start again when he heard some footsteps on the landing just outside the room. He turned round just in time to see the small, feminine silhouette outlined on the other side of the glass panel: it seemed to be hovering, checking him out, maybe. He could have sworn he was able to hear the soft breathing of the woman. Then he heard the metallic click clack of the heels hurry down the stairs.

Instinctively, Adam opened the doors and stepped out on the landing. He peered down the staircase over the banister and saw the top of a cloche hat and the gloved hand sliding over the wooden handrail: *it was her!* Adam couldn't help himself and called after her.

'Hello? Excuse me!' The sound of his own voice, urgent, almost pleading, made him blush. The figure halted its descent and her now familiar, remarkable face lifted towards him; the big green eyes acknowledged him. Then, without a word, the woman resumed her course and had reached the ground floor before the petrified Adam could react. The heels resonated on the floorboards and then the entrance door slammed.

Still standing on the third floor landing and staring into the empty staircase, Adam was once again surrounded by silence. After a minute or so, he shook off the trance-like state which had overpowered him and walked through the double doors again, this time without stopping on the threshold. He walked through a series of one, two then three identical large unused rooms whilst trying not to feel too self-conscious about the sound of his footsteps filling in the whole space. He finally reached a large double door boldly painted in a deep red colour; it was ajar. Adam was about to knock when a sonorous, controlled voice came from inside and made him jump.

'Mr Tuckfield, please do come in.'

Adam put his hand on the brass door knob and, inhaling deeply, pushed the red door.

The room was, again, surprisingly large but, contrary to the rest of the house, it wasn't plunged into darkness. It actually was incredibly light, even on such a drab, drizzly London day. This was due to the fact that the roof as well as an entire wall had given way to large glass panels that had transformed the place into some kind of roof-top conservatory. The three remaining walls hadn't been painted for years and were of an off-white colour. No picture or any other ornament had been hung on them. In the middle of the room stood a heavy Victorian-looking desk and, seated behind it, was the man who called himself Saturnin Bloom. Upon Adam's entrance, Mr Bloom stood up and walked towards his visitor with an impenetrable face.

'Mr Tuckfield, welcome! I hope you are well and have found your way easily.' The hand he had offered Adam was rather cold and strong, steely even. 'Please take a seat,' said Saturnin Bloom, gesturing towards a comfortable upholstered chair. He quietly returned to his place behind the desk. Adam struggled for a few seconds to find a suitable position in the chair – it was more an armchair than a seat fit for a job interview.

'Thank you for coming, Mr Tuckfield. First, I'd like to tell you that you are in luck, so to speak, as we haven't had a lot of applications and the other candidates were not exactly... appropriate. Allow me to do a little bit of talking first, if I may. The position is a live-in one, located at Whitemoor Hall, a historical manor standing in an Area of Outstanding Natural Beauty. You would work as a tutor for Dimitri Chronos, who is 11. Dimitri is a quiet, bookish, rather shy young boy with a vivid imagination. He lives with his mother and his stepfather, my employer, Lord Vangelis Chronos, who is an eminent scientist and scholar. I am Lord Chronos's assistant and secretary. I teach Dimitri maths and science, and therefore you would only have to deal with English, art and a little history and geography. Dimitri loves English and art, and is not that keen on the two other subjects.'

'You would be in charge of devising your own programme and lessons; you would have access to his previous governess's teaching journals and therefore, you will know what he has studied before and where you can start again. We would also like you to act as companion and, let's say... role model for the boy. Dimitri is a curious, unusual child but he is fiercely intelligent. Our household itself is far from being usual... The boy's mother, Sophia Chronos, has a fragile health and does not spend a lot of time with her son; as for Vangelis Chronos, well, he is an extremely busy man. If you were Dimitri's tutor, you would spend most of your time with the child or on your own. We do have a few people working for us; their numbers vary according to the work undertaken on a particular day, the season, etc. We have a cook, two maids, two kitchen assistants with one doubling up as a porter, an estate manager, a head butler and a gardener with two young apprentices. The tutor is free to mix with everyone in the house and will have free access to every part of the estate. We also work with the people from the nearby village, Whitemoor.'

Saturnin Bloom paused for a moment, observing the perfectly still and attentive Adam. Something imperceptible passed on the secretary's features; his eyes turned even darker for a while. He seemed to be appraising the young man in front of him, as if he were intent on discovering something hidden within him. It lasted only a few seconds and was gone. Mr Bloom then carried on.

'I cannot hide the fact that this will be a highly unusual and demanding position, but it will be interesting and rewarding for the right person. Needless to say, the pay is extremely generous. And of course, the tutor wouldn't have to worry about anything like paying the rent, getting the laundry or the cooking done; it is all included.'

Saturnin Bloom thus concluded his presentation. He had been rather solemn, speaking in a serious, impassive manner. His voice was deep and vaguely soporific, without any angles or harshness. During his allocution, Adam had plenty of opportunity to observe him. He had a lean yet surprisingly muscular build underneath the dark blue suit. He was also extremely tall, well over 6ft. His facial features were strong and stern, with very black eyes, a large yet hard mouth with well-defined lips that were not made for smiling; the nose was sharp, slightly hooked. But what gave him his unusual looks was the completely shaven head that accentuated his features and his air of authority and solemnity, something Adam wouldn't have expected from a simple 'assistant and secretary'. He briefly thought that he wouldn't like to meet Saturnin Bloom in a dark alley. Feeling that it might have been his turn to say something, Adam gestured to the room.

'This is an unusual building, Mr Bloom. For an art historian like me, this place is full of mysteries that beg to be unearthed.'

Saturnin Bloom's face surprisingly lit up, and he *almost* smiled.

'I am glad you like it… Lord Chronos acquired this house last year to use as a *pied-à-terre* for when he is in town. Unfortunately, things being as they are, there hasn't been any spare time to do anything about it… I hope you do not find this too distracting or sinister in any way.'

'Not at all!' blurted Adam.

'Well, then. Now, let's talk about you.'

Here we go, thought Adam, tensing ahead of the challenge.

Saturnin Bloom leant over, his elbows resting firmly on the shiny surface of the desk, his hands clasped in front of him. Adam noticed for the first time the silver ring on his right middle finger, and recognised the sun and moon dial that appeared on the seal and the letterhead. Mr Bloom's face looked as grave as ever.

'Mr Tuckfield. I'd like to reassure you straight away. I assure you that the events that took place at Belford High School last year will not have any influence on the decision we will take regarding the position.'

Adam felt himself go white, the blood drained from his face with shock; he then went hot and red with embarrassment. *How did they know?* In his head, he heard once again the sound of the palm of his hand meet the girl's flesh. He remembered the mixture of incredible anger, surprise and horror that had rushed all around his body when he had realised what he had just done. He also remembered the stunned little crumpled face of Ophelia Booth-Fielding which had been displaying such vile superiority and fierce adolescent cruelty only a few seconds beforehand. He remembered the red mark his hand had left on her white cheek and the thin trail of blood under her nose. He could still hear the screams of the girl's school friends and the insults – and the few blows – that had started pouring over him moments before his colleagues had come to his rescue.

'How do you know?' he asked with a choking voice.

Saturnin made a reassuring gesture.

'Let's say that because of his work, Lord Chronos has numerous contacts, including in the worlds of education and justice. We know about 'the incident'. We understand that you were not your normal self on that day. We believe that your actions were completely out of character and that you have paid a high enough price for your temporary loss of temper. What we are interested in are your teaching skills, who you are as a person and your ability to fit in with our household. We are entirely satisfied with all of this and your credentials are excellent. It would take more than this to spoil it for us…'

'I am not proud of what happened on that day. I have accepted full responsibility for the incident and have now put everything behind me now' – although it took so much time, he thought; the hysteria surrounding 'The Slap' had been so intense, even though the school had painstakingly attempted to hush the whole thing up. This man knew, and therefore Adam thought that he could be relatively frank with him.

'This position would be an opportunity for me to start afresh. I have never been a tutor before and I'd like to give it a try. I am up for the challenge.'

'This is exactly the way we would like you to think, Mr Tuckfield. New beginnings... You know, the human race is deeply flawed and I have never encountered anyone entirely good or bad. All humans are a mixture of reason and instincts constantly battling each other within the mind and the body. They should embrace those contradictions and learn from their mistakes... It should make them humble and a little wiser each time. At least, I expect that's the way it works...'

Adam was feeling confused; this was not the way he would have expected a job interview to go. Saturnin Bloom had dismissed the event that had cost him his position – and probably his place at the City and Guilds – as a mere incident without any bearings on his chances of getting the job. Actually, the secretary was talking to him as if he had already decided that Adam would be the boy's tutor. The young man wasn't sure whether this was a good or a bad sign.

Mr Bloom questioned him on his tastes in literature and art; he asked him about teaching and education. Adam was more and more under the impression that he was having an informal chat rather than sitting through a job interview. Despite all this, though, Saturnin Bloom never smiled or showed any kind of warmth towards him; he remained a cold, polite, distant yet vaguely sympathetic interlocutor. Adam had noticed a certain stiffness in his deportment.

They had been talking for about thirty minutes when Saturnin Bloom cut the conversation short, opened one of the desk drawers and took out a beautiful silver case.

'Do you smoke, Mr Tuckfield?' he asked Adam, opening the case in one brisk movement of the wrist.

'Occasionally I do, yes.'

'Well, maybe this is one such occasion.'

Saturnin Bloom presented the cigarette case to Adam. Inside were perfectly aligned dark brown tubes, each sporting a gold and silver ring around the tip. Adam's eyes met Saturnin's very dark pupils and the young man thought that he had better not refuse the offer. He carefully pulled one of the cigarettes out. The secretary stood up, walked towards the glass wall and opened one of the panels to let the air come in. The drizzle seemed to have stopped, but the atmosphere was incredibly damp. Despite the lack of visible radiator or any other heating device, the room felt pleasant and dry, when Adam would have expected damp patches and mildew.

Mr Bloom walked back to where his interviewee was sitting and produced a rather splendid silver lighter, decorated with exquisite exotic flowers. *This object must have cost a fortune*, thought Adam. The flame, high, elongated and clear, burst out of the implement with a satisfying 'swoosh'. The young man briefly felt its heat over his face while his cigarette was being lit up. He inhaled deeply and let the strange, spicy smoke swirl around his system before exhaling it. What kind of tobacco was this? It definitely was tobacco, and not some herb or marijuana of any sort, but it was incredibly sweet, a little as if the leaves had been dipped in honey. Saturnin Bloom, himself enjoying his cigarette, had spotted Adam's intrigued face.

'Special Egyptian cigarettes, made with a rare type of tobacco grown in one place only, a small valley in Southern Egypt... Lord Chronos is a keen Egyptologist and has travelled extensively around the country, although Egypt is not his only country of interest. He is half-Greek, you see, and has always been fascinated by the ancient Greek mythology... Whitemoor Hall is full of objects and art related to those two countries. As an art historian, I reckon you would also feel very much at ease in such a place. You will find plenty of things to do and study during your free time if you are so inclined.'

Silence fell between the two men for a while. Adam didn't move from his armchair and smoked his cigarette furtively. His eyes were studying every crevice and irregularity around the room. He was feeling uneasy, almost queasy.

Saturnin Bloom had returned to the open glass panel and was looking down to the wet and grey street below. His profile was stark, as if carved out in stone; his jaw was clenched. The smoke of his cigarette was escaping out of the room in gushes of fragrant particles that mixed with the toxic London air, while the police and ambulance sirens screamed across the dirty yellow sky. He knew what was going to happen next, of course. He had known for a long time, and now, the moment had come. He didn't feel nervous, as those like him were strangers to that kind of emotion.

In a minute, he would walk back to his desk and tell the young man who was uncomfortably seated in the armchair that the job was his. Then they would discuss the last details, and a date would be set. In less than a month, Adam would be joining them.

If Saturnin Bloom was incapable of feeling nervous or worried, he nevertheless couldn't help being apprehensive. Even he couldn't be in control of everything all the time. The whole thing implied some degree of risk, and there was so much at stake. They would need to be careful, patient and ingenuous. He had found Adam more damaged than he had expected, but this could actually play in their favour or, admittedly, it could spoil everything beyond repair. Who could predict how things would turn out? Not even he, Saturnin Bloom.

He briefly turned his attention to the people outside hurrying along the pavement. Most of them looked miserable, stressed out, timorous and empty. He pitied them and their directionless lives, and even though he had tried hard, he could only manage to feel contempt for them. Those little people... He had spent so long observing them struggle and wrestle that he had grown quite tired of them. A few had proven useful, and then some had revealed themselves as being exceptional. Take Dimitri, for example: Saturnin had guessed his gift, but hadn't managed to prove anything yet; and he needed the boy to acknowledge it before it could be of any real use. All the boy needed was a little bit of guidance... And then now, there was Adam, who remained blissfully unaware of the real job that was awaiting him.

Saturnin stubbed out his cigarette on a nearby silver ashtray and walked back to his desk. In doing so, he glanced at Adam's slightly slouching back. The young man was patiently, groggily waiting for Saturnin to say something; the active agents in the Egyptian tobacco had altered his senses and he had relaxed a little. Everything was cosy, now.

'Mr Tuckfield. I guess it is time for me to deliver the good news.'

Of course, Adam hadn't heard the footsteps next door. If he had turned round, he would have recognised the young woman who was now standing against the red doorframe behind him, her hat perched on her proud little head and her arms crossed. She was quietly listening to Saturnin Bloom and observing the effect the secretary's words were having on the young man's composure. When the two men shook hands over the desk, one of her black eyebrows rose and her red mouth smiled. She wanted to applaud but restrained herself. She had played her part, and now she deserved a drink or two.

FIVE

Adam's eyes were burning; he hadn't slept enough the previous night and had had a hell of a day; now it was 1am and he was still sitting in front of his laptop, the luminous screen bathing his features in a surreal, artificial light. He just couldn't stop, because he still hadn't found what he had been looking for and he had become hooked, obsessed with this apparent absence of information, this gaping non-existence of anything.

He had come back home in a feverish, hyperactive state, with thousands of thoughts going through his mind. He still hadn't realised what had happened to him; it hadn't sank down properly yet. He had done it! He had found his way out of the mess that had been his life for the past fourteen months. Now he had to start packing his belongings and get ready for some serious lifestyle changes. In a few days, he wouldn't be a Londoner anymore; he wouldn't be on his own anymore. He would be shedding his previous skin, which had become too damaged, too tight for his own good, and settle himself inside a brand new one, full of will, strength and ambition. He was determined to make this a success, whatever happened. It was his second chance and he was ready to seize it with both hands and run with it.

The strangeness of the circumstances that would be taking him from the capital to Whitemoor Hall was not putting him off, but rather made things even more interesting. He relished the eccentricities attached to the story of the Hall and its inhabitants. He wasn't sure how to address the episode on the Tube and couldn't determine the role that had been played by the young woman who had appeared to him in his dream. He was taking everything in his stride; he was ready for an adventure, the odder the better. He was tired of the mundane, the day-to-day, the average, the normal. He wanted to embrace something else, something more extravagant. Could you classify as extravagant the act of burying yourself within the walls of a country house? At least, it *was* something different; he would be going against the grain of the fast-paced, digitally-enhanced world. There, he might find his peace at last.

He was curious about the area and the house itself, and tried several websites with satellite views. He carefully checked the address, and he thought he had found the exact place. Yet, something odd happened: the land that would have been occupied by the Whitemoor estate was all but a blur, as if the equipment used to take the satellite images had experienced some kind of technical failure just as it had passed over the area. Adam reloaded the pages several times, restarted his computer, but he was still getting the blob of washed out colours, as if someone had taken a bad eraser to the picture and made a mess. You couldn't see anything: the estate seemed to have been swallowed up by the earth. Wherever he looked, the same blurred blot of void filled in the area where the estate should have stood. Whitemoor Hall seemed to be a ghost estate if ever there was one. Adam found the village of Whitemoor though, a few miles to the east of the Hall; there even was a 'whitemoor.org' website, with the predictable list of farmers' markets, Parish council meetings, slimming clubs and kids' activities, but no trace of a Whitemoor Hall nearby. He grew weary and was ready to give up when something turned up on his screen, at last.

The name of the website was rather ominous: 'The Gates of Delirium' was the glorified blog of 'professional graphic artist, amateur detective of the unexplained and keen rambler' Steven Steward. Mr Steward loved nothing more than travelling around the country and embarking on long walks that would take him to locations known for being the site of 'historical' mysterious happenings, ghost sightings and unexplained phenomena. He also loved writing – and was rather prolific, judging by the extensive articles that were posted on his website. Adam's heart sank. It was incredibly late, it had been a long day and he really didn't have any time to waste on some delirious ghost-hunting website. But he decided to hang on in there for a while, because after hours of unfruitful research, he had managed to find something that referred to 'Whitemoor Hall, Somerset'; the title appeared in red letters on a black background, followed by a rather long text illustrated with pictures of old pubs and fountains, lush footpaths and ancient stone and brick walls.

The article was dated 'August 6th 2004'. Whilst doing some research at the British Library, Steven Steward had come across some obscure reference to an elusive favourite of his: the 16th century alchemist Aloysius Dean, who, it was said, had been a talented apprentice to the infamous occultist John Dee, astrologer to Queen Elizabeth I. Aloysius Dean had disappeared for some years to pursue his research, and people had suggested that he had been somewhere in the West Country.

The book Steven Steward had been reading was a manual on the 'stars' of the occult throughout the ages written in 1970 by a Dr Tristan Winston-Dunst; the author had found out that Aloysius Dean had bought the remarkable Whitemoor estate in Somerset and had very probably had a special laboratory built there in order to pursue his experiments away from preening eyes and jealous colleagues and rivals. Unfortunately, Dr Winston-Dunst himself, when doing his own research, hadn't been able to find anything related to the history of the house; nevertheless, he had managed to get his hands on a few more details: Aloysius Dean had died in Venice in 1617 at the age of 80. There were no records of what had happened to his laboratory or work; no papers had been found relating to the fate of the estate.

The name of Whitemoor Hall had reappeared in 1835 when the then Lord Whitemoor, supposedly a descendant of Dean, had decided to demolish the existing building to rebuild it according to the taste of the times, turning it into a Victorian Gothic mansion of some proportion. The Lord had moved into the property in 1840 after some extensive foreign travels during which he had married, but the building work had carried on until 1847. Once again, there was a curious gap in the history of the house after the sudden death of Lord Whitemoor in 1856. The name of the estate had once more disappeared from official records, this time for as long as 70 years.

In addition to the link to Aloysius Dean, what had persuaded Steven Steward to go and have a look at the estate had been the strange tale told by Winston-Dunst in his book: the astonished academic had stumbled upon one unique piece of news relating to a severe incident that had occurred at the Whitemoor estate. In late November 1925, the police had been called to the house after one of the young gardeners had made a gruesome discovery: the people on the estate had apparently been struck overnight by something akin to a deadly virus. The young man who had made the call from the gardener's cottage had unfortunately died himself before the police had arrived, and the doctors called to the estate had only found corpses showing the grim symptoms of some kind of plague. The medical men had then given orders from inside the estate to block every access to the grounds and a safety perimeter had been put in place around the entire area. Then, a small group of men had been sent to bury the corpses.

The style of the article had been strange: the writer had sounded eager to go into details, but hadn't named anyone, either the inhabitants of the estate, the doctors or the policemen, seemingly '*to respect the privacy of the individuals involved and their stricken loved ones*'. Some people had been convinced that the government had been involved and that information had been suppressed to ensure that nobody knew exactly what had happened within the tall walls of the estate. It was obvious that the heavy hand of censorship had been at work. The journalist had deplored the fact that no villager had been told what had exactly happened, and those who had lost loved ones in the tragedy had had to accept the vague, unsatisfactory explanations that had been given to them by 'smug science men and officials from London'. Some wild rumours had been alluded to, but the newspaper had refrained from repeating them in print – once again '*out of respect for the individuals who had lost their lives.*' There had been no mention of the health of the doctors and policemen involved in finding out what had happened on the estate. It all sounded terribly suspicious, and everything had become mixed up or lost amid the hysteria.

In 1970, Dr Winston-Dunst had conducted his own investigation and had found that the estate had been left empty since the tragedy. Steven Steward himself, in 2004, hadn't been able to find anything on record and had decided to go and pay a visit to Whitemoor Hall in person.

If Mr Steward had found the village a pleasant one and seemed to have had a lovely time at the local pub, he had found the process of obtaining any kind of information about the Hall incredibly frustrating. Every person he had asked about the house had shaken his or her head in disbelief: 'What would you want to have a look in there for? There's nothing left, I reckon. The thing's been abandoned for decades, and it's probably gone dangerous, with all those ruined buildings and all. No, I haven't even had as much of a glimpse myself, you can't see anything, what with the very tall walls around it and thick trees… It's as if there was nothing there at all. It's a shame in a way, waste of good land! Maybe someone should go and have a look in with a plane or a helicopter.' The pub landlord, who obviously hadn't been born in the area, had shaken off the idea of the manor house in a good-humoured, devil-may-care sort of way.

Things had been quite different when Steven Steward had met 86 year-old Marjory Willis. The old lady, very dapper in her bright blue dress, had been only seven at the time of the tragedy. When Steward had asked her about the events of 1925, the soft folds on her face had somehow become more pronounced, and she had put her small, sinuous hand to her mouth.

'Oooh… I wouldn't recommend you trying to get in there, young man. It's not healthy. I remember my mother warning us about it, saying that if we ever tried to climb those walls and get to the grounds, we would fall ill and then die. Yes, she was not one for sweet talk, my mother, bless her. Anyway, the walls were far too high for any of us to even attempt to climb them. But you know, there had always been something of genuine terror in my mother's eyes… I think she remembered something that had happened there but had never told us the story. No one really has any idea of what happened in 1925, all we know is that all those poor people died. There had been a lot of them in there. Apparently, there was some kind of,' she pursed her lips, *'religious community* staying somewhere on the grounds and working at the house. Some poor souls who hadn't coped really well with the war, you see, the First World War… All dead! Them and the people who lived at the manor house. No, I haven't got any idea who those people were. My mother never told me. I was too little, and then I forgot about it. The Second World War came along, you know… Terrible! But that's the way we deal with things, us humans.'

After his chat with Mrs Willis, Steven Steward had then taken the footpath out of the village in the direction of the estate. After a while, he had encountered a tall, thick stone wall at least twelve feet high, good enough to dwarf any human who dared harbouring the thought of catching a glimpse of what stood beyond it. It had looked daunting, menacing and terminally unfriendly, but had still retained a certain elegance: after all, this had been the wall protecting a manor house and not a military fortress. Steward had decided to walk around it.

In his impatience, Adam skipped the rest of the article to get to the section that interested him the most: Steven Steward had never managed to climb over the wall, had never glimpsed if only a chimney or a gargoyle. Even when he had stood in front of the majestic, foreboding entrance gates – they had been locked, of course – the vegetation had been so lush and wild that it had created yet another wall, another layer of protection. The rambler hadn't been able to take any picture of the gates themselves as his camera had jammed and he hadn't been able to get it to work again on that day. The mystery of Whitemoor Hall had remained intact.

Upon leaving the area, Steward had promised to himself that he would return to Whitemoor, but he never did. A note on the homepage stated that in late 2005, Mr Steward had become a family man with two small children and hadn't been able to travel around looking for any more mysteries. He was mainly maintaining the website and adding a few things here and there to keep it going and to make sure it was good enough to be used as reference. He had carried on commenting on various topics, though. You can't stop a keen writer from writing.

Adam fell back against his chair, his lower back aching and one of his legs rendered numb. He rubbed his eyes vigorously with the palm of his hands and remained there staring at the screen. The house must have been in quite a state if the present occupants had purchased it after Steward's visit in 2004. It had stood empty since 1925! Adam wondered what had made Saturnin Bloom's employer pick Whitemoor Hall as a home for his family. Had he been in search of a high level of privacy, just like the previous owners?

The young man started reading the article again, in an attempt to make sense of Steward's report. His foggy brain began to drift then, and he clicked away from the page he was reading. Half asleep, he browsed through Steward's crowded, wordy website without registering any of the photographs of ancient monuments, grotesque statues, lopsided rooftops and ruined churchyards. His head felt foggier and foggier and his eyelids heavier and heavier. The screen became blurred and sentences stopped making any sense anymore. He closed his eyes and allowed himself to go to sleep.

When Adam woke up some hours later, a weak autumn sun was playing on his cheek with the shadow of his eyelashes; his whole body ached all over. He managed to sit up in his chair, feeling as if his bones and muscles had turned to concrete overnight. He glanced at the screen: Steven Steward's website was still there, full of words and stories. He was in a bad mood. 'What a load of tosh', he groaned, struggling to stand up. He sleepwalked to his bedroom and slipped under his duvet. For a moment, he thought he could smell the creamy perfume of vanilla on his pillow and hear the liquid rustling of silk.

The clock on the side table indicated 3pm when Adam next opened his eyes. He got up thinking about Whitemoor Hall and its inhabitants, past and present. He had given himself a new mission: he would unearth the house's history and solve its mysteries.

PART
III

Welcome to Whitemoor Hall

ONE

Adam stepped out onto the platform and stood under the artificial light, his three bags at his feet. The crisp Somerset air filled his lungs and made the skin on his face tingle. Soon, the cold would penetrate his clothes and freeze him to the bone. He had spent the best part of the day in an airtight train compartment and the contrast momentarily stunned him.

Night had now fallen; he glanced at his watch: 7pm; the train had only been five minutes late. Saturnin Bloom would be waiting for him outside. Adam picked up his bags and walked out towards the exit of the deserted station. Shrouded in the orange glow of the streetlamps, the Grade II listed building, built by Isambard Kingdom Brunel, looked somewhat bigger than it really was. The car park was virtually empty, apart from a battered old van and two anonymous cars. The place felt vaguely sinister and abandoned. Adam was used to the overcrowding of the capital, and this rather desolate place felt unnatural to him.

He looked around for Saturnin Bloom and finally caught sight of him. The secretary had parked away from the main entrance, in what looked like the darkest corner of the car park. He was standing with his back against the shiny surface of his car, smoking.

This time, Mr Bloom was wearing a dark coat over his suit and had a trilby on his shaven head to keep the chilly air at bay. He nodded when his eyes met the young man's, but he remained still, the smoke surrounding him like a protective screen. Adam thought he looked more like a shadowy Chicago gangster from the prohibition era than a scholar's secretary; there was definitely something odd about the man. As he approached the car, Adam recognised the fragrant spicy tobacco he had smoked on the day of his job interview. Up close, and despite the lack of light, the vehicle against which Mr Bloom had been leaning on revealed itself as being quite out of the ordinary. Adam studied the car, astonished.

'Mr Tuckfield! Here you are… Welcome to Somerset. I see that you are admiring the car: Morris Oxford Deluxe, four seater, 1924. It is a little bit dark for you to see it in all its glory, but I promise you will have ample opportunity to have a good look at it at your leisure in the forthcoming weeks.' Still the same monotonous deep voice: Mr Bloom didn't betray any pleasure, excitement or annoyance at having to come and pick up the new tutor himself.

'It's a wonderful car, Mr Bloom. How you have managed to keep it in such good condition, I couldn't say. It looks brand new!'

Adam didn't know anything about cars but was able to recognise a beautiful beast when he saw one, and he possessed the trained eyes of the art historian. So absorbed was he in the contemplation of the vehicle that he didn't notice the expression on Saturnin Bloom's face. His eyebrows had gone up a few inches on hearing Adam declare his surprise at the wonderful state of the car. The car was indeed brand new.

'I'm afraid the journey will be rather long, and you might feel cold. There are two woollen rugs on the back seat if you need them. You can put your luggage next to you or on the floor if you prefer.'

This had sounded like a polite order and Adam decided to obey without any question. He was to travel at the back of the car, with the secretary driving at the front, on his own. Whether it was a normal occurrence that a tutor would be driven around like a VIP or whether Mr Bloom merely wished to avoid engaging in any kind of conversation on the way to the house, the young man had no way of knowing.

Once seated in the car, he looked about him with curiosity, admiring the beautiful grey upholstery, glancing at the shiny wooden driving board. The hood of the car was up against the cold air, but Adam thought how exciting it would be to go for a drive sometime in the spring or summer along the winding lanes of the countryside. He was feeling strange; the very same morning, he had been at a smelly Paddington station full of bleary-eyed commuters queuing up to buy overpriced takeaway coffees. Tonight, he was in a small town in the middle of a rural county, about to be driven to the mysterious house that would become his home. Was he having an out of body experience? Because this didn't really feel like his life at all. Adam was brought back to reality when the vehicle coughed and hiccupped; the engine started purring amiably, and then, they were on their way.

The countryside was pitch-black. Adam couldn't see a thing beyond the windows of the Morris and he could only guess and imagine the gentle wilderness outside. Once or twice, they drove through sleepy villages; there, some street lamps would make his pale face appear on the glass panel, very much as if the ghost of a long-dead wretch were pressing its wan face to the window of the car, attracted by the life within. He had never been very big, but the past year had accentuated the regular angles of his face. His reflection appeared almost translucent.

A nagging apprehension took hold of him; he really wished Saturnin Bloom were the chatty type, it would help him relax. The journey so far had been heavy with silence, disturbed only by the purring of the engine; the driver seemed to have forgotten about his passenger altogether. Of course, Adam could have said something, but he just couldn't find it in him to do so; Saturnin Bloom intimidated him, he wasn't ashamed to admit it. There was something emanating from the man, a mixture of charisma and authority that he found disquieting. Adam himself had always been quite unassuming and he had never been comfortable around authority and power. He wasn't feeling *at all* at ease around the secretary and his opaque personality. He couldn't wait to arrive at the house and be relieved of the discomfort of the silent journey.

They had just driven through yet another village and Adam had decided to give in to his increasingly heavy eyes, when the sound of Saturnin Bloom's voice made him jump.

'The last village was Whitemoor, and therefore, it will not be long before we reach Whitemoor Hall.'

Adam had been so surprised that he struggled to force any sound out of his mouth. He finally managed to articulate:

'Thanks for letting me know, Mr Bloom.' Then he wondered: had his driver merely let him know about them finally reaching their destination or had it been some kind of warning?

It was another twenty minutes before the Morris exited the road, turning left into an entrance; then it stopped. Leaving the engine running, Saturnin Bloom got out of the car. Looking ahead of him beyond the vehicle, Adam could see, illuminated by the car's headlights, a long, seemingly endless drive disappearing into the night.

He then turned round and peeked through the small round back window: the red rear lights of the Morris were just enough for Adam to see that Mr Bloom had stopped the car just inside the walls of the estate. The secretary was now busy closing the high ornate gates, which were extremely tall and imposing and were made of metal – possibly iron – painted black. The right side of the gates sported an ancient-looking ornament representing the sun, whereas the left one had a similar symbol showing the moon. Set into motion by Saturnin Bloom, the gates joined in the middle with an almighty, foreboding 'clank' noise; for no justifiable reason, Adam sensed a shudder sweep over his whole self from deep within him. From the back of the car, he looked at the gates that had just closed as if the monstrous jaws of some ancestral beast had swallowed him whole.

He glanced at the time-worn symbols: the sun seemed to be looking straight at him from its cast-iron pedestal; the moon was being less direct, only casting a side glance, as if it were trying to avoid his gaze. They both looked angry.

Adam felt as if he had just been shut out of the outside world or had just passed something akin to a border control: he was now inside the Whitemoor estate. After a long, silent drive in the dark, he was about to arrive to his as-yet invisible destination; it was not far, it was *there*, somewhere beyond the wall of darkness, and he could feel its presence. It was only at the other end of the long narrow drive that stretched in front of him.

After having secured the locks on the gates, Saturnin Bloom walked back towards the car and silently took his place behind the wheel. Soon, they were on their way. Adam distractedly glanced at his wrist watch: 9.30pm. When he looked away, his eyes caught something strange away on the horizon above the drive: an orange effulgence was mixing with the ink of the sky, as if a building had been burning for hours before being reduced to a pile of glowing, red-hot live embers. It was then that, without any warning, the apprehension he had been feeling for a while turned into full-blown panic.

As the car drove through the grounds of the estate, the atmosphere in the vehicle and all around it seemed to change; the air somehow thickened, if such a thing were possible. Adam's pulse started to race faster and faster until he thought it would stop altogether. He felt a cold sweat run along his spine and dampen his brow. His skin started to prickle all over and his muscles turned into cotton wool. He knew that if he had attempted to stand up, he would have collapsed on the car floor like an abandoned puppet. He started shaking in his seat whilst his heart now beat in his ears, the thickened blood pumping too fast. He wanted to call for help, but his whole body was paralysed and refused to obey: no sound got out of his mouth. His vision slowly blurred and became distorted.

Adam stared at the darkness beyond the car windows in search of help, of something to hang on to. He saw nothing at first, because there wasn't anything to see. Then he began to notice flashes of colour moving behind the glass, just outside the advancing car. The night slowly merged into brightness; the trees, the drive and even Saturnin Bloom disappeared altogether and were replaced by a corridor of flowing, shape-shifting light. Adam's body temperature rose abruptly and his head started spinning, causing a violent nausea. Finally, a terrible explosion filled his head. Just before losing consciousness, the young man heard the cries of a very young child.

Then all went dark…

TWO

The clock in the lobby outside the scullery indicated 7.30am and Gladys was already convinced that today was going to be a rotten day. Not that there had been any particularly good days in her life so far. It just felt more rotten that average; you just had to have a peek outside at the vile, thick fog that surrounded the house that morning. She was thinking about how so very rotten her day was going to be while cautiously climbing the stairs, her eyes never leaving the contents of the tray she was carrying. With each of her steps, the china made a rattling noise and the white milk trembled in the jug, threatening to spill over.

Yes, it was going to be a rotten day... Her friend Genevieve had eaten something bad the previous night – probably something she had pinched from the larder before going to bed – and had been sick the whole night. She was being punished for being so greedy! When she had woken up that morning, Gladys had been told to attend to Lady Chronos until poor Ginny felt better, something she had never been required to do before. She should have been pleased, as it showed that Mr Simms, the head butler, trusted her enough now to let her cover for her more experienced friend. But she knew that this was a poisoned honour, and it hadn't been long before she had been proven right.

At 6.30am, Gladys had attended to Lady Chronos's first call. The lady of the house never slept well and was always up very early, although she would rarely make an appearance downstairs before midday. She had received the little maid sitting in her bed and propped up against a pair of huge white pillows with a mixture of surprise, contempt and barely contained annoyance. Gladys had answered her sharp, short questions about Ginny very carefully: Sophia Chronos's temper flares and bouts of 'hysteria' were notorious among the staff and could happen at any moment. As Mr Simms had told Gladys when she had started working at the house: 'One has to choose one's words and tone of voice very carefully when addressing Lady Chronos.' Gladys had never been very good with words, but her education at the abbey had remedied to her virtual illiteracy and she was now confident enough to risk 'choosing her words' herself.

Facing Lady Chronos on her own was something else, though. She had tried to keep her eyes down and had avoided making eye contact with her mistress, who had ordered her first morning tea and had unceremoniously sent her running down to the service block. Then Mr Simms had come into the kitchen and announced that she would also have to go and wake up the new tutor who had arrived the previous evening; Gladys was to bring him some tea and enquire as to what he would need for his morning ablutions.

The girl's foggy brain had momentarily cleared up at the mention of a new arrival. This had been the first she had heard of it. She thought it rather strange that no one had mentioned anything about it. Nobody had asked her – or Ginny – to prepare any of the guest rooms. She had gone to bed at 11pm as usual, and hadn't heard anything afterwards. Mrs Abbott, the cook, had been very cross about it indeed. *We should have been told*, thought Gladys, sulkily.

Once she had safely brought the tea to Lady Chronos and had left the mistress of the house to her daily musings, Gladys had returned to the kitchen to prepare the tray she would then take to the new guest. She wondered what he would be like… It certainly would be quite a change from Miss Finch. Gladys had never really known what to think of the former governess, who had always remained distant and isolated. She hadn't liked her that much, she decided, but she had never really had any good enough *reason* to dislike her, apart from the way Miss Finch had behaved with the young master. Gladys had pitied the poor boy, especially when the governess had kept him at the table for hours in order to get him to eat some foodstuff he had refused to swallow outright…

She was thinking about all this whilst taking the tray to the first floor of the East Wing. She paused for a moment when she reached the door of the room allocated to the tutor and rested the tray on top of the small wooden table outside the bedroom. Her arms and fingers had become numb, for she had gripped the tray too tightly. She then smoothed her hair and adjusted her dress. She wanted to make a good first impression on the stranger she was now about to wake up. A new face would certainly be most welcome in the house; everything had been so quiet.

True enough, she had found a kind of family at the abbey: they had welcomed her, educated her, given her the position she now occupied at Whitemoor Hall. Then there were the rituals; she loved the rituals, they were so full of lights, chants and beautiful objects. There was as well the appeal of all the mystery surrounding them. They soothed her, made her feel as if she were part of something *else*, something *beyond* the mere blandness of everyday life. They had taught her to control her emotions, to lock her sadness and anger away. She had changed so much since the abbey community had welcomed her with open arms; she had become calm and patient. She remembered how, before she came, she had constantly felt low and useless, ugly and gauche. She had thrown tantrums, gotten into fights with boys and girls, adults even.

Now, her life was more peaceful and dutiful and she was thankful for it, but somehow, she couldn't ignore this nagging feeling that would erupt sometimes amidst this peacefulness, the feeling that her life at the Hall was, well, a bit dull. In those rare moments of realisation, she would step out of the trance-like way she lived her day-to-day life and the awareness of her lot would be revealed to her in all its mind-numbing tediousness. But the girl found it hard to express that dissatisfaction, and even harder to act upon it; she was part of The Family. She wondered whether the new arrival would join them at the abbey. She hoped he would.

Gladys knocked on the door. No one answered and nothing stirred inside. Maybe he was still asleep and wouldn't answer at all? Maybe she would just have to take the tray back to the kitchen and wouldn't have to face a stranger in his bed?

Oh please, make him still be asleep...

*   *   *

Far, far away up there in the immensity of his unconsciousness, Adam heard a knock. Actually, he was awake now and emerging from the fog of sleep, but his eyes were still closed on the real world. Someone was knocking on a door, on *his* door. He stirred and groaned. He opened one eye, then the other. It hurt like hell. It actually hurt everywhere, and at first, he didn't manage to register his surroundings; he was concentrating too much on the sensations in his body. Moving his head was painful. His torso and limbs felt bruised and contused. Maybe he should just go back to sleep and not even attempt to get up.

The knocks made themselves heard again, this time more insistent. They echoed in his head; this was unbearable; he had to make them stop, and the best way to do so was to answer them.

'Who… Who is it?'

His jaw felt stiff, his tongue stuck to his palate in an unpleasant way. Was he hungover? He didn't remember drinking at all. There was a slight pause, as if the person on the other side of the door had been surprised by his question. Then the weak voice of a girl came from the corridor.

'Morning, sir. I have been asked to bring you an early morning tea, sir.'

What was he supposed to say?

'Co… Come in.'

Instinctively, he pulled the covers to his chest. The door slowly opened and a young girl of about 15 stepped in carrying a small tray. Her strawberry blonde hair was neatly tied back revealing a sad, rather bland face. She was wearing a simple and practical dress made of thick grey material and a white plain apron. She glanced towards the bed where Adam was lying and blushed violently; she stood there, the door still open behind her, petrified.

The young man's vision had finally come into focus, and he frowned with embarrassment and pain. There was still this dull ache behind his eyes he couldn't get rid of. The poor girl looked as uncomfortable as he was. The awkward moment passed as soon as he opened his mouth.

'Er… Good morning… and your name is?'

Jolted back to reality by the sound of Adam's voice, the girl cast her eyes down upon the white teapot.

'It's Gladys, sir.' Her eyes now remained stubbornly on the tray. The blush hadn't receded and she could feel it burning her face; it was causing her extreme distress.

'Ok, Gladys…' With some effort, Adam managed to get himself into a sitting position. His brain still refused to work and all he could do was to smile feebly. The girl, who had surreptitiously been looking at him just at that moment, turned an even deeper shade of red. Adam said in a reassuring voice: 'I'm sorry, I am probably not helping you that much… I've never had tea brought to me in bed by anyone, so I don't really know the conventions. What am I supposed to do here?'

Gladys breathed deeply and lifted her head. She was still trying not to stare at Adam, although she really much wanted to. His hesitant, all but confident voice reassured her a little. She cleared her voice.

'This is your early morning tea, sir. Everyone at Whitemoor Hall takes some tea early, before they have their breakfast proper. I'm just to place this on a table for you to enjoy at your convenience. I'll do this now and maybe you shouldn't wait too long otherwise it might turn cold.' The words had poured out of her mouth a little bit too fast. Flustered, the girl looked around the room for a place to leave her burden and spotted a small round table opposite the bed; she swiftly walked to it and deposited the tray. 'There you are, sir.'

'That's great, thanks, Gladys. By the way, I'm Adam. Adam Tuckfield.' Ah, he remembered his own name! That was a good sign...

The young maid's ears had definitely turned purple now and Adam could see that all she wanted was to flee. Just as Gladys was about to turn round to leave the room, a deep, monotonous voice made her jump.

'Mr Tuckfield! I see you are awake!'

Adam, still in his bed, gave a little start as well, as he hadn't even heard Saturnin Bloom's steps along the corridor. The secretary had appeared out of nowhere, framed by the door, as if he had suddenly materialised into the room. He looked huge next to Gladys, who recoiled from him and stood there, shaking, her hands fiddling with the folds of her apron.

'I hope you have everything you need for you to get ready this morning. Gladys, have you asked Mr Tuckfield whether he needed anything?' Saturnin Bloom stiffly glanced down at the girl. She didn't look at him, preferring to fix a spot on the floor.

'I was just about to, sir.'

Saturnin turned towards the bed; Adam hadn't moved.

'Well, Mr Tuckfield, please let young Gladys here know what you would need to wash, etc. I wanted to ask you whether you would join us – Lord Chronos and I – in about an hour for our breakfast. We will be taking it in the study downstairs, so we can save time and look at a few papers. Gladys, will you come back later and show Mr Tuckfield the way to the study? Thank you. Mr Tuckfield, I see you later for breakfast.' Saturnin Bloom exited the room, leaving behind two stunned young people.

Adam suddenly threw away the bedcovers and sat on the edge of the bed.

'Right, then. I guess I'd better get going. Let's have some of that tea!'

Adam poured himself a cup of tea. This was genuinely the best tea he had had in ages. His pasty mouth was instantly better, the flow of liquid having washed away the unpleasant feeling on his tongue. His brain was still not fully functioning, though. There was something odd about the way he felt: as if he were not fully there, as if it were not him who had just gotten up from this large, comfortable bed. He was wearing pyjamas he didn't recognise, he had been sleeping in a bedroom that was definitely not his; he could remember his name, and yet, he wasn't entirely sure that if anyone had asked him who he was, he would have been able to give them a satisfactory answer.

'The bathroom is here, sir!' Gladys was now invisible to him, her voice coming from behind the wooden door at the other end of the bedroom. He could hear her moving items around. 'I think there is everything you need in here, sir: towels, shaving things, soap, a brand new toothbrush!' She emerged from the small bathroom, flushed and satisfied with her little check. 'If you please, sir, I will go now and come back in about 45 minutes and take you to Lord Chronos's study. You probably would get lost if you tried to get there by yourself!'

Adam looked at her inquisitively above the edge of the cup he was finishing.

'Thank you very much, Gladys. Tell me... What is the name of the man who was here just now again?' His eyebrows were frowned with effort.

Gladys's eyes opened wide and her mouth formed an 'O'.

'Oh, sir... This was Mr Bloom, Lord Chronos's secretary.'

'Mr Bloom...' His face lit up with recognition. 'Oh, yes! Of course! *Saturnin* Bloom, isn't it?'

Gladys was feeling more and more confused.

'Yes, sir.'

'I am really sorry, Gladys, I am not making much sense this morning... I must have been unwell yesterday... My head feels like it is full of smoke and I have strange aches everywhere... I am not really sure... But of course, do go and do whatever you've got to do, you must be very busy. I promise I will be ready when you come back. I'll keep an eye on that clock, there!' Adam had spotted a large, beautifully crafted clock on the mantelpiece. Gladys nodded silently and left the room.

Adam's smile instantly vanished from his face. He remained standing in the middle of the bedroom, feeling dizzy. He went back to the bed and sat on the edge, his toes only slightly touching the wooden floor. He passed a shaky hand over his face, trying to gather his ideas and memories and to get a sense of the present. But how could he do it, though, when he felt so unsure of the past? Bribes of conversations and images had begun to flow around his head as if someone had opened a gate that had so far been kept tightly shut. He started to remember, but it was mainly odd details here and there...

The girl on the Tube, her small gloved hands holding the newspaper; the light, ghostly dust deposited on every single surface in the big, empty house in which he had had his interview with Saturnin Bloom; the way the spicy tobacco had prickled his nose and made him go all heady; the strange sensation in his stomach as the train had left the grey, soulless, draughty platform at Paddington; it had felt like a ship casting off on her way to unknown territories...Then the smell of varnish in the Oxford Morris and the imposing, surrealistic beauty of the cast iron sun and moon attached to the gates of the estate. Those mysterious fixed half-smiles were the last things he remembered from the journey. What had happened afterwards? Had he fallen asleep? Why hadn't anyone woken him up? Had he fainted? Had it been the fumes from the car? It was embarrassing, confusing and scary. It was not a good start to his new life.

The young man looked about him. So, this was Whitemoor Hall. It felt and looked familiar and alien; it had an air of timelessness and yet, it looked authentically old and venerable. He was pleasantly surprised: his room was spacious, with a high ceiling and two good sized windows. It was uncluttered yet cosy, and was decorated with a mixture of Victoriana and early 20th century furniture. There was a big double bed flanked by two perfectly formed side tables, two armchairs, a large wardrobe, a chest of drawers, a small round table with two chairs, a narrow writing desk and a bookshelf.

Adam stood up again and walked towards the wardrobe. Inside, he found various articles of dress neatly folded up or hung: underpants and pyjamas, shirts, trousers and jackets. They all looked new but were definitely in a much older style, and he felt as if he had been inspecting the props for a movie set in the 1920s. The clothes seemed to be exactly his size. His eyes fell upon two leather bags at the bottom of the wardrobe. He pulled them out and started to fish out their content and lay them out on the floor; a flash of recognition came to him: they were indeed his own bags and clothes, the dark pants and t-shirts and trousers, the few – now all crumpled – shirts.

At the bottom of the second bag, he found some pens and a brand new notebook, with spiral binding and smooth, creamy paper. There was also an incongruous mobile phone and a charger; Adam looked at the black device and left it where it was, switched off, mute and dead. What use would it be to him here? There probably wouldn't even be any signal anyway. It was probably better that way.

He glanced in turn towards the wardrobe and his own possessions now in a heap on the floor. Were the family expecting him to wear the clothes they had provided for him, rather than his own? Would it be right to indulge such an eccentricity? Neither the maid nor Saturnin Bloom had mentioned anything about the garments, and he had been left to his own devices to try and guess what was expected of him. Saturnin Bloom had obviously been busy, impatient to go back to his work. Gladys had looked shy and embarrassed.

Still unsteady on his feet, Adam crossed the room to one of the windows and peered outside. The building seemed to be floating on a sea of fog. He could just about make out the ground below, a white wooden bench and the contours of what must have been an ornate garden pond.

There was not a soul around, either inside or outside. No human-made sound had reached his ears since Gladys had left. The confusion in his head receded and was replaced by impatience: he couldn't wait to go out there and yet, he was apprehensive about it. It all seemed incredibly surreal... Maybe it was all just a dream.

He turned away from the window. He must have wasted so much time, and the young girl was supposed to come and pick him up... Would he still have time for a quick shower and shave? He looked across the room at the ornamented clock on the mantelpiece; something was not quite right about it. He couldn't really see properly from where he was, and so he went closer, anxiously staring at the face. The handles were ticking *backwards*. Incredulously, Adam closed his eyes for a few seconds, and then reopened them: underneath the arch dial featuring the moon, the handles of the elegant clock face were going undeniably anti-clockwise, back in time. Adam shook his head in disbelief. How did they expect him to be on time if the clock in his bedroom didn't work properly? He looked around for another one, remembered that he had a watch, fumbled for a few minutes looking for it and didn't find it until he opened the drawer in one of the side tables by the bed. There was his watch, showing 9.30; it had a long, single crack cutting through it exactly on the half hour mark: his watch had stopped and was now broken. He remembered that they had crossed the gates of the estate at *exactly* 9.30pm; he had looked at his watch then, and it hadn't been cracked. With no way of telling the exact time, all Adam could do was to get ready as quickly as possible and wait for Gladys to show up.

As he stood in the shower, naked and feeling oddly vulnerable, Adam knew that he was washing away the last remnants of the wretched London air off his skin. He wondered what the strange world of Whitemoor Hall was like outside the sturdy bedroom door. One thing was certain: it would be very different from the one he came from.

THREE

D imitri was dreaming of ghosts; not the ones who regularly came to disturb his quiet days – those ones weren't dreams; they were real, materialising at the end of a room, at the top of the stairs, in the middle of the courtyard or even on one of the numerous footpaths that criss-crossed the estate. Those ones, he could perfectly see them; besides, they were usually resoundingly silent.

The ones that inhabited his dreams that night were invisible, moving on the edges of his consciousness, within the folds of his resting brain. They were only noises, improbable sounds: the moving of some furniture, the shifting of undistinguishable objects, the rustling of sheets, curtains or clothes; low, conspiratorial conversations, whispers, thumps, creaks and squeaks. They sounded close. Then something in his sleep raised the alarm and he opened his eyes. He thought for a moment that he had gone blind, because he found himself staring into nothingness, or rather into an opaque, absolute blackness. He was not in the habit of waking up in the middle of the night; he always went to bed early and slept soundly until the morning.

Without a move, he lay there, listening to the ghostly sounds. He heard footsteps along the corridor, just outside his door – he stopped breathing then for two whole seconds; but they carried on, passed the study room, then... Were they in the other bedroom, the one on the other side of the study? Were the revenants using the unoccupied space as a meeting room, or for a party of some kind? He pondered what a ghost party would look like. At any rate, it would probably feel more alive than any of the rare 'family meals' at Whitemoor Hall. He smiled in the dark. He quite liked the idea of a spectral celebration... Dimitri had never been to a party. He wondered whether, after all, they were ghosts at all? Probably not. But then, who was moving things around in the other room?

He was seized with a burning desire to go and see what the fuss was all about, but he stayed put in the dark. He was alert and intrigued, his young heart pounding with excitement – never with fear, for he was never afraid of anything, how could he, with this strange power of his? He waited, expecting something extraordinary to happen. The noises lasted a little while longer, then a door was carefully shut and the footsteps went past his door again, all together this time. How many of them were there? He heard them cautiously going down the stairs, then could just make them up reaching the ground floor and dispersing in various directions. Complete silence was now restored. It was so utterly quiet and so infinitely dark that Dimitri closed his eyes against the void. He gave a sigh of relief, one that was mixed with disappointment.

They hadn't been ghosts at all. The noises they had made had been disappointingly real and practical. But who had it been? And what had they been doing? Nobody slept on this side of the East Wing apart from him. He had always been on his own since he had moved to this part of the house, when he had been deemed 'grown up enough'. How old had he been? Six? Seven? Yes, he had moved down here from the stifling nursery the day of his sixth birthday. He had been so happy, so relieved – and not a little proud – when he had realised that this big, grown-up room would be his and his only. It had become his refuge, his universe.

He had never seen any ghost in it. Adults rarely came to see him here. It was as if some kind of invisible barrier had been erected outside his door to protect his little world. Gladys and Ginny would come in, of course, but then they were hardly adults. Miss Finch had been in here once or twice when she had been in charge of him, but she had seemed reluctant to stay. They had spent most of their time together either in the study or in the large drawing room on the ground floor. Next, he tried to remember his mother coming to his bedroom. She had always kept her distance, as if she might be struck with some contagious virus if she walked over the threshold. She had never sat on his bed to read him a story.

And then, probably the most unexpected had been Vangelis Chronos's recent visit, when they had sat together at the table and pondered over Dimitri's 'treasure'. The boy had been thinking about his precious bundle ever since and had often regretted having handed it in. He hadn't dared asking his stepfather what had become of the leather notebook and the colourful, precious jewellery box. He wondered whether the scholar had managed to find who they had belonged to. Dimitri thought that the journal might have contained some interesting stories or secrets. Maybe the name of that solemn man who had appeared to him at the spring was written somewhere among the yellowed parched pages? What did Vangelis Chronos intend to do with the box? Most importantly, he, Dimitri, had been true to his promise and hadn't said a word about his discovery to anyone; who would he have told about it anyway? He didn't have anybody to talk to.

The image of the box appeared in the boy's mind and refused to go away. He closed his eyes and fell asleep again, surprisingly quickly. He dreamt of the beguiling insect jewellery and of the fresh, soothing spring where he had found his precious bundle.

FOUR

Whitemoor Hall was enveloped by a thick, pervasive and damp fog. Dimitri was standing at the window, fascinated by the vaporous, unstable texture of it. Every morning, he did exactly the same thing: he got out of bed and walked directly to the window, swept one of the heavy curtains to one side and had a peek at the outside world. He never tired of the view, which was different everyday depending on the weather, the season, the amount of dampness in the air...

That morning though, he couldn't see a thing beyond the arches of the rose garden. It made it look unreal, eerie, like a floating vessel on a sea of gauze. The surface of the pond looked undisturbed, like a vast smooth mirror. The blue lotus remained stubbornly closed and its stem looked slightly bent, as if flagging under the sheer weight of the air. It would make his mother sad. He wondered if she would be going down later on to have a look at the flower. How disappointed she would be when she'd find it shut tight against the outside world! Sophia Chronos had developed an obsession since seeing the flower for the first time. She had tried to go down and have a look at it every day. Today was the first time the flower wasn't triumphantly spreading its hued petals. Without the patch of bright colour, the garden looked abandoned, as if about to go to ruin. It had appeared so glorious under the sun at the height of summer. Dimitri hated the fast approaching winter.

He made a face, wrinkling his forehead and his nose... What would he be doing today? It had been five months since Miss Finch had left and he hadn't had any English lesson since her departure... Not that he was going to complain about it. He had been able to enjoy the pleasures of the summer to the full for the first time. He had had a few science and maths lessons with the severe Mr Bloom, but those were never regular. He was wondering whether he would ever have another governess. He sighed. So... Today... Like a flash, he remembered the strange noises of the previous night. Yes, of course! He would go and investigate what had taken place during the night! He would turn into a detective for the day!

He was about to get started on his morning ablutions when a rapid knock was heard on the door, which opened a little too quickly and nearly banged against the chest of drawers that was placed near it. Gladys entered the room, carrying the usual morning tray. But it was not the teapot or the cup that caught Dimitri's attention, but rather the queer expression on the young maid's face. The boy had never seen any colour on Gladys' rather pasty face; he had never caught as much as a smile on it. And yet, that very morning, he was astonished to see the girl's face radiating with a high pink colour, the tip of her ears the pinkest of all. Her usually dull eyes looked bright, and a vague half-smile was pasted on her thin lips. The boy simply couldn't stop looking at her as she busied herself pouring a cup of tea for him.

'Gladys,' he started.

The little maid lifted her head and actually looked at him, something she usually avoided, preferring to stare at the floor.

'Yes, Master Dimitri?'

'Are you... Are you *alright?*'

The girl, having finished, stood straight, her sparse eyebrows lifted, the strange smile still in place.

'Oh yes, Master Dimitri, I am well, thank you.'

Dimitri, looking younger than his age in his long white night shirt, came closer to the table and picked up his tea cup. He was still looking at the girl, frowning inquisitively.

'Did something unusual happen last night?'

'Last night?'

'Yes. I got woken up by some noises...'

'Some noises, Master Dimitri? Like what?' asked Gladys, opening her eyes wide, her eyebrows higher than ever.

'Well, like... like some people carrying and moving things in one of the rooms along the corridor. Is anyone changing rooms?'

A light of understanding shone on Gladys's face.

'Oh yes, I know! That'd be the new tutor who's arrived to give you lessons, Master Dimitri, that's what it is!' Gladys's colour rose alarmingly as she pronounced those words.

'A new tutor? You mean for *me?* To give me lessons, like Miss Finch used to do?'

'I s'pose so... Didn't you know? I'd have thought you'd have been told, as it's all for you, after all.' Gladys surprised herself; she was not used to voicing her own opinion.

'So, there's going to be a new tutor, and he will be sleeping in the big room on the other side of the study, just there?' With his thumb, the boy pointed to his left in the direction of the study.

'Yes, he's spent his first night here. I… I brought him his morning tea earlier, and now he's in the downstairs study with Lord Chronos and Mr Bloom. His name is Mr Tuckfield.'

Dimitri was confused: he was feeling a little bit shocked, intrigued, curious and annoyed, all at the same time. Nobody ever told him anything, even if it concerned him first and foremost! Nobody *ever* cared about what he thought, just because he was only eleven. How impatient he was to be all grown-up! He would show them, then! The wave of indignation lasted only a few seconds; the boy quickly came to his senses. He went closer to Gladys, and asked in a low, conspiratorial voice:

'You saw him, then… What is he like? Is he as old as Lord Chronos? Does he look as severe as Mr Bloom?'

He waited for the girl's reply, which came with yet another wave of flushing; her voice betrayed excitement, something that sounded rather alien to Dimitri's ears. There had never been a lot to get excited about at Whitemoor Hall.

'Oh, Master Dimitri, you're so very lucky! He's young and he looks ever so nice! He was really polite with me. I'm sure he's a very, very good teacher! You will like him a lot. Let's hope Lord Chronos and Mr Bloom will like him too!'

Slightly embarrassed by her gushing, Gladys gauchely asked whether Dimitri would like to have some breakfast brought up to the morning room then left, leaving a perplexed boy behind. Dimitri hurried his morning preparations and got dressed in record time. He then proceeded to start his investigation.

He cautiously opened his bedroom door and popped his head out: nothing on the right, nothing on the left. He stood on the threshold for a moment: no noise was coming from the above floor, where his mother's rooms were located. He could vaguely hear some sounds coming from the South Wing, where people were getting ready for the day. Even though theirs was not a big household, there was always something going on around the service block and yard: deliveries for the kitchen, the garden, the stables, even for the abbey. Sometimes, some strange boxes and parcels would get delivered for Mr Bloom or his stepfather. Even though most of the house's activity remained invisible to the boy, he was nevertheless sensitive to all that was going on; Whitemoor Hall was the unlikely centre of some important activity.

Dimitri's socks advanced silently on the deep red rug that ran all along the corridor. The boy passed the familiar door of the study. For a moment, he visualised the quiet room, with its two desks – one oak pedestal desk for the tutor, one smaller and simpler for the pupil; the shelves and the rows of books, manuals and encyclopaedias; the shiny globe and the map of Britain used in geography lessons; the 'art table' littered with paper, pens and brushes...

Dimitri stopped. He was standing in front of the door of the second bedroom, the one on the other side of the study. This was the room from which he thought the noises had come from the previous night. He stood there, unsure of what to do next. He put his ear against the wood and listened: the room was empty. It would be, as Gladys had told him that the occupant had been summoned to Vangelis's study. He wondered whether the door would be locked, or if he could get in and satisfy his curiosity. He stayed there, his head bowed in reflexion and biting the inside of his mouth for about half a minute, then put his hand on the cool brass of the handle. He was about to turn it when a door banged upstairs and some floorboards in the corridor above him creaked under someone's weight. Then somebody slowly came down the stairs. Dimitri, petrified, recognised his mother's painful advance and his heart tightened in his chest.

Sophia Chronos stopped on the last step, obviously surprised to have come across her son standing in the corridor with a guilty expression on his face. She frowned. Her pure visage already carried some unspoken irritation. Her voice was the usual mixture of tiredness and bitterness.

'Oh. I wasn't expecting to find you here. And pray, what are you doing standing in front of that door?' Sophia sighed before carrying on. 'I have been ringing Gladys, and she hasn't appeared yet. Where on earth is that girl? Why, oh why, has Ginny decided to get ill and leave me at the mercy of the capricious mood of a mere girl?' As usual, this had been uttered with a little more pathos than was required. Sophia Chronos hadn't been on the cusp of stage triumph twelve years previously for no reason.

'Now look at what I have to do. Even in my condition, I have to go and try to find the wretched girl myself.' Sophia went down the last step and stopped again at a good distance from the boy. She shot him a reproachful glance.

'You should be in the morning room having breakfast. Have you eaten?' She eyed him suspiciously, her dark eyes resting on the boy's pale cheeks. 'I will need Gladys to help me dress, you see…' She pulled at the sleeve of the frilly dressing gown she had put on before leaving her bedroom. 'One shouldn't have to go out of one's room without proper clothes on. It simply isn't done. I'll have to ask you to do something for me.' She had pronounced the last few words with a tinge of regret.

Dimitri's face lifted towards his mother's. He looked at her delicate features, the narrow, perfect oval of the face eaten away by the dark brown eyes. Her surprising white-blond hair was tied in a loose ponytail cascading down her back; it was thick with small curls. Her unusual mane, together with her perfectly white skin, her light brows and eyelashes, her straight, delicate nose and small, thin mouth, gave Sophia the allure of an angel that had fallen to earth. Dimitri thought his mother most resembled a graceful, ethereal ghost. Of course, he would love to do something for her, to be useful to her! It was always down to the maids – mostly Ginny – and to Vangelis Chronos to do things for Sophia. The boy nodded.

'Good. Could you go down to the service block and tell Mr Simms that Gladys hasn't been answering my calls. *Nobody* has been answering my calls. Tell him that I need someone to come and help me dress *immediately* because, as he knows perfectly well, I can never get started on *anything* until I'm washed, dressed and ready to face the day. Today, I am up early and I want to go out for a walk.'

'But it is very foggy outside. I couldn't see further than the back of the rose garden half an hour ago!' warned the boy.

Sophia looked at her son with a mixture of contempt and disapproval. The corners of her mouth lowered and her fingers fiddled with the folds of her dressing gown. Her voice turned blunt.

'But that is the point, you see. I want to go and have a walk in the fog, so I can disappear and lose myself in it.'

Her eyes went vague for a few seconds; Dimitri patiently waited. Without looking at him again, Sophia turned round and started towards the stairs she had just descended.

'I am going back to my bedroom now. Do go to the service block and send someone immediately. I'll be waiting.'

Dimitri started promptly, forgetting that he was not wearing any slippers or shoes. He reached the ground floor and crossed over to the South Wing into the service block. As he approached the latter, the sounds grew louder. He realised that he was only wearing his socks when he went from the comfortable rugs and carpets of the main house to the tiles in the corridor leading to the kitchen. His toes started feeling cold and the sensation travelled up his legs to reach his upper body; it made him shiver. Soon, he was standing outside Mr Simms's office. The door was closed, and this meant that he was engaged in 'business' – at any other time, the door was kept open. On the other side, the boy could hear the head butler's controlled tones.

'… been acting exceedingly strangely today. We would like to get to the bottom of this.' He then recognised the more forceful voice belonging to the man who managed the estate, Mr Suleman.

'Indeed, Mr Simms. We at the abbey would never condone this type of…'

A mighty clanging came from the kitchen and made Dimitri jump. He didn't wait to hear Mr Suleman's reply and ran straight into Cook's territory, only to stop dead on the threshold: Mrs Abbott, the cook, was sitting at the long table that took centre stage in the kitchen – it looked very much like she had just let herself drop into the chair in despair. She was holding her head in her hands, her face resolutely looking down. On both sides of her were piled up boxes of vegetables awaiting her attention; in front of her was open what she called her 'Cooking Bible', a thick, crowded manual only she was allowed to consult and which she kept locked up in a small wooden chest on the top shelf of one of the large dressers.

At the other end of the room, near the door that opened up onto the service yard, young Paul Briggs was crouching and picking up the copper saucepans, pots and bowls that were scattered all over the tiled floor. He looked sheepish and anguished, his narrow face very white apart from two red dots burning under each eye. Every now and then, he glanced anxiously towards the table, expecting Mrs Abbott to explode in a torrent of insults at any moment. Dimitri took in the scene.

'What's happened?' he asked tentatively.

The cook's head, still covered with her uncannily large hands, shook from left to right in disbelief. She then flung her arms in the air before hitting the table with the palms of her hands and simply exclaimed: 'Ha!' Paul hurriedly stood up, holding two saucepans in each hand like the grotesque extensions of his gangly, overgrown arms. Mrs Abbott turned her round, pleasant face towards Dimitri, and the sight of her favourite seemed to cool her down a little. She had been about to burst into a rage, as Paul had been dreading. But she then had changed her mind and swallowed her anger. She solemnly shut the cooking book and held it against her generous chest.

'I despair, Master Dimitri, I really do. I think I am surrounded by the most incompetent staff I've ever seen. Young Paul here has been showing off his comic skills and just went flying over the threshold with the box of piled up pans and pots he'd been carrying.'

Paul protested weakly:

'But, I wasn't showing off!'

The boy was promptly interrupted by the cook, who had suddenly stood up and already forgotten all about her short episode of desperation. She remonstrated severely:

'No, Paul, unfortunately, you were definitely *not* showing off. And that's a pity, because at least, it would have shown some initiative on your part. No, you were just daydreaming as usual, or worse, in that sort of trance that comes over you abbey people from time to time, even at 10 o'clock in the morning when the day has hardly started!' She then turned to Dimitri. 'I told Mr Bloom, I've repeated it to Lord Chronos: I don't know what they do to them up at the abbey, but they all have some queer behaviour and are not all there... Not ideal when you want to get things done! You never know what kind of mood's going to come over them and when. So Paul, here, was 'away with the fairies' while carrying a whole lot of pans, caught his feet in the door frame and there, dropped the box and all the nice pots rolled around on the tiles... I really hope none has been damaged or he's going to hear about it!'

Mrs Abbott kept shaking her curly head in disapproval. She walked to the dresser, placed the book inside its chest and turned the key in the lock.

Paul thought it better not to argue, and kept his mouth shut. He felt humiliated, especially in front of Dimitri, who was three whole years younger than him. From the height of his 14 years, he considered the young master as being no more than a child. Despite his age, though, Paul himself was far from cutting an imposing figure: very lanky and always looking like he was about to lose his balance, he had an inferiority complex that life at the abbey hadn't completely managed to erase. Mrs Abbott had been right though, he *had* been daydreaming, lost in a kind of torpor that would take him to another world full of lights and sounds, the world he would experience every Sunday during the High Ritual in company of the others… Then, he would forget all about his worries and insecurities and would join his companions in their communion.

'See what I've just been talking about? He's gone again!' Mrs Abbott was saying knowingly to Dimitri. The kitchen boy snapped out of his dream, crouched down and resumed picking up the pots. Mrs Abbott sighed.

'So, dear, what is it you wanted?' she asked Dimitri.

For a moment, the boy stared at her blankly, the reason for his visit momentarily eluding him.

'You must have come here for a reason, eh?' encouraged Mrs Abbott.

'Yes! Yes, sorry! I remember. Oh, Mrs Abbott, mother is going to be so cross with me… She's sent me to say that someone should go and help her dress, as she's been ringing Gladys, and Gladys hasn't gone up. She said that she'd want to get dressed immediately because she'd like to go for a walk.'

Dimitri had spoken quickly, without pausing. He felt dreadful for having wasted so much time. Mrs Abbott looked at him curiously. First, she exclaimed:

'She wants to go for a walk? With that fog?' She then lowered her voice and rolled her eyes. 'Gladys is in trouble! She's been called to Mr Simms's office a while ago, and Mr Suleman is there too, I'm not sure what the poor girl's done apart from acting a bit odd this morning... She came back from serving the morning teas in a right state! All excited and flushed – a little too much, quite unusual for her! – and she kept whispering to Rose, who looked quite disturbed by it all. I think Mr Simms didn't like it at all!' She shook her right hand. 'Now, what are we going to do? Ginny is not feeling any better and I can't send Rose up, your mother would scare the daylights out of her, poor thing.'

Dimitri wondered whether the 'poor thing' was supposed to be his mother or Rose. At that moment, just by coincidence, dressmaker Ethel Taylor walked in, a large basket on her arm.

'Morning, Mrs Abbott! Good morning, Master Dimitri! Have you seen that fog out there? Just plain horrible! Robert couldn't see a thing on the road and it's extended our journey by a good fifteen minutes… But we've made it, and I'm going to be here for quite a while today… I'm taking people's measurements to make some nice winter clothes! What about that? I thought I might come and ask whether I could get a pot of tea to take with me to the drawing room?'

'Hallelujah! Miss Taylor! You've been sent to us by the angels!' exclaimed Mrs Abbott, making Ethel start with surprise. 'We desperately need your help! Could you please do us a favour and run to Lady Chronos's room to help her get dressed? We are having a maid crisis at the moment, and she's been waiting for someone to go and help her for ages!'

Confused, Ethel managed to utter 'Oh, but, certainly, I mean, if I can be of any assistance...' before the cook seized her elbow and started to lead her towards the door. Mrs Abbott turned towards Dimitri without letting go of the dressmaker's arm. 'Dimitri, go and fetch Rose in the larder, will you? Ask her to prepare a pot of tea to be taken up to Lady Chronos's room – with two clean cups! – then she needs to make sure there's another one on the go to be carried to the drawing room as soon as Miss Taylor is ready to start work.' She then dragged Ethel Taylor out of the room.

Obediently, Dimitri went and found Rose, the scullery maid and kitchen assistant. They came back together to the kitchen and the girl started preparing the tea. Paul had finished picking up the pots, had left the box on the floor near the door and had disappeared. Dimitri wasn't too sure about what he should be doing, now that Mrs Abbott had left. He pretended to be interested in the boxes of vegetables that had been left on the table, but he was really observing Rose from the corner of his eye.

At 14, Rose was, like most of the others, part of the community who lived at the abbey and came to work at Whitemoor Hall every day. Much like the others, too, she was a very quiet, introvert creature who didn't communicate with anyone unless necessary. She was wearing the same grey dress as Gladys and Ginny; she was small and lean, with dark hair, dark eyes, a small mouth with slightly protruding front teeth, a pointy nose and a pointy chin. Dimitri thought that she looked very much like a mouse.

'Rose, is Gladys alright?'

Rose almost dropped the cups she was about to place on the tray. Her small black eyes darted in his direction, and she frowned slightly.

'I guess so.' The girl started arranging the cups, spoons and milk jug.

'What has she done wrong?' insisted Dimitri.

Rose stopped again, straightened up and started fiddling with the edge of the tray.

'Don't know.'

'Is it because of the new tutor?'

Rose blushed slightly.

'I wouldn't know, would I?'

'But I saw her this morning and she looked really excited! She told me all about him. Did she tell you about him too?'

Rose's mouth trembled and she seemed ready to say something, then she changed her mind and turned round to check on the boiling water.

'No.'

Disappointed and realising that he wouldn't get anything more out of the girl, Dimitri decided to go back to the main building. On his way out of the service block, he passed Mrs Abbott, who was trotting back to her kitchen.

'Is that alright now with mother? Is Miss Taylor helping her getting dressed?'

'It's all fine, Master Dimitri. Lady Chronos was getting impatient but she is now pleased to have Miss Taylor's assistance and exclusive attention. I have left them talk dresses and fabrics, so I guess all is well, now. I think we've averted one of your mother's crisis. I now need to go back to my vegetables!'

The cook hurried towards the kitchen. Dimitri was relieved: his mother's outbursts could be embarrassing. He wouldn't have liked it if she had made a scene with the new tutor just arrived in the house. He was feeling irresolute and hesitant, and ended up wandering into the galleried Great Hall.

As always, he felt minuscule there, his small frame dwarfed by the sheer size of the place. He didn't feel welcome in this spectacular space: the monumental fireplace was empty and cold, whereas the intricately carved oak panelling that covered the walls looked at times overdone and grotesque. He lifted his head towards the vaulted ceiling, so far away above his head; at eighty feet high, the Great Hall was one of the numerous exceptional features of Whitemoor Hall, but Dimitri had come to see it as some kind of monster. It was the mouth of the house, or maybe its heart. You would enter the building and be immediately struck by its crushing grandeur.

From the Great Hall, you could either go up the monumental staircase to the galleries with their innumerable doors, or pass through the curved wooden arches that led to one of the network of corridors that ran in every direction within the house. It was very much like a giant digestive system, Dimitri thought, thinking of the detailed and rather ghoulish illustrations found in his anatomy books.

Up towards the ceiling, the weak light of the foggy October morning was trying to pass through the large arched stained windows without much success. The boy was trying not to rest his eyes on the portraits that were aligned all around the gallery. He found those paintings vaguely disturbing and expected one of the subjects to step down from its canvas at any moment. Most of all, he could *feel* those people's presence. The Great Hall was at the centre of an incredible energy whirlwind; occasionally, the air would be crackling with electromagnetism, draughts, unseen presences and inaudible voices. Over the past few years, Dimitri had seen quite a few spectres there: a transparent, distracted young lady had looked down on him once, her elbow gracefully resting on the balustrade and her face cupped in her hand; her portrait, hung opposite the top of the stairs, was showing her sitting on a bench in the rose garden, happy and elegant. Her name was Lucilla. He didn't know who she was.

Another time, he had seen the ghost of an imposing nobleman, wearing his most outlandish outfit and looking quite angry, walk round and round the gallery mumbling to himself. There had been a few children too, running around and chasing each other up and down the red-carpeted stairs; they had disappeared suddenly after having run towards the big fireplace. Today, the ghosts were thankfully not in attendance.

The boy shivered. The place was chilly, lonely and too quiet; even the silence seemed to be amplified by the vastness of the hall. So much unused space! It seemed like a waste. He knew that if he spoke, his words would ricochet off the walls all around him. Sometimes he wished he could live in a cottage, like the Gardener's Cottage or the Guardian's Cottage located in the grounds. Both looked snug, comfortable and above all reassuring. Whitemoor Hall was too big, with too many unoccupied rooms and obscure corridors. It felt like an abandoned ship or a ghost town. Well, at least, it *was* full of ghosts… They actually outnumbered the living by an overwhelming majority.

Dimitri exited the hall via one of the doors on the left-hand side of the room and walked resolutely towards the North Wing where his stepfather's study was situated. He knew he was transgressing one of the silent laws of the place: he wasn't exactly welcome on that side of the house. It was particularly dark and stark, and looked suspiciously dusty. He stopped for a short moment in front of the heavy door he knew to be that of Vangelis Chonos's study; some people were having a conversation inside, but the door was extremely thick and the sound of the voices was far, far away. How long had they been in there and how much longer would they be?

Dimitri found a small alcove with a chair covered in worn out crimson velvet near the door. If he sat there, he would be quite invisible to anyone coming out of the room. He would stay there until they eventually came out. He was determined to catch a glimpse of the tutor before he was formally introduced to him. To keep himself busy while he waited, the boy took out his notebook and pencil and started studying the pattern of the ancient and rather stained carpet under his feet.

FIVE

Sophia Chronos stepped out of the back entrance and stopped, just as she was about to take the steps down to the rose garden. The feel of the air over her face first took her by surprise: her skin contracted, making her look even paler than she usually was, and her lips instantly lost the little colour they had. Her lungs gave a jolt and she had to breathe heavily at first to allow them to function properly.

She hadn't expected the morning to be so chilly. It was the first genuinely cold day of the autumn. She pulled her coat tighter around her and bit her lower lip, full of indecision. She had desperately felt the pull of the open air since she had woken up, but now that she was standing outside the door surrounded by the fog, she wasn't sure anymore. She took a step forward; she could just about make out the immobile surface of the water, but the boundaries of the rose garden had simply disappeared. The house and the grounds looked like they had been swallowed up or eaten away by the thick mist; it was as if someone had made the world disappear. She knew that if she went down the steps and advanced any further, she would eventually no longer be visible from the building. That's what she wanted: to walk into the fog until it made her invisible.

Her eyes searched for the patch of purple that should have been hovering over the water; they didn't find anything. Disappointed, she slowly walked down the steps with infinite care, making sure to position her feet, legs and hips in a way that wouldn't bring too much pain. Once she had reached the low border of the pond, she realised that she wouldn't be seeing her extraordinary flower today: at the end of the rigid stem was a little greenish-grey bundle showing only the tips of the purple petals: the flower was shut tight. It looked sorry for itself and very much the opposite of the triumphant, nature-defying bloom she had come down to admire most days. Dimitri had proudly told her that it was a Blue lotus, and that it was very rare. She had considered it a little miracle of colour, and had been fascinated by it. Flowers had been her salvation, and this one had captured her imagination. She had seen strange things in it: a glimpse of the hope and the vitality she had lost all those years ago; an ally against the dullness of her existence, a tribute to her past triumphs on the stage.

Reluctantly, Sophia turned away from the pond and started walking around it, to where she knew the narrow path cut through the lawn. She was crushing the white gravel under the soles of her ankle boots, producing a crunching noise that sounded much louder than usual in the foggy air. She might have been invisible to the eye, but the sound of her footsteps betrayed her. She enjoyed the embrace of the woolly air.

As she walked, she encountered some familiar features: the white statue of Artemis, the Greek goddess; the ancient oak, with its giant trunk and wrinkled bark… Then the moondial slowly emerged from the fog; as she came closer to it, she noticed it was grimacing. She had never noticed that before, and it disturbed her. She averted her eyes and carried on.

She had now stepped out of the gravel and onto the lawn; her steps were no longer accompanied by the crunch of the stones rubbing against each other and all was silent, apart from the few crows perched on the highest branches of the trees at the edge of the wood. She looked around her: she was entirely surrounded by fog; the house, the woods, the fields had all vanished, and she suddenly felt liberated, at ease in her protective blanket of gauzy air. Sophia stopped walking and closed her eyes, letting the air reach her weakened lungs, feeling the myriads of water droplets melt into the skin of her face. She could smell the wet grass and the earthy scent of some crushed mushrooms. The dull pain that constantly nagged at her loins had calmed down. She lifted and outstretched her arms on each side of her body and started spinning round. The wide sleeves of her coat flapped; she lifted her face up towards the sky and the absent sun. She started feeling dizzy and would have carried on until she'd collapsed on the damp ground but for the noise on the gravel ahead of her. She abruptly came to a halt, giddy, and waited a few seconds before opening her eyes. It took a moment for her vision and balance to stabilise.

There was someone there, moving rather heavily on the small stones. It couldn't be Dimitri as he was so slight. Nor could it be Vangelis or Saturnin Bloom, who were working away in their lair. One of the servants perhaps, looking for her? Sophia could feel all her muscles tense and her nerves jolt. The throbbing, infuriating pain in her loins intensified. Who dared break her peace, she wondered, her fists clenched, her nails cruelly cutting into her palms. She held her breath, lying in wait. The misty air in front of her was disturbed and a human form emerged from the fog, tall and imposing: it was

Eliott Mills, the gardener. He was carrying a toolbox and looked as grave as usual.

Sophia Chronos gave a sharp little squeal; the gardener stopped dead in his tracks and looked ahead of him, trying to see who or what had just cried out. His face betrayed his astonishment at discovering the lady of the house out in the garden on a damp foggy day, on her own and only wearing a light cream coat over her morning dress. He looked at her with questioning eyes, but didn't say a word.

'Oh, it's you, Mr Mills.'

Lady Chronos's voice was weak and faint; she rested her right hand on her chest, trying to bring her breathing and heartbeat under control. The gardener was annoyed and embarrassed, whereas his employer's wife felt trapped. A frosty silence came between them, two shadows facing each other in the intimacy of the fog; it was broken by Eliott Mills.

'Lady Chronos… I was on my way to the west garden to repair that fence that's been broken for a while. I can't really do anything else at the moment because of the fog, and so I thought…'

His voice was deep, slightly authoritative – a remnant of his military career. Sophia flinched under its strength and shuffled on her feet to try and ease the pain between her hips. She could feel the panic and vague disgust creep over her. She was standing on the lawn with the gardener, alone. She felt incredibly vulnerable and at the mercy of this powerfully built man. Her brain started processing his square face framed by dark brown hair and rather old-fashioned sideburns. His eyes were dark blue and intelligent, but Sophia barely registered them; instead, she concentrated on the large hands covered with dark hairs, the wide chest encased in a good cotton shirt and the long, powerful legs inside the dark trousers. He gave out a kind of menace, she thought, something wild and dangerous. She simply couldn't cope with Eliott Mills. She felt small and weak facing him, and hated him for it. She had always done her best to avoid the gardener for the best part of the five years he had been on the estate. He made her flesh creep, that flesh that had been tortured enough already.

Eliott Mills was looking at Sophia, patiently waiting for her to speak. She *had* to say something, surely. This was far too embarrassing for words. The poor woman looked chilled and terrified. Was she afraid of him? That thought worried him. He would never be able to hurt a fly, not anymore.

Sophia straightened up in an attempt to look dignified. With her most haughty voice, she announced:

'I fancied a walk around the rose garden, it… it looks so odd like this, full of fog. I thought it would lift, but it looks determined to remain. I was on my way back. I do not wish to keep you, Mr Mills, good day to you.'

She clumsily started back the way she had come. Maybe she could just sit on her bench for a while and wait for him to have gone away before resuming her walk…

Eliott Mills looked pensively at the slender, limping silhouette moving away from him, swallowed up by the fog a little bit more with each step. What a strange creature, obviously not made for this world. Of course, he had noticed that she had been avoiding him. There had been something disturbing in the way she had reacted to his presence.

The gardener made his way towards the west garden, thinking about poor Sophia Chronos. He felt for her young son, too. He had had the opportunity to observe the two of them together. The boy had always appeared as quiet, intelligent and definitely not unhappy, but you could see the dread in the mother's eyes, something deep seated and immovable. He had always been convinced that Sophia Chronos associated her son with a traumatic event; she hadn't wanted the baby, and the boy was now paying the price. He sighed, trying to push the Chronos family to the edges of his consciousness. He had to concentrate on his task, and then maybe, in the afternoon, he could go and pay a visit to Will. Mrs Abbott had given him two fresh loaves of bread, one for him and one for Will and his mother.

Soon, he reached the fence and deposited his toolbox on the ground, ready for work; Lady Chronos and his friend Will were still very much on his mind: they had something in common, those two. Crushed by life, dependent on others, suffering in the very core of their being. People like him had to be strong for people like them, always. Otherwise…

SIX

At last, Saturnin Bloom stood up. He glanced at Adam, then at Vangelis Chronos and declared:

'Very well! Mr Tuckfield, I think that this will probably do for today. Thank you very much for agreeing to join us for this little working breakfast. I sincerely hope that you have found it as instructive and useful as Lord Chronos and I have.'

'Oh, certainly, certainly!' Adam heard himself say in a slightly flustered manner.

The young man jumped to his feet, suddenly desperate to leave the somewhat overbearing, claustrophobic study; he needed some fresh air. When he had stepped inside the room around two hours earlier, he had thought that he would suffocate on the spot.

He wasn't too sure why the claustrophobia had seized him. Maybe it had been the crowded state of the place: three walls covered from top to bottom with shelves that were almost crumbling under the weight of hundreds of books; there were glass cabinets full of objects, bits of rocks and other minerals, small fragile-looking skeletons and mummified creatures Adam had been unable to identify; the fourth wall, behind the scholar's messy mahogany desk, was covered with ancient maps as well as scientific and esoteric artworks.

The room was dark: several layers of thick velvet hung on each side of the large window, and a net curtain obstructed the view, as if it had been of the utmost importance to keep the outside world at bay. Everything, from the furniture to Vangelis Chronos himself, looked antiquated and scientifically obsolete. Maybe the study was kept this way as a tribute to the past triumphs of science, and there was a modern laboratory somewhere else? There was no experiment bench in the room and yet, Adam could have sworn that he could smell a pervasive, somewhat chemically sour odour in the room, mixed with the spicy fragrance of Saturnin Bloom's exotic cigarettes. Concentrating and eating breakfast in such an unsettling environment had required all of Adam's willpower.

The meeting had revolved around some very practical aspects of Adam's job, and then Mr Bloom had described the way the household was run.

It had sounded deliciously old-fashioned and charmingly shambolic to Adam, who had been used to the fast-paced, chaotic modernity of urban life. Still, this down-to-earth conversation hadn't sounded quite right. The vague feeling of apprehension that had gripped him on entry had stayed with him the whole time, and now his strange ordeal was coming to an end at last.

Vangelis Chronos extricated himself from his comfortable chair and joined Saturnin and Adam as they made their way towards the door.

'I think it is now time for you to meet Dimitri,' announced Saturnin Bloom, 'although I am not too sure of the boy's whereabouts at the moment.'

Vangelis Chronos shook his head of white hair.

'Since Miss Finch left, the boy hasn't been keeping regular hours at all… He's been left to his own devices, I'm sorry to say.'

Adam wondered whether the scholar was really that sorry. During their meeting, he had been distracted the whole time, and Saturnin Bloom had taken the lead. Lord Chronos had nodded and uttered a few words of approval at regular intervals, had observed Adam silently for a while, had added a few kind words about his beloved wife. But overall, Adam's impression was that the scientist had been thinking of something else entirely, some complicated equation, perhaps? The whole thing was so clichéd, he wondered whether he had just walked into the middle of a big joke.

The door opened once again on the dusty, shadowy corridor. Vangelis was staying in his study to get on with his work, whereas Mr Bloom was to accompany Adam back to the East Wing and show him the classroom. Even though he had just had some food, Adam was still feeling slightly light-headed.

The two men walked silently side by side for a while. Adam attempted to familiarise himself with his new surroundings, and tried to memorise the way to the study; his sense of direction momentarily failed him. All through the morning, one important question had been burning his lips; now was the time to ask it.

'Mr Bloom…' he started, feeling his tongue stick to his palate, his mouth suddenly dried out. 'When I woke up in the bedroom this morning, I… I'm afraid that I failed to remember how I had got there from the car. I know it sounds utterly ridiculous, but I genuinely don't remember *a thing* from the moment you closed the gates and started the car again up to the moment I opened my eyes this morning to find myself in bed with a massive headache. Did I... Did I get ill at all at some point?'

Adam glanced sideways at Saturnin Bloom, who didn't betray any emotion and carried on walking unhurriedly. They had now arrived at the bottom of the staircase. Saturnin Bloom stopped, one foot on the first step. His eyes turned a shade darker; his stony face and shaven head shone in the pale daylight; Adam shivered like a child under his gaze.

'How so very strange, Mr Tuckfield. Maybe you have been much more tired than you thought you were. Nothing went wrong yesterday evening: I drove you up to the entrance where you were welcomed by Mr Simms, our head butler. He and I took you straight to your room, as you were understandably tired.' Saturnin Bloom stopped and scrutinised Adam's face, as if he were looking for some reaction on his part. The young man, too astonished for words, remained silent, plundering his mind in search of any small morsel of memory he could find: he kept drawing a blank. The secretary carried on. 'I remember that you accepted a cup of Mrs Abbott's special infusion after Mr Simms had told you that it would help you sleep. You do not remember this either? No? Well, this could be the answer to your momentary loss of memory and headache! Mrs Abbott's concoctions are based on ancient recipes she has inherited from her grandmother, who in turn had inherited them from her own grandmother. Although these teas are medicinal, they are also extremely potent. It will come back to you in time.'

Having pronounced those slightly worrying words, Mr Bloom turned round and started climbing the stairs.

Adam followed in a daze. Was he really ready to believe that his memory loss was due to a particularly efficacious herbal tea? The 'old' Adam, the one from a year and a half ago, would have reacted strongly to this and dismissed it straight away. The 'new' Adam, though, was more prone to accept things as they were presented to him without any protestation. He felt troubled but, above all, embarrassed – he should never have asked about the previous evening, because now he had made himself sound stupid, confused and hesitant, not exactly the ideal qualities for a tutor in charge of an eleven-year-old boy. Saturnin Bloom wouldn't stand for any weakness of character, he could feel it.

Since the job interview, Adam had been wavering between a heady new-found confidence and a state of vague, undefined apprehension. Something was escaping him. He decided not to dwell on it immediately; he would have plenty of time for it when he found himself alone in his bedroom.

They had now turned the corner of a corridor that looked familiar: they were back on the first floor of the East Wing. Mr Bloom stopped in front of the door to Dimitri's bedroom, knocked, then turned the door handle and stepped inside.

'Hello, anybody there?' When no one replied, the secretary turned round and looked at Adam: 'I didn't think I'd find him in here anyway. Let's go to the study.'

Saturnin Bloom opened the next door and invited Adam in.

'Here you are, Mr Tuckfield, this is your territory now: office, classroom, art room and study all rolled into one! I hope you will like it and find it at your convenience.'

The room smelled of dust, wood and paper. It hadn't been used for a while.

'I teach Dimitri a little science and maths when I have the time, but I always do so in the library downstairs. This room hasn't been used since Miss Finch's departure five months ago and needs some fresh air.'

Mr Bloom walked straight to the two tall and narrow windows and opened them in quick succession, letting the air rush in and chase away the stale atmosphere of the room. After having opened the second window, he paused, his attention attracted by something in the garden. Adam silently observed the secretary's tall, black-clad frame as he stood immobile, intently looking at something invisible to the young man.

When Mr Bloom turned round, Adam observed a temporary shift in his facial expression: the nostrils were slightly flared, the mouth was a little pinched, and the eyes squinted. He couldn't determine if Lord Chronos's assistant was angry, offended or pleased by what he had seen.

'It is still quite unpleasant out there, although the fog has thinned slightly. I will now leave you for a while; I am going down to the service block to ask if someone could find Dimitri and bring him over to you. I thought Gladys would be around, but she has disappeared too.' Saturnin Bloom left the room in a visible hurry.

Adam sat against the edge of the teacher's desk and looked around the room. He thought about what he would say to the boy and wondered how he would manage to build a good relationship with him. Dimitri would probably be a difficult child; imagine growing up in such a big, isolated house, with so few people around you, none of whom really paid attention to you! Did the boy have any friends his own age? Did he go to the village from time to time? He had obviously received a very old-fashioned education and had only been working with dusty old books. Certainly, his family could have bought him some recent manuals? What about computers?

Adam realised that he hadn't seen any computer or TV set in the house. During the interview, Saturnin Bloom had warned him that the household was somewhat eccentric… That was putting it mildly! They seemed to have rejected all modern amenities and stuck to the romantic idea of living in a house that hadn't undergone any refurbishment. Everything looked in a pretty good shape, though; they had been good at preserving things. He tried to remember what he had read on the 'Gates of Delirium' website: 'the house has stood empty since 1925'.

He suddenly thought about Saturnin Bloom standing at the window, looking intently down. What had he seen? Adam walked to the window ledge and peered outside. It was true, the fog had receded, and the rose garden was visible again from the first floor windows. And there, on one of the white wooden benches, sat the most extraordinary creature: it was a woman with cascading, luxuriant white-blond hair and a sheer cream-coloured overcoat. From his vantage point, he could see that her face was white and small, her profile exquisitely pure. She was immobile and had her eyes fixed on the closed flower that emerged from under its round floating leaves. She was lost in her thoughts. Adam thought for a second that someone had simply put a mannequin on the bench for effect. He smiled at the thought. After half a day at the house, he had already come to the conclusion that this was a place in which he had better expect the unexpected.

He heard a door open somewhere and spotted Saturnin Bloom walking out of the rear entrance door and go down the stairs straight to the bench. The secretary stopped in front of the white figure. The woman moved slightly; without looking at Mr Bloom, she made a faint gesture with her hand, as if chasing away a fly that had been annoying her.

Adam heard the secretary's deep voice, but he was too high up to catch the actual words. He then saw the woman's lips move, but she had spoken too low for him to hear any sound. The two people in the rose garden had a short exchange, the man seemingly asking the woman to do something and the latter refusing or protesting. Suddenly, she stood up, straight and fragile, a beaming white beacon in the receding mist. The contrast between the angelic but nervous woman and Saturnin Bloom's stolid and dark presence was disconcerting. Adam noticed that the woman was trying to keep her distance and avoided any kind of physical contact with her interlocutor. She started walking slowly ahead of him, whilst he followed, adapting his walk to her pace. He offered his arm to help her climb the stairs, but she stubbornly refused and managed her way up with some difficulty; she retained her wounded dignity all along. Her companion opened the door for her and soon, they had both disappeared inside.

Adam stayed next to the open window, looking down at the now empty rose garden. The lawn and the woods were still not visible from where he stood, but he could hear the crows in the distance. Behind him, the door opened, squeaking slightly on its hinges.

The boy was standing on the threshold of the study, his hand still on the door handle. He was relatively smaller than usual for his age; his face was delicate and pale, with tuffs of very blond, very fine hair falling over his right eye; he was looking at Adam with inquisitive blue eyes. The shorts of his grey suit stopped just above the knees and showed his very thin white legs. He was wearing high woollen socks, but no shoes.

'You're Mr Tuckfield.' It wasn't a question.

'I am indeed. And you're Dimitri, aren't you?'

Adam smiled; instinctively, he had used his 'teacher's voice'. The boy let go of the handle and went to sit at the pupil's desk, just in front of his new tutor.

'Do you like it here?' he enquired.

'Well, I have only just arrived; last night, actually. But I've seen enough over the past few hours to know that this is a wonderful house you have here, Dimitri. A big one too, I reckon it's going to take me a long time to find my way around.'

'Oh yes, it *is* a big house. I'll be your guide, if you want.' Dimitri paused; the tone of his voice had sounded slightly blasé. He glanced at the old blackboard that occupied the right-hand corner next to the tutor's desk. 'Do we really have to start having lessons again? I could just show you around and take you to my favourite places. There are a lot of things to see here.'

'Thank you very much for the offer, Dimitri. I'm afraid that teaching you is now my job. But Mr Bloom and Lord Chronos have also asked me to spend some time with you outside the classroom, and therefore, you *will* be able to show me around.'

The boy raised two almost invisible blond eyebrows.

'Have they? I wouldn't have thought they'd care about that kind of thing… I mean, they are the ones who decided not to send me to school and all that. They spend their time working and never do anything else,' he explained sulkily. 'I've been taking care of myself since Miss Finch left. I've read *loads*! And thanks to the books I've read, I've learnt *a lot*!' A sunny smile suddenly cracked the serious surface of the boy's face. Adam realised the importance of books for the boy, and made a mental note of it.

After a short pause, Dimitri carried on: 'I saw you get out of Vangelis's office earlier. You looked funny then. Did they say anything about mother?' Adam looked at the child, who seemed to like jumping from one topic to the next without warning. Dimitri noticed the tutor's frown and explained: 'I was sitting on a chair not far from the door. You couldn't have seen me, it's in a small alcove. Gladys had told me you would be in Vangelis's study and I was waiting for you, but Mr Bloom stayed and walked with you, so I followed you here without you noticing me.'

'Mr Bloom is probably still asking everyone where you are, he was looking for you.'

Dimitri innocently shrugged, then looked at Adam in earnest.

'So *did* they talk to you about mother?'

'They… They…' What had they said about Lady Chronos? He made something up on the spot: 'Your stepfather said that she would be very happy to know that you were getting your lessons again.'

Dimitri thought about this for a few seconds and pretended not to have heard anything.

'I wonder if she'll like you. She didn't like Miss Finch that much.'

'She didn't? Any reason for that?'

Dimitri looked Adam straight in the eyes with a very serious, almost chilling seriousness.

'Oh, she doesn't like anyone, really. Not even herself.'

The child lifted up the lid of his desk and started rummaging through the small objects and used exercise books that had been left inside the drawer. He then carefully took every item out one by one. Adam was still standing in front of his own desk, his arms crossed over his chest; he looked at the boy, puzzled. Had he heard that right? Had the child just told him that his own mother 'didn't like anyone, not even herself'? Adam thought it a terrible thing to say to a complete stranger. Had Dimitri wanted to provoke Adam's pity? He observed the calm, methodical way with which the boy emptied his desk drawer sporting a peaceful, unperturbed expression on his face. The young man didn't know what to say. With a slightly strangled voice, he asked:

'What are you doing, Dimitri?'

'I am getting rid of all those things I'd forgotten I had in there. If we start lessons again, I'd like to do it properly, with a clean and empty drawer, so I can put my new exercise books in there. I'd like some new ones. Do you think they'll let me have any?'

'Of course, they will… A fresh start, as they say. I can get them for you, if you wish.'

The boy smiled, then. Adam would have to make sure he fulfilled his promise.

'Are we going to have any lessons today?'

'Not today, I'm afraid. I am not ready at all, you see. I'm going to need a few days to get up to date with what you've been doing, and then I'll need to plan a few lessons ahead.'

'Ah, so I can start showing you things, then!' exclaimed Dimitri, delighted.

'Maybe a little bit later. I need to get started.' Adam paused to think. 'Tell me, what do you use for your lessons?'

'Well, we use those books,' he gestured to the shelves around the room, 'then I had some exercise books, but as I told you earlier, I'll need new ones. For art, I use the art table there. That's it, really.'

'No computer?'

Dimitri stared at Adam.

'Pardon?'

'Have you ever used a computer for your lessons?'

'A *what*? Is that a big book, like an encyclopaedia?'

Adam thought for a moment that Dimitri had decided to play a little game with him, but the child's face was full of the most sincere ignorance and curiosity. Was it possible that this 11-year-old boy had never even *heard* of a computer?

'A computer is a machine with a screen, and you can use it to look at images, write and communicate with other people.'

'Oh.'

'You've never seen a computer?'

'No.'

'Would you like to see one?'

'I suppose so.'

'We will have a look at mine, then, one of these days. I've brought it with me. What about TV, then, do you watch TV?'

'TV? Is that another machine?'

Not for the first time, Adam was under the impression that someone was pulling his leg. That was his luck: he had accepted a job in a household that had decided to live as if progress hadn't occurred in the past ninety years or so... It could prove to be interesting and refreshing in a way, and it would be a good 'detox' for him, but to exclude technology completely didn't appear to him to be the best thing to do, especially with a young boy in the house. He would have to adapt as well as he could. It would be back to basics for him and his teaching methods, then.

'Gladys said that your bedroom is the one there, next to the classroom. Mine is on the other side, to the right. We're the only ones on this floor of the East Wing,' explained Dimitri, playing with the edge of an exercise book cover.

Adam saw the boy open his mouth as if to add something else, then shut it again. He picked up one of the old exercise books his pupil had taken out of the drawer and flicked through it. It was a maths book, full of equations, operations and diagrams. The pages were neat, the boy's handwriting rounded and large. Dimitri shifted in his seat and then decided to speak.

'You see, last night, I heard noises in the corridor and sounds coming from your bedroom. I thought at first that the ghosts were having a party!'

Adam lifted his eyes from the pages of the exercise book and looked at the boy: Dimitri's face and voice were serious, matter-of-factly.

'*The ghosts?* Which ghosts?' asked Adam.

Of course, he should have expected it: every English country house had its very own resident ghost, and Whitemoor Hall was no exception to the rule. The boy coloured slightly.

'Well, I was asleep you see, and I think I dreamt! But then as soon as

I opened my eyes, I could still hear the noises and of course, I knew it must have been real people.'

Dimitri had spoken in a hurried voice. He avoided looking Adam in the eye and once again concentrated his gaze upon the exercise book in front of him. His little face had gone very pale again. The next question was asked in a calm, slow manner.

'Do you believe in ghosts, Mr Tuckfield?'

Now the boy was looking expectantly at the tutor, his eyes suddenly larger and animated. Adam was hit by a strange sensation, a feeling of discomfort; something on the child's face had stricken him as unusually grave. He laughed nervously.

'Ha ha! You've caught me unawares there, haven't you? What kind of a question is that, Dimitri?'

Unfazed, the boy insisted: 'But *do you* believe in ghosts, then?'

The smile disappeared from the tutor's face and he tried to compose himself. He wanted the boy to know that he was taking his question seriously, even though he had just blown it by sniggering in a most idiotic manner.

'OK, ok. So my answer is: no, I do *not* believe in ghosts. I don't at all. I believe in rational thinking and scientific proof and I...' He had forgotten he was speaking to an 11-year-old boy. He stopped, because he had just noticed his pupil's face fall under the weight of disappointment. Adam was convinced that Dimitri wanted to hide his feelings from him, but the boy wasn't able to conceal his chagrin. The teacher added precipitately: 'But, I admit that they make great stories. We could study a few together if you were interested...'

But the door that had been half open a few minutes earlier had now been shut. Dimitri had been expecting, hoping for an answer, and he had given the wrong one. Adam could feel that he had missed an opportunity to become the boy's ally straight from the start. He tried to think of a way of reassuring his pupil.

'Is Whitemoor Hall haunted? Does it have a ghost?' encouraged Adam.

The child fixed his gaze again on the old blackboard and sighed.

'I don't know. I don't really want to talk about ghosts anymore. It's boring.'

He got up and started picking up the exercise books and small objects he had taken out of the desk drawer earlier. He dropped them into a wooden box that had been lying on the floor behind the door, and announced:

'I'm going to take this to the kitchen; they'll know what to do with it. Then I can get my new exercise books. You won't forget to ask about them, will you? Can I go, now? You said you needed to prepare the lessons.'

The child was now impatient. Adam nodded and Dimitri, holding his discarded items, disappeared instantly. The tutor could hear the objects rattling around the box as the boy made his way downstairs, until the noise finally died out as he entered the South Wing.

The young man sighed: he wouldn't know today whether Whitemoor Hall had its own ghostly legend! Dimitri's interest in his reply had piqued his curiosity. He wondered what the boy's reaction would have been if he had admitted to believing in ghosts? Who knows what kind of wild stories a child like him could come up with whilst spending so much time wandering around such an evocative Gothic mansion.

Adam decided to start his English lessons with Oscar Wilde's 'The Canterville Ghost', a good way of engaging the boy's attention and maybe get him to start talking about ghosts again…

SEVEN

A dam had been expecting Dimitri or Mr Bloom to return, but instead, they had disappeared into the bowels of the vast house and left him behind to come to terms with the silence and stillness of the place. For a while, he didn't move; he let his brain take in the various details of the room; he was attempting to tame it, to make it familiar to his senses. He would be spending a lot of time in there, and he had better make sure that it was to his convenience.

He tried to think of something to do; He was there to work, wasn't he? He had to find something to keep his mind occupied so as not to ponder the strangeness of the situation and the eerie atmosphere of the house. He picked up the pad and pen he had taken to his earlier meeting with Saturnin Bloom and Vangelis Chronos, and sat at the teacher's desk. The notes he had been taking were mostly about Dimitri's daily routine – or rather the routine they wished him to adopt once again after five months of freedom: wake up at 7.30am, morning tea; get ready then breakfast served in the small morning room at 8.15am; lessons to start in the study at 9.00am; break between 11am and 11.20am; lunch break between 12.45pm and 1.30pm; more lessons from 1.30pm to 3.00pm. Then, there would be a one-hour break for Dimitri before he started his homework hour from 4.00pm to 5.00pm. On Tuesdays, Mr Bloom would take Dimitri in the morning for his science and maths lessons. The secretary was too busy to do any more than this, much to the joy of the boy who disliked the two subjects very much. Friday afternoons would be dedicated to art, and would last from 1.30pm to 5.00pm, taking in the afternoon break. Most days, dinner would be served in the dining room on the ground floor, from 6.00pm to 7.00pm. Dimitri was supposed to retire to bed at 8.15pm and the lights were switched off at 9.30pm very latest. The boy was a big sleeper.

After about twenty minutes at the desk, Adam realised that he wouldn't be able to concentrate and indulged his restless mind. He stood up a little too quickly, toppling his chair in the process; it fell backwards onto the ground and hit the wooden floor, producing a surprisingly resounding racket. The sound echoed around the small room and the movement disturbed some dust on the desk and on the floorboards; its ripples travelled through the walls to fill the corridor then ran through the whole length of the East Wing; it was as if the entire house had started at the sound.

The agitated young man remained standing behind the desk for a few seconds before going back to the window. At last, the pervasive fog seemed to be retreating slowly, reluctantly. Adam could see the end of the rose garden and for the first time the white, fleshy statues inhabiting it; beyond spread the vast expanse of lawn. The first trees of the wood were still mostly invisible to him, but he was now able to make out their black frames and the knotted branches on which were perched the noisy crows. In a few hours, the landscape would reveal itself completely.

Back by the desk, Adam's eyes fell once again on his notes: Saturnin Bloom had indicated that Miss Finch's diaries, in which she had written down the activities and content of her lessons, had been left in the room for reference. And here they were: a neat row of hardcover A4 notebooks, their spine covered with a very thin layer of dust. Adam picked up the one at the end of the row; his fingers left some marks on the dusty cover. On the front was stuck a rectangular cream-coloured label on which a meticulous hand had written in black ink and curly handwriting:

1st April – 31st May 1925

Adam sighed: these were obviously not what he had been looking for… Only some old documents that had been kept in the room as souvenirs of older, more prosperous times, perhaps. Adam had always been interested in history and antiques as well as in art and literature; it was this particular interest that had made him choose the restoration course at the City and Guilds. He had been looking for something to keep his mind busy, and he had found some items of interest… There was no harm in spending a bit of time looking at the notebooks; obviously, nobody cared much about what he was up to that day. He would look for Miss Finch's lesson plans later.

He opened the book. The very faint smell of some old-fashioned *eau de cologne* reached him. On the first page, in the same handwriting and ink as on the label, was once again inscribed:

1st April – 31st May 1925
Lessons and activities diary
By Miss Finch

Miss Finch? How odd. The governess working at the house in the 1920s had had the same name as the last one. He smiled at the thought. Life was really quite strange, sometimes.

The ruled paper wasn't white and smooth, but greyish and a little rough. The first entry started thus:

Wednesday 1st April, 1925

Morning

Checking of homework

Reading and analysis of the last chapter of Charles Dickens's 'Oliver Twist'

Vocabulary and grammar exercises, 'The Beauty of the English Language' textbook, pages 119-120

Correction of exercises and activities

Afternoon

History: Queen Victoria, lesson 2; chronology; textbook 'England in the 19th Century' pages 70 to 80, illustrations and activities pages 72-73

Correction of activities

Geography: Spain. Drawing of the map, with main cities and rivers; Textbook: 'Our World' pages 23-24

Adam started flicking through the book, opening it at random. On each page, line after line of the same, all very neatly presented: the date, followed by the more or less detailed description of the activities of that day, the textbooks used, the literature read, the countries studied... Adam's eyes had been scanning and skimming through the pages with interest for a few minutes when they stopped on a line that made his heart skip a beat:

Friday, 29th May 1925

Due to the glorious weather, I have decided to take Dimitri to the lake for his art lesson

Art lesson: animal drawing, painting the water and the sky

One single chuckle, uncontrolled and involuntary, rose in Adam's throat. Ha ha. Hang on a minute. Had he read that right? Adam went back to the beginning of the diary, and instead of opening pages at random, he started scanning through each and every page.

Tuesday, 7th April 1925

Morning: *sciences and mathematics with Mr Bloom*

Adam fumbled a little bit until he found the lessons for the following Tuesday.

Tuesday, 14th April 1925

Morning: *sciences and mathematics with Mr Bloom*

And it carried on…

Tuesday, 21th April 1925

Morning: *sciences and mathematics with Mr Bloom*

Adam went on reading one page after the other; black, curly inky names kept jumping at him from the pages: Mr Bloom, Lady Chronos, Dimitri… There must have been some sort of mistake. Or rather, this Miss Finch, the governess, must have been a cheeky one, playing at being an old-fashioned governess because it added some spice to her daily routine. After all, *she* was the one who had given her notice, and therefore must have been dissatisfied with her lot at Whitemoor Hall. Had it been her way of alleviating the boredom? The young man threw the notebook onto the desk and eagerly picked up another one at random, further down the row on the shelf. The label read:

1st October – 31st December 1924

Again, the name 'Miss Finch' appeared on the front page and again, he found references to yet the same people. Adam feverishly pondered the entries in various diaries for close to forty-five minutes. Dates were dancing in front of his eyes, unreal: *17th June 1924, 16th November 1923…* He foraged around the desk drawers, only to find an elaborate fountain pen, two small glass bottles containing black ink and some well-used pencils in need of a good sharpening, bits of paper and rulers, some old and unused notebooks, an empty scrap book, an unloved leather-bound pocket book – most certainly an unwanted gift, a discarded calendar – year 1924 – with various events and names scribbled on it: 'Lady Chronos's birthday', 'Katie's wedding', 'Visit to mother', 'Juliet's birthday', 'Dimitri's birthday', 'Dimitri's doctor appointment', 'Summer Fête', 'Village Christmas celebrations' and so on… All so normal and yet, so *unnerving*. An abnormal normality.

In the bottom drawer, he found yet another calendar, this time 1925, with only one date circled: *May 31st*. The word: _LEAVE_ followed by two exclamation marks had been written in capital letters across the empty box next to the date. The governess seemed to have looked forward to leaving the house very much…

So… 1925… Was it so much of a surprise then that everything in the house had felt out of, well, time? He was gobsmacked, because he now found he was barely surprised at the thought of Whitemoor Hall being a 1925 household, just as if he had always known, deep within him. No. No! NO WAY! *What* was he *thinking*? Adam shook his head then nervously passed his hand through his hair; he could feel a slight dampness along his hairline, and he noticed that he had gone weak at the knees. He swallowed with difficulty, so knotted was his throat. Now he had to think calmly, reasonably, practically. There must have been some simple explanation to this charade, and he was going to find out what it was. Much as he had thought, someone was playing a big trick on him; the whole 'recruitment effort', with the girl looking like she had come straight out of a silent movie – only in Technicolor and 3D – and leaving the paper on the train; the abandoned, echoing house in London; the classic car; the memory loss… This was all ridiculous, laughable. He felt like the character in a bad novel.

The young man inhaled deeply and walked out of the study, then straight into his bedroom. Once inside, he closed the door and stood just behind it, looking around the room and still getting this strange, eerie feeling that had been with him since he had woken up in the large double bed that very morning… He hadn't been able to define it; something like walking in slow motion, or seeing things not entirely in focus.

He walked to the clock on the mantelpiece, the one he thought had been ticking backwards earlier that day. The handles were precisely indicating midday. Adam fixed the minutes handle so intensely that his eyes watered. The imperceptible, irrevocable movements of the thin metal strip were indeed going backwards, edging their way towards the 'eleven' when they should have gone towards the 'one'. Adam's skin started prickling all over, from the roots of his hair to his toes. His body temperature rose then fell before rising again, and his heart rate increased exponentially. He suddenly felt like he would explode. He had to get out, talk to someone, and *make sure*. He rushed outside the bedroom, leaving the door open. Without thinking, he literally ran past the study, Dimitri's room and the morning room and down the staircase to the ground floor.

At the bottom of the steps, he stopped, confused, not having the slightest idea where to go. Where was he going anyway? He didn't know. His instinct told him to turn left into the small vestibule and he found himself in a long, rather dark corridor. He decided to ignore the various doors and archways and kept to his path, looking straight ahead of him, not noticing anything, neither the swirls on the dark green wallpaper or the paintings hanging on the walls. Finally, he reached the end and was forced to branch out into yet another wing of the house. When all he had heard so far had been his own laboured breath and the beating of his heart in his ears, Adam could now distinguish some far away noises and voices. Unknown to him, he had finally reached the South Wing of the house and was drawing close to the service area.

He didn't see Gladys turn the corner with a pile of warm, freshly ironed linen in her arms. They collided and cried out in unison. The shock got Adam out of the strange trance he had been in, but didn't diminish his increasingly frenzied anguish. When Gladys recognised him, she immediately turned bright red but didn't display the unusual chattiness she had had that very morning. She had been severely told off by Mr Simms and Mr Suleman, and was now trying to retreat to the behaviour that was deemed acceptable for a member of The Family.

'Sorry sir,' she whispered, embarrassed and out of breath. Her face cast down, she started picking up the linen that had stumbled to the floor. Adam crouched by her.

'Let me help you with this. It's entirely my fault; I was not looking where I was going.' Their hands accidentally touched on top of a towel and Gladys jumped to her feet, as electrified. Adam stood up as well.

'Tell me, Gladys… What's the date, today?'

The young girl looked at Adam with suspicion. She frowned.

'The date? It's… It's Thursday.'

'The *exact* date?'

'Thursday the first of October, sir.' Adam could detect some degree of alarm in the girl's voice.

'Which year? Which *year* are we, Gladys?' He had almost shouted.

The girl's cheeks went into a deeper red. She thought that he was mocking her, and this brought tears to her eyes. She stared widely, her eyebrows lifted as high as they could go.

'It's Thursday the first of October 1925, sir!'

Gladys hadn't expected the effect her words had on the new tutor. Mr Tuckfield looked as if she had just hit him in the face with all her might. She stepped forward, expecting him to fall to the floor in front of her very eyes. She sensed his distress, but didn't understand what could have caused it. What had she said? She had only given him the answer to his question, and a silly question it had been, too! He had perfectly known the date, he was a tutor after all!

The young man lifted his hands to his face and rubbed his eyes; for just a moment, his whole body appeared to sway as if a strong wind had been blowing around him. Then he suddenly stepped towards the girl and grabbed her by the shoulders, his icy fingers hurting her flesh through the fabric of her dress. He looked hard into her face, his usually boyish, attractive features now distorted by confusion and panic. Positively horrified yet paralyzed, the girl shrieked.

'It cannot be, do you hear? It *cannot* be 1925. How on earth could it possibly be 1925? You're lying!'

He hadn't shouted, but had uttered the words in a laboured, horrible way, his voice strangled and hoarse, hammering his truth through clenched teeth. Gladys would have preferred him to shout at her, because this was far worst.

'Mr Tuckfield, PLEASE!' she pleaded.

Adam immediately let go of her, with a baffled expression on his face.

'I'm sorry,' he managed to whisper whilst holding his hands in the air, before he turned around and started walking rapidly in the opposite direction. He was disappearing from Gladys's view just as Mrs Abbott reached the girl's side.

'Is that you who screamed? Was there anyone else here? What's wrong with you today, Gladys?'

Gladys's narrow face was now extremely pale and she was about to burst into tears… Mr Tuckfield had been so nice to her… Poor man, he had looked so scared, so lost… What had happened to him? Swallowing her salty tears, Gladys turned to the cook and lied with a trembling voice.

'Oh, Mrs Abbott, what a stupid girl I am… I was turning the corner when I saw a black thing run across the corridor just in front of me! I bet you it was Midnight! I dropped the linen… I apologise, Mrs Abbott.'

Mrs Abbott, her two hands on her generous hips, harrumphed and frowned.

'That cat! He knows he's not allowed beyond the kitchen, but he always finds ways to wriggle his way through when no one's looking. Now, what's going to happen if he goes walking about the house and Lady Chronos spots him? Oh well, I haven't got any time to waste running after a silly animal, me. I'm sure he'll turn up sooner or later.'

The cook was already returning to her kitchen. Gladys felt relieved but sorry she had used the cat in that way. She was more worried about Mr Tuckfield though… If he were in trouble, maybe the abbey community could do something? They were always ready to help those in need…

*   *   *

They were all insane, that's what it was! He had been looking for a job that would give him back his sanity and return him to some degree of normality, and he had fallen into the hands of a bunch of nutters who were rehearsing for who knew what 1920s play. Or maybe, they were re-enactors whose hobby had gone to their heads and who had formed a strange historical commune? Nowadays, everything was possible! So why not? After all, they were not hurting anyone, not really. He would just have to adapt and accept their eccentric requests and see how long he could last.

As this trend of reasoning was making its way around his brain, the panic started to dissipate, the hot fuzz of it evaporating in the chilly air. He could still feel the energy of his panic attack make his nerve endings crackle and he carried on walking straight ahead. He could easily get completely lost.

He finally reached the front entrance lobby, with its geometric tiles and large half-moon mirror. He wondered whether the heavy-looking, medieval revival oak door would be unlocked. It was. The young man pushed against the heavy wood.

He found himself outside and felt disorientated at first; he was standing underneath Whitemoor Hall's tower situated above the entrance porch. From there, he could see the drive winding away from the house, with its rigid rows of trees either side. An irresistible urge to run away, to escape from this ominous place seized him. He started following the drive, walking fast at first. He could hear each of his steps on the gravel, their sound encouraging him to carry on. He didn't turn round to look at the building. He wasn't sure why, he just couldn't do it, as if he were afraid of glimpsing something terrible if he did. He didn't look around him, at the lawn, the trees or the edges that would flower once again in the spring; he didn't admire the stonework on the garden stairs and the fence; he didn't stop to look at the beautiful if extremely damp countryside around him. He was locked inside his own head, the panic rising in his chest once again for no apparent reason.

He reached yet another curve in the endless drive and started trotting, then running. He was fleeing the clutches of an invisible monster; he was pursued by an effluence of irrational fear that had taken control of his mind and his movements. He ran without noticing the chill of the countryside air that penetrated his thin shirt; he was numb, as if he were trying to escape some kind of drunken hallucination, his eyes burning and his head throbbing.

At long last, he reached the end of the drive where he stopped in front of the huge iron gates and tried to catch his breath. He was now back to the place where he had fainted in the car the previous evening. It was a strange, atmospheric spot. The grey sky appeared through the mangled branches of the trees, which were shaking from time to time under a weak, rather chilled autumn wind. Adam could see the asphalt of the road on the other side of the ornate gates, but he couldn't hear any engine on the isolated country lane. It was quiet, as if the now fast retreating fog had stunned nature and made it hesitant.

The sun and the moon that had so impressed him bathed in the red lights of the Morris looked far less menacing in daylight, but their grimaces still inflicted their unpleasantness upon Adam; they made him feel observed, judged. 'FOOL!' they seemed to be saying.

Don't be such an idiot! They are just iron adornments, not living entities, he thought. And yet, they still looked as if they were guarding the exit and had been planted there precisely to prevent people like him from leaving.

Adam thought about the 'Gates of Delirium' website, especially the section in which the author had described how he had walked along the tall brick wall for so long and had stood outside the gates without ever being able to find a way in or catch a glimpse of the house. He was exactly in the opposite situation: he was inside, dying to get out, and it looked like he couldn't. He eyed the sturdy padlock and its thick, heavy chain. There was no pedestrian side gate, and the wall was far too high for him to even think about trying to climb over it without a good ladder. Adam knew these were only gates. He wanted to believe that, in the future, he would be given the opportunity to get out of the estate and explore if he so desired. Looking at the road on the other side, he could feel some kind of strange longing, as if he knew, in his heart of hearts, that he would never be able to reach it again.

He stepped forward towards the gates and stood against the cold metal bars. His fingers grabbed them, making him look like a prisoner looking at the outside world from inside his prison cell. Still holding a bar of metal in each hand, he looked up towards the top of the gates, the hard spikes pointing up towards the sky. In frustration, he tried to shake them; of course, they didn't bulge. The two sculpted faces were considering him, their frozen rictus mocking his useless efforts.

'Oh for fuck's sake!' he shouted out loud, before returning to lean against the metal bars of the gates. The iron felt cool against his burning brow for a minute. He closed his eyes, the panic and stress having worn his nerves out.

'Tut tut tut. It's not nice to swear. Besides, there's no point at all, you know. You won't get out.'

She was there. She looked so out of place, just like the day she had appeared to him on the Tube train a few weeks back. She was wearing a little dark blue felt cloche hat low on her forehead, her eyes just visible under the brim. The bottom part of her face was disappearing behind the big fur collar of a beautiful dark blue wool velour coat. The contrast between her dark clothing, her pale skin and her red mouth was startling and made her look more than ever like an apparition.

Adam had turned round with his back against the railings, the moon face looming above him. The young woman came closer then grabbed one of the metal bars in her gloved hand.

'What a horrid thing this is, is it not?' She looked up at the sun and made a face. Her voice was surprising: velvety and slightly playful on the surface, it had a smoky, deeper undertone. 'Those sculptures are beastly, but I guess they were not made to be pretty. They are supposed to sow fear in people's hearts!' She had pronounced the word 'fear' with a mock-horror tone and chuckled quietly afterwards. She turned round and joined Adam.

Now the two of them were standing side by side with their backs against the hard iron of the gates, looking straight ahead of them at the damp drive and the near-naked trees. The young woman shifted her head and body so she could look at Adam. She observed his boyish, regular profile. She liked the strand of hair that was falling over his face; she wanted to reach out and touch it with her leather-clad fingers, but she refrained from it. She could sense his anguished confusion.

'It's nice to be able to speak to you at last,' she said quietly.

Adam detached himself from the railings and stood unsteadily, his hands in the pockets of his trousers.

'Are you for real?' he asked, looking intently at her.

'Am I for...? Ha!'

She laughed joylessly. The cloche hat swayed, the fluffy fur collar fluttered. Shiny white teeth sunk into the bottom red lip. The excitement of at last finding herself face to face and alone with Adam had been dampened, buried under the weight of the bitter realisation that there was too much explaining to do, and that once this would have been done, he would probably hate her.

'It's all because of you!' exclaimed Adam.

'I'm sorry?'

'All this!' He gestured wildly in a motion that encompassed the horizon, the trees, the sky and the gates. 'Just because you left that stupid newspaper on the Tube for me to pick up!'

He was back against the railings, steadying himself, rubbing his face with both hands. When he removed them, his hair was sticking out above his forehead, making his charm more rakish still. 'Because you left it there on purpose, didn't you, so I could pick it up?'

She was glad her hat and fur hid most of her face.

'Yes, I did,' she finally admitted, her head sinking slightly between her shoulders. She wasn't proud of herself at all, now, although she had been then. She could see how miserable she had made him. 'I was *asked* to do it,' she said.

Adam could feel something unravel inside him: the bizarre sensation that had bothered him since their Tube encounter, the strange build up of tension and expectation; he had somehow known something had not been quite right. He had lived through the past few weeks as if in some kind of dream, going through the motions automatically, guided by an outside force. He was here now, and whatever the reason, he had to understand.

'Who...' He couldn't go any further; the woman turned to face him and put both her gloved hands on his shoulders, her small face lifted towards him, an odd playful gravity about her.

'Not here. Would you come with me?'

Without waiting for his answer, she started on her way towards the house. Her steps were small but fast, and after a few moments of hesitation, he had to almost run to catch up with her. He settled next to her and they walked silently side by side for a minute or so. At last, he asked:

'Where are we going?'

'To my house, I mean, it's not *really* my house... I live in the Guardian's Cottage on the other side of the lake. I'd rather not walk past the Hall, if you don't mind, so we'll have to go round the lake and cut through the lawn.' She glanced at him. 'You really *do* look cold, you know. You're wearing close to nothing. You're going to catch a nasty chill, and you won't be able to start your new job.'

Adam thought that whilst she seemed to know a lot about him, he knew nothing about her, not even her name. At least, he was *almost* convinced that she wasn't a hallucination, after all. He shivered, with both exhaustion and cold.

'You see? You're frozen to the bone, poor darling.'

She put a hand on his back and rubbed it vigorously, in a familiar, affectionate way, just as she would have done if they had been old friends, or even lovers.

'I've got some cardigans at home that will do splendidly; but we're not there yet!'

The young woman left the path and started walking across the lawn. The rich earth was sticking to the heels of her little boots. Suddenly, the Hall appeared on their left; it looked like a contented and venerable monster resting on its belly in the middle of its vast and prosperous territory. Fragments of torn fog had attached themselves to the bushes and the trees, reluctant to dissipate.

They soon reached a tranquil man-made lake in which the water was only disturbed by a few brave ducks. Vaporous strands of mist hovered over the water, adding to the atmospheric gloom of the scene. A few benches had been set up all around it, and Adam could perfectly imagine the very same spot in the spring or summer, the few bushes and edges in bloom, the lawn welcoming and dry, as bouncy as a thick carpet.

They carried on walking, leaving the lake behind them, joining a narrow track as it winded its way away from the house in the opposite direction.

'Where is this one going, then, if we can't get out by the main entrance?' Adam pointed to the dusty path.

'This is one of the exits towards the village of Whitemoor, about three miles away. They all join the main road eventually; there is another one over there,' she pointed to the east, the view now obstructed by a small coppice that seemed to sprang up in the middle of the estate, 'and it comes out of the service block, passes the stables and goes out by the south exit towards the village. That's the way most deliveries arrive at the estate. Everyone else prefers the small road we're on at the moment.'

They were now approaching the small wood and as they went around it, a snug little cottage soon appeared.

'I know what you're about to say: *'It's lovely!'* Well, when you've lived in there six months, you come back and tell me about it. Me too, at first, I found it quaint. But I was not exactly myself when I moved in, and I've since come to my senses. Not that it really makes any difference…'

Her voice had hardened; the velvety tones were replaced by sharpness.

She unlocked a small wooden gate and walked up the short cobbled path to the tiny front porch. The naked, twisted branches of wisteria vines covered most of the wall on either side of the entrance door.

'Do be careful not to bang your head on the door frame. This cottage was not made with tall people in mind.'

Inside, the lounge was such as you would imagine: it was furnished sparingly yet rather cosily with items that must have been as old as the house itself but in good enough condition. The flowery curtains were drawn and the wooden floor was covered with patterned rugs of an exotic provenance.

The two sofas had seen better days but their weathered appearance added to their charm. The only object that looked new was a portable wind-up gramophone in one corner. On a narrow dresser by the window, an assortment of half empty bottles, used glasses and a full ashtray were clues to an earlier gathering of merry souls – unless they were the remnants of a melancholic solitary drinking session. Adam averted his eyes.

The young woman opened the curtains, allowing the pale October light to reveal a little bit more of the messy room. There were cushions and pillows everywhere, on the floor and on the sofas, on the armchair… Some scribbled sheets of paper and newspapers were lying about, covering the coffee table and the floor underneath. She read Adam's disbelief on his face. As she started removing her hat and gloves, she warned:

'I know it looks like a crazy, alcoholic grandmother lives here. It's not the case, unless I am much older than I think I am. Although to you, I…' She stopped.

'Yes?'

Adam looked at her unusual face, now framed by her short, wavy bobbed hair. It had been flattened by the cloche hat, but it suited her well. A shadow of regret and sadness passed over her face and she shook her head.

'Nothing. Not now… Let's get comfortable first. Do take a seat.'

She gestured towards one of the sofas.

Adam was feeling lost, overwhelmed by the contrasting emotions he had been going through over the past forty-eight hours. His panic had definitely gone now, and been replaced by a strange mixture of excitement and heightened expectation. He felt as if he had been wandering around a theme park, and he was about to know more about this stranger whom he had thought had only been a dream. Yes, she was a stranger and yet, she now felt familiar to him; when they had met at the gates, it had been like finding an old friend again.

Whilst removing her coat, the woman walked through an arched door into a small, rather primitive kitchen and called out from there.

'What would you like to drink? Tea or alcohol? Any of those should warm you up.'

Adam glanced at the crowded tray on the dresser.

'Tea will be fine, thanks.'

She appeared on the threshold of the kitchen, wearing an elegant day drop waist dress of red brick colour. Out of nowhere, Gladys's voice rang in his head: *Today is Thursday the first of October 1925, sir...* Adam's hostess caught his eyes on the bottles and dirty glasses.

'Oh, come on... If you must know, I had a small, intimate party last week with a few friends I had managed to smuggle into the estate. I just haven't had the will to clear up since. I only drink in company.'

She was so at odds with her surroundings that Adam refused to believe she actually lived in the cottage: she looked so sophisticated and vivacious in her perfect dress and was not at all suited to the genteel setting. He couldn't stop looking at her; his eyes were irresistibly drawn to her glorious, exquisitely groomed face.

She had returned to the kitchen and all he could hear for a while was the clicking noises of the cups and crockery and the hissing whistle of the kettle. Adam didn't move at all the whole time she was out of the room. He felt stunned.

'Would you be a pet and clear that table for me?' she asked from the kitchen. He did as he was told.

The tray was now on the table, and they each had a burning-hot cup of tea waiting for them in round white cups; the young woman had joined Adam on the small sofa, smiling.

'How positively divine! I can't believe you are here, having tea with me!' Her green eyes were gleaming with a strange, seductive light.

'But I don't even know your name!' exclaimed Adam.

'Oh... I guess we might as well have some kind of formal introduction: Maeve Hayward, journalist and spy, at your service. 'Maeve' comes from the Gaelic 'Maebh' and means *'intoxicating, she who makes men drunk'*. Don't you just love it? I really wonder what my mother was thinking of at the time... Poor mummy...'

The name suited her all too well... Adam tried to change the topic of the conversation.

'Why did you say you were a spy? Who are you spying for? And, more importantly, *who* are you spying *on?*'

Maeve put on a serious face. She took a sip of her tea, careful not to smudge her lipstick.

'I am not sure how much I am allowed to tell you. I think you'd better hear the truth from the mouth of Uncle Vange. My uncle is Vangelis Chronos, by the way. I 'spy' for him, although the one giving me my 'orders' has mostly been our friend Saturnin Bloom. And for the past few weeks, well, it's *you* I've been spying on. You guessed right, I left the newspaper in the carriage on purpose, for you to pick up.'

'And if I hadn't picked it up? If someone else had been faster than me?'

'Then we would have organised another little encounter. We just *had* to have you hooked!'

'But how did they know who I was? Why did they want me to come here?'

Maeve shook her head.

'I'm sorry. I don't know the answer to that. I'm only an assistant. I don't ask questions and I don't think I would get any answers if I did.'

'But how... I mean, *why* are you doing this? Why are you living here? You're not exactly the countryside type!'

'I'll take that as a compliment!' she sniffed.

She started rummaging through a small basket placed next to the feet of the sofa and found a packet of cigarettes, a slim, elegant tube that Adam identified as a cigarette holder and a sleek, precious-looking enamel and silver lighter. She presented the packet to Adam, who accepted one. Maeve blew a cloud of smoke towards the ceiling.

'Look. I know this sounds insane, but you'd better do as I did: don't ask too many questions. Accept the craziest things as fact or reality, as you like, it'll be better for your sanity.' She took her eyes off his face and fixed the wall opposite. 'You'll find that... a lot of things you previously took for granted before you came to Whitemoor Hall are going to be challenged. Nothing is what is seems. A lot of strange things are going on, but it's all underneath the surface, never too far from it, but it never *really* shows itself... It's all suggested in the atmosphere, don't you think? I've just embraced it like the silly little idiot I am, without digging into the why and how of things, a novelty for me. I guess... Discovering the truth in that case would be far too terrifying for words. I've chosen self-preservation. I don't think I had much choice in the matter anyway.'

She looked at him again. Her face had lost this effortless, natural sultriness it had possessed earlier and had grown paler underneath the ivory powder; Adam noticed for the first time the dark circles around her eyes. She resumed her explanation.

'I haven't been here that long, and I expect... hope... that I will be allowed to go back to my life when the time comes. Not now though, it's too early.'

'Where did you live before?'

'London, of course! I still have a little flat there I'm renting... I've been sharing with a friend. Not at all like this!' She gestured at the room with her cigarette holder. 'It has all the latest fashionable furniture, all geometrical patterns and clean lines. I miss it awfully.' She shifted in her corner of the sofa, obviously uncomfortable. 'I'm a journalist you see, and I was living the high life there... Working hard, but playing hard too! I mean, nothing too outrageous, we're not aristos... We're *working* people, a tad intellectual, not as vapid as the other lot... Not that much into dressing up all the time, but we like our little gatherings after work, our cocktails, our jazz and liberal approach to life. Such a cliché, isn't it? I started quite young, I just got lucky. I suppose I have some talent for journalism, you know, the knack for a good story, a certain writing ability, a love of culture and controversial social issues...' Maeve was growing animated, her cheeks turning pink, her eyes glittering once again. 'Oh, that was really, really exciting for me, I really thought I was going to make it in a world in which women have rarely been able to shine... These are changing times, and I've made the most of it. I just charged forward...' She paused, checking on Adam's reaction. 'I am not boring you to death, am I?'

'No, of course not. Do carry on...'

'I... er,' she stammered, 'got into trouble. Look, I'm not sure I want to get into this.'

'You don't have to if you don't want to,' said Adam softly.

Maeve had started to show her more human side and he was now feeling more at ease.

'I prefer not to tell you now. Later, maybe, when we... when we know each other a little bit better. Let's just say that I'm lying low until the storm has passed.'

She winked, and they both fell silent while finishing their cigarettes.

'Maeve, I want to know the date. Today's date. The *year.*'

Maeve sighed.

'Are you sure?'

'I've asked at the house. The answer made me lose my temper.

I've... I've been wondering...'

Maeve repositioned herself on the sofa yet again, straightening herself in her red dress. Her elbows on her knees, she covered her face with her hands for a few seconds as if she were thinking about the consequences of the words she was about to utter. She lifted her head and said:

'Today is Thursday the first of October 1925.'

The date echoed around the young man's head, found its way to his heart and stomach. He breathed deeply as if to unblock his lungs. He had heard it before, Gladys had told him, back at the house. He had snapped, then. He had thought that by running away, he could somehow escape and get back into the 21st century. He stared at his companion.

'That's what the maid said when I asked her. 1925 was the year that kept appearing in the diaries in the study room. I thought that someone was playing a practical joke on me. I thought...'

'I'm sorry. I would have preferred it to have been a joke, believe me! It wouldn't have been so difficult for me to be sitting next to you like this.'

'I just can't believe it. It's IMPOSSIBLE!' Adam was shaking his head in disbelief.

'I know. I had the same reaction when they told me what was expected of me. I was actually physically sick. They didn't really reveal a lot, just enough for me to know that for some reason, they had found a way of travelling through time. I don't know which one does it: Uncle Vange, Saturnin Bloom, more likely both. They have an unusual way of getting you to side with them. I don't know what it is. Hypnosis? Drugs? I just can't fathom *how* they do it, but they *do*. They will get you to do whatever it is they brought you here for.'

'But I'm... I'm just *me*! I'm *nothing*! I am just a failed teacher trying to get my life back! I just wanted a quiet place, a quiet job. I...' Adam had once again started shaking. The waves of panic were coming at him, making him light-headed. 'Why couldn't I just get out through the gates? What if I managed to climb over the wall with a ladder or something?'

'If you tried, *something* would happen. The wall would grow higher as you went up, or you would bang your head on some invisible barrier.'

The room grew a notch darker for Adam, as if a veil had come down in front of his eyes and his head started to ache again. His brain was trying to cope with the information he had just received, with the enormity of what

Maeve had just told him.

1925. *That was 89 years before his own present.* The Second World War hadn't happened yet, and the world was just about recovering from the first one... In 2014, Maeve, who looked like she was in her mid-twenties, would be a very, very old lady if she were still alive. He looked at her, horrified at the thought of the lively, lovely girl who was sitting in front of him being over 100 or even long dead. He wouldn't even be born! Nor would his parents and not even his grand-parents...

Suddenly, the tears started pouring out of his eyes; soon, he was crying inconsolably, without being able to do anything about it. He found himself in Maeve's arms and carried on sobbing until the tears ran out.

EIGHT

He knows,' announced Saturnin Bloom, closing the door of the study behind him.

It was close to 4pm and the light had already started declining outside. Within the walls of the crowded room though, the curtains had been drawn again and the gas lamps and the candles had been turned on; the place looked more like the inside of a church than a working office, but Vangelis Chronos didn't like using electricity in his quarters as it interfered with his experiments.

Lord Chronos's very own cabinet of curiosities was bathed in an ominous orange glow; the scientist liked it that way, because it was in keeping with the authenticity of his art and work. The man himself was seated deep in his chair behind the crowded desk. His gaze left the document he had been reading when the secretary had entered and his eyes were now fixed on the brass planispheric astrolabe in front of him.

'I will not do you the affront of asking how you know this.' Vangelis's voice was calm and steady; it was that of a wise, learned man more used to deep thinking than action. Reflecting, he passed a knotted hand over his white beard. 'Just *how much* does he know?' he queried.

'He seems to have become aware of the fact that he is no longer in 2014 but in 1925. He might even have accepted it, which would help.'

'He is bound to come to us with questions, sooner or later. Are you proposing to answer all of them?'

'It will depend which ones he asks. We need to get him on our side, but we will have to do so carefully. Your niece will once again prove incredibly useful, you'll find.'

'Maeve?' Vangelis shook his head. 'I wonder why I've agreed to involve her in our endeavours. We are ruining her life.'

'She had pretty much done most of the work herself when you went to get her!' mocked Saturnin Bloom, a sneering rictus appearing on the corner of his mouth. The scholar looked at him from the depth of his upholstered chair.

For the past thirteen years, Vangelis Chronos had had to put up with Mr Bloom's antics and his blatant contempt for the human race.

During that time, the scientist had learned to indulge his assistant's egotism and destructive tendencies, his power trips and manipulative behaviour. He had often been worried and even at times had been scared for his life. But he knew he had agreed to his side of the bargain and he had to stick to it for the sake of his work, his family and his own safety.

Now that Adam Tuckfield had arrived, they had entered a dangerous phase in their work. The forces at play went beyond Vangelis's own comprehension and he knew it. Who knew where the consequences of their actions would take them? Whatever the price they would have to pay, he would have to protect Sophia... His thoughts were interrupted by Saturnin's gloomy voice.

'You are not having second thoughts about it all, have you?' The secretary's stature seemed to have expanded and his besuited figure was looming over Vangelis.

'No, of course not. I find the whole thing rather fascinating, from an academic and scientific point of view. This has gone beyond my wildest dreams already. No, it's the fleeting nature of humans that worries me. Adam is not one of your followers, his brain hasn't been whipped into shape. He is still a wild card, an unpredictable element of the plan. We will have to tread carefully. And about Maeve... Do you mean that they could get romantically involved?'

'I can... sense something. I have for some time, when we went after him in London.'

'Then we will need to be even more cautious. That kind of feeling can turn into an incredibly powerful force and could derail our plans if we are not careful,' Vangelis warned. *And don't I know it*, he thought.

He had a man killed because of Sophia. Every day was a risk. His terrible weakness for her had made him act like a fool, had threatened his life's work and his sanity. His obsession was a severe, unshakable rival to his scientific and academic work. The fact that she had stubbornly refused herself to him since the day of their wedding had tormented him, sometimes making his flesh agonise for nights and days on end. He had known before they were married; she had told him then why their marriage wouldn't be consummated. And yet, he had always kept some little hope in his heart, thinking that one day she would relinquish her body to him. He was still trying to earn her love, bit by bit. He was getting old now, and day after day, the prospect of sharing her bed looked further and further away. He regretted it, but had recently realised that he had resigned himself to it. If only she could at least *like* him and show a little affection...

Saturnin Bloom nonchalantly brushed an invisible spot of dust off the sleeve of his impeccably tailored suit.

'It is not my intention to give Adam the choice, Vangelis. He *will* have to help us and accept his destiny. When he knows what is awaiting him, he will rise to the occasion. No one can refuse that kind of bargain. *You* most certainly didn't.'

A subtle change swept over Saturnin Bloom's face: it suddenly seemed to glow, as if a flame had lit up inside him; the skin took an unearthly leathery aspect. His deep-seated eyes turned entirely black, the white disappearing under the inky spread of the iris. His rictus grew cruel, savage and superior. It was the grin of an all-powerful creature contemplating yet another triumph.

NINE

Adam couldn't believe he had fallen asleep at the cottage, exhausted by his tears. He had woken up at around 4pm to find Maeve reading Edith Wharton's 'The Age of Innocence' by a roaring fire. If he had believed in guardian angels, he would have counted Maeve as his own personal one. She had given him the strength to face the strange situation he was finding himself in. She had agreed to be his guide through the era – hadn't Dimitri offered to be his guide around the estate? What was it with people all wanting to guide him?

'Do I look so lost?' he asked Maeve as he was getting ready to go back to the house.

'You kind of do, you know,' she had answered. 'You don't play the man's man, you are just you. You let your emotions show, and you don't know how refreshing that is. You're just different. Maybe that's because you're from the 21st century? By the way, has anyone told you that you were devilishly charming?'

She was teasing because she was afraid of becoming serious. Her throat constricted as she looked at him tugging at the chunky cardigan she had lent him.

'Don't remove it! Please do keep it. You can always give it back to me later.'

'Are you sure? There might be something in the wardrobe up in my bedroom; I haven't had time to have a good look at it yet.'

'Please keep it. It was… It was one of my older brother's.'

'Oh, he doesn't mind you stealing his clothes, does he?'

Maeve averted her eyes and clenched her jaw.

'He's dead…'

'I'm… I'm sorry.'

The young man's gaze dropped to the woollen garment, all comfy and reassuring with its large wooden buttons; he tried to imagine Maeve's brother wearing it. It sent a frozen shiver down his spine.

'Jolly good! Now, off you go!' She ran to the door and opened it. 'Brrr. You are going to need that cardigan. It's really chilly out there… Can't you stay a little longer? I could make us some cocktails.'

'They're going to start looking for me. I probably haven't made a very good impression, disappearing off like that on my first day.'

'Don't worry. They are all too absorbed in their respective obsessions to notice. The kid *might* be wondering where you are, though...'

'I will try to be good and work on my lessons for the next few days. That's why I'm here for, after all... When will I see you again?'

'I'll be here. I have no intention of going anywhere. I'm trying my hand at writing a few articles to submit to some magazines and papers. I'd like to get things moving so I can get out of here. I'm trying to make *plans*...' She tried to sound as light-hearted as possible. Adam looked at Maeve, feeling oddly energised by her carefree personality. He would learn a lot from her.

'Thank you for rescuing me this afternoon.'

Instinctively, he kissed her on the cheek; her skin smelled of face powder and that vanilla perfume that accompanied her everywhere; she was warm from having sat next to the fire.

'You're more than welcome, 21st century boy,' she murmured.

He had walked up to the small gate and was about to open it when Maeve called out.

'Adam! Do be careful at the house. Remember what I've told you: things are not what they seem.'

Instead of going back to the main entrance, Adam found himself heading towards the service courtyard. While the sombre façade of the house appeared to him as rather austere and unwelcoming, the reassuring domestic sounds that resonated around the service block attracted him: running water, clanking kitchen noises, voices; there was a whirlwind of steam rising in the washed-out sky above the small 19th century religious building.

The young man followed the track up to the small church; he then soon found himself in a paved courtyard surrounded by low red-brick buildings on three of its sides. He immediately recognised Gladys, who was checking some pieces of cloth she had left out to dry. Nearby, a gangly youth in a flat cap who seemed to have outgrown his clothes too quickly was picking up some wood logs from a cart and piling them up against the wall.

'Good afternoon, Gladys.'

The two youths looked up at the same time. Adam nodded to the boy, before turning his attention to the one person he knew.

'Gladys... I wouldn't want to bother you too much, but... I went out for a walk and kind of got lost... I'd like to go back to my bedroom but I... I'm afraid I don't think I know the way yet. Would you mind taking me back, please?'

'Oh, of course not, Mr Tuckfield.' She quickly glanced at the gawping boy by her side.

'This is Paul, sir. He helps around the service yard... Paul, this is Mr Tuckfield, Master Dimitri's new tutor... from London!'

She had said those last two words with stars in her eyes and pink cheeks.

Paul clumsily removed his cap.

'How d'you do, sir.'

'Hello, Paul. Glad to meet you.'

'I am going to take Mr Tuckfield to his room, Paul. I will let Mrs Abbott know on the way. I'll come straight back,' declared Gladys.

Adam followed the girl to the large and odorous kitchen and was promptly introduced to the mistress of the place, Mrs Abbott. After having looked him up and down, the cook declared:

'You'll excuse me for saying so, Mr Tuckfield, but as Gladys will tell you, I always speak my mind: you look like you are in need of some good, fortifying food. A young man like you needs proper sustenance, especially if you are to teach Master Dimitri the whole day and then take some exercise in the evening.' She then lowered her voice and her tone became conspiratorial.

'Now. Please mind that I am *not* complaining or anything, but you'll notice very quickly that the people in this house have very strange eating habits. It's my daily struggle. They almost never sit together around the table in the dining room and they all require this and that to be carried up, down, right, left and centre to various places, all at different times... Most of them are adults and it's only right that they do whatever they like, if you ask me. At the end of the day, that's why I'm here, I'm a cook! It's Master Dimitri I'm worried about. He probably takes after his mother, who's got the appetite of a bird, but she's a Lady so it's her nature... Master Dimitri, you see... He doesn't eat. He is very, very fussy and I don't think his muscles are building up properly. Have you seen how small he is? How pale and delicate? That's not natural...'

'When Miss Finch was here, she would be very strict and would sit for hours trying to get the boy to eat. We have tried so many different ruses to get some good, nourishing foodstuff to pass his lips. I am sorry to say that we haven't always been successful, far from it! He only tolerates certain types of food, removes the butter from his toasts, avoids milk, refuses meat, and loathes cream. He has never asked for sweets and puddings don't interest him, apart from very liquid custard of all things! You're a man, Mr Tuckfield, and a young one at that. You're a teacher. The boy will be looking up to you and expect to find a role model in you. Please show him the way, sit down with him at breakfast, lunch, tea and dinner and show him how to appreciate the food I cook for him. I love the child dearly and would never forgive myself if he were to die of starvation!'

Mrs Abbott concluded her emotional speech by grasping Adam's hand and squeezing it energetically, with tears in her eyes.

The young man was rather stunned by the cook's statement and the confidence she had in the influence he would exercise on his young charge. He had never been told he was a role model and he didn't feel like one at all. This was one of the reasons why he had taken up the position at the girls' school where 'The Slap' episode had occurred. He had naively thought that teenage girls would be easier to handle than boys. This had been his downfall.

'I... I will do my best, I promise, Mrs Abbott.'

'Thank you, Mr Tuckfield. I trust you.'

She let go of Adam's hand and allowed her mind to return to tonight's dinner. She rubbed her hands together. Adam noticed how rough, chapped and red they were. It didn't seem to bother her in the least.

'It's time to start making soup again, with that weather... A good vegetable soup, Mr Tuckfield, what do you think?'

'Perfect, Mrs Abbott...' Adam grinned inanely at the cook.

'Wonderful! You can take him away, now, Gladys, I don't want to delay him any longer!'

Once again, Adam found himself walking along shadowy panelled corridors, but not in the erratic way he had exited the house a few hours earlier. He was being guided by Gladys's neat little figure at a leisurely pace; the girl was obviously in no hurry to go back to her tasks in the courtyard. The tutor was trying to concentrate on remembering small details of his itinerary but it was not easy to memorise. He felt the urge to speak in order to break the monotonous journey through the recesses of the house.

'Tell me, Gladys, how long have you been at Whitemoor Hall?'

'Oh! A long time, sir. I arrived here from the village when I was seven.'

'And you've always worked at the house?'

'Oh no, sir. Nobody works before they're 14, here. They make sure we get a good education first.'

'*They?* Who are *they?*'

Gladys stopped in her tracks and turned round to face Adam, the colour rising in her cheeks. Her face was reproachful, as if he should have known who she was talking about.

'But the people at the abbey, of course. *The Makhaut*, 'The Family'! They took us in, me and my mum, after my dad died in the war... My mum was in a right state, she was.'

They had reached a landing Adam recognised because of the beautiful painting of a Devon cliff by stormy weather he had noticed before.

'The abbey... Nobody has said anything about it to me. Is it part of the estate?'

'Yes. To the east, just beyond the edges of the wood. That's why you can't see it from the East Wing, but it's there alright... It's beautiful... I was so excited when we came; I was just a little mite and Mum was so ill. They took care of her, nursed her, and educated me... Now mum works for them as a seamstress, and when they asked me what I wanted to do, I said I wanted to be like my friend Ginny and work at the big house... So here I am. I've been a maid for a bit less than one year, I'm still learning... Are we going now?'

Adam nodded and they resumed their journey to his room, which they reached a few minutes later. He thanked Gladys and sent her back to the courtyard and her domestic chores.

Once alone in the room, he let himself fall backwards on the bed and stayed thus, his eyes fixed on the decorative plaster ceiling, his hands resting on his chest. The short exchange with Gladys had piqued Adam's curiosity. The abbey.... Was there a convent there? Who were those people? Did they have anything to do with the Hall at all? Questions, always questions... That's all he was getting. Too many questions but so very few answers... He shut his eyes and for a moment, let the silence of the room envelop him. His mind was flicking through the day's events in a rather chaotic manner.

At first, a simple, short chuckle shook his chest, and then another rose in his throat. Soon, he was laughing out loud at the fleur-de-lys mouldings on the ceiling. His laughter exploded around the large bedroom, expanding, spreading with ease along the wide walls.

Adam was laughing at himself for having been so naive and having fallen into the trap so obviously set up for him; he was mocking his weakness of the past year, his loss of confidence and his incapacity at getting back on his own two feet. He was finding his situation absolutely hilarious, in a preposterous, grotesque kind of way. He just couldn't believe what was happening to him, and his best protection against it was that resonant laughter; it was assuaging his fear and his incomprehension.

That's when he heard the knocks. They hadn't come from the solid oak door. It was a more hollow sound, as if someone had been rapping on an empty wooden box. Tensed, he lifted his head from the bedcover and listened.

Knock knock knock!

It seemed to be coming from the wall to the right of the bed, the one the bedroom had in common with the classroom. Adam jumped out and walked towards the place where the sounds originated. Then the voice came:

'Sir! Mr Tuckfield! Hello?'

'Dimitri? Is that you?' Adam was talking to a wall.

'You were laughing at something. Are you well?'

'Yes, of course, I am!'

'Could you open the passage for me, please? The thing is broken this side of the wall… If you push on the red book that's in the middle of the small shelf to your right…'

Adam easily spotted the book in question and picked it up from the shelf. It was of course a fake one and was attached to a contraption that disappeared inside the wall at the back of the shelf. He heard a clicking noise, like an unlocking mechanism being released and to his amazement, a section of the panelled wall sprang open, like in all good old-fashioned horror movies. Instantly, Dimitri poked his head round the corner then stepped on the threshold of the secret passage, a wide smile on his face.

'Hello, Mr Tuckfield! Where have you been? I've waited for ages!' The boy pouted.

'I, er, went for a walk.'

'You should have told me! I would have pointed out interesting things to you!'

The boy sounded genuinely disappointed.

'Well… We can go together another time, can't we? I needed to think about next week's lessons… What about you? What have you been doing?'

'I've been drawing. I'm working on something,' the boy said enigmatically.

Adam gestured at the open panel.

'How do you know about this?'

The boy's face lit up.

'I just do. I've discovered a lot of things during my explorations around the house.'

'Is that what you do in your free time?'

'Yes. I explore all the time. I am like an adventurer in my own house. I am lucky, it's a big one…' He lowered his voice before confiding: 'There are loads of secret passages around the house. This one is boring. There are much better ones. Some run inside the walls, in between rooms… It will take me ages to find out about all of them.' Dimitri's voice became a whisper. 'I have decided to draw a map of all of them, with all the rooms that are locked up and all the secret corridors and passageways. It is going to take me years!' concluded the boy gleefully; he seemed to have found his calling. Adam watched him with curiosity: the boy's face was at last showing some kind of happiness.

'Does anyone else know about it?'

'No. Only you.'

'Oh.' Adam was perplexed. 'But why tell *me*?'

'I know you can help me do it! You *will* help me, won't you?'

Against his better judgement, Adam decided here and there to play the game.

The next hour or so passed quietly. They had closed the passage again and taken their places in the study. Adam had sat down at the teacher's desk and opened Miss Finch's latest notebook, and he had been taking notes with a pencil on a few pieces of blank paper he had found in the drawer. Dimitri had been quietly minding his own business on the art table. The tutor had glanced over at the child a few times: the boy had been absorbed in his work, forgetting about the adult's presence in the room. Sometimes, he could be heard whispering softly to himself.

Footsteps resonated up the stairs and on the landing, then stopped at the classroom door. Sharp little knocks were heard and were followed by Gladys then Saturnin Bloom. While the little maid stayed by the entrance, the secretary walked towards Adam's desk after having glanced at the boy in the corner.

'Mr Tuckfield! I am pleased to see that you have already made yourself comfortable in this room and managed to keep Dimitri busy until this late hour!'

Adam looked at the round, simple clock that had been screwed in above the door: it was 5.35pm. The clock was reading exactly the same way as the one in his bedroom and as the large, ornate grandfather clock that was dominating the entrance hall: the handles moved anti-clockwise, as a constant reminder that he didn't belong to Whitemoor Hall's present.

'Mr Tuckfield, I am here to present Lord Chronos's apologies as well as mine. Dinner will be served in the dining room at 6pm, but unfortunately, we will not be able to keep you company tonight as we are in the middle of a crucial experiment. I do hope you will not keep it against us and will enjoy the company of Dimitri and his mother. We will most certainly make up for it very soon, as we will be celebrating Lord and Lady Chronos's wedding anniversary next week. We will have Miss Hayward with us at the house on that day; I think you have now properly met.'

Saturnin Bloom's face was as imperturbable as ever. Adam tried to hide his trouble: how did he know that he and Maeve had met again? That spooked him a little, but he tried not to show it.

Dimitri had stopped drawing as soon as the secretary and the maid had entered the room but hadn't turned round or moved. His eyes were still fixed on the table but he was listening attentively. Mr Bloom turned briefly towards the boy.

'Dimitri, I will ask you, for the sake of surprise, not to tell your mother about the little dinner we will be having next Saturday. If you could think of a gift for her, it would please your stepfather immensely.'

'I will, sir' answered the boy, sternly.

'Very well, then. Mr Tuckfield, I wish you a good evening and a good night. Maybe I could come and see you in the morning in here, say, 10 o'clock, so you can tell me about your first day and whether you need anything to start your lessons. Gladys will be at your disposal again tonight and will probably stay in charge of this corridor as Genevieve will be fully occupied with Lady Chronos when she comes back tomorrow after her short illness.'

Saturnin Bloom then promptly left the room. Dimitri waited until the secretary's steps had reached the bottom of the stairs and turned to Gladys.

'Has Ginny been ill today? What's wrong with her?'

'She has been unwell, Master Dimitri. She... She's eaten something that didn't agree with her.'

The boy looked knowingly at Adam: 'You see, sir, that's what I always think when I look at the food they put on my plate. Most of it looks and smells so revolting that it could only make you sick.'

Gladys protested weakly:

'But Mrs Abbott's food is very good!'

She stopped herself, conscious that she had raised her voice. Dimitri didn't seem to notice.

'I am sure she is a very good cook,' he said to Gladys reassuringly.

'Will any of you sirs need anything before going down to dinner?'

Dimitri looked up at Adam from his art table.

'No, I don't think so. We'll be alright, won't we, Mr Tuckfield?'

'Yes, I guess we will. Thank you, Gladys.'

'I will then go down to the dining room and assist Mr Simms to make sure everything is ready for you.'

Dimitri sighed as he started clearing up the pens and papers.

'I guess I'd better go and wash my hands. Shall we meet on the landing in front of my room in five minutes or will you need more time to get ready?'

'Five minutes will be fine, Dimitri.'

They exited the classroom together, turning the light off as they did so.

TEN

Adam wasn't convinced that he would be able to swallow anything of his dinner that evening; the set up was simply too overwhelming. They were welcomed in the room by Mr Simms, head butler of the house, a massive yet rather placid man with a big voice and even bigger hands. He announced that Lady Chronos wouldn't be joining them either, news that Dimitri received with obvious relief. Sophia's place had been cleared, and Dimitri and Adam had been shown to their respective seats at either end of the table.

They looked at each other: the young tutor felt quite disconcerted and terribly silly. At the other end of the long dinner table, Dimitri was considering his new-found companion in a serious manner, looking small and very blond against the heavy-looking sculpted wooden chair.

The child had sensed Adam's vulnerability and had been intrigued by it. He had detected the dark remnants of the young teacher's past which had been clinging to his skin like the last strands of the chrysalis cling to the butterfly after its metamorphosis. He had felt an affinity with him. He too had uneasy secrets he didn't dare share with anyone.

Much like the rest of the rooms in the house, this one was high of ceiling and panelled with dark, carved wood. The large portrait that dominated the room was hung just above the monumental fireplace, in which a seasonal fire was now burning. It represented a formidable looking fiftysomething Victorian gentleman, who looked like a cross between an adventurer, a pirate and an aristocrat. He had been painted wearing a rather eccentric suit of rich dark green material and holding a large volume, the title of which remained indecipherable. His dark brown hair was luxurious and his moustache perfectly waxed. He had been set against a dark backdrop of thick, mythical woods. The painting made a vivid impression on Adam.

Behind Dimitri, at the very other end of the room, stood a large bay window leading onto a terrace sloping towards the front lawn; by daylight, you could see the stables and the rolling countryside to the left, the small wood where the Guardian's Cottage was located, the tranquil lake and the grazing fields beyond.

If it had a lovely view, Adam was unable to admire it that very evening, as the heavy green velvet curtains had all been drawn to keep out the darkness of the night. A large circular chandelier was hanging over the dining table and was throwing a muted light on the polished surfaces of the furniture.

Adam was feeling almost as small as his young charge, and ever so slightly more ignorant of the ways of the house. He was seized once again by this eerie, surreal feeling he had been experiencing the whole day: a very strong sense of unreality.

'Don't worry too much, Mr Tuckfield, and don't let the house get to you. Do as I do, treat it as if it were a game. I eat here on my own a lot; you get used to it!'

'You eat on your own in this big room?'

Their voices sounded too loud in the empty space, disturbing the solemn peace. The only sounds were the crackling of the wooden logs in the fireplace and Mr Simms's footsteps in the corridor. The butler entered, deposited the tureen and a bread basket in the middle of the table and served the soup; he then disappeared as he had come, without a word. The smell of vegetables and herbs started spreading around the table and mixing with the one of the burning wood.

Adam suddenly realised that he was rather ravenous indeed. The bread crust was golden and looked terribly appetising. He bit a sizable chunk and started eating his soup: his teeth made crunching noises, the spoon hit the ceramic at regular intervals. The young man was conscious of the sounds he was making in the silent room, but he was now too hungry to care.

At the opposite end of the table, Dimitri hadn't moved at all. He had stayed there, his two forearms resting on each side of his steaming bowl. Only his thin index fingers were moving, tapping softly against the wood. He was trying to avoid looking at the thick, generously nourishing soup in front of him; the boy was now staring as Adam was finishing his.

'Aren't you eating your soup, then, Dimitri?'

The boy made a disgusted face and wrinkled his nose.

'No. Don't like the look of it.'

'You should. Soup's supposed to be good for you, and this one is really delicious. And it's cold outside, it will warm you up!'

As soon as he had finished his sentence, he regretted having said it. He noticed an immediate reaction in Dimitri's face and body, some kind of tensing.

'I feel warm enough, thank you very much,' was the sharp reply.

Adam bit his lip and cleared his throat.

'It must be a little bit lonely eating on your own in this big room,' started Adam, his eyes scanning the sheer size of the dining room again.

'It's alright. I sometimes eat in the morning room next to my bedroom, it's much smaller. Now that you're here though, we can have our meals together. The others are always bothering me about my food, but I know you won't.'

'That's true, I won't, because it is not in my job description to also act as your nutritionist as well as your teacher.'

Dimitri had no idea what a nutritionist was but thought it better not to ask. Instead, he started to methodically strip the bits of bread of their golden crust and put it in his mouth. He noticed Adam's questioning stare.

'I like bread crust.'

'Only the crust?'

'Only the crust of fresh bread. I also like toast.'

The boy shifted in his chair, uncomfortable. Mr Simms reappeared and asked whether he could clear the table, while Gladys had followed him carrying a large tray laden with chunks of meat, vegetables and potatoes. A small jar of very hot homemade vegetable gravy accompanied it.

'Thank you, Mr Simms. We'll help ourselves, Gladys, thank you very much.' said Dimitri.

Silently, the butler and the maid walked off again.

When they were alone, Adam eyed the meat, unsure about what to do.

'You don't eat meat!' exclaimed the boy, delighted.

'No, I don't, I'm afraid. I'm vegetarian.'

'Me too!' Dimitri proudly announced. 'I read an article about it in *The Daily Chronicle* once. It was written by someone called George Bernard Shaw.'

'Do you think your cook will get cross with me on my first day?'

Dimitri, who had carried on stripping the bread of its crust, shook his head confidently.

'No, she won't. She's used to it.'

Oh, well, I might as well make the most of the vegetables and potatoes, then. Don't you want any?'

The boy shook his head and resumed nibbling his crust pensively. The dining room fell silent apart from the sound of the flames and embers, and the noises made by Adam's fork and knife against the plate.

'Tell me, Dimitri, do you know who this person is, in the painting there?' Adam gestured towards the image hung above the fireplace. The lighting of the room as well as the fire combined to give the face of the subject a shadowy, mysterious quality. The man had obviously been vigorous and energetic, even though he had reached his sixth decade.

'Yes, I do know. He's Lord Whitemoor. He is the one who's built the house. It sounds like he was fun.'

'Was he? In what way?'

'Apparently, he was an adventurer, and an archaeologist too. He was an Ancient Egypt expert, just like Vangelis! There are a lot of his books in the library; they are really big books, very heavy!' Dimitri turned to the painting, admiringly. 'I want to be like him when I grow up. Or like Eliott, I haven't decided yet.'

'Who is Eliott?'

'He is the gardener. He is really strong! But he doesn't speak much.' The boy paused, then started again: 'He was married to an Egyptian lady, you know!'

'Who? The gardener?' asked Adam, slightly baffled.

Dimitri looked at the tutor reproachfully.

'Of course, not! Lord Whitemoor.' He nodded at the painting. 'She was very beautiful and she was the daughter of a very important man in Egypt. They had a big celebration and then they came back here to live at the Hall.'

'It must have been difficult for her! It is very hot, in Egypt, isn't it?'

'Maybe...' Dimitri thought for a moment. 'She died of pneumonia,' he added matter-of-factly. 'I can show you her portrait, if you want. Would you like to see it?'

'Now?'

'No, not now.' The boy stopped and listened up, as if to check that nobody was coming their way. 'We have to wait until Sunday, when there is nobody in the house.' Dimitri lowered his voice even further. 'It's in one of the rooms we are not supposed to go to. There are *whole* corridors that are locked, you know!'

'And you still manage to get in?'

'Yes. It is part of my exploration. I like it there, it is very strange, like in another world or on another planet.'

Another world, or another era, thought the tutor.

Adam's eyes were drawn to the portrait again. He was finding the contrast between the colourful, exuberant individual and the twisted, gloomy background fascinating. And it really felt as if there were a third person in the room. Mr Simms and Gladys reappeared and asked them whether they wanted any pudding.

'Is there any custard?' ventured Dimitri.

'I can ask Mrs Abbott if she has made any,' replied the butler.

Dimitri looked at Adam and explained:

'She would have made some. She knows it's the only sweet I'll have! Do you like custard?'

A few minutes later, Dimitri was presented with a bowl full of glistening, pale yellow custard. He started spooning the cream slowly. The boy's was very liquid, just the way he liked it; Adam's was thick and quivery; the strong, creamy vanilla smell reminded him of Maeve. He wondered what she was doing at that precise moment. He distractedly picked up a biscuit from the small plate in front of him and nibbled at it.

'What would you like to do after dinner?' the boy enquired enthusiastically. 'We have a little bit of time before bed.' He didn't give his tutor any time to reply. 'I know! I can take you to the library and we can have a look at some books!'

*   *   *

Adam spent an hour in the impressive library of the house. He had never seen that many books in one room. The volumes covered the walls from floor to ceiling. There were two wooden ladders and three stools propped up against the shelves. Dimitri pointed at his favourite books and showed Adam where Lord Whitemoor's and Vangelis's bulky volumes were being kept. Two walls were for works of fiction, poetry and biographies; the other two for academic and scientific works. Adam kept going to and fro between the walls, his eyes jumping from one shelf to the next, from one book to the other. He finally spotted the book he had been looking for: Wilde's 'Lord Arthur Savile's Crime and Other Stories'. It was lucky they had it at the Hall.

'Here it is! We will start our English lessons with this!' he exclaimed, tapping the book cover lightly.

'Which book is it?'

'This is Oscar Wilde's collection of stories, 'Lord Arthur Savile's Crime and Other Stories'. There are a few stories in there I think you might like. For example, 'The Canterville Ghost'. You remember earlier when you asked me whether I believed in ghosts? Well, it gave me an idea. You'll like it.'

It might have been a trick of the light in the room, but Adam saw Dimitri go distinctly paler, and for a moment, he thought that the child was about to faint. Quickly recovered, the boy then turned his attention to a spectacularly preserved collection of Dickens's work, all leather-bound and fully illustrated; they were his favourite books.

*   *   *

The contrary clock on the mantelpiece indicated 8.20pm when Adam finally found himself back in his bedroom. He closed the door behind him and switched the light on; his eyes took some time to get accustomed to the room.

By 9pm, Adam had showered yet another time, brushed his teeth and put on the pyjamas that had been left for him. He laughed at himself: ready for bed at 9pm! But he could feel extreme tiredness stalking him, even though his head was still buzzing from his first day.

Nobody else apart from Dimitri seemed to be around in the house now. He knew he could ring the bell if he fancied a late cup of tea, but he decided against it, thinking that Gladys probably had better things to do than attend to his every needs. He was feeling uncomfortable having people wait on and clean after him.

The curtains had been drawn, and he slipped behind them to have a look outside. It was perfectly still out there. The darkness of rural nights had always taken him by surprise, so used was he to the permanent orange glow of the city. It was more and more difficult to find perfect darkness in England. One had to get further and further away from civilisation in order to achieve the perfect night sky, complete with stars if you were lucky. That night, there were no stars in the sky; the clouds had put a heavy lid on the countryside. There was no light on their side of the building and Adam could only guess the rose garden, the pond, the lawn and the woods. Looking at the blackness outside and thinking about his day made Adam's heart lurch, and a vague anguish seized him. He felt alone and lost, away from his past life. But wasn't it what he had wanted after all?

Adam still couldn't believe that he had time-travelled to 1925. His instincts told him it was so, but his reason was rebelling against the idea and prodding at his brain. He thought it better to block it from his thoughts before it drove him insane. He would have to behave just as if he were finding it all normal and regular.

On a very 21st century impulse, he went to the wardrobe and pulled his travel bags out. From the smaller one, he took out his mobile phone and charger; from the second one, he fished out his laptop. He then looked everywhere for a plug and couldn't find any. He pressed the 'on' button on his phone, but almost immediately, the irritating alarm told him that the battery was now empty. He threw it on the bed, impatient; the phone bounced on the cover and crash-landed on the floor on the other side. Adam then flipped open the lid of his laptop and pressed the 'start' button. He waited, staring absentmindedly at the screen, waiting for the software to do its thing.

Instead of the swirling brand logo that usually appeared on the screen before log in, the light in the center of the screen whirled around then seemed to collapse and fade on itself. For a second, the screen was back to black, then suddenly it was streaked with horizontal, humming and buzzing interferences. Adam had never seen anything like this on a computer. The sounds started changing and became like the electronic version of some kind of chants. He could distinguish several disembodied voices, some sort of electronic choir.

Then, without warning, the screen seemed to overheat and implode: it first was filled with light; then, like a flame being put off, it abruptly died and Adam found himself sitting on the floor near the bed, with the laptop still open just above him on the bedcover. Imprinted on his brain was the fuzzy outline of a face, the one that he had just seen on the screen in the half second before the screen had gone black for good. He was convinced he had seen it, but he would have been incapable of describing it. It had been female, fierce and dark, with wide open, maniacal eyes. 'She' had been screaming, her mouth a gaping black hole.

'What the bloody hell was that?' he asked aloud. His eyes darted to every corner of the bedroom. He pulled himself together and started frantically hitting the start button on the computer, to no avail. A slight smell of overheated metal and burnt plastic indicated that the computer had probably died right there on the bed. The young man sighed. No computer, no mobile phone. Welcome to the 1920s... This time, the transformation was complete. 21st century technology eliminated, he would have to rely on his brain and survival instinct.

What had happened? What was it he had seen there, in the middle of his dying screen? His eyes fell on his hands and saw that they were shaking. He slammed the lid of the laptop down, went to pick up the lifeless phone on the floor and put the lot back inside the travel bags. He decided not to get any of his own clothes out. He would be wearing the ones his hosts had 'generously' provided for his sole use.

Adam wiped the thin layer of sweat on his forehead and sat on the bed against the pillows. He knew he wouldn't be able to turn the light off, and felt idiotic. He tried to resist the urge to go and take refuge in Dimitri's room. *How pathetic.* Him, the so-called teacher and adult, was dying to go and find the protection of an 11-year-old boy. He would have to toughen up if he wanted to last. He wished he had one of those cigarettes he had smoked with Maeve at the Guardian's Cottage.

He felt exhausted and yet too nervous to sleep. He had to find something useful to do. Where had he put this book he had picked up in the library? He would start planning his lessons the following day, and he might as well get started tonight while he couldn't sleep. He had always found reading comforting; it provided a refuge from reality. But was he *actually* living in reality right now? Adam passed a clammy hand over his face. *Breathe*, he told himself. *Try to block unpleasant thoughts and impressions. Think about something agreeable, Maeve, for example.'*

With the book on his lap and his back propped up against the pillows, Adam closed his eyes and tried to conjure up the image of the young woman, sitting across the armchair in her red dress, reading 'The Age of Innocence' by the fire. It did the trick. After a few seconds, he felt much better and reopened his eyes. Trying to focus his mind, he turned his attention to his book. In the index, he found the page for 'The Canterville Ghost' and started reading: *'When Mr. Hiram B. Otis, the American Minister, bought Canterville Chase, every one told him he was doing a very foolish thing, as there was no doubt at all that the place was haunted.'*

Somewhere in the house, a floorboard creaked.

PART IV

The Book
of Thoth

ONE

At last, Sunday arrived. *Not too soon*, thought Dimitri. He had been wide awake when Gladys had come in with his morning tea. He had been in such a good mood that the forlorn, apprehensive face of the girl had annoyed him a little. She wasn't the happiest of people, but Sundays didn't seem to particularly agree with her for some reason. She was not the only one: all the other staff – bar the always cheerful Mrs Abbott, who didn't belong to the community – put on their 'Sunday faces' every week.

It had always baffled the boy. What were they doing at the abbey that required them to adopt this sour, solemn face every Sunday? He had never been able to know. Several times, he had stood outside the 13th century gatehouse, in front of the high and sturdy wooden drawbridge with the deep water-filled moat at his feet. When the light was low, you could see strange multi-coloured lights coming from inside through the large windows of the main building, as if fireworks were being let off indoors. He had asked Vangelis about it, but he had only received vague, evasive answers; it was always along the lines of 'You will know, one day. I will explain it to you. At the moment, do not worry about it.' Wasn't his stepfather aware that this type of reply only fuelled his curiosity?

But today, Gladys and the others were not going to spoil his excitement. Today, he was going to take Mr Tuckfield to see the hidden portrait he had found whilst exploring. He had been good those past few days and had left his tutor alone as he worked on his lesson planning. He had remained focused on his work for the whole of Friday and Saturday. Mr Tuckfield had been polite enough and had made small talk at dinner time. Dimitri had noticed a slight change in the young man: he had become a little bit more self-confident, less jumpy. He had seemed more at ease around the house, had grown more observant. The boy was rather pleased; maybe it meant that the tutor liked Whitemoor Hall, after all. He had looked so ill on that first day.

'Has Mr Tuckfield got out of bed yet?' asked the boy.

'Mr Bloom told me to leave Mr Tuckfield sleep and to bring him his tea a little later, around 8.30am,' replied Gladys, joylessly.

Dimitri was disappointed. He glanced at the little clock on his bedside table: 7.45am. He drank his tea whilst looking by the window. The fog was back to its normal morning level. It looked like the day would be a much nicer one. Eliott Mills would probably start on his round of the gardens soon.

He looked down at the water in the pond below and wondered how long it would be before it started to be covered with a fine layer of ice in the morning. Dimitri loved the frost. It made everything look like a big iced cake, or jewellery. It had always fascinated him. Because he was on his own most of the time, he had taken up observing nature in its most intimate details.

He was surprised at how the presence of the new tutor had changed the atmosphere of Whitemoor Hall, after only a few days; he had been acutely aware of the young man's presence. Their respective bedrooms were on the same floor, and only the study separated them. It felt as if together, they were forming an independent unit within the house. Whereas before it had been him and *Them*, now it felt like *Us* and *Them*. He thought he might have found an ally, someone who could guide him through knowledge of the world while he in turn would guide him through the maze of corridors.

Dimitri washed, got dressed and sat on the bed with one of his notebooks. He had to try and remember how to get to the hallway leading to the room where the portrait was hung. He carefully reproduced the route they were to follow on a loose sheet of paper, because he didn't want Mr Tuckfield to know about his notebooks. Even though he wanted to be friends with his tutor, there was a limit to how much he could trust him. He had to retain some kind of higher hand and some secrets. His map was his life's work...

It would be nice to be able to share some of his discoveries with his teacher, but there were some deeply personal things that he knew he had to keep for himself for his own safety. The ghosts, for example. Mr Tuckfield had said he didn't believe in them, so he couldn't really show him what he had seen, could he?

TWO

Adam shouldn't have been there, and he knew it. A somewhat childish impulse of curiosity had made him sign up for the day of exploration, but a part of him regretted it, while the other tingled with anticipation. Reason was incessantly tugging at his mind as he made his way along the convoluted corridors with Dimitri as his guide. To him, the house was as confusing and disorientating as a maze and yet, the boy seemed to be moving around it unhindered by doubt, holding a piece of paper very tightly in his little white hand. They had gone up and down several staircases. But now, they seemed to be as high up as it was physically possible to be in the house, just under the roof. They were standing in front of a heavy-looking double door which was tightly shut.

'This entrance is locked, but I have discovered that through here,' he pointed at a stained glass panel to the right of the door, 'you can get to the old servants' staircase and get to the other side.'

Dimitri applied the palms of both hands to the panel and pushed briefly. The whole piece swung around and Adam caught a glimpse of a rough narrow stone staircase behind it; a draught brushed past his face. Once on the other side, the young man felt a chill and frowned at the smell of damp.

'It's a little bit grim in here,' he commented, spotting the accumulated dust and numerous spider webs in the weak light of the tiny square windows. Without replying, the boy busied himself with a key he had produced from his jacket pocket.

'I think it might be a little too rusty now… The key is not working very well,' complained Dimitri.

After a few attempts during which the boy managed to make the skin of his fingers bleed, the small key finally turned inside the lock and the door swung open with an unpleasant squeaking noise.

'Careful, it's really low, and there's a step!' warned Dimitri.

Adam followed the boy reluctantly. On the other side, they found themselves in yet another corridor, this one very different from the passages criss-crossing the main parts of the house: it was low of ceiling and rather wide, and it was deprived of any ornament whatsoever; its yellowing walls and peeling floorboards looked – and smelled – unhealthy.

Dimitri suddenly stopped on the threshold, and Adam almost walked into him as he stepped through from the service staircase. He immediately noticed a certain stiffness that had come over the boy's body, as well as his clenched fists. He shifted to the right so as to be able to see the boy's face.

'Dimitri?'

The skin on the child's face had tightened and Adam could see the extreme pallor of the cheeks and their goose bumpy texture, with each and every hair standing on end, as if in extreme freezing conditions. His eyes were fixing a point somewhere further ahead in the corridor. There was absolutely nothing to see, just dirty walls, small windows of dubious cleanliness and a poorly preserved wooden floor. Dimitri's breathing sounded louder and irregular, as if he were having difficulties getting the air to his lungs. He seemed to have suddenly got into a trance.

'Dimitri? What's wrong?'

Adam placed his hand on the boy's shoulder; the child let out a little squeal of surprise and jumped out, as if electrified by his teacher's touch. His eyes were bigger than usual.

'What?'

'You don't look very well. Have you seen a giant spider or something? I wouldn't be surprised if we found rare species lurking in corners around here…'

First uncomprehending, the boy's eyes returned to the point they had been fixing a few seconds earlier, then reverted back to the tutor's reassuring face.

'I'm fine. The portrait is there, in the room at the other end of the corridor.' He pointed to the door standing a few metres away from where they stood.

Dimitri started walking cautiously. He took a step to the left and made sure his body stayed in contact with the wall. The whole time, his eyes remained fixed on a particular spot halfway down the corridor, as if there were something there he was trying to avoid. Adam observed the procedure with incredulity, wondering whether the boy was putting on an act for his benefit.

Once Dimitri had walked past the place that worried him so, he accelerated his pace and almost ran to the door which he pushed rather forcefully. It wasn't locked: the sturdy iron padlock was broken and hung from the wooden panel.

'I didn't break it. It was already like that when I came here the first time,' explained the boy before stopping in the middle of the room. He then patiently waited for Adam to join him. On the threshold, the young man came to a halt and fixed the opposite wall.

'Here she is!' exclaimed Dimitri, who seemed to have recovered from his unexplained earlier trepidation.

The room was square and small but had a surprisingly high ceiling. The walls and floor were stripped to the stone and it felt incredibly cold. A heavy atmosphere of sadness and unbearable loss permeated the very fabric of the space. There was no furniture; nevertheless, the only object in the room filled it by its cheer presence. It chilled Adam to the core of his being.

It was a huge painting, a life-size portrait: it took almost the whole height of the wall. It represented an exotic, fierce-looking woman draped in a rich, deep purple ball dress of a complicated mid-19th century design. She wore her stunning brown head high and proud, and her square shoulders were bare. She had a wide forehead, an aquiline nose and violet eyes.

Adam's head started spinning and all moisture left his mouth; he took several steps backwards until he reached the wall. He covered his face with both hands, his back against the freezing surface, the cold stone reaching his skin through the shirt and jacket he was wearing. When he removed his hands and lifted his face again, his eyes met Dimitri's gaze. The boy's furrowed eyebrows indicated his confusion and vexation.

'But I thought you wanted to see the painting! You don't like it?' queried the child.

It was impossible for Adam to answer. At first, he was too distressed to look at it. Then he forced himself to lift his face up: it *was* her, the woman in his dream. He was absolutely certain about it; he couldn't be mistaken. It *was* the very same woman who had straddled him as if he were a wild stallion, then had seized a gold dagger and plunged it into his arm. He tried to steady himself and think rationally. Yes, he was sure it was the same individual, albeit this one looked somehow different. In his dream, she had been a crazed, roaring, potentially murderous amazon; the woman in the painting was a more restrained, civilised version.

She was portrayed standing in the rose garden which was in the full bloom of spring. She was obviously dressed for a glittering social event:

she was wearing the richest version of the most fashionable evening wear of her time, but all the trimmings of ladyship struggled to tame and contain her real nature. An attempt at a more 'English' hairstyle had had to submit to the thickness of her jet-black curls; her whole body looked like it was about to escape the constraint of the restrictive corset and layered petticoats underneath the full skirt. She literally looked like the wolf attempting to dress like a rather daring lamb. The violet eyes had a strange depth to them and the half-smile that hovered over her lips could have been interpreted as mocking, even cruel.

The contrast between the innocent and fresh explosion of life in the natural background of the painting and the woman's plush presence looked provocative.

'Yes, I... Yes, I like it. I mean, it's... it's quite a portrait!'

'Isn't it?' interjected Dimitri, satisfied. 'I was sure you'd like it.'

'So this is the lady who was married to the Lord in the dining room?'

'To Lord Whitemoor. Yes, it is!'

'What a couple they must have made!' whispered Adam, impressed.

'It must have been more fun around here when those two were alive,' commented Dimitri sulkily.

Somehow, 'fun' wasn't the word that came to Adam's mind just then. He walked towards the portrait to see its details a little better. The paint was layered, rich and thick, the colours incredibly vibrant. It made you want to touch the fabric of the dress, take the smooth hand of the woman and smell the perfume emanating from the rose bushes.

'I wish I had a chair or a ladder at hand; I'd like to see it better,' announced the tutor.

'There is an old wooden stool in the small cupboard outside the door. Do you want it?'

Dimitri ran to fetch the stool; when he came back, Adam perched himself precariously on top of it, and his eyes came almost to the level of the woman's head. He tried not to think about the dream he had had weeks before he had set foot on the estate. He pushed the event to the back of his mind and started studying the painting. The light was far from ideal.

'Are you looking for something?' asked Dimitri, one hand on the stool, looking anxiously up at his tutor.

'I don't really know, Dimitri. I might be.'

A strange sensation was coming over Adam. He had started to feel uneasy looking at the portrait; the whole thing felt almost indecent, as if the image was about to come to life and he had been staring at the real woman for all that time. He could almost feel the warmth of her skin and smell her heavy perfume. He closed his eyes, trying to come back to his senses. He was being mesmerised by a painted portrait! After all, they were only layers of coloured paste spread on canvas!

When he reopened his eyes a few seconds later, he noticed the pendant nestling on the woman's collarbone: it was an exquisite example of insect jewellery, a delicate and intricate winged scarab framed by multi-coloured stones and swirls of gold leaf. She was wearing assorted earrings, bracelets and rings, all full of Egyptian exoticism. He wondered whether she had deliberately chosen those particular pieces for the portrait, yet another way of asserting her origins or of reassuring herself in an alien environment. Adam felt like talking to her, but remembered the boy and swiftly climbed down the stool.

'I wonder why this portrait is kept in such an unwelcoming place and behind closed doors. It deserves to be in the dining room, together with her husband's. Why isn't it?' remarked Adam.

'I don't know… Maybe no one knows about it.'

'Have you said anything to your stepfather about this painting?'

The boy shook his head.

'No. I'm not too sure if he'd be interested. He'd prefer a portrait of my mother. He's been trying to convince her to pose for a painter, then for a photographer. She was horrified! Poor Vangelis, he cannot get mother to do anything nice for him!'

Genuine regret permeated the boy's voice.

'I just can't get my head round the reason why this portrait has been isolated in this manner. It is a real treasure, a masterpiece!'

Adam suddenly felt self-conscious; his voice had sounded over-enthusiastic. Whilst talking, he had been closely inspecting the surface of the work in search of a signature.

On the lower part of the frame were inscribed the words: '*Lady Amunet 'Amy' Whitemoor, The Rose Garden, Whitemoor Hall, June 1846*'.

The work was definitely anonymous, which added to its mystery. Adam suspected that there was more to the painting, that it had a story to tell.

The woman who was portrayed had had an intimate relationship with the place, he could feel it, but something had happened in her lifetime that had condemned her incredibly faithful image to be outcast and relegated to a cold dusty room as far away as possible. The woman's husband had remained master of the dining room, whereas she had been banished from the living quarters. Now, thinking about it, he thought that he could see why: contrary to the portrait of her husband whose image exuded intellectual charm and rakish energy, Lady Whitemoor's painting had an air of malevolence about it which probably would have put anyone off their food...

'Where would you like to go, now?'

Dimitri's voice, fresh and loud, reached him through the fog of his brain and resonated around the empty room. Adam had been completely lost in his thoughts. Meanwhile, his young companion had grown impatient; the time had come to leave the room, and he knew that he would only do so reluctantly. Oddly enough, he would have wanted to remain a little longer in the presence of the woman who had assaulted him in his dream. Her grip had felt so real and so strong, then.

'We could go and have a look at the abbey if you want,' proposed Dimitri, obviously in a hurry to leave the inhospitable room.

Adam walked to one of the narrow windows and had a peek outside:

'Where are we exactly?'

He could see the small coppice behind which Maeve's cottage was nestled and the red roof of the stable block to the left; the winding drive making its way towards the main gates to his right. If he looked carefully enough, he could catch a glimpse of the North Wing of the house.

'We are in the tower above the porch!' he exclaimed.

Stool in hand, Dimitri paused on the threshold, carefully scanning the empty corridor in front of him. Obviously reassured, he stepped out. Just as he was about to leave the tower, Adam thought he could feel a pair of violet eyes on his back.

THREE

They made their way across the lawn and along the woods. Adam breathed in the fresh air and took in the autumn landscape with relish. Everywhere he looked, there were woods, fields, hedges, bushes and trees covered in fragile autumnal leaves. It was endless, spreading as far as his eyes could see. It was incredibly quiet apart from the screeches of the resident crows perched as usual at the top of the trees bordering the thick woods. As if he had been reading his mind, Dimitri gestured towards the trees.

'The Wise Man's Spring is somewhere in there, it's my favourite place. There's also the rock formation, 'The Green Rock', with a proper cave! If you sit still for long enough, you can observe all kinds of animals.'

To their right, the lawn stopped to give way to the soft curve of a slope. A wide path led to a house quite similar to the Guardian's Cottage, only this one was surrounded by several small outbuildings and its courtyard looked cluttered up with gardening equipment.

'That's the Gardener's Cottage, up there, on Greenside Hill. Elliott Mills lives there.'

Just at that moment, a tall, powerfully built man wearing a cloth cap and a solid tweed jacket opened the gate, pushing a bicycle. The wicker basket at the front of the bike was full of parcels wrapped up in brown paper and tied up with string. When he saw the boy and the young man, the gardener stopped, hesitant. He finally seemed to make up his mind and started down the path towards them. When he reached the two walkers, Dimitri saluted him warmly.

'Good morning, Mr Mills. How are you today?'

'Good morning, Master Dimitri. I am well, thank you.'

'This is Mr Tuckfield, my new tutor. He comes from London and he is not used to the countryside, so I am taking him on a tour. We are going to have a look at the abbey!' Dimitri had delivered his greeting and introduction in a fast, shy voice. He was thrilled to be able to introduce Mr Tuckfield to the gardener.

Eliott Mills responded discreetly and politely to the greeting, but didn't smile. Adam thought that he looked slightly worried and a little wary;

he was definitely not a talker.

'Are you going to the village?' enquired Dimitri, boldly.

The gardener scratched the back of his head, dislodging his cap slightly and making it fall low on his forehead. His eyes remained on the parcels in the basket.

'I am, Master Dimitri. I might also do a bit of work in the kitchen garden later, once I have delivered my parcels.' He surprised his interlocutors when he addressed Adam.

'I wouldn't hang around the abbey too long, if I were you. Unpleasant bunch, the lot of them.'

He then bid them goodbye and was on his way. When he had reached the crossroads where the tracks met, he climbed on his bike and started pedalling vigorously towards the southern exit. Soon, he would be on the little road leading to the village of Whitemoor.

'Mr Mills works so very hard. It's nice to see him take some time to bring some parcels to his friend.'

'Oh, has he got a...,' he thought of an appropriate word and the one he found came out all wrong: '*a lady friend* in the village?'

Dimitri looked at Adam severely.

'Oh no! Nothing like that! Not Mr Mills!' The boy frowned, obviously disturbed by Adam's suggestion. 'Mr Mills was in the war, you know. He fought very bravely. He got a medal too. He and his friend Will were in the same platoon and were the only ones who survived.' Dimitri's face betrayed an intense emotion. 'Mr Reynolds – Mr Mills's friend – was very seriously injured. When he was released from the hospital, he came back to live with his mother in the village. Mr Mills was with him. He heard that Vangelis was looking for a gardener and he got the job! I think they had offered to take Will in at the abbey, but Mr Mills got really angry about it and refused. He said that he would take care of his friend himself. Mrs Abbott said he was really rude to the people of the abbey!'

Dimitri smiled sadly before carrying on with his story.

'Mr Mills goes to see Will with some parcels Mrs Abbott gives him, at least once a week. Apparently, his friend's mother is on her own and really struggles to make ends meet. I think it is so generous of Mr Mills to do that. He hasn't got any family of his own, you know... I admire him so very much! Don't you?'

The big eyes were now glistening with tears. Dimitri sniffed loudly and added:

'I know all this because Mrs Abbott told me. She is very nice, Mrs Abbott. She is like Mr Mills; she doesn't like the abbey people very much either.'

The boy perked up a little. He added:

'You look sad, now! Don't be. The war is finished now, and there's nothing we can do but carry on living.'

The boy patted his tutor's hand reassuringly and started walking towards the abbey. Much like a zombie, Adam followed his pupil. What an extraordinary thing to say for an 11-year-old! Not for the first time, Adam felt like the child in the pair. He carried on walking, the nagging feeling of inadequacy never completely leaving his side until they arrived at the abbey.

*   *   *

The 13th century Cistercian building struck Adam as a rather remarkable place. It had obviously been refurbished and preserved with care by its consecutive inhabitants. The cloister buildings were huddled together in the middle of a softly hilly landscape, making the ensemble look like a small village set in a peaceful corner of the English countryside. People lived and worked there, were cared for and educated away from prying eyes.

You couldn't reach the abbey any other way than by going through the gatehouse; it was surrounded by a water-filled moat. The drawbridge was up, leaving the buildings frustratingly out of reach. Adam and Dimitri started walking along the moat, their eyes searching the grounds and the windows for a glimpse of human activity, without success.

'So if this is an abbey, are there monks living here?' asked Adam, trying to remember what he had learnt about the dissolution of the monasteries under Henry VIII.

'Oh, no… They're not monks.'

'Gladys mentioned something about *a family*? Or 'The Family'? Do you know who these people are?'

Dimitri shrugged.

'Not really. Vangelis always says he'll explain to me when I'm older, mother doesn't know a thing – or doesn't care. Mrs Abbott and Mr Mills disapprove of them but I'm not sure they know very much about what's going on. Mrs Abbott said that they have helped a lot of people during and after the war. Mr Simms, Mr Suleman, Gladys, Ginny, Rose, Paul… They are all from the abbey, and they don't look like monks, do they?'

Dimitri conjured up the images he had seen in his history books: perpetually hunched men with tonsured heads, covered in long shapeless cloaks and wearing sandals.

'Is your stepfather happy to have them on the estate?'

'S'pose so. They were here before he bought the house, so I guess he agreed for them to carry on when he moved in. I don't mind too much, personally. I just wish I could go in and have a look!'

Adam noticed that curiosity made the boy's eyes shine as he was looking longingly at the inaccessible buildings; the child's imagination was probably running wild. Nevertheless, the young man was growing wary: it seemed to him that the inhabitants of the abbey were nothing more than a cult. How peculiar that a scientist like Vangelis Chronos would agree to support an organisation such as this! There must have been certain advantages for him or he wouldn't have tolerated them on his land. Adam wondered what the people in the village thought of it.

They had gone halfway around the moat when they reached a small chapel surrounded by a copse. Nestled to the side of the building was a graveyard no one seemed to visit anymore. They pushed the rusty gate and stepped onto the uneven path. Some stone slabs had gone missing and had left muddy holes the visitors had to try and avoid; the ones left were covered with moss, which made them treacherously slippery. Brambles and other weeds were wrapping themselves around broken tombstones, creeping over one or two immobile angels and lopsided crosses. Most of the names, dates and epitaphs had been weathered away by time and a few were entirely covered with a layer of russet-coloured leaves. The place reminded Adam of Highgate Cemetery, although on a much smaller scale.

Surrounded by the silence of the countryside, completely undisturbed, this tiny burial ground had a gripping quality to it. It was infused with the sadness of negligence; it was a forgotten spot.

Dimitri left Adam's side to walk round the corner of the church. He called after his companion:

'Mr Tuckfield! Come, come! Have a look at this!'

In a separate plot, away from the building and the other tombs, stood a lonely mausoleum which had seen better days, but could still strike visitors with its exotic solemnity: the entrance gates were dominated by a pharaonic arch and flanked by two Egyptian columns decorated with stylised lotus flowers. 'In Memoriam' was the only visible inscription on the structure.

'This is Lord and Lady Whitemoor's mausoleum! Their coffins would have been placed in there. Lord Whitemoor describes it in one of his books. He had it built at the same time as the house. It looks like an Egyptian temple, doesn't it?' enthused Dimitri.

So Lord Whitemoor's infatuation with Ancient Egypt hadn't stopped at his chosen career and wife. He had wanted to pursue his passion into death too... This fact left Adam thoughtful.

Behind the first set of gates, a second wrought iron padlocked fence blocked the passage to the stairs that let down into the invisible vault. Adam's eyes lingered on the disappearing steps.

'So alive in their portraits, and yet so very dead,' he whispered.

He was aware of Dimitri's light breathing, the white vapour of the boy's breath escaping from his mouth at regular intervals, a reassuring sign of life. Adam discreetly observed his young companion and saw that he was still at the happiest he had seen him so far. He obviously enjoyed the freedom of the open air exceedingly.

'I wonder if Nutty's around today,' the child said suddenly, his nose up in the air.

The strange eeriness of the atmosphere was disturbed by his unexpected comment.

'Nutty?' echoed Adam, incredulously.

Dimitri had started looking around, as if he had quite forgotten about the excitement that could be derived from staring at an eccentric mausoleum on a cold October morning.

'He's the resident red squirrel!' he explained.

'A red squirrel? I wouldn't mind seeing one of those!' exclaimed Adam, suddenly laughing with relief at the boy's very wholesome interest for a small furry creature. They both wandered around the graveyard for another ten minutes, their faces lifted towards the high branches of the trees, but without success. Nutty wasn't going to show himself.

'Oh well. I guess he might be hibernating or something.'

'Do squirrels hibernate?' asked Adam, catching his breath again after having jumped here and there looking for a ball of red fur.

'I don't know,' admitted Dimitri.

'Well, then. We'll have to make it the topic of one of our lessons.'

A wide smile appeared on the boy's pale face.

They walked to the chapel and pushed the wooden door. Instead of the expected wooden pews, altar and pulpit, they were confronted with a completely empty space. Naked stone was all there was to see. In a little niche carved inside the southern wall burned a single small candle made of deep red wax. The smell permeating the air was rich and fragrant, as if someone had burnt some musky incense earlier in the day.

Dimitri pulled a face and used his hand as a fan in front of his nose.

'Ugh!' he uttered, inhaling noisily. 'What's that?'

'Obviously, this chapel hasn't been used for years and yet, there's this lit candle here... and someone's been burning some kind of incense...' observed Adam.

They had to whisper in order to prevent their voices from being amplified by the rough surface of the walls. There was no trace of the Christian rituals that had once been conducted there. Some marks on the walls showed that items had been removed, unscrewed, torn away – taking a little bit of the plaster that was still hanging on in some places.

Indecipherable scratches, like some worn out graffiti, appeared here and there around the room. Some looked like unknown symbols belonging to a language Adam had never seen before. His gaze came back to the candle: it was definitively burning, but its size didn't seem to have changed since they had arrived.

'I don't like it here,' declared Dimitri firmly.

'You have been here before, though, haven't you?'

'In the graveyard, yes, often. Not in here, though. The door and the windows used to be boarded up. Maybe the people from the abbey have started using it again?' Dimitri was still rubbing his irritated nose. 'Let's get out!'

Soon, they were back in front of the moat. They were about to start again on their walk when Dimitri suddenly pulled Adam's sleeve.

'Look!'

The boy pointed to the right of a cluster of buildings. An orderly column of about twenty people had just started coming out of an arched passage to walk the short distance and then disappear again through another entrance in another nearby construction. From where they stood, Adam and Dimitri couldn't see their faces; a row of very closely planted trees was obstructing their view and some bushes in the grounds of the abbey were in the way. They could see that the individuals wore long white tunics adorned with heavy gold jewellery and carried baskets and various other types of containers. They moved quickly and purposely, and they all disappeared again in less than one minute.

Tutor and pupil looked at each other.

'It's the first time I actually see anyone here. They *did* look a little like monks, didn't they?' remarked Dimitri.

Adam was trying to rapidly process the short scene he had just witnessed. There had been women and men in that group, some small and slight, some tall and strongly built. The long flowing white tunics with the wide sleeves and chunky gold collars somehow felt familiar. It came to him suddenly: these were the same clothes and adornments the woman had worn in his dream. Adam started to feel light-headed; he was troubled by all the strange coincidences he was coming across at an accelerated rate.

'I wonder what the time is,' he ventured.

Dimitri dipped his hand in the breast pocket of his grey suit and got out a small round Victorian watch attached to a thin silver chain.

'It's almost midday!'

'You know what? I feel really hungry, don't you?' exclaimed Adam with forced cheerfulness.

The boy looked chagrined.

'Do you?'

'I wasn't hungry at all this morning at breakfast but now I feel like I could do with something a little more substantial.'

Adam also wanted to get as far away from the abbey as he could. A sudden panic, similar to the one that had seized him on the day of his arrival, was creeping over him, and he wanted to avoid making a fool of himself in front of Dimitri. In addition, he thought he could feel real hunger cramping his stomach. The boy gave in with a sigh.

'All right, I could have some hot tea, I guess. Let's go back to the house, then. We can get in through the service yard.'

They started on the path away from the abbey and back towards the house. They had been walking for about a minute and a half when, coming from the abbey buildings they had left behind, a strange sound made the air vibrate.

It had started as nothing more than a very loud breath or gust of wind, but had grown and grown, swelling like a giant wave of sound; and now, the hypnotic, rhythmic evocation seemed to have spread to the whole landscape around them; it covered the fields and mixed with the water of the rivers; it got caught in the branches of the trees and chased away the startled birds that had been perched on them. The whole of Nature seemed to be groaning in unison, expressing the grief of humanity as a whole in an unknown tongue. It was terrifying and otherworldly.

They didn't talk, just stopped and looked at each other. Then they started walking again, their pace accelerating until they were both going as fast as they could without running. They only stopped, out of breath, when they reached the reassuring clutter of the service yard which protected them from the haunting hymn.

FOUR

Dimitri was finding it difficult to get the image of the ragged girl out of his mind. She had been sitting in the corridor up there in the tower, her back to the wall. When the boy and his tutor had emerged from the unused service staircase via the narrow door, she had lifted her face and her eyes had penetrated Dimitri's soul through and through. The misery that had been burdening her clear blue gaze had wounded and frozen him. He had wished then that Mr Tuckfield had been able to see her, that desperate shadow of a girl lost in the locked corridor, the only and reluctant guardian of Amunet's portrait. It was a heavy burden to carry on his own.

The girl had slowly stood up on her unsteady legs; even death couldn't bring strength to her weakened limbs. She hadn't tried to communicate with him, but they had stayed there, looking at one another and acknowledging each other's presence. Dimitri remembered how the slight figure had remained immobile as he and his tutor had made their way towards the room where the portrait had been hanging. When he had pushed the door, he had thought he had heard a faint, choked sigh behind him. But he hadn't turned round and instead had resolutely stepped inside.

The ghost of the lost girl had already disappeared when he had gone to fetch the stool for Mr Tuckfield, but her disconsolate little face and the waves of grief that had poured out of her had stayed with him over the following days.

As he had done for all the other encounters, Dimitri drew the girl and wrote a short paragraph about her; he knew he wouldn't be able to faithfully portray the unearthly quality of her features and form. He could only try and remember the main details of the ghost's appearance: the length of her hair, the shape of her clothes… He had noticed the translucent, grey quality of her skin – was there really any skin left? He couldn't resolve to call it her 'flesh' either, as it wasn't flesh anymore, was it? He carefully wrote down the date and place of the apparition so he could remember her.

Unfortunately, the boy knew that he would never know either who all those people were or what their story was. Even the man who had walked on water at the Wise Man's Spring had remained a complete mystery. Dimitri was convinced of the existence of a link between the man in white and the objects he had found hidden in the hollow by the pond. But relinquishing the items to his stepfather had meant losing them for good, and therefore abandoning any chance he had of ever knowing the true nature of his treasure. The jewellery box and the leather bound notebook had never been mentioned again, and the boy hadn't dared ask about them. Now that his thoughts had turned to the Wise Man's Spring ghost, something came knocking on the door of his memory. A sparkle, a faint light had lit up somewhere in his mind. What was it?

Dimitri got up and walked to the oriel window behind the small armchair, which he pushed aside; he then started removing by hand the loosened screws that discreetly kept one panel attached to the others. Once removed, the space showed a large hollow in which the boy had placed all his notebooks: his secret ghost diaries, the statements of all the apparitions he had seen since he had been able to write; hidden in there were also the plans of the house he was working on: this was his secret stash!

He picked up the notebook in which he had written about his encounter at the Wise Man's Spring and flicked through the pages until he found his illustration; that was it: the man had been wearing the same layered white tunic as the men and women at the abbey. There was a link between the ghost, the items he had found in the pouch and the obscure community. His heart rate accelerated: he felt puzzled, excited, worried and confused. Should he be telling anyone about it? Mr Tuckfield, perhaps?

On Dimitri's bedside table was the book his tutor had shown him in the library: 'Lord Arthur Savile's Crime and Other Stories'. The boy was supposed to start reading 'The Canterville Ghost' for his lessons later in the week, but he had left it untouched so far – and it was now Tuesday evening. He wasn't sure he wanted to read it. Mr Tuckfield had told him that it was a very entertaining story, but the boy hesitated. He was a child with a serious mind and most certainly didn't think ghosts were a laughing matter; then he was worried that whilst studying the story, he would betray himself and let his secret slip out. At the same time, Dimitri was burning to share it with someone! He craved the relief of unburdening himself.

He had always had to deal with the ghosts all on his own, without anyone to reassure him and explain to him why he could see people after they had died, as they wandered around the world of the living aimlessly, without anyone being aware of their presence. He had secretly read books about séances, psychics and revenants; they hadn't helped him that much, but had rather scared him. He understood that his strange powers singled him out and made him different. He thought that the books he had consulted were hysterical, over-exaggerated, with a scientific value very close to nil. He hadn't recognised himself or what he had been experiencing in any of them. He had decided to stop reading that kind of literature out of disappointment, disillusionment and despair. He would find out the answers he needed himself. But it was a lonely thing to do. If Mr Tuckfield offered a helping hand and a sympathetic ear, why not take advantage? It was time for decisions.

He had just replaced the loose board back into place when the door opened without warning and Sophia Chronos's ethereal form floated into the room, looking so immaterial that she could have very well qualified as one of her son's spectral apparitions. She was shrouded in an ivory-coloured dress and her hair was loosely tied back in a bun that let her curls escape all around her face. Lady Chronos's icy presence always made the room temperature fall by a few degrees, much like ghosts did. Dimitri had sometimes wondered whether his mother was a real human being or only a pretend one.

The boy waited for her to be seated in the armchair – the very same one behind which his notebooks were hidden! Sophia suppressed a groan as she lowered herself slowly onto the seat. She then looked around her son's bedroom with hazy eyes.

'The décor in your room has really become old and tired, Dimitri. I have been wondering whether we should perhaps move you to somewhere a little bit more appropriate, like the main room in the West Wing. It has a better bathroom and the wallpaper is fresher.'

Sophia Chronos was trying to give her voice a steady, calm tone. The boy was on his guard, knowing that any wrong word or gesture could derail his mother's attempt at composure. Nevertheless, he was horrified by her suggestion. Just when Mr Tuckfield had moved into the room next door, his mother wanted to remove him to the other side of the house? He couldn't let that happen! Not now!

'Thank you for thinking about my comfort. I do like it here, though. I have become very attached to this old room.' The boy started cautiously. 'Besides, it is so very convenient for the classroom.'

'Oh yes, *the classroom*!' echoed Sophia; her brown eyes looked towards the window and blinked. 'I have been told that you have been spending an awful lot of time with your new tutor. I don't remember anyone mentioning a new tutor to me.'

That wasn't true, of course, as Vangelis had painstakingly explained to her where and how they had recruited Adam and how good it would be for the boy to resume his education. But Sophia's memory had always been highly selective.

'Of course, he cannot be worse than that *dreadful* Miss Finch,' she spat. *The lying, scheming, gossiping, rotten bitch she was!* she thought, remembering the former governess's tight curls, pinched mouth and clipped delivery with disgust. 'I wonder why we bothered keeping her that long.' She sighed. 'I haven't yet had the pleasure of meeting Mr...?'

'Mr Tuckfield! His name is Adam Tuckfield.'

'Mr Tuckfield...' She sniffed. 'I expect you'll introduce me to your new teacher, then, as nobody else is willing to do so.'

'Yes, yes, of course! Mr Tuckfield is very nice, you'll see. I like his face. He is quite young.'

Sophia looked at her son with a strange expression.

'Is he?' She blanched. 'Young? I mean... Is he a *young* man?'

'Quite young.'

Sophia looked away. Her mouth seemed to gasp for air.

'I will... I will try and come to one of your lessons soon. Or maybe I'll come down to dinner one evening. I shall meet your Mr Tuckfield.'

Sophia Chronos smiled her forced, sad smile. Without a word, she raised herself from the armchair with difficulty and walked across the room; and then she was gone, very much like a ghost. Soon, the only trace left of her visit was a faint, floral scent of roses and powder.

FIVE

If Adam had thought that giving 'The Canterville Ghost' to read to Dimitri had been a clever move, he now doubted himself. The story had obviously upset the child.

'I have read it because you asked me to. But no, I didn't like it.'

'And do you think you can tell me why that is?'

Adam was standing in front of Dimitri's desk with his hands in his pockets, waiting patiently for the boy's answer. He had come to realise that he might have made an error of judgement. Dimitri was obstinately keeping his eyes on the cover of the book in front of him. He shuffled in his seat with a sulky lip.

'I don't know.'

'You don't know?' Adam was observing the boy with curiosity. He had adopted a rather furtive attitude and the tutor could see him struggle. His pupil obviously wanted to speak but was censoring himself. Finally, the boy looked at his teacher and exclaimed:

'The way he writes about the ghost... I don't know... It's not right.'

'Why is that?' asked Adam softly.

'He's making fun of him!'

'Well, at the beginning, certainly, the story has a light tone, it is closer to comedy than to a horror story, but this changes towards the end, don't you think? It all gets more serious when the young Virginia befriends the ghost and helps him find peace...'

Dimitri's countenance suddenly seemed to disintegrate. His face grew a shade paler and his eyes filled with tears; his lips quivered. Soon, tears were rolling down his cheeks. Adam was flabbergasted; he hadn't counted on tears at all... He removed his hands from his pockets; he could feel his ears burn with embarrassment. He wanted to console the child but didn't know how.

'Dimitri... Are you alright? What is it that has upset you so much?'

The boy silently shrugged. Adam looked up at the clock above the door: almost 2.45pm. The natural light in the classroom was already declining, the sky having remained overcast for most of the week. It was threatening to rain again.

'What I propose we do is to take our break early. We've already worked well today. I will choose another story for our English lessons. Then whenever you are ready, you come and tell me what has unsettled you about Mr Wilde's story. All right?'

For a brief moment, Adam thought the boy was going to throw a tantrum. But he just nodded through his tears with an uncertain smile.

'Can I go to my room to splash my face with water, please?'

'Of course you can.'

Dimitri quickly left the classroom; he knew that the only way for him to regain his composure was to leave the room, the book and the teacher behind. He had felt threatened in his certainties and he wasn't used to having to explain himself to anyone…

He was feeling wretched: the Canterville story had struck a chord with him and it had stirred his feelings far too much. He had disliked the way the ghost had been portrayed as a grotesque, wicked master of disguise who could be seen and heard by everyone and who could get buckets of water dropped on his head, kept tripping over bits of strings stretched across corridors and generally got bruised and battered. He *knew* this was not true, and it felt like a great injustice. *His* ghosts had been disembodied people, if such a thing could ever be. He could see them alright, but something about them – the appearance of their skin, their demeanour, their lost, imploring expression and, above all, the lack of any sparkle of humanity in their glassy eyes – something always told him that the individual he was seeing was not from this world but had come from The Other Side.

Most of them had been reduced to silence, even though they seemed to want to speak to him, desperately. The young soldier he had seen near the stables had been eager to tell him his story, opening his hollow mouth without any sound coming out of it. The more he had tried, the more diaphanous he had become, until the boy had only been able to distinguish the faint outline of the uniform. The ghost had then disappeared entirely without having managed to express himself. Dimitri had been able to sense his suffering, the loss of his innocence to the unspeakable horrors he had witnessed. This particular encounter had left him feeling unwell for two whole days. The only one that had felt somewhat different had been the man at the Wise Man's Spring; he had appeared strangely real.

*   *   *

'I am really not sure I am up to the task!' admitted Adam, forcefully exhaling the smoke of his cigarette.

'What on earth do you mean? It is only your second week, remember?'

Adam and Maeve were sitting side by side on the tiny wooden bench underneath the rugged wisteria; the only light was coming from inside through the window, and in front of them spread the blackness of the estate. It was cold, but they both needed air. Tightly wrapped up in a huge woollen cardigan that had also belonged to one of her brothers, Maeve was enjoying Adam's company. She had felt very lonely during that last week and several times had been tempted to call at the big house, but she knew she wasn't exactly welcome there.

'Has the child been difficult?' she asked.

'No, not particularly. I mean, he definitely is not the type of kid I've been used to.' Adam was at a loss to explain the social media and smartphone addicted, fame-hungry materialistic teenagers he had left behind in the 21st century. Yet, if he had thought of them as being over-protected in an increasingly connected world, he had been wondering whether Dimitri's isolation was a blessing or a curse.

'He is a clever child, mature way beyond his years,' he admitted. 'He seems to be very knowledgeable about a lot of things, but all this knowledge comes entirely from books. He hasn't had a lot of experience of this world, nor any kind of interaction with children his age, and this cannot be right. Certainly, his mother and stepfather should have his best interest at heart.'

Maeve's shoulders were shaken by a soft bout of quiet laughter.

'Oh, Adam. You are so sweet. Can't you just see that neither Vangelis nor Sophia care enough about Dimitri? He is a hindrance to both, that is what he has been for the past eleven years. In Sophia's case, he has completely ruined her future, her health and her life. No wonder she can't bring herself to even *like* the poor mite.'

'How can you... I mean, what makes you say this? You are being extremely cynical here. I thought cynicism was more widespread in our shallow 21st century.'

Maeve turned her face towards him. She felt a surge of anger flow through her.

'Shall I remind you that a few years ago, this country got out of the worst conflict Europe and probably the world had ever seen. Millions of young men died and apart from a few, no one seems to even remember why. Ask around you at the house, see how many of the staff have had loved ones taken away from them in the most horrific circumstances. My two brothers died there, and several cousins. It has driven my mother mad. She is in a home and probably will never get out. Society changed, people changed. The scars of the conflict are not only physical, they run too deep to be able to be expressed properly. If that doesn't make you cynical, I don't know what does.'

She reached for her cigarette case and lit up shakily. Her anger disappeared as fast as it had come.

'My mother is Vangelis Chronos's sister. She and her brother led very different lives, but even though they rarely saw each other, Vangelis had kept a soft spot for his little sister. After the death of my father – dad was a journalist, like me – he had been sending money to her regularly; I only discovered that recently. The only reason he came to my rescue when I got into trouble is because I am his sister's daughter. I've always been wondering about this evasive uncle of mine; he sounded exciting, always going off to Greece and Egypt... I've always imagined him being something of a mad scientist and some kind of adventurer.'

'During my first year at the newspaper five years ago, I spent a lot of time with my nose buried in the archives, especially anything to do with culture and entertainment. I stumbled across a short article about the marriage of the *'enthralling actress Sophia Augarde, who disappeared suddenly from the stage a year ago after the tragic death of her husband-to-be, and Lord Vangelis Chronos, a highly respected scientist and scholar'*. My curiosity was piqued, and I started asking around about this Sophia Augarde. I was told that she had been a very promising actress before the war, one destined for stardom and celebrated as much for her great and delicate beauty as for her scintillating talent and personality. In the theatre world of 1913, there had been some rumours about an affair between Sophia and one of the great stars of the stage, a Shakespearian and tragedian called Henry Emery. I've seen pictures of him and read reviews; he was quite something, you know, the dashing, dark brooding type, some kind of Mr Rochester... not at all like you!' She laughed softly at Adam's dismayed facial expression.

'He was probably a beastly man in private, you know... But women have always gone weak at the knee for those types, the silly cows. *I* for one, have more civilised tastes... Anyway... One day, he announced publicly that they were to be married, hence cutting short all new gossip, and then he promptly died of a mysterious illness. I haven't managed to get a lot of details about his demise, but some accounts talked about 'a dreadful bloody mess'. What kind of illness this could have been, you tell me. But it was all hushed up because of his fame and wealth. And then, something strange happened: Sophia disappeared completely. Whoosh, just like that! Her fellow actors, her audience, no one saw her again.' Maeve sighed deeply.

'She was pregnant, you see. She thought she was going to marry Emery and had become careless. The pregnancy was a very, very difficult one. The birth was even worse. Horrific. The doctor thought she wouldn't make it as she had lost a lot of blood and she was damaged internally. Gosh, this always makes me feel awfully queasy.' Maeve shivered violently.

'You have seen how she limps. She is riddled with pain and is being drugged up by Saturnin and Vangelis; I think she's developed an addiction to this Victorian panacea that is laudanum. Have you seen her? She cannot function properly. It's heartbreaking, really... So... After the birth, she found herself all alone – no known family – physically and mentally damaged with no hope of returning to the stage, and her dreams of limelight in tatters. She soon ran out of money, and she was completely damaged goods. Her options were running out, when tadaa! Out of the blue appeared one of her old admirers, a much older and wiser man full of money who proposed marriage on the spot.'

'Vangelis?'

'Bravo, darling! You've been following.'

The feeble light from the lounge fell on Maeve's grin. She looked like a devilish elfin.

'So that's the story? Your uncle took his bride and stepson to come and live in his big house, away from their miserable life?'

'That's pretty much it. Vangelis had bought the house in 1913. They all moved in here soon after the wedding ceremony.'

'Well, thank you for that, Maeve. That was quite a story. Poor Dimitri! No wonder he takes refuge in his imagination. Reality is not too much of a comfort. I hope he's feeling a little less isolated since I arrived.'

The young man fell silent for a while, now very conscious of the darkness surrounding the small house. He wondered what the child would be doing now. He himself had departed for the cottage immediately after dinner, leaving Dimitri in the classroom where the boy had wanted to spend some time drawing.

'Still. All this doesn't even start to explain the fact that he got so upset about Oscar Wilde's portrayal of a ghost in a short story. It really felt like it was... personal, you know? There is something not quite right about this ghost thing.' Adam shook his head.

'Children often take refuge in their imagination when things don't go well in their world, don't they? The same way adults find solace in alcohol, drugs and the heady pleasures of the flesh. But kids still have this charming capacity to believe in imaginary worlds and fantastical beings, and they are sincere in their will to believe in them. Dimitri spends whole days on his own, without anyone to tell him what's real or not. No wonder he's developed a warped sensitivity to that kind of subjects. His surroundings fuel his beliefs; I bet you it wouldn't have been the same if he had been living in a terraced semi somewhere in a London suburb.'

Maeve was rather proud of her explanation, and she savoured it in silence. She then took to scrutinising the darkness that spread beyond the gates of the cottage. During the short silence, Adam was conscious of her regular, controlled breathing. The smoke of their cigarettes mixed up with the air and filled the space around them like a protective screen. The young woman started speaking again in a low, dreamy voice.

'It's incredibly dark out there isn't it? If I am being perfectly honest, I understand the hold the house has over the boy. Down here at night, sometimes, when I stop doing whatever it is I am doing, I suddenly become conscious of the fact that I am all alone in this small cottage beset by darkness. I am not used to it: my London flat is full of light and the building full of people. I am still adjusting. I leave a small light on in the corner of my bedroom, like a child!'

Listening to Maeve, Adam suddenly got the impression that the blackness of the countryside around the cottage had become yet even thicker and was closing in on them. He remembered the small chapel near the abbey, and the overgrown churchyard. Only the weak glow of the little red candle would be providing any light there.

His companion interrupted his thoughts.

'Sometimes, if you look long enough into the darkness out there, you start seeing shapes and hearing noises. It has happened that I've felt as if someone were watching me from outside. At other times, I have noticed some strange glows coming from the south-east of the estate. On those nights, if you come outside, the air is filled with a strange buzz.'

Adam looked at Maeve: she had put out her cigarette and was now shivering. Was she cold or scared? He wondered whether he should put his arm around her to warm her up, a gesture that might seem far too familiar. She didn't leave him time to make any decision. She rubbed her hands together and jumped to her feet.

'Brr. I can't even feel my fingers anymore,' she declared. 'I think we have been out too long! Do you fancy a hot drink?' She opened the door and stepped inside the lounge.

Adam was about to follow Maeve when his pen fell out of his pocket and rolled on the ground, coming to a halt underneath the bench. He crouched to retrieve the item; as he stood up, his eye caught something indeterminate: the darkness itself seemed to have shifted silently; he was filled with the certainty that he had seen something, but he was unable to describe it. He hurried inside, slamming the door a little too vigorously. He didn't even want to think about walking back to the main house now.

In the end, thanks to one or two glasses of strong spirit and a good torch, he managed to gather up enough courage to make it safely to the house before the front door was locked for the night. Needless to say, it hadn't been his favourite walk.

SIX

Adam had been battling with his evening suit for the past thirty minutes and wished he had been able to call someone to advise him on how to tie his bow. He was feeling nervous; tonight, for the first time since he had arrived, he would find himself in the same room with the other inhabitants of the Hall. Sophia Chronos had never attended any lesson, as she had promised her son; Vangelis and Saturnin Bloom had remained invisible, locked away in their part of the house.

The young man wondered what kind of strange chemistry would result in all of them being together between four walls; thankfully, Maeve had been invited and he tried to think about her as much as possible; he was now connected to her by an invisible thread that couldn't be severed; she was his guardian angel…

'Come in!' he called out, replying to a series of knocks on the door.

In the mirror, he saw Gladys enter the room followed by a smiling Maeve. The young maid looked confused and only managed to mumble:

'Miss Hayward to see you, sir.'

'Hello darling, I hope I'm not intruding? I've just arrived and the place is frightfully empty! So I've asked this charming young lady here to take me straight to your room. I kind of had to convince her, didn't I?' She winked at the poor Gladys, who went bright pink.

The young maid's eyes were two perfectly round saucers; she was gawping and feeling embarrassed by the familiarity with which Maeve had addressed the new tutor.

'Thank you, sweetheart, you can leave us, now.' Gladys hesitated, her eyes darting from Adam to Maeve and back several times. She then nodded and trotted out of the room, closing the door carefully behind her.

Adam was standing, defeated, the undone bow tie hanging pathetically around his neck and still astonished to see Maeve in his room. She was looking ravishing in her peach-coloured beaded chiffon flapper dress; the light colour of the garment was in stunning contrast to her dark glossy head and velvety red lips; her huge eyes were rimmed with kohl; Adam thought that he could just get lost in the green jungle of them.

'What?' she quipped, suddenly realising that he was staring at her.

'Nothing!' He quickly turned round towards the mirror and tugged at his collar.

'I don't know what to do with this. I've never worn formal dress like this, bow tie, dinner jacket and all. It's very nice of Mr Simms to have provided a suit that fits perfectly, but he could also have made sure it came with an instruction manual.'

The young woman grabbed his arm and ordered him to turn round once again to face her.

'Very well, young man. Let me do it. I've had the opportunity to do this quite a few times. I am now an expert!'

She grabbed the two ends of material. Adam lowered his eyes to her face; his nose filled with the scents of her hair, make-up and perfume. Her mouth twisted in a funny way as she concentrated on her task. For a second, he closed his eyes. She was so close, as she had been in his dream all those weeks ago. He couldn't help wondering who were the men whose bows she had tied up.

'Done!' She patted him on the chest softly. 'Look! What do you think?' She made him face the mirror again. They stood side by side looking at each other's reflection, grinning.

'Perfect! Will you teach me?' Adam lifted his right hand to his neck. The bow was not too tight, but he was not used to having one and could feel a small discomfort. 'I'll see how long I can endure that thing before I tear it off.'

Someone then knocked on the door. Dimitri walked in, holding a large square parcel wrapped up in silk paper and tied up with a ribbon.

'Mr Tuck…' The child stopped when he spotted Maeve.

'Hullo, there, Dimitri. How are you, dear child? I haven't seen you in ages!' exclaimed the young woman.

Blinking, Dimitri ignored her and addressed Adam.

'What is *she* doing here?'

'Come on, Dimitri, I think you are being a little bit rude to Miss Hayward. She's just said hello to you!' Adam could feel his ears burn.

Very matter-of-factly, Dimitri turned to Maeve and offered his hand.

'Oh. I apologise, Miss Hayward. How do you do?' he asked sulkily; his little hand felt cold against Maeve's flesh and he avoided meeting her gaze. The boy then stood undecided, his packet tucked under one arm.

'So, what have you got there, all wrapped up?' enquired the tutor.

'It's a present for mother and Vangelis. It's their wedding anniversary tonight.'

The boy almost sighed. He didn't seem to be looking forward to the reunion downstairs.

'Oh, that's very nice of you... Shall I be so daring as to ask what it is?' asked Maeve.

'It's a painting I've done.'

'That's a great present indeed! Your mother will be pleased,' exclaimed the young woman. Dimitri only shrugged.

'That's what you've been working on all week! I cannot wait to see the result,' added Adam encouragingly.

'Are you still living at the Guardian's Cottage?' asked Dimitri, his grave little face now turned towards Maeve.

'I am indeed.'

'Do you like it there?'

'Well, it is very comfortable and...'

'And you never get scared?' inquired the boy, with genuine gravity and interest plainly on show on his face.

Maeve went a shade paler under the layer of ivory powder.

'Scared? Me? What do you mean?'

'I don't know... Just asking...' The boy looked at the clock on the mantelpiece and changed the subject entirely, oblivious to his two companions' surprised faces. 'Shall we go downstairs? I think we are supposed to be there at a quarter to six.'

Adam grabbed his dinner jacket and the trio came out of the room; they were about to go down the stairs when two women appeared on the staircase coming down from the second floor: Ginny was giving a supporting arm to Sophia Chronos who took in the small group in one sombre gaze.

'Ah! And who do we have here?'

They walked towards the trio who patiently waited for them to catch up at the top of the staircase. Sophia was wrapped in a long satin evening gown of pearl colour over which she had thrown a metallic gold lace shawl. Her hair was piled up high on her head, and her slender neck looked far too fragile to take the weight of it.

'Oh! Maeve Hayward... I had heard that you had been invited, but I was not expecting to see you coming out of one of the first floor bedrooms. Whose room is that, anyway?' she asked, looking straight at Adam. Her haughty, low voice was chilling.

Adam took a step forward, Sophia Chronos a step backward, as if something about his person had stung her from a distance.

'This is my bedroom, Lady Chronos. May I introduce myself: Adam Tuckfield, Dimitri's new tutor.'

'Mr Tuckfield... I have to express some surprise at seeing my son and this young person here exit your room in this way.'

'We were having a pre-dinner meeting, Lady Chronos. Nothing untoward about that. Adam and I have known each other for quite a while, and it came as a surprise to find him working as a tutor in this very same house!' lied Maeve.

Sophia Chronos's mouth betrayed her distaste. There obviously was no love lost between the two women.

'I wouldn't normally have deemed it appropriate for someone belonging to Miss Hayward's London set to become a live-in tutor for my son,' she started. Adam opened his mouth in protest, only to feel Maeve pinch his arm. 'But as my husband has assured me that you were perfectly suitable for the position and you have passed a rigorous application process, then I will try and forget this unfortunate detail.'

'You will see, dear Lady Chronos, that you will not come to regret Vangelis's choice,' confirmed Maeve, smiling sweetly at her uncle's wife. 'Dimitri and his tutor have already become firm friends, which can only be good news for the future!'

Sophia turned to her son.

'Is this true, Dimitri? You and Mr Tuckfield are getting on well?'

'Yes, it is true.' Dimitri was holding his wrapped up canvas behind his back, only knowing too well that he couldn't hide it. Fortunately, his mother didn't even notice it.

'You see, Mr Tuckfield, this child spends far too much time on his own, and in my circumstances, I simply cannot attend to his needs at all.' Those lines had been well rehearsed, accompanied by a weak, falsely motherly smile. They were all aware – Dimitri included – that Sophia Chronos indulged her illness. After having lost her power on the stage, she had found yet another way of putting on a show and obtain the attention she craved so much.

'Well, I guess we had better go downstairs now, dinner will be served soon.'

Sophia offered her arm to Ginny, who had remained silent the whole time, her eyes cast down. She was tall and plump, her dark brown hair neatly tied back away from her ruddy cheeks. Adam thought it funny that she was the exact opposite of the rather sickly-looking Gladys; the girl must have been excruciatingly patient and tolerant to be able to endure the rather thankless position of Sophia Chronos's maid.

The small group started down the stairs, adjusting their pace to that of Lady Chronos. Everyone looked slightly apprehensive apart from Maeve, who had been involved in so many embarrassing social situations that she was past caring and worrying. Dimitri's face was immobile and grave; he was holding on to his canvas, taking great care not to catch it on anything or drop it.

Adam was uneasy about being caught by Sophia getting out of his bedroom with Dimitri and Maeve. He was stupidly alarmed by the lady of the house: her cold, haughty beauty, cast against her physical suffering, was disturbing; he found her attitude towards her child repugnant, but at the same time, he felt sorry for her because of what she had been through. There was also something else… She seemed to recoil from him and he had caught her eyes on him… He was convinced that he had seen horror in those eyes.

Ginny was patiently supporting her mistress, her strong arm being used as a crutch, an infallible support; she stopped when her lady had to rest – which was rather often – and started again when Sophia did. The maid was also extremely vigilant and made sure that Lady Chronos didn't trip, as her balance was not always very good – the impracticality of her gown adding to her difficulties.

'Can you really believe that it has been eleven years since you and my uncle got married?' exclaimed Maeve.

'No, it is very true: I cannot,' replied Sophia in a cutting, bitter tone, without looking at her husband's niece.

'Are we to expect a speech of some kind from dear Uncle Vange?'

'He didn't the previous years. I certainly hope not. Speeches are so tedious. But you never really know, with Vangelis.'

Sophia had spoken with a forced, tired indulgence. She was used to her husband's eccentricities and to his sporadic shows of affection. Oh, he was affectionate and attentive every time he was with her and if she didn't care too much for it, it had become relatively bearable with time. What she hated was when all this accumulated affection came out in the open and Vangelis suddenly *exploded* with love; then he became insufferable, throwing into doubt the contract they had drawn, the conditions they had agreed on. In those moments, she was reminded that he wasn't just a good-natured fatherly figure but her *husband*, someone she was supposed to love and have respect for. Someone whose bed she should be sharing. When her thoughts turned to this particular part of the marriage vows, a black veil would come down in front of her eyes.

'Tell me, child, what have you been learning with Mr Tuckfield this week?'

Dimitri's shy description of the week's lessons filled the time it took them to reach the dining room. Adam was asked to add a few comments. Sophia didn't seem overly interested, but everyone thought it better than walking through the house in a dead, uncomfortable silence.

SEVEN

*V*angelis and his assistant had arrived in the dining room a few minutes earlier and were standing in front of the portrait of Lord Whitemoor. Mr Bloom had changed into a dinner outfit that matched Adam's, and Vangelis had swapped the purple coat he had been wearing with a red one, richly decorated with intricate gold leaf patterns. The scholar looked particularly pleased.

'Ah! And here is the rest of the company! Welcome! Welcome to the dining room, everyone. There's a fire, and the big radiator is on as well as a special treat, so I hope everyone, including the ladies, will feel comfortable enough to enjoy the evening.' Vangelis walked towards Sophia and seized both her hands in his. 'My dear, how beautiful you look tonight! This gown is simply angelic! Yes, that's it! You look just like an angel!'

The scholar then bowed and deposited a kiss on his wife's hand. Sophia's lips wavered into something resembling a smile; it disappeared within seconds.

'Ah! Mr Tuckfield! Thank you so very much for coming to our little, er, family gathering. As you probably know, this is an extremely rare opportunity for us to be together. By the way, pray do excuse us for not being in attendance this week, but we absolutely had to keep unsociable hours... Moreover, I daresay that all these experiments manage to curb our appetite somehow.' Vangelis Chronos next turned to his niece. His watery eyes didn't seem to recognise her at first, then he exclaimed: 'Maeve! How charming of you to come.'

'You are the one who invited me, Uncle Vange. I was not going to miss this opportunity to come to the big house!'

'Oh, yes, of course, *I* invited you... And how are things down at the Guardian's Cottage? Not feeling too lonely?'

'Well, I'm doing all right. I have started writing again, you know, trying to get back into the swing of things... I have a few ideas for articles... Actually, I was going to ask you, would that be all right if I used the phone more frequently? I need to...'

She was interrupted by Mr Simms's entrance.

'Sir, we would like to ask, are you all ready to start dinner, sir?'

'Oh yes, well, certainly, Mr Simms, yes, we are ready. Just give us a few minutes so we can get settled around the table, and then you can start!'

Vangelis Chronos looked at Saturnin Bloom and nodded. The assistant took over and almost solemnly walked to one end of the table. At the other end, Maeve had the time to whisper in Adam's ear before her name was called and she was shown her seat:

'Saturnin Bloom's face is enough to spoil *my* appetite!'

*   *   *

The atmosphere around the dinner table was a little solemn. Despite the radiator and the roaring fire, Adam was conscious of some persisting chilly air circulating around the seated guests, like small invisible spirits mucking about at their expense. He had never felt as much of a stranger as now: looking at the people around the table and seeing them looking so *authentic* in their 1925 clothes was unreal; he wasn't entirely part of *their* present. It was a very bizarre sensation, just like sitting around a table in the company of ghosts. *Ghosts...* Maybe they were all *his* ghosts: the people around the table, the maids, the cook, the gardener, the people at the abbey... They were haunting him for whatever reason... Maybe they were stalking his dreams, and the whole thing was only one long dream, and he was going to wake up in his bed at Jimmy's flat...

His head started spinning; his fingers loosened around the table spoon which hit the plate with a high pitched clatter and he jolted. Suddenly, all eyes were on him: Saturnin's piercing, bottomless black eyes; Vangelis's watery, washed-out blue ones; Sophia's dark brown irises in which the passion for life had long been extinct; Dimitri's gaze, so serious and already questioning; Maeve's cat-like emeralds, full of surprise and concern.

'Mr Tuckfield? Are you all right?' inquired Vangelis.

Adam was mortified. He could see a lock of his hair fall in front of his eyes but didn't dare move at all. He swallowed and managed to find his voice again.

'I am so sorry... I sincerely apologise. I think... I think my bow tie might be slightly too tight and it might have caused me to go a little dizzy.'

He squeezed his finger in between his collar and the skin of his throat. Vangelis, having recovered from his surprise, smiled sympathetically and nodded vigorously.

'Exactly what I always say, young man: to do proper work, a man needs to feel comfortable in his own clothes. It's very important. Look at me: some would say I am an eccentric, and that a man of my, er, reputation should pay more attention to the way my peers dress in the London circles – oh yes, I have been told that many times! – but I have never given in! To *think* properly, to resolve the great *questions* that are put to me, to *compose* those great essays, pamphlets and books, my body needs to be at ease with itself. If it is, then my mind can work properly. Look at this coat, for example. It comes from...'

'Vangelis, PLEASE!'

Sophia had visibly been growing more and more irritated by her husband's unnecessary outburst. She looked at him as if he had been the naughtiest child in the universe. She sat very straight, the shimmering material of her gown playing with the light of the chandelier and the flames in the fire. Very fine locks of her hair had become loose and framed her face like a halo. Adam noticed that her left hand had closed on a small roll of bread on one side of her plate. Deprived of blood, her knuckles had gone white. When she released the bread, the crust had been crushed and the roll reduced to a small ball of inedible dough.

Saturnin Bloom suggested Adam should remove the bow tie. There was a small bathroom at the end of the corridor he could use. For Adam, leaving the dining room felt like having a bucket of cold water thrown into your face after having been sat too close to a fire for some time. He soon found the small room, got in and locked the door. He then started undoing the bow Maeve's hands had artfully constructed. He paused for a few seconds, appalled: his hands were shaking. In the large ornate mirror, he looked like a flustered child: his hair was falling in front of his eyes, his cheekbones and lips were ablaze, his eyes were red... In short, he was in a bit of a state...

He turned the tap on and splashed his face with cold water. His hot skin tingled under the cool liquid. After having dried his face with the soft white towel, he stood for a few seconds, looking at the reflection in front of him: was he still sure about who he was anymore? He was under the impression that his old self, the one from the 21st century, was slowly melting away, or rather, was being diluted in the bracing air of 1925 England. His memory was patchy, and his mind went blank if he attempted to think about his past life. Maybe it was for the best, but what if everything *did* get erased? Would he be able to live in the skin of a complete stranger? Was it possible to be yourself without being yourself?

He took a deep breath and straightened himself. At the back of his mind, the same urge he had felt when he had run down the drive one week earlier was showing its twisted little face. Only this time, he knew it would be impossible to find his way around because it was pitch black, out there. And anyway, the gates would still be locked. He was stuck inside the unyielding walls of Whitemoor Hall, his existence now entwined with that of its inhabitants. How quickly it had all happened! How long had he been away from the dining room? Five minutes? Ten? He ought to go back and face them. *He had to.*

When he entered the room again, he was welcomed by Vangelis from the other side of the table.

'Ah! Here you are, young man! Mr Simms is about to bring the next dishes… Feeling any better now?'

'I am feeling much better, sir, thank you. I apologise again.' Adam slipped into his chair.

Soon Mr Simms and Gladys were back with some more hot dishes and the incident was not mentioned again for the rest of the meal. Adam could still catch Dimitri's curious eyes on him from time to time; Maeve, when addressing herself to him, would search his face, looking for a clue as to what had happened to him.

Vangelis was by far the most voluble person around the table, closely followed by Maeve, whilst Saturnin Bloom and Sophia Chronos both seemed enclosed in a stubborn silence; they represented the day and the night, the light and the darkness, although Adam found Sophia's blinding presence even more sinister than Saturnin Bloom's shadiness.

The secretary was growing more tenebrous by the minute; even the light from the chandelier didn't seem to completely reach up to his seat. He was intriguing, and his relationship with Vangelis didn't seem as clear-cut as the young tutor had originally thought. The older man was the enthusiastic scholar, the genial genius. He was an entertaining host keen to share his knowledge on everything under the sun: birds and plants, the horror of London in the summer, the tomb of Tutankhamun, news stories. In fact, he was ready to talk about anything as long as it was not his past and present research and experiments, which seemed to be out of bounds.

But the observant Adam couldn't help noticing the subtle influence Mr Bloom was exercising on the man he was supposed to assist. Vangelis all too often looked his way as if seeking some sort of approval or support. A simple word or sentence from the assistant could stop the scientist in his track. Saturnin Bloom behaved like a shadowy puppet master, and Adam couldn't help wondering what the truth was behind their odd partnership.

On the other side of the table, Sophia stood as the supreme ice queen: in her immediate vicinity the air was cold and rarefied, as if a coating of frost had deposited itself around her. She either looked down to her barely touched plate, or straight in front of her, her eyes fixed on a spot beyond the walls of the room. Only her body was present at the dinner table; her mind was far, far away.

At last, it was time to leave the table. The little group moved to the adjacent living room, a vast, comfortable space littered with sofas and upholstered chairs. They were to have coffee there.

Dimitri timidly approached Vangelis and whispered something in his ear. The scientist nodded, and a smile appeared on the boy's face. He trotted out of the room and came back with the wrapped up packet he had left hidden in a corner of the dining room. He approached Vangelis and his mother who were sitting next to each other on a stout little Chesterfield sofa and presented his special gift.

'Dear Mother and Stepfather, here is a little present I have made for your wedding anniversary. I do hope you like it.'

Behind Adam, Maeve murmured 'Oh, Bless...' The young man couldn't decide whether she had said it in earnest or if this was one of her usual sarcastic quips. He turned round and pointed at two chairs nearby.

'Let's take a seat, Maeve. You're not going to drink your coffee standing up, are you?' he whispered.

Saturnin Bloom didn't sit down, preferring to position himself away from the others. He was standing behind a plump armchair, his hands resting on the top of its back. He was observing the unwrapping with distracted interest.

Sophia slowly peeled away the layers of silk paper. The ribbon and the delicate sheets fell to the floor, completely covering the hem of her gown. She looked as if her legs were melting into the floor.

At last, Vangelis exclaimed 'Aaaah!' whilst looking expectantly at his wife; he had the face of a malicious, ageless goblin. Lady Chronos's graceful white hands tightly held onto the frame. Her face, at first emotionless, betrayed surprise. Her eyes still on the canvas, Sophia uttered a passionless 'Thank you'.

Vangelis's wrinkled, weathered face filled with a smile.

'Young man, you can be proud of yourself: this painting is a success!'

Dimitri, who had been standing in front of his mother and stepfather with his hands behind his back, flushed with pleasure.

From where they were seated, Adam and Maeve could only see the back of the frame. The latter had been fidgeting in her seat, and finally, she couldn't help exclaiming:

'Oh, go on, then, we want to see the picture too!'

Sophia's eyes lifted and fixed themselves on Maeve, cutting right through the young woman. The contempt Adam saw in her eyes suddenly brought back to his memory the look Dolly had given him when she had announced completely out of the blue that she was marrying another man because he, Adam, was not worthy of her. He felt a light stab to the heart, then the episode retreated back to the darkest recesses of his mind as fast as it had appeared. Sophia's fingers tightened their grip on the frame, blocking the flood of blood to the tip of her fingers. Vangelis carefully put his hand over his wife's.

'Please, Sophia. Let Adam and Maeve see how talented your son is.' The scholar had spoken softly, with emotion and care, more like a father to his reluctant, capricious daughter. Sophia's forehead crumpled for a few seconds, then she whispered, with a very faint smile on her lips:

'Very well...'

She let go of the frame and Vangelis passed it on to Maeve.

The painting represented the rose garden in late spring or early summer, with all the roses in full bloom. Adam recognised the ornamental pond with the little white benches around it. In the middle of the pond was the magnificent lotus flower: its petals were a striking sky blue, its heart a splash of pale yellow and its stem, strong and upright, emerged from the midst of the large flat leaves floating on the tranquil surface of the water. The ensemble was incredibly vibrant and colourful, the details exquisite. Adam had only seen the garden deprived of its greenery and smothered in fog. He had noticed the flower at the centre of the pond but it had remained stubbornly closed since he had arrived.

'If the rose garden really is as gorgeous in the summer as you've painted it, then I cannot wait to see it. This is very good, Dimitri. Congratulations.' Adam was genuinely surprised by his pupil's talent.

'Just wonderful!' agreed Maeve.

Suddenly, without a word and with great effort, Sophia stood up and came over to Maeve's seat. She grabbed the painting with both hands and took it off the young woman's grip. She then stood awkwardly in the centre of the room, holding the frame in her stretched arms, her head tilted right, then left, the generous mass of her hair threatening to tumble down any moment. Her body was swaying slightly. Vangelis jumped to his feet to be near his wife just in case her legs gave way.

'Where shall we put it?'

'My dear, your bedroom would be the best place, wouldn't it?'

'Oh… Yes, perhaps it would… I will think about it for a while before I make a decision.'

The scholar gently took the painting off his wife and called Mr Simms who materialised almost immediately.

'Mr Simms, could you please take care of this painting and have it brought up to my wife tomorrow morning in her room so she can decide where to hang it?'

When the head butler had departed with the frame under his arm, Vangelis once more turned to his wife.

'Now, my dear, it is my turn to give you a wedding anniversary present.'

Lady Chronos, who had gone back to the sofa, shifted uncomfortably. She looked around the room.

'You really shouldn't have, Vangelis. I'm afraid I haven't bought you anything. You know I haven't been very well those past few months, and I never go anywhere anyway.' There was regret and weariness in her voice. Vangelis left the room, leaving the remaining four occupants struggling for conversation.

'Oh, I wish I could paint as well as you, Dimitri!' sighed Maeve. 'I often think that I'd like to do the view from the entrance porch of the cottage. It is so pretty and atmospheric! Would you paint it for me? Or maybe you could paint the house itself, so I can take it with me when I leave. I'd hang it in my bedroom in London, you know, to remind me of the time I've spent here!'

The boy looked at Maeve with a serious face.

'Yes, if you wish, I'd like to do that!'

'Are you leaving us soon, then, Miss Hayward?'

Sophia, Adam, Maeve and Dimitri all started at the sound of Saturnin Bloom's deep voice filling the silence of the living room. The secretary had hardly uttered a word the whole evening, and they all had quite forgotten about him, only registering him as some kind of dark, immovable presence out of the corner of their eye. He was still standing behind the armchair, as immobile as a statue. He was now looking intently at Maeve, a corner of his mouth slightly lifted.

Something passed between the young woman and the assistant, something that turned the usually buoyant Maeve into stone; her eyes betrayed fear, and Adam noticed it. Since he had arrived at Whitemoor Hall, his senses had been sharpened: he could catch concealed looks, fleeting impressions, furtive movements in other people, an ability he didn't have before. He wished he had been that sharp two years previously; it would have helped him spot the stormy clouds gathering over his head before disaster struck and turned his life upside down.

The heavy atmosphere was broken up by Vangelis's return. He was carrying a packet tied up with a red and golden ribbon, which he presented to his wife with a mischievous air; he could barely contain his excitement.

'My dear wife, please accept this very, very special token of your husband's love on our wedding anniversary.'

Vangelis Chronos sounded rather emotional; Sophia took the parcel and placed it on her lap. She started unwrapping her second present of the evening, her long white fingers fluttering over the shiny ribbon and the delicate tissue paper, and finally revealed the most astonishing Egyptian jewellery box. Dimitri gasped, immediately recognising it as the one he had found at the Wise Man's Spring. Vangelis didn't wait for Sophia to ask for help.

'In order to open the box, you have to put your palm here, like this.'

Vangelis covered the sheer scarab with his palm and pressed downwards. The 'click' resonated and the box opened, revealing its glittering entrails. Sophia's face changed entirely: her sad eyes lit up, her cheeks flushed with pleasure, and her lips recovered some of their colour. She temporarily forgot her chronic pain altogether; she simply couldn't believe what she was seeing. Her brown eyes reflected the glint of the jewels.

'Oh! Oh! But how did you… This is simply… Oh!'

Her fingers sank in the pile of tangled jewellery; she took a handful and brandished it towards the other guests.

'Look! Look how beautiful they are! Are they really mine now?'

Sophia's hand was disappearing under a scintillating nest of inestimable creatures. Her gaze met that of Saturnin Bloom and she suddenly froze, her arm outstretched, her hand, heavy with jewels, suspended in mid-air. Something in his appearance made her face go from absolute delight to utter horror in the fraction of a second, and her smile was instantly erased. Everyone's eyes switched from her to the secretary.

Saturnin Bloom's face had darkened significantly. His features had become somewhat more prominent. The white of his eyes had disappeared, as if the ink of his iris had spread to fill in the entire socket. His shaved head seemed to be pulsating, his mouth was twisted in an unpleasant rictus and he struggled to contain an all-encompassing rage.

Suddenly, he moved, faster than anyone would have expected, and was near Sophia, dominating her with all his height, crushing her fragile frame with his overbearing presence; he had seized her wrist in his powerful hand and they faced each other over Lady Chronos's upturned hand full of jewels… She looked close to fainting.

'You will not, under ANY circumstances, wear ANY of those jewels, do you hear me? You will NOT wear any of them.' His voice had changed somehow; it had acquired an odd metallic undertone and his breath felt unnaturally hot. His grip tightened around the delicate bones of Sophia's wrist. The lady of the house could feel panic rise within her and she glanced at her husband. The scholar had jumped to his feet and was looking at his secretary with astonishment and anger.

'How DARE you touch her!'

Without releasing Sophia's wrist and still keeping his eyes on the jewels, the secretary hissed:

'Where did you get it?'

'Saturnin…'

'WHERE DID YOU GET THE BOX?' insisted Saturnin Bloom, barely containing the violence in his voice.

Vangelis Chronos was obviously quite ruffled and trembled in his richly embroidered robes; even his beard looked indignant.

'This is not the time or the place. Do let go of her, you are hurting her...'

Saturnin Bloom released Sophia's now burning wrist; the young woman quickly placed the jewellery back into the box and held the coffer tight against her stomach, her whole body now shaking and hurting with indignation and fear.

The assistant turned to Vangelis Chronos.

'We go to the office now and you tell me where you got this box. NOW,' he ordered. There was no discussion possible. The secretary crossed the room to the door; but before he exited, he turned once more towards Sophia:

'Do NOT wear those jewels, EVER. I have warned you.'

The secretary disappeared, leaving the door ajar and the room dead silent.

Maeve and Adam were still seated side by side, too stunned for words. Dimitri stood still, as pale as a sheet and close to tears; Sophia had remained on the Chesterfield; her head was bowed and her arms crossed around her waist, cradling her precious box.

The quietness felt unbearable to Maeve, who stood up.

'Uncle Vange...'

Lord Chronos had the appearance of a man who had just been hit in the face; he was looking intently at the floor, stunned. There was no trace of the jovial host and loving husband. All that was left was a tired-looking, ageing scholar faced with a grave problem to solve: he would have to explain himself to Saturnin Bloom, whatever the outcome. He knew that he had breached his side of the bargain, and he would have to make amends for it; this could cost him dear, dearer still than he could ever imagine. He had to find a way of soothing the rage he had been responsible for igniting. He left the room without another word.

The atmosphere in the large living room was grim. Sophia was sobbing inconsolably, waiting for Ginny to come and take her back to her rooms. Dimitri, mortified by the turn of events, was sitting on the edge of one of the armchairs and was picking at the fringed fabric, wishing he could just disappear down a hole with immediate effect. He wanted to go upstairs to his room and find refuge in his own world – but he hadn't been formally dismissed. Maeve was observing Adam, increasingly concerned.

Adam wasn't too sure where the anger had come from. Something had clicked just as Vangelis had exited the room; a red mist had descended in front of his eyes, an electrifying wave of pure anger fed by everything the young man had gone through over the past few weeks. This rage was born out of not understanding the forces that had taken control of his life since he had first cast his eyes on Maeve on the overheated Tube carriage. He had been fearful and meek until now, but some doors had just opened within him, releasing a brand new vital energy. He jumped to his feet; when his voice resonated around the room, it surprised everyone, including himself.

'That's it! I've had enough. Now, who's going to tell me what the hell is going on in this house?' His throat hurt as the words came out hoarse, harsh and fast. He was standing, his face reddened, his hair standing on end in every direction and his beautiful evening suit crumpled. He turned towards Maeve, suspicious and hurt by her silence.

'YOU got me here, so YOU should be the one to explain yourself. Who is Saturnin Bloom? What kind of experiments are they doing down there, in their so-called 'laboratory'? What is this farce about it being 1925? Do you all think I'm such an idiot that you can feed me your fantastical stories and play your tricks on me?'

The young woman shot a glance in the direction of Dimitri, who was looking intently at his tutor. She shook her head.

Sophia's sobs had been cut short by Adam's outburst. She was staring, feeling utterly drained and empty, her brain unable to comprehend what had led to this disaster of an evening. She craved the soft, reassuring refuge of her bed, the only place in the world where she felt safe. Soon, Ginny entered the room, concern written all over her plump, soft features.

'Ginny, take me to my room, please. I will go to bed now.'

The young maid frowned: it was still early, and this was supposed to be Lord and Lady Chronos's wedding anniversary, but she had heard the raised voices in the lounge and seen Saturnin Bloom storm off. She was very scared, suddenly. The careful balance that had been struck between life at the house and at the abbey seemed to be dissolving. Their peace, she could sense, was at risk. Surely, Lord Chronos and the elders at the abbey would never allow this to happen?

Ginny offered her hands to Lady Chronos, who stood up and leaned against her. The pain in Sophia's lower abdomen had returned with heightened vigour, spreading all over her body. All she wanted now was to open her little cabinet, take the laudanum bottle out and let the sweet bitterness of the concoction soothe her weary head and body. *Sleep, sweet oblivious sleep...*

Adam was about to protest, but Maeve stopped him:

'Let her go, Adam, she doesn't know anything.'

'But *you* do. You *know.*'

'Not that much; at least, not as much as you'd like me to.'

They both turned towards Dimitri.

'What about you, Dimitri. How much do you know?'

The boy looked at them with wide eyes.

'About what?'

The boy was wondering what his tutor could possibly mean. Had he discovered something about the ghosts? Was he challenging him to reveal his secret? No. It was something else, something related to the events of the evening.

Maeve put her hand on Adam's sleeve.

'Let Dimitri go to his room, Adam. He won't be able to tell you anything. Please, be reasonable!'

Adam glared at Maeve and shook her hand off his arm with a jerk.

'Reasonable! REASONABLE! Why is it that everyone always wants me to be reasonable?' He opened his arms in sign of powerlessness. 'That's what I've always heard, 'be reasonable' and I've listened! I've been reasonable my whole fucking life! And what good has it done for me?' The young man's voice was indignant, angry, bitter. He laughed, briefly. 'You are asking *me* to be reasonable, in the middle of this madness? Here, in this house? With all of you completely off your heads? You must be having a laugh!'

By then, Adam was almost crying with frustration. Maeve had made a move in the direction of the petrified Dimitri. She spoke to him calmly.

'You can go to your room, now, Dimitri. I am sorry this evening has been spoilt for you. Tomorrow's another day, eh? Good night, try to sleep.'

Still in shock, Dimitri murmured:

'Yes, Miss Hayward.'

Adam looked at the boy hurrying out of the room. Suddenly, his anger retreated to its lair somewhere deep within him. He remained speechless for a while. Maeve's automatic reaction was to try and lit up a cigarette to calm her nerves. It took her at least three attempts: her hands were shaking uncontrollably and her thumb kept slipping against the metal of her lighter; she painfully broke a nail.

'Ouch!' she winced. She brought her injured finger to her mouth and sucked on the ripped nail. She then went to ring for Gladys. Adam was observing her, immobile. He could almost smell the fear emanating from the young woman.

'I am still waiting for an answer,' he said suddenly. 'Who is Saturnin Bloom? What are they doing down there?'

Maeve inhaled then exhaled deeply, her eyes never leaving Adam's face. Her charming red mouth had hardened.

'He's a secretary, an assistant! That's what he is… What have you been imagining?'

'You're not a very good liar, Maeve.'

It was her turn to lose her temper.

'I *am* a good liar, actually! If only you knew how *good*! I'm almost ashamed of how *good* a liar I am! Saturnin Bloom is an ambitious secretary who's got some hold over my uncle, but how? He might be blackmailing him, for all I know. I haven't got the slightest idea! And actually… Actually, why don't *you* just go and ask them *yourself*?'

She stamped her foot in frustration, then furiously crushed the butt of her cigarette in the nearest ashtray and declared:

'I've had enough of this. I've been given a bedroom for the night, so I'm going there now. Good night.'

Gladys had appeared on the threshold. Maeve turned to her, eager to escape the poisoned atmosphere of the living room.

'I'd like you to show me to my room, Gladys, if you don't mind. Thank you.'

She gave Adam a last reproachful look and left with the maid.

The tutor was left on his own in the empty lounge. The fire was still roaring in the fireplace but he couldn't feel any warmth. His nerves were tingling, and he felt disgruntled and frustrated. They had all abandoned him to his anger and he had nobody to turn to. This time though, he was not going to give up. He wanted to know, so he would follow Maeve's advice and go and confront his employers. But how would he make his way to the office? The house was such a maze of corridors and rooms, and his sense of direction was muddled.

He closed his eyes for a moment, trying to recall the day Gladys had taken him to Vangelis Chronos's study; he attempted to work out where in the house he was at present and in which direction he should go in search of the scholar's quarters.

A strange whistling noise caught his ear. It was something akin to some sudden gush of air or gas circulating in an empty pipe, and it was somewhat amplified by the size of the room. It seemed to be coming from somewhere above the fireplace and was definitely getting louder. After a few seconds, the whistling turned into what Adam could only describe as a humming or chanting cavernous voice pouring in from the chimney flue. Taken by surprise, the young man turned round to face the hearth.

Suddenly, the voice's anger exploded into the fireplace and the fire swelled: the orange flames turned red, grew enormous and erupted up, filling the smoke chamber and the flue, jumping out into the room as if a giant had been blowing on the fire. Over the hellish roar of the flames, Adam could distinctly hear the voice turn into an almost inhuman scream which pierced his eardrums and filled his head with the terrifying image of an inferno engulfing human forms. For a second, he could even smell the burning skin and singed hair, then everything stopped: the flames died out as suddenly as they had started and silence was restored. All that was left of the fire were a few blackened logs smothered in grey and black ashes. A few embers were still glowing weakly, but the furious flames had consumed all the wood and coal in a few seconds and the fire was now dying.

Bewildered, Adam passed his hand over his hot face. He hesitated before getting closer to the hearth. Now just on the edge of the firebox, he could feel the heat of the stone. He stayed there, listening up, expecting the monstrous voice to return. Nothing. Suddenly, behind him, he heard the squeak of the door hinges. He jumped and tuned round: Dimitri was standing on the threshold.

'Dimitri! What are you doing here? I thought you had gone to your room!'

'I didn't want to go up and I hid round the corner.'

'But why?'

The young boy twisted his mouth, raised his eyebrows and shrugged.

'I don't know.'

He fixed the floor sulkily, waiting for his tutor's reproach. As none materialised, Dimitri lifted his face again and studied his teacher, who looked hot and scared and whose eyes darted around the room as if he were looking for something.

'Did you hear it?' asked Adam. Seeing the look of incomprehension on the boy's face, he explained: 'Just now, about three minutes ago. If you were hiding outside the room, you must have heard it. The voice, the scream... Then the fire!'

Dimitri thought that maybe he shouldn't have stuck around. His tutor had lost his mind!

'You... You haven't heard anything? *Anything at all?*'

'No.'

Had his tutor seen one of his ghosts? the boy wondered.

'Dimitri. You have to take me to your stepfather's study. I think he owes me an explanation.'

'Are you very cross with all of us?' enquired the boy timidly.

Adam put his hand on Dimitri's shoulder.

'Not with you, Dimitri, not with you... Come on, take me to Lord Chronos's office.'

Adam gently pushed his pupil towards the double door.

*   *   *

They walked along the gloomy corridors in silence. Adam didn't have a clue about what he would say once in front of Vangelis Chronos, but his determination grew as they approached the part of the house that had been surrendered to the exclusive use of the scholar and his assistant.

As they turned the last corner, they could hear the angry voice of Saturnin Bloom. Then when the young man and the boy were less than two metres away from the office door, the voice fell silent.

'Thank you for guiding me, Dimitri,' whispered Adam. 'I think you should go up to your room now. I need to see your stepfather and Mr Bloom alone. I will see you tomorrow morning.'

Dimitri looked disappointed but relented. He slowly made his way back to the main hall, not without looking back a few times. Finally, the boy's small frame disappeared at the other end of the corridor.

Adam was standing in front of the thick wooden door, trying to control his breathing. There was no noise whatsoever coming from inside the room. Then he heard Saturnin Bloom's voice, so close that he could have been whispering in his ear:

'Mr Tuckfield... So you've come. What can we do for you?'

The door opened slowly and a waft of the now familiar spicy smoke from the secretary's exotic cigarettes escaped from the room. A look of confusion appeared on Adam's face: Saturnin Bloom couldn't have been behind the door just now, as he was standing at the heavily curtained window just behind Vangelis Chronos's desk. He was lifting the curtains with one hand and peering at the perfect darkness outside. Vangelis was slumped in his chair, his head in his hands. Adam couldn't see the scholar's features, but Lord Chronos exhibited the signs of intense despair or suffering.

The secretary turned round. His face was still the stone-hard mask it had put on back in the living room, and his eyes still had the appearance of two black holes of the soul. He slowly removed the cigarette from his mouth.

Adam's hair stood on end and he felt his insides turn into liquid. He desperately tried to find his anger again, as it would give him courage. And that's when he thought: *there is definitely something about Saturnin Bloom. Something... Inhuman...*

EIGHT

ophia Chronos was sitting at her dressing table, her eyes fixed upon her own reflection. It was the only presence that really did reassure her; she didn't trust any other human being. She preferred to be alone with her own image, in the safety of her fabric-smothered bedroom which was as soft as a cocoon.

Her long white-blond hair had been brushed and her svelte body wrapped up in a delicate nightgown. Every day, she was surprised by what she was seeing in the mirror: how comes someone so ethereal, so bright, had to be hidden from the world in which she had been destined to shine? How could this elegant, graceful body of hers hurt and torment her so? It was just so unfair. She was now a prized jewel too precious to be confronted with the horrid reality of the world. Gone were the soft, youthful curves of her stage days. She had been literally glowing then, showering her audience with her sheer luminescence. The flesh had melted away, together with all her dreams. She was a drastically different creature now…

The usual dose of laudanum she had taken earlier to numb her pain was swimming about in her system, helping her to get out of her own treacherous body. She had deposited the Egyptian coffer in front of her. In Sophia's cloudy, confused consciousness, Saturnin Bloom's voice echoed again and again: *You will not, under any circumstances, wear any of those jewels.*

She shuddered as she remembered his hand closing in on her wrist. Her whole body had revolted then, it had hurt so much… She had thought that his intention had been to crush her bones, but she hadn't let go of the box, oh no! She would have preferred to be battered to death by her husband's secretary rather than have surrendered the case and its glittering contents. They were *hers*.

Something in her had been shaken to the core when the insect jewellery had burst out of the casket. The colourful, exotic wood and the entangled precious stones and metals had awakened a fascination that she hadn't felt for years. It was as if they had represented the promise of something else, something better. Or maybe it had just reminded her of the many happy hours she had spent backstage in the company of the costume designers. How fantastical her costumes had been!

She tried not to think too much about the provenance of the jewels. Why had Vangelis given her the box and its precious contents? The jewels were Victorian, all prefect specimens of the best insect jewellery of the era. Were they family heirlooms?

Sophia was now looking pensively at the case; before trying anything on, she would need to disentangle the pieces. She stood up and picked up the box, walked to her wide bed and poured the contents on the coverlet. Apart from a few lone pieces, the jewels came down in one big lump. Lady Chronos then sat on her bed and started the painstaking work of detaching the pieces from each other. She became completely absorbed in her work, forgetting about the time and place. She was getting absolutely hypnotised by the gorgeous pieces she was laying out in front of her.

Soon, Sophia's bed was covered with a bestiary of extraordinary creatures, all rivalling with each other: necklaces, pendants, lockets, brooches and earrings, a few rings that were unfortunately too large for her long, delicate fingers. They represented dragonflies, bees and spiders, butterflies and scarabs.

She was working slowly, her senses distorted by the laudanum and her disbelief in the face of her rare good fortune. For the second time that evening, she forgot the lingering pain that had been plaguing her for the past eleven years.

At long last, every single piece of jewellery had found its place on the bedcover. Sophia scrutinised the unusual treasure spread out in front of her: gold, silver, diamonds, pearls, amethysts, rubies... Her heart beat had increased and her breathing was short and fast; she didn't dare making too much noise or any sudden movement for fear of waking up the dozing creatures sprawled all over her counterpane.

She decided to choose the one she'd like best to try on. Her eyes stopped on a bronze patina brass filigree pendant representing a dragonfly with a beautifully pure aquamarine stone embedded in its body. This was definitely one of the most handsome pieces of the lot. Picking up the pendant, she sat back in front of her mirror. This was the type of jewel you would wear with an evening gown; it was meant to glitter under cascading chandeliers and to throw rays of light across a ballroom. It was of exquisite taste, but was meant to be on show and dazzle an audience.

Sophia let her nightgown slip to the floor and, now in her nightdress, lifted the pendant and tied it behind her neck whilst trying to keep her long hair away. Once secured, she let the dragonfly fall onto her chest where the cool metal met her skin, just a few millimetres above the lacy edge of her gown. Just as the dragonfly touched her chest, Sophia gave a little gasp; a sharp burning sensation stung her like a wasp. It barely lasted more than a second. She attributed it to the laudanum which sometimes would make her skin feel itchy and uncomfortable; she was used to the temporary unpleasant reactions brought upon by the drug, but these were nothing compared to the pain she'd had to endure without it. Ignoring the burn, she started to think about the kind of dress she could wear with the dragonfly.

She had one cupboard full of rustling ball gowns she had virtually never used. Sometimes, when she knew she wouldn't be disturbed, she would put one on and wander around her rooms pretending she was attending one of those gay *soirées* she used to go to when she was a rising star of the stage. At other times, she would pick up one of the Shakespeare plays she kept in her little morning room and would read through a scene aloud, imagining the enraptured audience in front of her.

She was smiling at her reflection now, as she admired her dragonfly, and then… her eyes glazed over and her smile disappeared as a strange sensation came over her. It had started out of nowhere, something deep within her, as if a capsule had melted inside her chest, releasing its content. It now felt like the blood in her veins had been replaced with some cold liquid metal which spread to her whole body, and her heart vigorously pumped the foreign substance through her veins and arteries. It was such an odd feeling, this chilly flow travelling along her limbs, behind her eyes… It was neither pleasant nor unpleasant, and certainly didn't hurt.

Sophia didn't dare moving and scrutinised her frozen, immobile reflection, looking for some external signs of a sudden disease. Apart from the fear written all over her features and her extreme pallor noticeable even in the low light of the bedroom, she didn't notice anything alarming about her appearance.

The strange phenomenon seemed to have dissipated the effects of the laudanum and her head felt incredibly clear. She was still wondering whether she was just experiencing a new side-effect of the drug; but it usually had the opposite result: it clouded her mind and sent her into a dazed and confused state of mind and body; it wrapped her in a cocoon of gauze, slowed her metabolism and shut down her senses. This was something else entirely: some kind of alien energy was growing within her, and it made her aware of every single cell in her body. The substance was flowing in her breasts and groin, sending mini-electric shocks through her flesh; goose bumps covered her entire body and she let out a surprised exclamation.

Then she started feeling faint. Her energy levels dropped dramatically; she swayed on her stool and had to hold onto the edge of her dresser for support, as her upper body fell forward towards the mirror. Groggy, she shook her head and caught yet another glimpse of herself: the image was now blurred and she couldn't focus her eyes on her reflection. In the mirror, the outline of her face and body wasn't sharp anymore and seemed to be morphing into something else.

Soon, a horrified Sophia realised that the eyes that were looking at her were no longer hers: those were almond-shaped, a deep violet colour and Kohl-rimmed; they were the eyes of an exotic, ferocious and sensual creature… The complete opposite of Sophia.

She panicked, lifted her hands to her face and frenetically rubbed her eyes and cheeks. When she looked again, the violet eyes had disappeared and a sensation of heavy, irresistible tiredness swooped over her. Her mind and body felt utterly, hopelessly broken.

Shaking, Lady Chronos sleepwalked to her bed, picked up all the pieces of jewellery and put them back into their box, which she placed under the voluminous pillow next to her own. She then slipped under the covers and pulled them over her head before falling into the deepest of sleeps.

*　　　　　*　　　　　*

The night had once again enveloped the little chapel on the other side of the abbey. It had always been one of the quietest areas of the estate, and even the animals seemed to be wary of the place. Maybe it was due to the pungent, heavy incense that was left to burn there most days and nights. The heady swirls would escape through every crack in the structure and pour into the churchyard.

At exactly the same moment the dragonfly pendant met Sophia Chronos's skin, the lonely red candle inside the church was snuffed out by a gust of air. The smell of the incense suddenly became heavier, filling the small space with a thick, unbreathable cloud.

Outside in the churchyard, the blackness of the night thickened around the old stones. The oppressive darkness was filled with complete silence — the kind of silence that makes you want to scream.

As the cloud of incense spread, noises started disturbing the nocturnal peace around the vaults. If someone had been present, they probably wouldn't have been able to identify the provenance nor the nature of the disturbance, for the sounds came from nowhere and everywhere at the same time. They were horrible, terrifyingly organic: the gurgling of blood and the tearing of flesh, the wet, slippery noise of organs and the cracking of bones. They were the cries of dead cells being once again injected with life.

Then the churchyard was filled with the deafening beat of a monstrous heart pounding against the walls of its stone prison and with the choking sounds of lungs that were learning to breathe again.

NINE

Lord Chronos seemed to have recovered and was now standing as upright as he could in his chair. He looked like a man resigned to whatever was about to befall him. His eyes had the haunted quality of those who have seen beyond physical reality.

'So, Mr Tuckfield,' said Saturnin Bloom, 'I guess you are here because you have a few questions to ask us.'

Adam's heart was pounding in his ears. The study felt even more stifling than the first time around. He was wondering whether there would be enough air for the three of them. He took a deep breath.

'Lord Chronos, Mr Bloom. You will excuse me if I sound incredibly rude, but after the scenes I have witnessed tonight, yes, I *do* have some questions: what is going on, and why am I here? All I want is the truth. Most times, I'm not sure whether I am awake or whether I am dreaming. Every morning, I have to pinch myself to make sure I am really here. I'm no longer ashamed to admit that I don't understand what is happening to me, and I want to know.'

Vangelis Chronos sighed.

'I have been wondering how long it would take you to start asking questions.' The scholar shook his head. 'It took you longer than I thought.'

'That's because I haven't been thinking clearly; everything has happened so quicky. I think I've been in denial; I was afraid of the truth. I am not anymore. I've understood that if I want to remain sane and properly do the job I am paid for, then I need to understand my circumstances.'

'Quite.' Vangelis Chronos looked expectantly towards Saturnin Bloom, who was finishing his cigarette in silence.

'Very well, then. What would you like to know?' the secretary enquired sarcastically.

'I have come to realise that I am supposed to have somehow gone back in time. Apparently, this is 1925… Is it?'

Vangelis Chronos nodded gravely.

'Yes, Mr Tuckfield. This is indeed the year 1925.'

'So I suppose that you have a time machine of some sort hidden somewhere, although I do not remember getting into any device of such kind recently.'

Adam just couldn't believe he was having that conversation. Saturnin Bloom picked up yet another cigarette from the ornate silver case on the desk and lit it up. His features seemed to have gone back to their more 'normal' appearance.

'No, not a time machine, Mr Tuckfield. There's no need for any man-made device to travel through time.'

'No? So how do you do it, then?'

'Whitemoor Hall is a very special place, in so many ways. You've had the opportunity to admire our entrance gates?' asked Vangelis Chronos.

'The big ones, with the sun and moon faces?'

'Those very same. You see, they open on the road that leads to the house. But this is no ordinary drive; it is what is called a wormhole, some kind of portal, or bridge, between different times.'

Adam was desperately trying to keep a straight face, whilst his two interlocutors looked serious, almost solemn.

'So… We drove from the station in 2014, then we turned into the drive, and… When I woke up on the first morning, I wasn't able to remember what had happened to me…'

'Your body suffered a shock as the car went down the drive; a perfectly normal reaction from the human body being transported from one period of time to the other,' confirmed the scholar.

'But… who are you? What are you doing here and why me?' exclaimed Adam.

Saturnin Bloom and Vangelis Chronos exchanged a look. The secretary nodded, as if he were the one allowing his employer to explain further. Vangelis Chronos crossed his hands in front of him, his elbows resting on his desk.

'We need to ask you to leave all you know to be true behind, Mr Tuckfield. The reasons why we are all here are complex and might seem far-fetched and extraordinary to you. You will need to suspend your disbelief and trust me. We will not be able to reveal all today, simply because there are certain elements that we do not know ourselves. Nevertheless, I will try and explain as simply as possible what is at stake here.'

Vangelis Chronos hesitated and cast a glance towards Saturnin Bloom, who was enjoying his fragrant cigarette while not missing anything of Adam's reaction. The scholar started his explanation.

'This house – or rather a previous version of it – used to belong to Aloysius Dean, a disciple of the prestigious alchemist John Dee, Queen Elizabeth I's favourite scientist and astrologer. Aloysius met John Dee in 1558 and assisted him in many of his secret experiments; he also helped him write numerous volumes on alchemy. After having secured a substantial inheritance, he purchased this estate in order to pursue his experimentation in peace and away from prying eyes. Much, much later, in 1840, a direct descendant of Aloysius Dean, the anthropologist, archaeologist and egyptologist Lord Whitemoor decided to start refurbishing the then derelict Whitemoor estate, and the building work started immediately.'

'Also that year, on a mission to Egypt, he became infatuated with, and subsequently married Amunet, the daughter of an Egyptian diplomat and genuine Egyptian princess, who became Amy Whitemoor. They came back to England and settled in the house, with the building work carrying on well into 1845. One thing Lord Whitemoor didn't know was that his now wife was also the Great Vestal of the Cult of Thoth, a marginal, secretive group worshipping the Egyptian god Thoth, god of Time, Wisdom, Astronomy and patron of the scribes. Amunet had brought her entourage with her, who themselves all belonged to the cult, and soon, they took over the empty abbey in the grounds of the estate; they started recruiting more members around the countryside – most of them lost souls, abandoned children and desperate women – and built up a small, self-contained community.'

'Needless to say, this proved extremely controversial. When Lord Whitemoor discovered his wife's activities, he decided to put a stop to it and things deteriorated rapidly. This frayed situation came to an abrupt end in 1856 when Lord Whitemoor succumbed to a mysterious illness. His family, who had always been suspicious of Amunet, began a battle to remove the widowed Lady Whitemoor from the estate and contested their late relative's will. People at the time described how Lady Whitemoor did not display any of the behaviour expected of a respectable grief-stricken Victorian widow.'

'About a year and a half after the death of Lord Whitemoor, the two most vocal opponents to the will, the deceased's brother and sister, were killed, together with their whole families, in an accident on their way to a picnic. Amunet was then free to run the estate as she wished, and thanks to the money from Lord Whitemoor's estate as well as her own, she managed to grow the cult further.'

Vangelis Chronos paused at that point; his voice had grown hoarse. He reached for a glass of water and refreshed his parched throat while Adam tried to process the mass of information he had been given. Ensconced in his chair, Saturnin Bloom had remained unnaturally immobile. Adam was finding this dark persona more irritating than intriguing now. The secretary was overplaying it.

'The story doesn't end there, I'm afraid,' said Vangelis Chronos. He removed his small round glasses, rubbed them clean and replaced them carefully on his slightly beaked nose. He then cleared his voice. 'We are now getting to a delicate part of the story, and I will ask you not to interrupt, Mr Tuckfield, even if your head is screaming at you to stop the nonsense. Understood?' The scholar's eyes, piercing behind his round spectacles, made Adam understand that this was no joke. He nodded.

'Very well, then... A few months after the 'accidental' death of Lord Whitemoor's family members, a visitor announced himself at the abbey, and having asked to be received by Amunet, revealed himself to be the god Thoth himself...'

At that moment, Adam's mouth opened; Vangelis Chronos lifted his hand in warning.

'No, Mr Tuckfield, you have promised!'

The young man reluctantly reclined in his chair once again.

'The god Thoth had lost most of his powers due to centuries of in-fighting with other gods and numerous exhausting campaigns. Having heard about the spectacular success of the English cult – and disheartened by the lack of Thoth-worshipping communities in Egypt, Thoth had decided to seek refuge in this green oasis where he would be allowed to rest and find a way of regaining his lost powers. For fear of losing Amunet's support, which would be crucial for him to regain his occult powers, he purposely omitted to tell her about having lost his powers and instead, told her that she had been chosen to be his concubine and that he would reward her with eternal life.'

'This power of granting immortality to a few chosen mortals was no longer in his hands, and it is only when Amunet contracted pneumonia – her constitution had been weakened over the years by the English weather – that she understood that Thoth had been manipulating her to obtain her favours. Even though mortally ill, the fierce Amunet cursed Thoth and, just before passing away, rejected him and invoked Anubis, the god of the

THE BOOK OF THOTH

Afterlife, instead. Thoth shrugged off her delirious ranting and, after her death, decided to stay put at Whitemoor and recuperate from his gruelling life of travelling and campaigning. He went underground on the estate and kept a low profile, knowing that his time would come. Quickly, the abbey community dwindled, as no new recruit passed the gates for years on end and members were not allowed to reproduce.'

The scholar fell silent. Adam felt the first pangs of anger stir within him: Vangelis Chronos was mocking him. He had come to the study seeking answers, and all he got was a tale worthy of the 'Lord of the Rings' trilogy. He'd had enough. He rose from his chair.

'Right. Very nice story but I am obviously wasting my time, here.'

As quick as lightning, Saturnin Bloom had jumped out and pushed Adam violently back into the chair.

'You stay where you are,' he roared at a stunned Adam.

The secretary was now standing over the tutor, his towering shadow enveloping the young man. Vangelis Chronos shook his head sadly.

'I am not sure this is working, Saturnin.'

'He doesn't know half of the story *yet*,' replied the assistant.

'Ok! Sorry!' exclaimed Adam. 'I promise I will listen to the end. But first, could you please tell me what this has to do with me?'

'Well. I told you that Lord Whitemoor's brother and sister were killed in an accident with their families. They were in a two separate carriages. Both were accompanied by their spouses and children: the brother had three little ones and the sister four.'

'And they all died?'

'Both carriages were engulfed by what some witnesses have called 'fireballs'. The weather on that day was glorious, bright sun and blue skies; there was no storm and therefore, they were not struck by lightning.'

'How absolutely terrible,' whispered Adam. Suddenly, he remembered the images, the noises and the smells in the living room earlier, when the fire had swollen up and roared: he had seen writhing human forms and the outline of a wheel; he had heard adults and children scream in agony. He had smelt the burning flesh and the hot metal. Something like an electric shock went through his body. Adam snapped back to reality and looked fiercely at the scholar, who sustained his gaze.

'Amunet is the one who killed them all,' declared the scholar.

'She somehow conjured up the fireballs and sent them to annihilate her enemies; at least, that's what she *thought*...'

Another unnerving, maddening pause. Adam was now at boiling point; he knew something was coming. With a small smile, Vangelis resumed.

'Unknown to her, one child didn't get killed. He was ejected from the carriage on impact and landed in a ditch full of freshly cut grass. The god Thoth, who had witnessed the carnage, took it upon himself to save one descendant of the great alchemist Aloysius Dean. The child was moved and found miles away, placed in an institution and adopted soon after by Mr and Mrs Tuckfield, of Bath.

'Mr and Mrs Tuckfield?' Adam's eyes almost popped out of his head. Vangelis's smile widened.

'Yes, Mr Tuckfield. This little one year-old boy was your great-great-grandfather, and therefore, you are Aloysius Dean's direct descendant.'

A heavy silence fell on the trio. The walls of the studio seemed to have moved forward and the space looked smaller than before. In the glass cabinets, the strange, deformed creatures appeared to have shifted in their jars; they looked at him with mocking, surly eyes. Adam was glad he was sitting down, as he was now feeling faint. Saturnin Bloom, still standing near the young man's chair with his arms crossed on his chest, was enjoying himself immensely.

After a few minutes, Adam found his voice again; he turned to Vangelis.

'You said that after Lady Whitemoor's death, the god stayed on the estate. For how long?'

'He never left,' was the dreaded reply from a cautious Vangelis.

'Never? But... But where is he now?'

Vangelis Chronos theatrically extended his arm towards Saturnin Bloom, palm upturned, long velvet sleeve brushing the top of his wide desk.

'He is here, standing right in front of you...'

Saturnin Bloom *almost* smiled, but it was not pleasant: his face had turned darker than ever and his eyes looked like two glistening black holes opening on an unknown world. His very white teeth glowed under the lamps, small, sharp and pointy.

The god Thoth started laughing, triumphant, satisfied of his little effect on the stunned mortal in front of him. The moon began to shine brighter, its unearthly light illuminating every corner of the estate, piercing through the thick curtains that had been drawn against the threat of the night.

A heavy silence ensued… In Adam's feverish mind, the wildest theories were forming. Part of him just *knew* that everything was true and yet, his brain didn't accept it at all; it rejected the whole lot of it with superhuman force.

Saturnin Bloom walked to a dresser and unlocked a drawer. He came back, carrying in his hands some kind of silver cup decorated with one single symbol:

'Do you recognize this symbol, Mr Tuckfield?'

Saturnin Bloom had placed the side of the cup close to Adam's face.

'Why, I…'

Instinctively, his right hand reached to his left upper arm.

'Well?' insisted the secretary.

'I have a small tattoo of the same symbol on my left arm.' He started to roll up the sleeve of his shirt. The symbol on his skin was exactly the same one as the one engraved on the cup. The secretary's unpleasant grin made another appearance.

'Do you remember where you got the idea for this tattoo from?'

Adam couldn't. He had simply drawn it one day – he couldn't remember how old he was or where he had seen the symbol – and taken it to the tattoo parlour of his choice. It had been an unexplained urge.

'This is John Dee's glyph, the one he explains extensively in his *Monas Hieroglyphica*. It is supposed to represent the mystical unity of all creation. Only he *didn't* design it. He *stole* it from the Cult of Thoth,' explained Vangelis, now animated. 'You will find that all the members of the cult, all the people who work on the estate here apart from the cook and the gardeners, who do not belong to it, have the same symbol stamped at exactly the same place on their left arm. In a way, you branded yourself, Mr Tuckfield. You knew where you came from all along, you just needed to be guided.'

Adam swallowed with difficulty. His throat had turned dry, and a cold sweat was forming at the base of his back.

'But why now and not before?'

It was Saturnin Bloom's turn to reply.

'I have known about your existence and that of all your ancestors all along, but there has never been any need for you to be told about your connections to the mysteries of alchemy and ancient gods... until recently.' The secretary was pacing the room now. 'After Amunet's death in 1867, the house stood empty. Our small community dwindled drastically, but I thought it better to not be too overzealous and not attract attention to us. The faithful carried on working the land on the estate but the house wasn't occupied by anyone but me. The group has always preferred the abbey. It is far more convenient for worship and other activities. Then in 1913, Vangelis Chronos bought the estate.'

The scholar nodded and explained:

'I had come across some documents stating the existence of a secret laboratory built by Aloysius Dean under the house, and as an alchemist myself – yes, science leads you off the beaten track more often than you think! – it was imperative that I found his premises, and maybe some of his writings.'

'And have you found anything?' enquired Adam.

'More than I had ever hoped for!' exclaimed Lord Chronos, a glint in his eyes, looking ever more like the mad scientist he really was. 'I found the laboratory, his hidden manuscripts... A wealth of incredible material, which I am sure contains the knowledge every alchemist would die to get their hands on. The great tragedy of our kind is that we have never been taken seriously, and if we did, we would be thrown into the flames for heresy!' Vangelis Chronos was showing signs of extreme outrage. 'Then Thoth... Saturnin... revealed himself to me, and we...'

'Struck a deal,' interrupted Saturnin Bloom. 'But we won't get into the details of that, of course. I am afraid that you might not understand it very well. In short: I am helping Lord Chronos with his scientific and alchemical experiments, as I have a bottomless knowledge of languages, symbols, religions and universes, and I assist him under the identity of Saturnin Bloom in his more official research. It amuses me. In return, he helps me try and find a cure for my loss of power. I have retained a few, such as the ability to open wormholes, but without the Book, I have no hope to ever regain my almighty powers…'

'The Book?'

'The Book of Thoth is an infamous magic book that belongs to Thoth. It is full of spells and knowledge; incommensurable knowledge,' explained Vangelis Chronos. The scholar really was in his element, narrating the wonders of the gods and the unknown world of the supernatural. He savoured every moment, enjoying himself as he described the ever more impossible events that had occurred on the estate to a completely overwhelmed Adam.

Saturnin Bloom roared:

'It was MY book, MINE, and the bitch stole it! I don't know where she hid it all that time, but when Amunet was about to die and invoked Anubis, she somehow managed to send the Book to the Underworld, the doors of which are entirely shut to me. I wouldn't even know where to look for it anyway. Only the dead know, and I have lost the power to communicate with them.'

'We didn't know the whereabouts of the Book until recently. It is thanks to Dimitri…'

Adam suddenly sat up from his slouching position.

'Dimitri? What has he got to do with all this? Leave the poor kid alone!'

Vangelis looked straight into Adam's eyes and silenced him.

'Calm down, Mr Tuckfield. I am coming to this part of our already complicated story.' He sighed. 'I'm afraid Dimitri will have a very important role to play in all this. Last month, the boy went for a walk in the woods there,' he vaguely gestured in the direction of the tall trees bordering the lawn, 'and did a detour via the Wise Man's Spring, a favourite spot of his, if I am not mistaken. He found a bag hidden between some rocks near the pond. Inside, there was a leather notebook, which we now have in our possession, and an ornate jewellery box, which you saw in the lounge earlier.' The scholar stopped, looked towards Saturnin Bloom and cleared his throat.

'The notebook, the boy gave to me as it was full of texts written in a language he didn't know. I recognized Egyptian and in turn gave it to Saturnin here for translation. The box, I…' Lord Chronos bowed his head as if in shame.

'Stupidly, and against your better judgement, you kept it hidden from me to give to your airhead of a wife on your wedding anniversary, not knowing how dangerous it was, and doing so, breaking our agreement,' interrupted Saturnin Bloom with a voice full of angry contempt. It took Vangelis Chronos all his courage to carry on narrating his story:

'We started work on the notebook immediately. We discovered that it was a diary written by Jahi – which means 'The Dignified' – who was the appointed scribe of the cult at the time Amunet was mistress of Whitemoor. As a sacred scribe, he could only write down in the official books the authorised facts and approved events taking place at the abbey.'

'Amunet had been censoring her most disturbing actions and had threatened Jahi until the very end not to report the facts surrounding her almighty row with Thoth, and most importantly, her death. He had witnessed the vestal's treatment of the god and had been suitably horrified when she had renounced him and invoked Anubis instead. For Christians, it would be like selling your soul to the Devil! Becoming one of Anubis's followers at the door of death is an unthinkable act for any member of the Cult of Thoth. Jahi loved the Truth in its purest form, that's what his training had taught him since he was a boy. He witnessed Amunet's stealing the Book from her god; he saw her renounce him and give herself to Anubis. He was a silent presence in the room when she sent the Book to the dreaded Underworld, and he was the only one who knew that she had been buried with the key.'

Adam was making a huge effort to try and follow the story.

'The key? What key?'

'No mortal is allowed to read the Book. If he or she does, then they and their loved ones die. The rolls that constitute the Book have been locked inside a golden box, which is contained in a silver box inside a box of ivory and ebony encased in a sycamore box which is found in a bronze box contained in an iron box. The key opens all the boxes if accompanied by the correct spells. Amunet managed to get it buried with her inside her sealed sarcophagus.' The obviously exhausted scientist paused. 'It was all there, in this diary.' He tapped the chunky notebook lying on the desk in front of him. 'Jahi didn't betray his vows and didn't tell anyone while he was alive. Before his death, he took care to hide his journal and Amunet's jewels in a place where someone would find them one day. So we know where the key is, and we know that the Book is hidden somewhere in the dark recesses of the Underworld. Now we need to make contact with this Underworld and get our hands on the The Book of Thoth.'

'I still don't understand how the boy fits into all this.'

'We have a suspicion – we haven't got any proof, mind – that Dimitri can see ghosts, that he can communicate with the dead.'

Adam rolled his eyes. Alchemy, ancient gods, Egyptian cults, and now ghosts? His rational mind felt ready to give in under the pressure of so many unbelievable facts. *And yet.* Adam remembered that as early as their first lesson together, Dimitri had asked him whether he believed in ghosts. And what about the boy's reaction to his reading 'The Canterville Ghost'? His emotion and outrage at the way the ghost had been portrayed in the book had been genuine. *What if...?*

His train of thought was once again interrupted by Vangelis Chronos.

'The boy likes you and trusts you. He has found a friend in you. We want you to find out whether he can communicate with the dead. We need confirmation of this. And then, when you have gained his full trust, we want you to ask him to get the Book out of the Underworld for us.'

Adam's brain had stopped processing information by then. Everything was just too unbelievable, exaggerated, even grotesque... Saturnin had noticed the increasingly incredulous expression on the tutor's face.

'You don't believe a word of what we have been telling you, do you?'

The god Thoth didn't know which mortals he found the most irritating: the gullible, fearful, uneducated ones who for centuries had allowed religions to control and abuse them, or the ones who, like Adam, were so anchored in scientific reality that they couldn't or didn't want to believe in anything and dismissed the likes of him as pure fantastical inventions.

'You are a product of your educated times, and I congratulate you,' he declared slowly. 'However, I'm afraid we are here to completely destroy your certainties.'

As he spoke, he had come nearer the armchair in which Adam was seated. Suddenly, and without any warning, Saturnin Bloom clasped his large hands around Adam's head. The young man's mouth opened to scream but no sound came out. Instead, an explosion occurred in his brain. And then, the extraordinary images started pouring into his mind, and *he saw...*

PART
V

Amunet rises

ONE

The two weeks that followed the disastrous wedding anniversary remained stubbornly grey, muted and uneventful. The house was large enough for people to successfully avoid each other; it was the ideal accomplice. Only Dimitri and Adam had resumed their companionship, keeping their routine of lessons, breaks, study and homework. Their whole world was contained in the short length of corridor between their two bedrooms.

The weather definitely added to the gloomy feel of the house and prevented them from getting out and about in the grounds: the sky was low and dirty yellow-grey, and it felt as if the very fabric of the house were absorbing the weak autumn daylight. In the study, they had to turn the lights on by 2pm every day, sometimes even earlier. The pervading dampness in the air made things even more unpleasant.

Several times, Adam declined Dimitri's invitation to accompany him on his exploration of the house; the boy spent two whole weekends exploring new recesses while Adam worked on his lesson plans.

Alone in the study, he would listen to the house itself: from time to time, noises made by the other – mostly invisible – inhabitants of the house would reach him and distract him from his work. He would lift his head, alert, trying to guess the origin of the sound: the distant service yard and kitchen; Sophia Chronos's rooms; the gardeners working somewhere in the grounds. In the very still building, any faraway noises would sound unreal. The young man sometimes compared those sounds to those emitted by the internal organs of a great beast, for that was what the house felt like: it was alive, constantly shifting, creaking and expanding.

One Sunday evening, Dimitri didn't appear at all for dinner; the complete silence in the room combined with the mute painted presence of Lord Whitemoor behind him was too much for Adam, who lost his appetite entirely and left the room without having eaten anything more than a bowl of soup.

Another day, Dimitri timidly came down to the dining room covered in dust and cobwebs, and Adam was obliged to send him to the small bathroom round the corner so he could clean himself up. When he came back, cobweb and dust-free, the boy looked a little tired, but satisfied. Adam tried to question him about his exploration, but the child answered rather succinctly before concluding:

'You'll have to come with me next time and see for yourself!'

TWO

Adam didn't feel like a stranger from another era anymore. Two weeks earlier, he had emerged from Lord Chronos's study a changed man. He was no longer an outsider; he had found an intimate, personal connection with Whitemoor Hall and it had somehow altered everything: he had taken the place that had been reserved for him. He was the human piece of some gigantic jigsaw, and it had all fallen into place in the end. Even the impression he had had of not being entirely 'in synch' with the rest of the house had faded, although the clocks were still ticking anti-clockwise.

When he had emerged from the scholar's office, he had been able to find the way to his bedroom without a second thought; he had acquired an entirely new, instinctive sense of direction. He had looked around him with brand new eyes: at the floorboards and the patterned carpet; at the dark wood of the furniture, the hanged tapestries and paintings he encountered on his way from the ground floor study to the first floor bedroom: they had all appeared strangely familiar.

Amazingly, his mind was not burdened with the fantastical visions he had experienced after Saturnin Bloom had put both his hands on either side of his head. Said visions had been absorbed and digested by his brain; he knew he had seen them, but he couldn't describe any of them as no human-made language was fit for them. Their incredible power had tamed his natural scepticism. He had accepted their truth as *his*. Had they done the same to Maeve, he wondered? Was it the way they had managed to convince her to play a part in luring him to Whitemoor Hall?

He suddenly felt the urge to see the young woman again. They had parted on such bad terms the evening of the wedding anniversary. That night, he had felt that he had lost his guardian angel. Would it feel different to stand next to her now that he had undergone that strange mental initiation? Would they stand next to each other as equals?

Another Saturday came, and Adam decided that it was time for some fresh air. Dressed and booted, he let himself out of the back entrance door and stopped at the top of the stairs overlooking the rose garden. He was once again surprised by the freshness of the air and the rural silence surrounding the house. For someone used to the city, an undisturbed countryside always held some kind of magical quality.

The water in the pond was as still as usual, and the lotus flower was tightly shut against the inclement of the weather; the large rounded leaves floated on the surface of the water among the scattered, crumpled, decomposing leftover leaves blown from the edges of the wood by the wind.

The sculpted goddesses looked cold on their pedestals, their plump white flesh glistening with damp in the morning air. Adam stopped to look at the stubborn flower: it was obviously still alive and complete within its green cocoon, but seemed to have gone into contented hibernation. He would have to wait until spring to see it in all its colourful splendour.

Adam then turned round to face the building. The lower block to his left had all its windows shuttered. He imagined Dimitri roaming around somewhere within the dark stone house, walking along shadowy corridors and pushing doors stuck to their frame by years of disuse. At least, someone was making the most of Whitemoor Hall!

Standing there on his own in front of the elegant façade and shivering a little, Adam let his eyes wander from window to widow: here was his bedroom, then the two tall narrow windows there were the study, then immediately along was Dimitri's bedroom. All the other rooms on their floor were shut apart from the extra bathroom accessible from the recess at the end of the corridor and the small morning room.

Something caught his eye on the second floor, just above one of his own bedroom windows: the curtains were still shut but a white, ghostlike presence seemed to have slipped behind them and stood out against the dark material: Sophia Chronos was now staring intensely at him. Her hair was down and cascading over her shoulders; her white neck disappeared within the folds of her garment. Her otherworldly face was perfectly immobile and was almost touching the window. If he hadn't noticed her breath leaving condensation on the glass panel, Adam would have thought she had left the realm of the physical world. Sophia's brown eyes had an intense, almost feverish expression that took Adam by surprise and shook him to the core when their eyes locked.

Suddenly, out of the blue, she lifted her arms and hit the glass on both sides of her face with the palm of her hands and surprising force; Adam heard the sound of her flesh come into contact with the glass; his ears resonated with it and his heart jumped in his chest; the violence of the gesture surprised him and he didn't know how to react to it. Sophia then closed her eyes and left her hands slide down slowly along the glass panel.

When her fingers had left the glass and her arms had dropped back to the sides of her body, she opened her eyes again, but this time didn't seem to see the young man anymore; she simply turned round, parted the heavy fabric and disappeared again inside her room. Adam was left transfixed and disturbed by Sophia Chronos's strange behaviour. Had she been trying to tell him something? He had noticed a definite change in her eyes: they had exhibited some kind of unusual fervour.

He glanced up again, but all he could see now was the opaque mass of the curtains. He shrugged and took the direction of the path exiting the rose garden before going round the North Wing. In passing, he glanced at the ornate moondial with its grinning moon face, very similar to the metal sculpture adorning the entrance gates.

Leaving the green house behind, Adam took the track back towards the *porte-cochère* and carried on in the direction of the small wood behind which Maeve's Guardian Cottage was located. He walked fast, trying to warm up. He thought about Maeve's small fireplace and hoped she would have a nice fire roaring in her cosy lounge. He kept his eyes on the horizon, and sure enough, he soon spotted the trail of smoke rising above the tree tops. As he walked around the small wood, he noticed an unknown, stylish vehicle – not dissimilar to Saturnin's Oxford Morris but flashier – parked a short distance from the house, under the trees. His heart sank: Maeve was not on her own. At the same time, his nose caught the wholesome smell of burning wood and his ears the unmistakable notes of jazz music.

So used was he to the austere atmosphere of the house that in the first instance he refused to trust his senses. He opened the small gate and stopped in front of the door: now, in addition to the music, he could hear voices. A sudden, high-pitched bark made him jump; the creature was just behind the door, most certainly feeling his presence ahead of the humans in the room. He heard an unknown female voice exclaim: 'Mary! What's wrong with you NOW?' Then, seemingly turning away from the door to speak to someone else: 'I told you we shouldn't have brought the dog, Gilbert. She's been making too much fuss since she's arrived here.'

Adam was tempted to turn round and leave, but the thought of Maeve being there in the room gave him a little courage and he knocked. On the other side the door, almost inaudible through the barking, the woman said:

'Oh! Oh dear... Someone's outside! Shall I open the door, Mae?'

She had obviously taken the decision not to wait for Maeve's reply as the door opened immediately and Adam found himself standing on the threshold faced with a tall, elegant woman holding a tiny nervous dog under her right arm. She was wearing an expensive-looking velvet caftan over a long dark purple dress and a little embroidered cap. Her make-up was rather dramatic and accentuated her strong features; her manners were theatrical.

'Oh! And who are *you*?' she asked, holding the little dog protectively as if Adam was intent on harming the animal.

Behind her, the young man glimpsed the warm fireplace and the legs of a man sat in the armchair. The coffee table was cluttered with a multitude of bottles of all shapes and sizes, and full baskets were scattered on the rug. Adam was cold and desperate to get to the fire.

Maeve emerged from her small kitchen.

'What is it, Gabby?' A shadow passed over her features when she spotted Adam. 'Oh! It's you. Don't stand there, come in, you're going to make the lounge all cold!'

Adam could sense that the young woman was fighting contrary feelings: on her mobile face, he could read surprise, annoyance and delight... She was pleased to see him but didn't wish to show it... That made him feel good.

The be-suited male visitor stood up to welcome Adam, and soon, the four of them were forming a small circle in the middle of the room.

'Gilbert, Gabby, this is Adam Tuckfield. He works as a tutor for my uncle at the big house.'

'Does he really?' questioned Gabby, raising an eyebrow and smiling knowingly at Maeve, who chose to ignore her.

'Adam, these are my dear friends from London, Gabby and Gilbert Ramsey. Please avoid mentioning their visit at the Hall, if you don't mind... Uncle Vange wouldn't be impressed, and Mr Bloom would turn apoplectic! I am not supposed to bring people here...'

'We're *persona non grata*! But the poor girl has been feeling so very lonely here on her own,' interrupted Gabby, putting her free arm around Maeve, 'so we've come to cheer her up!'

Gilbert flashed his most devastating white smile and talked in a studied nonchalant way.

'Indeed. And we haven't come empty-handed!' He gestured widely towards the bottles and overflowing baskets on the floor. 'There's everything we need for the cocktails that will sustain us through the night!'

'And food...' added his older sister.

'Ah, yes... Food... If we ever feel the need! Will you join us, Mr Tuckfield?'

Adam glanced at Maeve. He wanted to have a heart-to-heart conversation with her, not to take part in a drunken Charleston session. The presence of those two brash individuals seemed entirely incongruous on the sleepy estate: they talked loudly and rapidly, wore colourful clothes, heavy perfumes and cologne, and were obviously intent on having as good a time in a former Guardian's Cottage as they would in a trendy jazz club in the capital. Gabby looked intrigued by Adam.

'And anyway, what is a young and handsome man like you doing working as a tutor in this lonely place?'

'Earning a living, I suppose,' replied Adam, looking straight at her.

Gabby pouted pensively, then exclaimed:

'Oh, what a bore! Anyway, Maeve darling, where's that coffee you've promised us?' She deposited the small dog on the floor and flung herself onto the sofa. 'Oh, I can feel we are going to have a loooovely time here!'

Maeve disappeared into the kitchen and Adam used this as an excuse to steal five minutes alone with her. The kitchen was tiny, and Maeve kept bumping into Adam as she busied herself with the coffee. They talked in hushed tones.

'What are you doing here?' Maeve hissed.

'I just wanted to see you. It's been two weeks.'

'Has it really been two weeks since that awful evening? How amazing! Anyhow, I'm not sure I want to talk about it, especially not now, with those two here.'

'How long are they staying?'

'Two days, why?'

'I wanted to see you alone.'

'Well, you can't.'

They were both standing side by side in front of the small work surface. Maeve was busy laying the cups, saucers and crockery on the tray. Adam's hands were resting on the surface and his eyes were fixed on the field outside;

he was feeling tense, hesitant and a little ashamed. The warmth of Maeve's hand on his brought him back to reality. He turned his head towards his companion; her eyes appeared huge in her pale face; she was looking at him with a strange expression. All tension suddenly disappeared from his body, as if he had just been freed from a spell.

'Adam, I'm so sorry...' Maeve started.

'Need any help?' Gabby's clamorous voice rang in their ears. She was standing on the threshold of the kitchen posing as if her photograph were about to be taken.

Maeve, who had her back to Gabby, closed her eyes and sighed. When she turned round, she had her playful face back on.

'No, it's fine, Gabby, thank you very much. I am just waiting for the kettle to boil!'

Gabby marched to the work surface and seized the tray anyway.

'Let me take this to the lounge. I have been bone idle since we've arrived!' Then, as she exited the kitchen, she bellowed: 'Gilbert? Would you mind clearing that table so I can put the tray on it? We're having coffee, dear. Cocktails are for later!'

The four of them settled around the coffee table with the small dog curled up at his mistress's feet. Adam agreed to stay briefly for coffee before returning to the house to do some more work, and he promised that he would come back in the evening 'for cocktails'.

In the presence of Gilbert and Gabby, Adam had a glimpse of Maeve's 'flapper' life in London: surprisingly modern, seemingly carefree, and fuelled by cigarettes, cocktails, music and extravagance. He understood that girls like Maeve were clinging to their freedom at all cost, even though it sometimes meant going through hard times.

'So then, Mae, when are you re-joining our ranks?' asked Gabby after having described one raucous picnic her friends had organised on Hampstead Heath that summer. 'After all, it's been six months and I think you should be out of danger by now. They've probably all forgotten!'

Maeve made a face and took a cigarette out to conceal her discomfort.

'I... I need to make sure I'm ready. I've been working on a few articles.'

'Go on!' pleaded Gilbert, 'I'm sure Mr Flint would take you back straight away. He got rid of you only because he was pressurised into doing so!'

Adam turned to Maeve.

'You were dismissed from your newspaper job?'

Maeve's face turned one shade paler and she began toying with the spoon in her hand. She was about to reply when Gabby intervened.

'What, you don't know the story? Ah, but last year, Mae was involved in a scandal, dear boy, a real one!'

Maeve hid her face in her hands. Adam was worried she would burst into tears, but when she lifted her head, he could see she was actually laughing.

'Hardly the society scandal of the century! Don't look like that, Adam, it was just a bit of fun…'

It was to the smoothly elegant Gilbert's turn to speak.

'Let me tell you all about it, my dear chap. Mae here is a bit of a heart-breaker… Oh, yes, you are, darling! Don't deny it! She's got all those chaps wanting nothing more than to get together with her and she, the stubborn little idiot, insists on keeping her independence and not committing to anyone.'

His sister interrupted, waving a small biscuit.

'We're all rather commitment-phobes, because we're having such a grand time!' she announced before presenting the treat to the little dog at her feet.

'I'm not being awkward,' protested Maeve, 'I just don't really fancy any of them! The ones I've been with were OK for about two days.'

Gilbert smiled knowingly.

'Yes, well, all of them *except* John Norman, rising star of the company that publishes *The London Herald*, the newspaper for which Maeve was working – I still work there myself. Unfortunately, Norman was married and had a child. The affair became very public and Maeve was asked to leave the newspaper after Norman's wife – an heiress, don't you know – made a terrible fuss. Some people also started spreading rumours that Maeve was pregnant when she left the paper. Poor Mae, from star writer to scorned woman in a few hours…'

'I wasn't pregnant!' exclaimed Maeve, looking at Adam with a look of genuine panic in her eyes.

Gilbert carried on his story.

'Norman's father is a rich, powerful publishing magnate who didn't take to the whole story too kindly either. He is a big promoter of family values.'

'Ha ha!' Maeve put her hand on Adam's arm. 'Well, if I told you the stories a few of my little party friends have told me about him…'

Gabby interrupted her sharply.

'Unfortunately, Mae dear, there's no escaping the fact that double standards *do* apply: you're not rich, you're female, young, pretty and independent, and this makes for an explosive combination. You really should have been more careful.'

'I wasn't ashamed of it. John was…' she started. Gilbert interrupted her:

'You're just lucky your uncle came to the rescue,' he declared.

'What happened?' asked Adam.

'Well, our friend here was being harassed by some quite sinister people – no doubt paid by Norman Senior. Some journalists at rival papers decided to run the story and add a bit to it. No doubt Maeve's uncle read the article in the newspaper and decided to intervene.'

'I had run out of money…' admitted Maeve, sheepishly.

'Even though your uncle sounds utterly mad,' interrupted Gabby, 'and this place is so remote that I probably would *die* if I stayed more than two days, I really do think it was positively marvellous of him to take you in.'

'I had to lie low for a while,' concluded Maeve, twisting her mouth.

Gilbert perked up a little.

'Now that John Norman has been sent to Los Angeles and that people don't talk about it in the office or at our little gatherings anymore, we can only assume that it should be safe for you to come back to us, Maeve. Most of us do understand; Everyone's at it, you two just got caught. As I said before, old Flint always had a soft spot for you and your work, and he would give you your job back in a heartbeat. He's been asking about you a lot!'

'It's entirely up to you, honey. When you think you're ready, give us a call and we'll come and help you move back,' offered Gabby.

Maeve smiled at her two friends.

'Thank you both. I really appreciate it.' She waved her hand in front of her as if to clear the air. 'But enough of this, it's awfully tiresome. Tell me, any good parties this autumn?'

This was Gabby's territory, and after having looked grave and worried about Maeve's future, she had now come to life again.

'Oh, yes, there have been some good ones. We've had so much fun! But I didn't tell you about my new party trick!' Gabby started laughing her raucous laugh again, disturbing the little dog; Mary jumped up and started barking.

'Shush! Shush, you silly canine!' she exclaimed.

She pushed the dog away and the indignant creature retreated to a quieter corner of the rug in front of the fire.

Gilbert passed his hand over his face.

'Do you really have to tell them about your 'party trick'?' He looked annoyed.

'Of course! It's so much fun!' Gabby turned to Maeve and Adam. 'I've been feeling rather creative these past few months and I've been putting together a little act that has been *really* successful each time I've been out. You know how some of those evenings can drag out forever... People need to be entertained; they need something *piquant* to keep them awake! So I've been telling them that I have some special powers and can communicate with the dead. I have become a spirit medium!'

'Oh, Gabby, you haven't!' exclaimed Maeve sceptically.

'Yes! And it's been a jolly success! People ask me to their parties especially for my little show, now! It really *is* entertaining.'

Maeve was now serious.

'Gabby. You don't... You don't believe you have such powers, do you?'

Gabby's face froze in a questioning expression: she looked at her friend quizzically.

'Don't be silly, Mae. Of course, I haven't such powers! Who has?' She started laughing again, wholeheartedly. 'It's just a bit of *fun*, darling! It's all nonsense, of course! All this silliness about dead souls floating around us and trying to communicate with us... People seeing ghosts... It's all rather ridiculous! You know me, I'm all for science! But you see, you just have to put up a good theatrical performance and people believe in it, or at least *pretend* to believe in it! It's a game. I write little speeches all the time, now, inventing some names, some stories, and I make them fit in with whoever is present on the evening. I do *séances*, speak in different voices and knock on the table once or twice, you know, that kind of thing... It's all part of the show! It's just pure thrills!'

Gabby was obviously very proud of her new-found talent.

Her brother looked slightly embarrassed by her new game, remembering some cringe-inducing moments at a few recent parties when some people had been genuinely shaken by her 'show'. After all, the end of the war wasn't that far away, and there were still people desperate to contact the loved ones who had vanished in the muddy fields of France. Much like a lot of his friends, Gilbert was a sceptic about nearly everything, and considered mediums and psychics as nothing else than charlatans exploiting people's foibles and misery. Gabby's party tricks were another proof that you could really get gullible people believe anything if you wanted to.

'I know!' exclaimed Gabby. 'Tonight, I'm going to do a little demonstration for you! You'll see, it's such a laugh!'

Maeve and Adam exchanged a look of alarm. They understood each other immediately.

'Gabby, maybe it's not really a good idea...' started Maeve.

'Yes! I insist! I know, you think you're going to get really bored. But you see, the important ingredient in this trick is audience participation, so after you've had one or two cocktails, you'll just join me in my séance, and we'll just have some fun together!'

Gilbert chuckled.

'Gabby just wants to show off...' He sighed. 'Go on, Maeve, indulge your old friend.'

The unease that Maeve had just felt had disappeared. She remembered the atmosphere of those parties she used to go to, the incredible whirlwind of energy, the intoxicating trance-like state you would find yourself in after an hour or so of drinking and breathing the potent air charged with cigarette smoke, strong perfumes and alcohol vapours; after a while, the part of your brain that controlled any rational behaviour would shut down and let the rest go loose. It was then that people could make you do almost anything...

She imagined Gabby, wearing one of her outrageous gowns, rallying the crowds around her and ostentatiously starting a strange parody of a séance with the dimmed lights creating shadows that would start moving in the mind of her inebriated audience. She envisioned the heavy breathing and coughs, the consciousness half-drowned in a sea of alcohol... Yes, it was probably easy to make-believe in such an environment... Maeve herself would have been the first one to encourage Gabby in her little act if she had been present.

'All right, you always win!' she conceded.

'Bravo! I knew you would relent!' Gabby saw Adam stand up, ready to go. 'Mr Tuckfield, you *do* have to come back to have some cocktails and to see my little show!'

Contrary to Maeve, Adam hadn't been able to shake the sense of dread that had come upon him at the mention of the mock-séance. But something told him that he had to be present. He promised to come back later in the day.

THREE

I t was close to 11pm and the mood had seriously mellowed. By then, everyone was bathing in a pleasant alcohol-induced sort of light torpor, the conversation had slowed down, and the subject matter had moved from the lights of London to life in the countryside. Gabby had just given a speech on what she thought her alternative, rural life would have been. She was an entertaining and witty host with strong narcissistic tendencies which could sometimes be infuriating. Her brother clearly adored her but was also embarrassed by her. Gilbert tried to present himself as a gentleman and a dandy with a dash of daring reporter, and it worked; Adam envied his confidence.

Maeve was more subdued that evening because Adam was present and she didn't want him to see her feistier side. She wished he had never heard about her affair with John Norman. She was feeling troubled. After all, all she wanted was to become the best journalist in town, and she had messed it up. She was ready to start again on a better footing. *When she is back in London…* *When she is back…* Would she ever be allowed to go back? Somewhere deep inside her brewed the dread that had never left her since she had arrived at Whitemoor Hall. Adam might be able to help her lift the veil on her own fear.

'Well! 'Tis time, my dear friends!' exclaimed Gabby. She lifted both arms over her head and stretched like a big cat, making her numerous bracelets jingle and tinkle. Her three companions looked at her, bemused.

'Time for what?' enquired Gilbert.

'Why, for our séance, of course!' exclaimed Gabby, whilst readjusting the little cap on her head that had gone all askew. 'First, we need a table and some chairs.'

Groaning, Gilbert slowly got up and tried to smooth out his creased suit.

'I guess we haven't got the choice, pals… What Gabby wants, Gabby gets! Isn't that true, Mary?' declared Gilbert, looking down at the little dog which had been observing her mistress closely and was getting excited by the sudden flurry of movement.

For the next twenty minutes or so, Maeve, Adam and Gilbert busied themselves preparing the lounge under Gabby's supervision: a round table was brought in from the room next door and four chairs were found in various places around the cottage and dragged back to the lounge. All the curtains were secured against the moonlight and candles were placed at various points around the room.

'No electric lights at all during the séance, too bright, too artificial! I will allow only the fireplace and a few candles. We need the room to be as dark as possible whilst still being able to see each other. We need to create a favourable *ambiance*!

Maeve added some logs to the fire and for a few seconds looked into the orange flames; her eyes glassed over. She wished she could stay there, crouching in front of the fireplace, and not get involved in Gabby's grotesque idea. Holding a fake drunken séance in the middle of a glittering London party was one thing; attempting the same in an isolated cottage on the Whitemoore estate was another. She shivered.

If she had still been in London, she would have laughed it off and taken part light-heartedly. Now though, after all she had seen, the whole idea made her so anxious that she felt nauseous. She eventually shook off her dread and started lighting the candles one by one. When this had been done, she turned the light switch off. Immediately, the room took on a different personality: it appeared shrouded in a solemn, almost mythical low glimmer. Gabby looked around and smiled.

'Just perfect! I think we're ready. Do take a seat, all.'

She was standing by the table, very straight, already assuming her role of 'medium'.

Everyone sat down around the table: Gilbert had a half-mocking, half-blasé smile on his face. Adam was fighting contradictory feelings: he felt slightly silly and yet couldn't help being tense. Maeve's nausea hadn't receded; her jaw was clenched and her hands grasped the edge of the table. The candlelight and the glow of the fire revealed new angles on everyone's face and created shadows and dark corners all around the room. Earlier, Gabby had put a new record on the gramophone, some sombre classical music this time – it apparently added a layer of atmosphere.

'What I usually do is ask everyone to hold hands on the table. So let's just do that.'

Maeve's hand felt icy cold in Adam's despite the pleasant warmth coming from the fire and the wood burner; her fingers were rigid. He gave her a reassuring squeeze and glanced at her with a smile that wanted to say 'Do not worry, this is just a silly game', although he wasn't sure he believed it himself.

'Excellent!' murmured Gabby. 'Normally, at this point, I have to put on a rather silly voice, you know, all mysterious and incantatory. It is not as easy to do as you think, and I have to concentrate. So please, from now on, play the game, and remain silent. I always tell my participants: the main thing is, make sure you keep holding hands, otherwise it breaks the circulation of energies! It's a good one, isn't it?'

Gabby sat very straight in her chair and closed her eyes, as if she were trying to listen and locate some sounds only she could perceive. The recording had finished by then, and for a few seconds, the only noises they could hear were the ones coming from the fireplace: the whoosh of the flames and the crackling of the burning wood. Then Gabby's voice started again, melodramatic and showy.

'We invite the spirits to join us here tonight. You are welcome among us. Speak through me if you may. Is there anybody here?' The last sentence had been pronounced in a higher, louder tone of voice; almost a comedy voice.

Gilbert chuckled and whispered:

'Usually, that's when she starts...'

The young man stopped suddenly and Adam, who was holding his hand, felt it clench his own flesh. Mary the dog started growling in the direction of her mistress.

'Gilbert, anything wrong?' Adam asked. He glanced at the other man, who was looking at his sister with a baffled look on his face. Gabby's three companions all let go of the hands they were holding all at the same time and remained seated, looking at the woman in the cap who had started shaking from head to toe. The dog had gone from aggressive growling to pitiful whimpering, as if in pain or in fear of something.

'Gabby? Gabs?' called her brother, who put a protective hand on her shoulder and retrieved it with a cry. 'Ouch!'

'Gil! What's the matter?' asked Maeve.

'I... I am not too sure... It felt like... like I had put my hand on a burning stove.' He turned again to his sister, who now had bowed her head forward, her chin touching her chest; she was still trembling all over.

'It looks like... like she is in a trance or something,' commented Adam.

Gilbert looked at him with despair and incomprehension in his eyes.

'Well, usually, she *pretends* to be in a trance! But it's never like this... This one just looks so... so *real*!'

The three of them couldn't leave their chairs; they were petrified. Suddenly, they heard a sonorous 'click' coming from the direction of the gramophone that had long finished playing. An odd, plaintive sound came out of the machine and the strangest, most surreal noise filled the room. The cold hand of anguish seized the three companions.

'What the hell is that?' exclaimed Gilbert, chilled to the bone, as he jumped out of his chair towards the machine.

'Oh my God!' he exclaimed, his voice made hoarse by a mixture of fear and disbelief, 'The machine is playing the wrong way around!'

'What do you mean, 'the machine is playing the wrong way around'?' asked Maeve sharply.

'It... It is playing *backwards*... Can... Can those things do that?'

The warped, distorted notes chilled everyone to the bone. It was a horrible, unnatural noise: it was the sound of a cacophonous storm, the anti-melody of Hell. Soon, their ears would start protesting under the assault.

Then the sound of a swirling gust of wind was heard – no window or door had been left open – and all the candles were snuffed out all at the same time, plunging the room in even deeper shadow with only the now weak fire as its only source of light. The gramophone stopped and its sinister racket ceased abruptly.

Gilbert froze next to the machine, sweat pearling on his forehead. Adam and Maeve were frozen in their chair.

Very much like a puppet directed by invisible strings, Gabby's upper body was suddenly propped up again against the back of her chair with an unnatural violence that could very well have caused her neck to snap; her arms were propelled into the air only to land violently on top of the table. They remained thus, lifeless, on each side of her now rigid body.

Gilbert ran to the light switch and fruitlessly worked at it for a few seconds. He swore under his breath.

'The electricity's gone!' he exclaimed with disbelief. As if in response to his remark, the main light bulb as well as the two smaller reading lamps in the room started crackling with current and emitted a multitude of mini-thunderbolts. Then all went quiet again for a short time before Gabby's eyes opened suddenly and a rasping sound came from the depth of her throat: she was now gasping for air. When that ceased, the torrent of language started.

The voice wasn't Gabby's but a stronger, oratorical one. There was some kind of echo to the words, that of an ancient, long-gone language thousands of years old. It was a tongue made of myths, legends and prayers; a language utterly alien to the environment of the cottage, to the green fields and the winding lanes of the English landscape. The unknown words penetrated the three individuals present in the room and appealed to their inner fears, planted the seeds of utter horror in their hearts.

The strangely fascinating discourse went on for several minutes without interruption, until Gabby stood up abruptly, knocking her chair off.

'The Underworld is our home,' the strange voice uttered in guttural English.

As Gabby went silent again, something even stranger happened: an odd glow, faint at first, seemed to spread over her from the inside of her body. Her skin became almost transparent, illuminated from within, and her clothes were lifted away from her body by rays of pure energy that finally poured out of her through her dress, to finally form a human-size column of light which soon evaporated in all directions, sending threads of lightweight glowing matter to every corner of the room. Adam, Maeve and Gilbert felt the vapour-like substance fly past them, like a sudden draught of wind and the caress of the lightest of fingers.

At the same time, the lounge filled with hundreds of disembodied voices imploring, whispering, hissing and calling out. They couldn't be distinguished from one another, so intertwined they were. Then they stopped, as abruptly as they had started, and the whole room, which had been as bright as a sunny summer day, was once more plunged in gloom with only the orange embers of the fireplace providing light. Soon, flames grew back on the blackened wicks of the candles and the fire roared once again in the fireplace. The electric lights came back on their own accord, making the trio blink and the dog run and hide behind one of the sofas.

Gabby's body lay collapsed on the floor, one wide sleeve of her coat covering her face, her embroidered cap resting near her head.

Gilbert was the first to speak, his smooth self-confidence all but vanished, his hair limp over his ears and his forehead glistening with perspiration.

'What the hell was that?' His eyes were going from Maeve to Adam, wild with bafflement, searching desperately for some kind of reassurance.

'I don't think I know,' admitted Adam.

'We've been experiencing an instance of collective hallucination. Do you think it's the cocktails?' Gilbert needed to hang on to some rational explanation. Maeve sprang into action and kneeled next to her friend.

'I think we should attend to Gabby first. We'll ask all the important questions afterwards.' She put her hand on her friend's forehead: it was burning with fever. She turned and looked up at the two men. 'We need to get her into bed. Could you two please help me carry her upstairs to the guest bedroom?'

Gilbert and Adam managed to take the collapsed Gabby up the narrow stairs, which was no mean feat due to her height and loose garments. They finally deposited her on one of the small twin beds in the guest room; then Maeve took over and sent the two men downstairs. When she came down twenty minutes later, she found them silent and shaken, smoking and staring at the coffee table which was covered with the leftovers of the evening's cocktail-making activities. The mood was no longer a festive one.

*   *   *

In the study, under the single light of the desk lamp, Dimitri had started labelling some brand new rooms he had added to his map of the building. He was just about to put pen to paper when something akin to a premonition made him sit up, put his pen down and listen to the thick silence.

The clamour came out of nowhere: hundreds of voices filled the air around him; they were full of despair, pain and anger, and they resonated with the anguish of the ones who know there is no way out.

The boy's instincts made him recognise those voices immediately: he had seen their mute owners wander around the carpeted corridors, the panelled galleries, the cold dusty rooms, the abandoned stables and isolated woodlands of the estate, unable to speak to him. They were the voices of the dead of the Whitemoor estate. Something or someone had disturbed and alarmed them. Dimitri felt uneasy, and for the first time since he had become aware of his strange power, he was scared.

FOUR

$\int$aturnin Bloom had left Vangelis Chronos alone in the laboratory, surrounded by his boiling pots and gurgling jars. The dirty practicalities of alchemy were not really for him. He was only interested in the end result.

The scholar, on the contrary, revelled in his feverish activity: consulting the obscure volumes he kept close at hand at all times, mixing highly volatile powders and liquids, soiling everything in his vicinity... all this to satisfy his constant desire to perfect his *Magnum Opus*, his Great Work. Sometimes, Saturnin just had enough of all this, and sought out some fresh air out in the grounds.

The god Thoth was standing in one corner of the rose garden, just behind the moondial. The moon, his alter ego and companion, now felt very remote from his reach. He had retained some of his control over Time, and he had managed to open up and use the wormhole on which the estate was built, but his frustration grew every day. He was anxious about his powers diminishing any further and he was sick of the mediocrity he had been condemned to for so long.

He had spent over a month translating Jahi's diary and had been marvelling at the extent of Amunet's betrayal. It was all there, written on the cracked yellowing paper in the sacred scribe's delicate and steady hand. That great vestal of the Cult had tried to steal the show. The arrogance!

True, he had admired her strength and cunning as long as they had worked in his favour, and he had enjoyed their physical relationship. She had thought his bodily fluids would transfer some of his divinity onto her and she had expected to be granted immortality in return for her favours and hard work. By then, he had lost a lot of his powers and had been licking his wounds. But even if he had still been in possession of them all, he would never have given immortality to this dangerous, power-hungry mortal; it would have elevated her to a divine status. He thought that divinity was a birth right and not something you could *acquire*. He had never trusted the violet-eyed vestal anyway, not even in death. The fact that on her death bed, she had renounced him and embraced Anubis, his own bitter rival, had sowed the seeds of a vexation that had accompanied him ever since.

And now, he was waiting for Sophia Chronos in the rose garden. He hoped that the Lady of the house wouldn't disappoint: the autumn fog had returned, and he knew there was nothing she liked better than going out in the garden when it was shrouded in the thick layers of vaporous mist. And indeed, he couldn't see the house or even the pond at all from where he stood in wait, ready to check for himself whether his instinct had been right.

Right on cue, he heard the double door open and close again; then came the clicks of heeled shoes upon the stone staircase. To his surprise, Sophia's steps didn't sound like they were as cautious as usual; she was moving in a freer manner. The crunch on the gravel indicated to him that she was coming his way. Sheltered by the fog, he grinned.

'Good morning, Lady Chronos.'

Saturnin Bloom's voice had the effect he intended: Sophia Chronos jumped and instinctively turned towards the source of the voice. She stood, her slender frame swaying slightly like a beautiful flower in the wind, with her gloved right hand on her chest; she tried to tame the rhythm of her heart and her intake of air. Saturnin's dark frame emerged from the fog.

When he came closer, the secretary noticed a change in Sophia: her usually pale oval face was suffused with pink; her brown eyes, ordinarily cold and vague, were animated and looked at him with an unnerving intensity. It suited her, but it would take him a while to get used to it. His eyes suspiciously scrutinised her. He mockingly remarked:

'Dear Lady Chronos… Always taking your walks in the fog! Do you wish to get lost one day?'

Sophia Chronos blinked under the unrelenting depths of Mr Bloom's cruel black gaze. Her first reaction would usually be one of disgust and distrust... She was expecting it to overcome her as she stood so close to him, with only the moondial standing between them. But it didn't come, not this time. Was it because of the change she had sensed in herself? Just this morning, she had woken up with a strange tension in her body, some kind of longing for movement.

Saturnin Bloom's eyes searched her person. Then he saw it: nestled among the ruffles of her dress and framed by the lapel of her coat was the glittering dragonfly pendant. The secretary saw the specks of the red mist of anger dance in front of his eyes. Of course, the silly woman hadn't been able to resist and had completely ignored his warning. He felt a shudder of anticipation and dread travel up his spine. What a human feeling this was, 'dread'. If he had been even half the god he used to be, he wouldn't have felt anything like it. But the loss of his powers had given him human traits he could have done without. And he was genuinely *dreading* the consequences of the woman's actions, while at the same time, his combative nature rejoiced at the potential challenge that was yet to come. Mr Bloom's face managed to not betray his inner thoughts.

'I haven't seen you since that terribly embarrassing night two weeks ago, Mr Bloom. The night you hurt my wrist and shouted at me. That was not very nice of you, to say the least.'

Absentmindedly, Sophia rubbed her wrist, remembering he had almost crushed her delicate bones. It made the hair on the back of her neck stand up.

'It was for your own good, believe me,' he retorted sharply.

Saturnin Bloom remembered the blind anger that had overcome him at the time. Seeing Amunet's jewel box for the first time since her death had awakened the pure hatred Thoth had felt at his vestal's ultimate betrayal. Sophia's awe at the sight of the jewels had been pathetic, almost vulgar. But humans were mostly vulgar anyway, and so easily dazzled by shiny things. But he knew that today, anger wouldn't lead him anywhere, and so he fought against it until it finally retreated behind the closed doors of his brain.

Sophia Chronos looked defiantly at the man she knew as her husband's secretary.

'You have never explained... I found your attitude frankly unforgivable, Mr Bloom. I hope my husband has talked to you about it.'

Sophia feigned outrage but didn't feel it, not anymore. She had found wearing the pendant soothing, for some strange reason. Her lethargy has lifted and the itches and cold sweats she had been suffering from had virtually ceased since she had started wearing the piece of jewellery. The pain in her hip and pelvis had improved and she wasn't limping as much. She was feeling better in her own skin, literally.

'I see that you are wearing one of them now,' observed Saturnin Bloom, 'the dragonfly, isn't it?'

Sophia's hand travelled to her neck and she touched the pendant, feeling the shape of it under the thin wool of her pale grey gloves. She didn't move when the secretary joined her on her side of the moondial, lifted his hand to touch the pendant with his own fingers and extracted the jewel from its nest of lace. He looked at it, rubbed a thumb over it.

'Yes... The dragonfly...' he murmured.

Sophia's breathing quickened; Saturnin Bloom was so very close to her, the closest he had ever been. Within her, her instincts were fighting a real battle. Her horror of being touched had always made her whole body react violently as soon as someone invaded her preciously guarded personal space. Even the dressmaker and Ginny, her personal maid, were not allowed to touch any flesh other than that of her face or arms. The rest was out of bounds.

Twelve years earlier, she had allowed a man to touch her and to make love to her and the result had been nine months of agonising pregnancy, the horror of a long, bloody, unbearably painful birth, a near-death experience and the beginning of eleven years of chronic pain... And of course, the end of her glittering stage career; everything she had always hoped for had dissolved in the pure agony of her body and soul.

She had often wished she had died there and then when she had been told that she had been carrying a baby, that something alien had been growing within her and sucking on her insides like a monstrous parasite. The terror that had torn her mind apart had been indescribable. But Henry had been alive at the time, and she had tried to convince herself that she could do it for him despite the sticky disgust and the paralysing fear. And then he had died before their wedding day, and the horror had started.

She had seen Vangelis Chronos's torment so often when he had looked at her. Even though he had agreed at the time of their wedding that he would have to renounce any consummation of their marriage, he had tried several times over the years to woo her out of her celibacy. She had always regarded Lord Chronos as her social saviour, the one who had taken her – and the child – in, but the truth was that he had always repulsed her, even more so than any other man. He had buried himself in his studies and had left her alone, playing the role of attentive guardian and benefactor. But she had caught his eyes on her, and had seen regret in them.

Now, with Saturnin Bloom's body so close, she felt the revulsion replaced by something else she couldn't understand. Her skin didn't creep, her hands didn't grow cold. Something emanated from him; some kind of animalistic power. She closed her eyes for one second and in her mind, their two frames merged into one... She opened her eyes again. Saturnin Bloom had left the pendant fall back on the dress and was observing her with a grave face.

'Very interesting object. I guess out of all of them, I am glad you have chosen this one. A truly unique specimen.'

He was now searching her face for something, a sign or a shadow. Was it there, in the flushed skin of her face, on the slightly plumper lips and darker eyes? What had Sophia started when she had put the pendant around her neck? That slender, white, long neck he had wanted to wring so many times out of sheer frustration with her staggering weakness and her towering arrogance. He knew he could snap her cervical vertebrae with just one hand. The only way to prevent any accident was to walk away from her.

'What do you want, Mr Bloom?'

'Nothing special, Lady Chronos. I just wished to see how you were and report to your husband. He's been worried about you and feels guilty about working so much. He's been so engrossed in his new experiment, you understand, that he hasn't found the time...'

'I am perfectly well, Mr Bloom,' interrupted Sophia Chronos. 'You can go and say so to my husband. Tell him also not to interrupt his experiment on my behalf. I understand the importance of his work.'

Now impatient to get away from the secretary, Sophia turned towards the path leading out of the rose garden in the opposite direction.

'I will most certainly inform your husband of your good health. Good day, Lady Chronos.' Saturnin Bloom bowed slightly; Sophia knew his reverence was nothing but ironic. She could feel his eyes bore into her back, burning their way through her thick coat, her long jacket, her dress and her underslip... A deep shiver ran along her spine. She was more than ever determined to find Eliott Mills the gardener.

FIVE

Adam and Maeve were standing in front of the cottage outside the small wooden gates. They had just watched Gilbert's sleek car disappear on the horizon towards the southern exit. None of them had moved.

They had all spent the night at the cottage. Maeve had slept in her bedroom and Gilbert had insisted on taking one of the sofas while Adam had settled for the second one.

As soon as she had been up, Gabby had insisted on going back to the capital to see her doctor. She had woken up groggy and had maintained that she couldn't remember a thing about the séance. She had complained about feeling quite nauseous and drained still. She had sat, transfixed, as her three companions had attempted to describe as best as they could their experience of the previous night. Gabby's wide range of reactions had included shock, disbelief, nervous laughter, embarrassment and horror, but she had been completely unable to get her memory to work satisfactorily; everything had been erased from her mind. She couldn't describe anything of what she had felt during the previous evening, even though Gilbert had been very insistent. Everyone had been left shaken to the core by the experience.

The brother and sister had left with a heavy heart but also with a sort of impatience. The bright lights of London would be reassuring after such a strange ordeal. They had promised to come back and help Maeve move whenever she was ready, but somehow the young woman knew that they wouldn't.

The car had disappeared and silence had come back to the estate. It was still early – about 9am – and it was Sunday. Soon, the staff would be making their way to the abbey as they did every week.

'You could have left with them. Why didn't you?' asked Adam, his eyes still on the track.

'I'm sorry?' Maeve's voice, thin and weak, alarmed Adam. She was not looking at him; her face was still turned towards the exit where her friends' car had just been. Her eyes were glistening with tears.

'Didn't you hear what Gilbert said?' replied Adam. 'You can go back now, resume your career, your life… Everything is forgiven, or if not forgiven, conveniently forgotten. You obviously want it so much. You're wasting your talent, here. You should be there, in London, writing and going to parties… Living! You could have taken the ride with Gilbert and Gabby and come back here to pick up the rest of your things later.'

Maeve sniffed, her jaw tightened; she turned towards him. What he saw in her eyes and on her face, he wasn't entirely sure: affection and irritation, pity and indecision. She sighed; her whole face froze into a mask of coldness and a shadow spread across it.

'But you do not understand, Adam. I can't.'

'But why not? There's nothing keeping you here. You were just waiting for the storm to pass, weren't you? It has passed, now.'

Maeve, betraying her impatience, closed her eyes and rubbed her forehead before shaking her head. Then the green eyes, full of tears, looked straight at him again.

'But I *cannot* leave, Adam. Now and probably *never*.' She had wanted her voice to be firm but it wavered.

'What do you mean? Maeve?' Adam turned to face the young woman. She had bowed her head and was trying hard not to burst into tears. He put his hands on each of her arms, gripping tight, shaking her slightly. A strand of hair fell in front of her eyes. Adam wanted her to look at him, but she was desperately avoiding his gaze.

'Maeve? What did you say? You can't leave? But I thought…'

Adam could see that she was fighting against the rising hysteria. Maeve had hung onto her hopes and had tried to keep a lid on her fears; now they all seemed to be flowing back to the surface of her consciousness. She shook Adam off and took a step back from him.

'I know! I know… I have tried to convince myself that I was staying because I wanted to, that I was OK staying in here in this gloomy cottage ruminating about what I should have done and not done, what hopes I had about getting my old life back, about getting published again and making something of myself. But I think I've probably always known that it wouldn't be possible for me to go back. That it was final. After what I've done, what I've seen. I cannot get out of the estate, Adam. Like you, I'm a prisoner. Like you, I am playing into the hands of Saturnin Bloom and my uncle. Don't you think that I haven't tried to escape?'

'Soon after I'd arrived, I did exactly what you've done; I tried to get out the way I had come, by the main entrance. Like you, I found the gates locked and bolted. Then I went for the other two entrances: I walked along the track that is supposed to lead to the main road. I walked and walked, I even ran! The track never stopped, *it never ended*! As if someone or something were adding to it the further I went. I never saw the gates. After three hours, I stopped and turned back, angry and frustrated; I was in such a state! Everyone says it's only a twenty minute walk to the Village Gate entrance. I never found it. I got blisters and I bled.

'Then a few days later, I tried the lane that comes out of the service courtyard and runs along the stables and is supposed to join the road a little bit further south. I had to walk thirty minutes, only to see the track cut short by the tall wall that surrounds the estate. No gates. It looked as if someone had built the wall across the track, just to stop me from getting out. This is the way Gilbert and Gabby just went. Everyone else can get in and out, but I... *we* can't. The few times I have said something about leaving in the presence of Saturnin Bloom, he's mocked me. He is always teasing me about my departure because he knows I can't get out. I've seen too much, I know too much. He's forced me to help him get you here. Now we are both captive. I don't understand what this is all about. There is something terribly wrong with it all. Something malevolent, dangerous.'

'You are shaking, Maeve. Come here...'

Adam took the young woman in his arms. She was not crying, but she was now wrapped up in a thick blanket of despair. Her head was throbbing and her eyes were burning because of the lack of sleep. Her arms limp about her body, she allowed herself to let go and felt Adam's slight frame wrap itself around her. She could feel him through their clothes and wanted to melt into him. He had called her his Guardian Angel, but now they had swapped roles and she was the one in need of a guardian. Her usual strength was eluding her.

Adam's chin was buried in Maeve's short locks. She was very small against him, and she looked and felt like a precious vintage doll. He had often thought she was not real at all, looking as she did like a character out of an early Cecil Beaton picture.

The young man felt clumsy and confused. He wasn't suited to the role of strong man at all; he didn't want to be. What did Saturnin Bloom want out of them? Why did he need to take control of everyone's life? Only because he was a god? Adam hadn't even believed in gods before he arrived. As he was the last direct descendant of the family, he could see the point of keeping him here. He had accepted his status, in a way. But Maeve? Saturnin didn't need her anymore, not really. She wasn't an essential tool for him, was she? He could erase her memory and let her go and carry on with her life, couldn't he? Or did he take pleasure in manipulating humans just for the sake of it? After all, wasn't it what gods did, playing games with the weak little mortals and making them think that they were in control?

'Let's go inside,' whispered Maeve, 'I feel like I'm about to collapse here and there. I couldn't sleep last night and even though it's still early, I feel exhausted.'

Maeve fell asleep on the sofa immediately. Adam picked up the flowery blanket from one of the armchairs and covered his friend with it. He then battled for a good twenty minutes to start a fire in the lounge. He wanted to get rid of the pervading feeling of dampness in the air. He also needed a walk. He thought it would help him organise his thoughts and put things into perspective. Physical exertion would do him good and flush out any toxic thoughts.

He briskly made his way towards the lake. The light was low and the skies uniformly grey. As usual, there was not a soul in sight, even though Adam couldn't ignore that feeling he had of being observed: it came from the house, as if the building had eyes. He walked around the lake, absentmindedly staring at the undisturbed, smooth surface of the water, and then took the direction of the house. He crossed the main track onto the lawn, keeping his distance.

As he approached the long Victorian green house, he thought he heard muffled voices coming from inside, and slowed down his pace. He stood there, just outside the glass and brick structure. After barely a minute, the door at the other end of the glasshouse flung open as a woman's voice, full of scorn and frustration, warned: 'I haven't finished with you. I will come and find you again. You won't resist long!'

Sophia Chronos angrily walked towards the rose garden without ever looking back, her open white coat floating about her; her silky white-blond hair, earlier pinned at the top of her head in perfect Gibson Girl style, was now escaping from the pins and trailing behind her like the tail of a comet. Adam knew that something was not quite right, but he couldn't think of what it could be. Then it came to him: Sophia Chronos was not limping anymore. Her rage was carrying her away from the greenhouse faster than he would have thought possible.

For approximately twenty seconds, Adam remained stunned. He was about to make a move when a man came out of the same door and stopped on the threshold, looking in the direction of the rose garden: it was the gardener. Behind him, immobile against the wall, Adam was wondering what to do. He wasn't sure about what he had just witnessed. Then Eliott Mills turned round and for a split second, the tutor saw the immense distress and confusion on the man's very flushed face; these were replaced by surprise and consternation when Eliott saw Adam; blood drained from the former's face. Without making a move, he declared, as softly as his deep voice could manage:

'It's not what you think.'

Adam took a step towards the gardener, looking at reassuring him.

'I do not think anything,' he declared.

The two men stood face to face for a few seconds, unable to utter a word. Then the powerfully built Eliott Mills seemed to go into complete meltdown: his features were distorted by a rictus of pain and despair; he covered his face with his two large hands, let himself fall heavily against one of the glass panels of the greenhouse and let himself slip down until he hit the ground. He remained like this for a while, his back against the wall, sitting in the wet grass with his two knees up against his chest, moaning.

'What am I going to do?' he finally exclaimed.

Adam crouched next to him.

'Mr Mills... Please try and recover yourself. Maybe you could tell me what's happened?'

Eliott Mills removed his hands from his face. His eyes were bloodshot and his features were still bearing the marks of intense psychological suffering. He looked at the tutor with an intense stare, in which remained the incredible resilience and cold determination of the courageous military man he had been; but those eyes were also haunted by fear.

'I... I don't...'

The words didn't want to or couldn't come out. Eliott Mills had spent the past seven years bottling up his feelings, seeking calm and isolation, making sure he was doing his job as best as he could so he could provide for himself and for Will and his mother. This had meant a huge personal sacrifice. Working, working and always working, and obliterating his own feelings, hopes and dreams. They had all been shattered by the war but he had – just – remained human enough to feel those emotions stirring within him, often… He had learnt very quickly to tame them and block their way to the surface.

He hadn't really had a proper conversation with anyone during those seven years; The only person he talked to outside work was Will, but his friend probably didn't even hear him. He had given himself one goal in life: to make sure he survived and helped Will and his mother so they could get through. And now this incident with Lady Chronos had fallen on his head like thunderstorm; it had disturbed his carefully put together balance and had kicked him in the face so hard that he could barely breathe. He didn't know what to do, he was panicking! He, Eliott Mills, who had survived the war! He was panicking because of a woman's lust for him!

Adam's sympathetic voice reached him among his thoughts and brought him back to reality.

'Take your time, Mr Mills. If you do not wish to say anything, I will respect this.'

At last, the gardener lifted his face towards the young tutor, a face so different from his own. Whilst Eliott's was all square jaw, strong features and rugged angles, Adam's was open, softer, almost feminine with his long lashes, big blue eyes, round cheekbones and well defined lips. He looked like someone at ease with his feelings and how to express them. Eliott wished he could do it too.

'No! No… I will tell you. I have to tell *someone*. Maybe something can be done. I just don't know…' His voice died off. He turned his head towards the rose garden, where Lady Chronos had disappeared earlier. He then stared at the lawn in front of him, between his feet.

'I was tidying up the greenhouse. I always do this in the autumn. I get rid of dead plants, I prepare the ones that are left for the winter, I give the place a good clean and I do some repairs if needed. It is quite pleasant to work in there, especially on a morning such as this one, chilly, grey… It is warm and there aren't any draughts, I make sure of it.'

Eliott Mills obviously loved his job. He was proud of his meticulousness and of his good organisation.

'I was also having a look around with my lunar calendar. I have decided to take up lunar gardening, you see, and I am learning how it works. I would like to apply it to the plants I grow in there.'

Adam thought the gardener was trying to buy himself some time and was dragging his feet, so to speak.

'But, Lady Chronos...?' he ventured.

The gardener rubbed his face with his hands again and kept his eyes on the ground.

'I was too busy to hear her come in. You know, she looks like a ghost, doesn't she? She seems to move like one too, without making any noise at all. I was on my own in there, and it is not that big a place. I was not very far from the door; I should have heard her come in. She... She looked different.'

'Different? In what way?'

Eliott Mills shrugged.

'I don't know. When it comes to my fellow humans, I am not very observant. Just... different. More... self-confident, more talkative? I mean, she would never have sought my company, she used to avoid me like the plague. I've always wondered what it was that made her so... so *afraid* of me. She would never voluntarily come into the greenhouse knowing that I am on my own there. But this morning, she told me she had been looking for me.'

Eliott Mill's face went red again.

'And what... Why had she been looking for you?'

The gardener suddenly jumped to his feet and started pacing up and down. Adam stood up, his knees painful for having been crouching a bit too long.

'She was just behaving in a strange way. She was looking at me funny. It was... It was embarrassing. Then she started talking... She had a queer voice, not like her usual, rather cold voice. I am not sure what she was saying, because I... She was getting closer and closer and I... It disturbed me. So I didn't really listen to start with, I had to concentrate on keeping some distance between her and me... She...'

Eliott Mills paused again. He was not going to tell Adam, who after all was a stranger, what Lady Chronos had told him. He was not going to describe to him the way she had flung herself into his arms and had begged to be kissed. That she had clasped her arms around his neck and had asked him to make love to her there, in the greenhouse. He wouldn't dare.

It was too excruciatingly embarrassing.

'She tried to seduce me,' declared Eliott Mills, trying to keep his voice in check, 'I don't know... She just lost her mind... It was a terrible sight.' He paused again, then looked at Adam, his old determination back on his face but his eyes betraying a slight panic. 'I do not know what to do, you see... I cannot go and tell her husband, or her husband's assistant. He is bound to repeat everything! I have rejected her quite... forcefully, I'm afraid. I just panicked. I think I have upset her and she sounded very bitter when she left. She said she would come back... So it's either she will make up a story to get her husband to send me away or she will come back over and over again until I...'

'Until you stop resisting?' Adam held Eliott's gaze for a few seconds. The gardener shook his head.

'No, I won't stop resisting. I won't relent. I *cannot*. Before the war, maybe... Maybe I would have given in more easily. Not anymore. There is no place for that kind of thing in my life. My mind – as well as my body – seems to have been disconnected from everything like that, you know... I am not sure whether it is physical, psychological or both. I've never really taken the time to think about it.' There was no regret in Eliott Mills' voice, only that fortitude that seemed to carry him. 'The only love I have is the one for my best friend Will and his mother. You see, Will and I... We were in the same platoon. I don't know how, but over the years, we just kept each other company and we survived. We were the only ones left. The only ones...'

Eliott Mills's voice wavered, swollen with emotion. Adam was listening to him, transfixed, his mind racing with strange thoughts. There he was, a 27-year-old man from the 21st century, having a conversation with someone who only seven years earlier had still been in the trenches. Maybe he shouldn't even think about it, because how could he visualise the enormity of what this man had been through?

The gardener started talking again.

'In 1918, a few months before the end of the war, we both got wounded. I was the lucky one. But Will... He is in a wheelchair now, and half his face bears some very deep scars. His mind, his spirit has gone. Oh, I have nightmares and cold sweats and the like, but I guess I am stronger than him, physically and mentally. He has very bad days and bad ones... Never good days. He doesn't speak, ever. His mother only has him left, now.

She had been a widow for a long time when the war broke out, and Will's two brothers died in the war as well. She is doing her best for him, but there's no money, and she has suffered so much, it has broken her. So when the war was over, I came to see Will and his mother straight from France, and I never left. I have no family of my own.'

'I moved into their spare room and earned a living doing jobs around the village to pay for the three of us. Then five years ago, someone from the village told me that there was a head gardener's position at the 'big house'. I had been a gardener before the war, a good one. I used to work for the City of London. This job was perfect because it is so well paid, and I have accommodation, so I do not take up the extra room at Will's house. I share some of my wages, and Mrs Abbott gives me food for them as well, which really helps.'

After a short pause, Eliott Mills concluded: 'So you see, this is why I do not know what to do. What will the outcome be? I cannot walk away from the job. I have to do everything I can not to be dismissed. I have to provide for Will and his mother. I would never forgive myself if they fell into abject poverty because of me. They wouldn't be able to pay the rent and would get kicked out of their house. Will wouldn't be cared for as well as he is now, and I would never find anything as good in the area. I need to deal with this. But I do not know how.'

The image of Sophia Chronos' fierce, frenzied eyes as she had looked down on him from her bedroom window came into Adam's mind. What on earth was wrong with Lady Chronos?

SIX

Dimitri had a restless night. His ears were on alert, preventing him from falling asleep. He was on the lookout for footsteps in the corridor, a cautiously closing door, even some whispering voices; anything that would indicate that Mr Tuckfield was finally back in his bedroom. The boy got out of bed several times and, ignoring his freezing toes on the cold floorboards, made his way to the study; there, he stood with his left ear against the wall that separated the small classroom and the tutor's bedroom. Nothing... Not a sound...

Each time he was back under the covers, he remembered the screaming, chilling voices he had heard the previous evening. They had curled his blood with their inhuman, disembodied overtones; they were sounds no human being should ever have to hear, even someone like him. He could cope with the silent apparitions, but a whirlwind of ghostly voices screaming their way out of The Underworld had rendered him perplexed and, yes, rather scared. He knew that something had happened, but he just didn't know what. He needed to tell someone.

In the morning, the boy found himself in a rather gloomy mood. Yet again alone in the study, he half-heartedly carried on with the illustration he had started the day before. Ten minutes into his work, he heard some noise in the bedroom next door. Mr Tuckfield was back! Where had he spent the night?

The boy was dying to go and see his tutor but decided to remain in his chair: the perfect picture of the angelic child absorbed in his work despite all those dark thoughts racing through his mind. One name kept coming back into his head: Maeve Hayward. He had sensed a bond, an unspoken complicity between her and Mr Tuckfield.

Dimitri found the young woman in turns attractive and repulsive. He didn't really understand what she was about. She was pleasant to look at, with her lustrous hair, her big green eyes, her painted lips, her powdery face and her colourful outfits. She was so different from the other people in the house who, with the exception of the vivacious Mrs Abbott, were all dull, quiet and rather forlorn, as if constantly pining for something else, somewhere else, far away from Whitemoor Hall.

The boy was disturbed by Maeve's sparkling, voluble personality and cheeky self-confidence. He wasn't used to it at all and found it disquieting. And now, she seemed to have stolen his tutor. Was it at all possible that Mr Tuckfield preferred to spend time with his stepfather's niece rather than with him, Dimitri? It wouldn't be fair. Mr Tuckfield was *his* tutor, hired to teach *him* and keep *him* company. The young man hadn't been at Whitemoor Hall long, and already, the boy had decided that he wanted Mr Tuckfield to be his friend too. He was the only one who could understand him and his aspirations. He was the only one who had shown any genuine interest in what he was doing and thinking. He felt comfortable in his company, safer than he had ever been.

He wondered… If he were to tell Mr Tuckfield about the ghosts, would the tutor lose interest in Maeve and spend more time exploring the estate with him? Surely a confession would pique his curiosity…

'Oh, you're already in here! Good morning, Dimitri.'

The door of the study had just opened and Adam Tuckfield had stopped on the threshold, not expecting to find his young pupil at his desk on a Sunday morning. The boy didn't reply immediately to the tutor's greeting. Instead, he feigned to concentrate on his work. He composed his face: bowed head and puckered lips, frowning. He uttered a feeble 'Morning' without lifting or turning his head.

Dimitri heard his teacher's quiet footsteps behind him and felt his eyes on his back.

'Have you had a good Saturday, Dimitri?'

'Mmmh…'

'Don't you want to tell me all about it? I didn't see you at all yesterday afternoon, so I guessed you'd been exploring.'

'Well I would have wanted you to come with me but you were busy elsewhere!'

It had come out loud and clear but with a sulky and reproachful tone. Dimitri had spun on his chair as he had said it, dislodging the book he had been working with; it fell on the floor with a neat slapping noise. He looked at his tutor with alarm, aware of how that must have sounded. He had answered back.

Mr Tuckfield had a few sheets of paper and a pen in front of him; his two hands were resting on the smooth wooden surface of his desk, and he was studying his pupil with incredulity.

'Are you feeling well, Dimitri?'

The boy crossed his arms, frowning more than ever.

'I was looking for you yesterday evening. I've got something to show you.' He paused, then carried on with what he thought was a meaningful look in his eyes. 'You didn't sleep in your bedroom last night. It's not good.'

The young man was temporarily rendered speechless. *Touché.* Dimitri felt quite satisfied.

'Well, I... I...' The teacher paused. 'How do you know that anyway? Have you been spying on me? No, don't tell me! I don't want you to have to denounce yourself. It wouldn't be fair... You know, Dimitri, I am quite entitled to have some time for myself at the weekend.'

'But...' Dimitri was quite vexed. He now realised that he had crossed the line, because Mr Tuckfield looked quite cross with him. Maybe it was time to change tactics.

The boy bent over and picked up his book from the floor. He held the cover in front of Mr Tuckfield's face.

'See, I have been reading 'The Canterville Ghost' again, and I am trying to draw a portrait of the ghost,' the boy said in earnest.

Relief came over the tutor's features, but Dimitri was not about to give up that easily. He had been fired-up by his discovery the previous day, and was now desperate to share it with his tutor, even though he resented his betrayal. He jumped out of his chair, still holding the book in one hand.

'Please, do come with me to the tower again! I have something to show you... Something strange... I don't know what it is, but I think it might be important! Please!' The boy's voice was pleading, impatient. As Adam did not reply, he reiterated: 'Please, Mr Tuckfield! You are the only one who's seen the portrait before, you have to go and have a look at it again... Something's happened to it.'

The teacher glanced suspiciously at him.

'What's happened to it? I thought nobody went up there.'

'Oh, I am sure nobody's been up there! You have seen it yourself, there's nothing on that floor. It's not something someone has done. It's... it's *inside* the painting.'

'What do you mean, 'inside the painting'?'

'I don't know... You'd have to see it for yourself. Shall we go now?'

*   *   *

And there they were again, the two of them, making their way along the bare corridors of the unused parts of the house, going up narrow staircases, opening creaky doors with only their own echoing footsteps for company. It felt like a real life computer game, thought Adam; one of those in which you need to open one door after another to move onto the next stage. He was surprised by the idea; the very thought of a computer game felt alien in his mind, so used was he to his enforced 1920s environment.

Any thoughts about his previous 21st century life were far and between; they felt like dreams, vague flashes of memory, floating images and sound snippets. They belonged to someone else.

Once again, they had to go via the servants' staircase, squeeze through the narrow door leading to the passage in the tower. As he had done the previous time, Dimitri hesitated before stepping into the corridor, but there was no sign of the translucent ragged girl. Finally, they pushed the heavy door of the tower, and Dimitri stepped to the side to let Adam look at the picture.

At first, the young man's eyes struggled to accustom themselves to the low level of light. The uniform greyness of the sky permeated everything, and the tall narrow windows allowed for minimum light to enter the space.

Again, Adam's heart gave a jolt at the sight of the woman. There was something so unnerving about this portrait and the memory of his dream was still troubling him…

Hang on, thought Adam. What had Dimitri said? 'Something's happened *inside* the painting.' The young man narrowed his eyes and concentrated.

The changes were subtle, and you needed to have observed the artwork attentively first time around to notice anything. The colours in the portrait had dulled, making the whole painting look somehow less concrete, more evanescent, as if it had been exposed to the elements for too long. The jet black hair had turned a paler shade of brownish-grey and looked flatter, duller. The rich chocolate of the skin was now closer to milky brown and the violet eyes were now a washed-out grey; the formerly sumptuous dress had lost all its lustrous quality.

It was as if something had sucked out the very essence of the painting, the sheer boldness of execution that had made such an impact on Adam.

In the background, the rose garden was devastated: it had been an explosion of colours with the roses in full bloom – so well executed that Adam could have sworn that he had smelled their sweet perfume. Now all that was left was the desolate vision of an abandoned garden: the roses were faded and defeated, their petals and leaves brown and shrunken by decay strewn all over the dirty-looking gravel. The faint odour of rotting plants wafted through the room.

Adam didn't move for a long time, his face lifted towards the portrait; he was trying to make sense of what he was witnessing. He then turned to the boy, who had remained silent the whole time.

'How is that even possible?' wondered Adam out loud.

Dimitri shrugged.

'I don't know. It was already like that yesterday when I came in.'

'Could it be that something has damaged it over the past few weeks? Has a window been opened?'

The boy shook his head. Adam's eyes reverted to the artwork.

'It almost looks as if… As if Lady Whitemoor were actually fading away from the painting, taking the vitality of those roses with her.'

Dimitri stood with his hands behind his back, his little mouth twisted with indecision. A theory had started to form in the further recesses of his brain, born out of his numerous brushes with ghostly visions and strange phenomena. Adam noticed the change in the boy's attitude.

'Dimitri? I'm wondering whether you know more about this than you care to admit.'

The boy was looking at the floor so intensely that the little brown marks on the irregular boards had begun to hypnotise him. His 11-year-old brain was working hard to come out with a decision, the right one. What if he made a mistake? But his tutor was offering him the opportunity to at last unburden himself. Now was the time to tell someone. But would Mr Tuckfield believe him? And what if he were to go and tell Vangelis and Saturnin Bloom? What if they called the doctor and then sent him away to one of those terrifying asylums he had read about? He lifted his head and looked straight at his teacher.

'Maybe she is coming back,' he ventured.

'Coming back? From where?'

'*From the dead.*'

Adam felt himself grow pale. His hands turned cold and a shiver travelled down his spine. This is not what he wanted. After what Vangelis and Saturnin had told him, he should have seen it coming. He looked at Dimitri curiously.

'Now, then. What exactly do you mean by that?'

The boy's voice came out weaker and more hesitant than before.

'That… that someone painted Lady Whitemoor's portrait when she was still alive, and then she died, and now she's coming back. She is getting *out* of the painting.'

Adam frowned.

'That's an interesting theory. So her image is gradually fading as she comes back to life?'

'She's not coming back to life. She's just coming back.'

The boy sounded like an old and wise man, admonishing his tutor for his ignorance of this all important difference.

'OK! My mistake… Tell me, Dimitri, do you know a lot about that kind of thing?'

'What thing?'

'Well, I mean… What are we talking about here, then? Ghosts?'

Again, a small twitch of the mouth. Dimitri wasn't entirely sure about his tutor, whose tone softened somehow before he pressed on with his questioning.

'Dimitri. I remember two things. The first is that the first time we met, you asked me if I believed in ghosts. When I explained that I didn't, I clearly saw the disappointment in your eyes. I took it as a natural questioning coming from a curious and intelligent boy who reads a lot of books. Then came the day when I gave you 'The Canterville Ghost' to read. You became upset, and I could see that this was genuine distress and yet, I couldn't understand what had upset you so much. Now, I am going to ask you one simple question, and you can answer by 'yes' or 'no' if you so wish: have you seen or can you see ghosts?'

Dimitri inhaled deeply; his answer came out sounding like a huge sigh of relief:

'Yes.'

Adam put his hand on the boy's arm, as much to stabilise himself as to encourage his pupil. The remains of his personal non-belief system had just collapsed on the dusty cold floor of the tower.

'And do you get... scared?'

'No, not really.'

'What do they look like?'

'I don't know... like people, I guess. But not... real. Here, but not really here.' The boy was struggling to convey the immateriality of the apparitions. He carried on: 'They look a little ill and sad, and often, they cannot speak. I mean, they *try* to speak to me, but no sound comes out. Only once I've been able to hear one of them.'

Dimitri thought about the man with the white tunic and his soft, melodic voice. The boy felt something in the air, this familiar, barely perceptible change in the atmosphere of the room. The tower was a miserable and cold place, but the temperature had now dropped several degrees further. Dimitri froze, alert, his eyes darting around and his hair standing on end.

'What is happening, Dimitri?'

'Shush... Wait.' The boy gestured to his tutor to be quiet, then he murmured: 'Can you feel the cold? I think she is here...'

Adam adopted his pupil's hushed voice.

'Who? Lady Whitemoor?'

Dimitri shook his head.

'No. The little girl who was here last time.'

The boy walked cautiously to the door and had a peek outside. On the dirty floor of the corridor and exactly at the same place she had been the previous time, sat the little ragged girl. She was distractedly twisting a strand of her long fair hair while humming a song – although Dimitri couldn't *hear* her humming, he just *knew* she was. She let go of her hair, looked at Dimitri and smiled. Tears came to the boy's eyes as he was overwhelmed by sadness.

Adam had followed the boy and was now standing on the threshold of the room. He couldn't see anything beyond his pupil: the hallway was as empty as could be. Without turning round, Dimitri gently addressed his tutor.

'You cannot see her, can you?'

Adam's eyes were burning under the effort he was making to try and spot any sign of the girl in the empty space.

'I'm afraid I can't. What does she look like?'

'She is small and frail and looks quite sick. She has long blond hair and a blue or grey dress that's rather damaged, with rips here and there. She is sitting cross-legged on the floor here.' He pointed at the bottom of the wall halfway along the corridor.

Adam slowly advanced towards the spot Dimitri had indicated. The little girl jumped to her feet as quickly as she could and vanished into thin air just as Adam's hand was about to make contact with her hair. Dimitri could have sworn that she had opened her mouth to scream, but of course so sound had come out. He sighed.

'She's gone, now.'

'She's gone? Where? How?'

'She just faded away!'

Adam looked at the floor near the wall where the ghost was supposed to have been. How could he be sure that the boy was not making it all up? But then, a few weeks earlier, when he had still been ensconced in his miserable 21st century existence, he wouldn't have listened to anything this boy would have said. He would have tried to put all that nonsense out of his head as quickly as possible. Now though, he tended to think that the child was actually telling the truth. If Saturnin Bloom and Vangelis Chronos could travel to the 21st century and bring him back to 1925, and if an ancient Egyptian god could walk this earth pretending to be a scientist's secretary, then yes, he was ready to believe that ghosts existed, why not? After all, the way he looked at it, it was probably the most believable thing he had heard since he had met Maeve on the Tube...

'There is something we could try,' said Dimitri, suddenly...

'Sorry?'

The boy flushed slightly.

'I'd like you to believe me, you know, that I really see ghosts. There is one thing we could try to prove to you that they *do* exist. I might be able to make you *feel their presence...*'

Adam felt the cold fingers of dread tug at his heart.

'But I *do* believe you.' A glance at Dimitri told him that the boy was not entirely convinced. He probably needed to gain some credibility points. Adam remembered the séance at the cottage the previous night; meddling with spirits appeared to be everything but safe. Imagine something went wrong?

'Are you sure about this?' he asked the boy.

'It might not work, but at least we'd tried! I need to go back to my room to get my map.'

Dimitri was now behaving like a real little expert. He looked so earnest and knowledgeable, serious and curious. He was like a small scientist, protective yet extremely proud of the discovery that he had been keeping all to himself for all those years.

After a last glance at the portrait, the pair pulled the heavy door shut and made their way back to their quarters in the East Wing. None of them spoke. Adam had his head full of the vanishing portrait and Dimitri couldn't stop thinking about the lonely little ghost in the tattered dress.

Once back in the more familiar part of the house, Dimitri asked his tutor to wait in the study whilst he went to his room to fetch his map.

Adam had played along with it; he was finding Dimitri's seriousness and quiet determination rather touching. He understood that it had been a huge decision for the boy to reveal his unsettling 'gift'.

The young man felt rather nervous and walked to the window. He could feel the cold air behind the glass, and was tempted to go out for a bracing walk rather than plunge once again into the claustrophobic innards of Whitemoor Hall. He could push further towards the abbey, maybe. He hadn't been there for weeks, since that first time when he and Dimitri had ran away, pursued by that bloodcurdling howling choir. He had decided to indulge his pupil though, and he would stick to it. Something important might happen, and he wouldn't have missed it for all the fresh air in the world.

He peered into the rose garden below, lost in his thoughts, and was still there by the window when, 10 minutes later, Dimitri reappeared holding a wide sheet of paper.

'I have it now!' He waved the paper in the air.

'Maybe now you could explain to me where we are going?'

'I'd like to take you to the ballroom.'

'The ballroom? I didn't know there was a ballroom here.'

Adam thought about the gloomy, mirthless atmosphere of the house. A ballroom was the last thing he'd expect to find at Whitemoor Hall.

Dimitri shrugged, although he understood what his tutor meant. There hadn't been a ball at Whitemoor Hall for decades. The boy had read about balls and they sounded like fairytale-like affairs. He would have loved to have witnessed one of those glittery events, maybe hidden behind a door…

From there, he would have been able to listen to the music, observe the musicians – nobody played any music in the house, and he only knew about it because, once again, he had read about it. It was not that easy to conjure up in your mind the idea of instruments, notes and melodies when you had never heard any music before. He had often wondered what it would be like… Something akin to vibrations reaching you through the air and exploding in your ears.

'It's downstairs, in the West Wing,' he replied, pointing at a large rectangular shape on his map, then running his finger along the traced lines on the paper. 'You can access the corridor from the right-hand side of the Great Hall; it leads to a series of several rooms that are no longer used now: the billiard room, the music room and the ballroom. It is not very far from the service corridor that leads to the kitchen. The dining room is on the other side.'

'I see. So we are making our way to the ballroom, and then what?'

'You'll see when we're there! Let's go!'

As they were coming out of the study, they heard some strange huffing, puffing and shuffling noises. Soon, Mrs Abbott appeared, cautiously wobbling her wide body down the stairs; one hand was holding a large kitchen cloth and the other was gripping the banister for support. With immense relief, she finally walked down the final step, very much like a seasick boat passenger setting foot on dry land for the first time in weeks. She spotted the young man and the boy and shook her head at them, while trying to catch her breath. Her large moon face was flushed and a glistening layer of sweat was covering her wide forehead. She looked very displeased indeed. She struggled to speak at first, pausing every other word.

'Pfff… pffff… No, no, no… I tell you what… Mr Tuckfield… That was… the very last time… I am… going up… and down… those stairs…' She gestured at the staircase behind her as if they were the most contemptuous things in the whole world. She spotted a chair against the wall and let herself fall on it heavily, her two hands on her thighs.

'What's happened?' enquired Dimitri.

Mrs Abbott's displeasure was obvious.

'It's Sunday, isn't it? So everyone else has disappeared off to whatever they do at this cursed abbey of theirs. Once again, I have been left *on my own*, dealing with everything down there,' she pointed at the floor, 'and Lady Chronos needed some tea and biscuits, and of course, I've had to go all the way up there,' she pointed at the ceiling, 'to bring them to her. I have been saying it for months; this cannot carry on like this! When Miss Finch was around, she helped me a little bit every week. I know that she was a busybody and that it was a way of putting her nose where she shouldn't have, but at least it gave me some respite... My knees have been hurting awfully these past few weeks. I want a kitchen maid who is not part of this... this... cult there, and who will work even on Sundays if I tell her to. Otherwise, I am throwing in the towel, honestly, I am!' She threw her hands up in the air.

Dimitri looked genuinely alarmed and joined his hands in a pleading gesture.

'Oh no, Mrs Abbott! Don't go! Please! You're the best cook we've ever had!'

Mrs Abbott ruffled the boy's fair hair with affection, obviously touched.

'Actually, sweetheart, I'm the *only* cook you've had since you've arrived here, and you don't really eat anything, but I appreciate the compliment all the same. Thank you. See, I am not in my prime anymore and going up and down all those flights of stairs is killing me... If I had one person to help me on Sundays, it would really make a difference; someone from the village would be nice. I do appreciate Lord Chronos's goodwill, you know, taking those damaged people on and giving them a position, but sometimes I think they abuse that very same generosity. I've worked in a big house before and the rules were so much stricter! Not that it bothers me personally, but I do think there should be a few more rules in place...' Once again, Mrs Abbott shook her head despondently. 'So there, you two. What are you up to? Are you going for a walk?'

'Yes, Mrs Abbott,' replied Dimitri.

'Dimitri is going to show me some of the things he has learned about the house over the years.'

'Ah! He is clever, he is, Master Dimitri.' There, she lowered her voice and put on a conspiratorial facial expression. 'I'm glad he's got you as a teacher. That governess, Miss Finch... She was not nice to him. Too strict, wasn't she, Master Dimitri?' The boy acquiesced timidly. 'It's good for him to have a young man that can stimulate him. I mean, it is good to read books and spend a lot of time on your own, it stimulates the imagination and all that, but too much of a good thing, you know, as they say...'

With effort, the cook rose from her chair with a determined look.

'Well, then. I need to go back to the kitchen to have a look at what I've got for lunch and dinner. I also have to prepare the list for the market tomorrow. Would you like something to eat before you go?'

'No, thank you, Mrs Abbott. We'll be fine,' replied Adam.

'Very well, then. Enjoy yourself.'

And the cook shuffled down to the ground floor.

When no noise could be heard from downstairs, Dimitri and Adam started on their way to the ballroom.

*   *   *

The carved, gothic style double doors turned on their hinges with a certain amount of difficulty brought on by decades of disuse. Adam and Dimitri sneezed as their presence dislodged the dust that had accumulated in every nook and cranny of the long rectangular room.

The spectacular plasterwork on the vaulted ceiling had most certainly been impressive in its heyday; it was now yellowing and peeling and had been eaten away by damp; cancerous stains were spoiling the previously smooth plaster and spreading like gangrene along the walls whose colour was now impossible to determine – some kind of dirty, faded blue, perhaps. The vast white marble fireplace was covered with grime and dead insects, and the huge mirror that hung above it had seen much better days: its silvering had been badly eroded by moisture over the years, and its surface was now covered with an ill-looking, cloudy black spread.

Adam walked around, speechless. His face went up to the big plaster rosettes from which dropped the heavy-looking chandeliers; no light had shone in there for more than sixty years; there were four triple windows through which the pale light of the day was tentatively coming in.

It was a sad sight. That large room had been designed purely for pleasure and entertainment; it now stood so empty and pointless, with nobody to admire the craftsmanship of the plasterwork or the woodcarvings on the doors... There were no revellers to feel special under the hundreds of lights carried by the enormous chandeliers.

'So why have you taken me here, Dimitri?' asked Adam, his voice unexpectedly amplified by the vacant space.

The boy had been wandering around the room slowly.

'Shuuuush!' he ordered, stopping in his track, eyes darting around the ballroom, hand in the air. Adam joined Dimitri in the middle of what would have been the dance floor.

'Are you expecting something to happen?' he whispered.

'I don't know… I thought that maybe… Let's be silent for a while.'

For several minutes, they stood there side by side: the man and the boy scrutinised the room, their breathing shortened. Adam didn't know what to expect, and was looking for a movement in the heavy curtains that framed the windows, for a shadow in the distressed mirror or for a sudden gust of sooty wind coming in from the chimney.

Dimitri was concentrating hard. All the sightings he had witnessed hadn't been solicited; he had never asked to see anyone. The ghosts had all come to him uninvited, catching him unawares at first, until he had learned to recognise the signs… This time, though, he *wanted* them to appear when asked to. He was not like the psychics he had read about, those men and women who stood around tables and joined hands and invoked the spirits of the dead, harassing them into appearing and bullying them into manifesting themselves to the living. The boy had always thought that he didn't have any right to do this, nor did he have the will or even the *need* to communicate with them.

But this time, it was different. He wanted the ghosts to appear so he could try and see whether he could nudge Mr Tuckfield into seeing or at least feeling them. He didn't really know how to do it, so he just closed his eyes and tried to conjure up in his head the image of what a ball should be like and mentally asked for the ghosts of the dancers to materialise.

As nothing at all seemed to be happening, Dimitri felt his resolve begin to flag. To his right, he could hear his tutor breathe – they were both facing the monumental fireplace – and he had to admit to himself that he was glad he was not on his own. He twisted his mouth in a sign of disappointment and sighed. Then he said in a very low voice:

'I do not think there is anyone here today.'

Just at that moment, Dimitri felt the air around him change, as if particles suddenly crystallised; the light in the room, which had been low and wintery despite the large windows, turned brighter. The boy looked up to see if his tutor had noticed anything, but the young man was still looking glumly at the fireplace, his eyes vaguely glazed over.

To be true, Adam had grown impatient but had tried to hide his restlessness for fear of upsetting the boy, who was dead serious about the whole thing. The child had opened up to him, so he shouldn't let him down. He thought it to be his duty – 'duty', what a strange word! – to do his best to humour the child's unusual interests. He had come to the conclusion that not doing so could damage the boy irreparably.

In front of Dimitri's eyes, small lights started to rapidly glide along the floorboards, as if some crazed luminous insects had been executing a strange mating dance. They jerked and fluttered, swirled and whirled around the room. Then after a few seconds, some cloudy, misty threads joined the dots of light. The boy watched them, fascinated. *They* had arrived; *they* were there, around him, ready to reveal themselves... It was only a matter of seconds. The boy seized his tutor's arm and pulled him away.

'Let's clear the floor now!' Dimitri ordered his bewildered teacher, dragging him to the window at the end of the ballroom, as much against the windowsill as possible.

'What on earth is happening?'

'They're coming... They need all the available space to dance!'

The young man stared at his young charge in astonishment.

'To *what?*'

Dimitri looked severely at his tutor and explained, in a voice indicating that this actually was the most logical thing in the world:

'*To dance*. They are having a ball and we should get out of the way.' His eyes went back to the room.

It was miraculous to see. Slowly, the air filled with movement, invisible at first apart from the flickering of the multitude of hazy will o' the wisps swirling around at floor level. Then the ghostly lights started to rise, turning into human-shaped white shadows. Soon, the scene was revealed to Dimitri's curious eyes: couples waltzed gracefully, while onlookers fanned themselves or twirled their moustache. An orchestra was playing at the other end of the dance floor, filling the ballroom with a music Dimitri couldn't hear.

The room was now full of immaterial bodies covered in the fineries of their time: this was the ghostly re-enactment of the last ball that had taken place at Whitemoor Hall in 1854, at a time when Lord Whitemoor still thought he could rescue his disastrous marriage by throwing sumptuous social events for his exotic wife.

If the room was crowded, not a sound was coming out of the exuberant attendees. It was all very similar to watching a silent movie without the usual tinkly piano soundtrack, with the spectral, ethereal protagonists conveying their whole being through gestures and facial expressions.

Dimitri was very excited by what he was witnessing, even though he found it incredibly frustrating not to be able to hear the music or the conversations.

'What do you see?' enquired Adam, prompted by the boy's starry-eyed expression.

'It is full of people,' whispered Dimitri. 'A lot of them are dancing. The men are wearing evening suits and the ladies long dresses, jewellery, ribbons and flowers. There is an orchestra playing there,' he pointed at the wall at the other end of the room, 'and some people are sitting and standing on one side; they are talking and watching the dancers.' Dimitri now had a big smile on his face and his eyes shone with pleasure. 'But I cannot hear anything. It is a great shame.' He stood upright, his fists clenched with excitement, his eyes jumping from one couple to the other. Then the pairs came to a halt, separated and turned to applaud the orchestra, all at the same time. The musicians bowed to their audience, and threw themselves into their next piece of music. New pairings were formed and the dancers started moving again. Dimitri resumed talking to his tutor without taking his eyes off the action.

'Honest? You haven't noticed anything, not even the change in lighting or temperature?'

Adam realised that he was indeed freezing.

'I feel cold, yes, but I cannot see anything,' he said regretfully.

The young man stared at what was, for him, the still crumbling, dusty, empty ballroom. He tried to visualise what Dimitri was seeing, without success.

An idea suddenly came into his head. After a second hesitation and to the boy's horror, Adam stepped out of his corner, walked straight into the centre of the room and turned to face Dimitri, who could only watch as his tutor found himself surrounded by the dancers who would move past him – some went straight through him even – oblivious to the presence of the living man in their midst.

Adam remained there, his arms stretched on either side of his body, his palms upturned. He closed his eyes; then something extraordinary happened: he could feel the air being displaced around him. Soon, he became aware of the hems of wide, long dresses brushing past him. Dozens of bodies were close to him now, moving around him. He recognised that particular feeling you have when you are at a party, in a room full of excited people, only one of the many at that particular place looking for entertainment and excitement. He so wanted to open his eyes, but he couldn't, he simply couldn't! Just in case he broke the spell.

He remained there, standing firm under the now burning bright chandeliers. And then he thought he could smell a heady mix made of floral perfumes, spicy cigars, leather, cologne and soap. He was no longer at Whitemoor Hall in 1925 but further back in time, when Amunet reigned supreme over the Whitemoor estate, claiming more and more of her husband's influence and good health with every passing day...

The double doors opened slowly, letting in the dusty atmosphere of the unused corridor outside. Dimitri, still standing against the windowsill but entranced by the scene in front of him, barely registered the human form that had entered the room at the other end.

The effect of the intruder's presence was instant: the orchestra stopped playing, the swirl of couples came to a halt, the silent conversations died out. Adam opened his eyes and all perception of the ghostly presences was instantly lost to him.

Dimitri saw the dozens of mouths open to scream, and panic spread around the room as the ghosts acknowledged the person who had just disturbed their festivities. The human shapes melted away and joined up to form one big mass of cloudy matter that began to swirl towards the ceiling before splitting into hundreds of tiny luminescent strands that instantly disappeared into thin air. Dimitri was left stunned and momentarily half blind; Adam instinctively turned towards the intruder.

Sophia Chronos was standing a few feet away from the door, imperious. In her white garments, she looked as ghostly as the spirits that had just left the room. She stared with distaste at the empty space and at the columns of dust floating across the room in the weak daylight.

'I believe you owe me an explanation as to what you've been doing in such a place?'

The unexpected presence of his mother made Dimitri quickly come back to his senses.

'Mother!' he whispered under his breath.

'Lady Chronos! How have you found your way here?'

Adam took a step towards Sophia, who turned to her son's tutor, eyes flaming.

'Have you ever thought that I could be feeling claustrophobic, staying in those rooms of mine day in and day out? I *too* get bored. I *too*, need distraction, and it doesn't come often at Whitemoor Hall, believe me. I was… I was on the threshold of my bedroom about to get out and call out after Mrs Abbott when I heard you speak to her downstairs. I don't know what went through my mind. I followed you from a distance and stayed outside the ballroom for a while. I wasn't sure whether I should make my presence known. And now I'm here.' She smiled; it was a strange, dreamy smile.

Sophia Chronos looked exhausted. And indeed, she was. Her mood swings and the ups and downs in her energy levels had been far more extreme than usual, lately. Previously, they had all been down to her laudanum consumption, but she had stopped taking the drug. After all, her hip and loins were not hurting as much, were they? And it also meant that she wouldn't have to go and pester her husband for some more any time soon. It had felt liberating. So why, if she was genuinely better, did she feel so queer at times? It was as if… as if a *foreign body* had somehow found its way inside her and taken possession of her senses. She was no longer herself.

Sometimes, she would find herself out on the lawn, or walking along a corridor without remembering the reason of her presence there. It was exactly the way she had arrived at the ballroom; she was standing there, face to face with her son and his tutor, unable to remember feeling the impulse that had made her follow them all the way to this abandoned room; at the same time, a part of her knew exactly what she was doing.

She started walking across the room slowly, her limp barely there now. She was only feeling a slight discomfort; years of pain had left an imprint on her brain and prevented her from positioning her feet properly. Time would give her the confidence to walk without fear, she knew it. Her long dress trailed behind her, the heels of her soft leather slippers hitting the blistered floorboards at regular intervals.

Dimitri and Adam were staring at her. She was not welcome in the ballroom, not at all. She had interrupted their experiment and scared off the ghosts they had taken so long to conjure up; she had broken the spell, her presence tearing up the thin thread that had, for a few minutes, connected the realm of the dead to that of the living. Despite this, they couldn't take their eyes off her ethereal silhouette advancing across the ballroom, fragile and yet, strangely menacing.

'Tell me, Mr Tuckfield, do you often follow my son in his adventures around the estate? I've heard that if you are not working on your lessons, you still spend a considerable amount of time in the company of the boy, even on Saturdays and Sundays.' Sophia turned to Adam and cocked her graceful head to one side. 'Mr Tuckfield, you spend five days a week between the four walls of the study teaching the child. You do deserve a rest!'

Adam swallowed, still recovering from his sensory experience of a few minutes ago; its abrupt end had left him out of balance. He was finding it hard to concentrate on what Lady Chronos was telling him; his head was floating in some kind of gauzy, woolly cloud.

'It is part of my employment contract, Lady Chronos. I am to spend a lot of time with Dimitri in order to, er, provide him with a solid education and life skills.' His voice was shaky, far from assured.

As for Dimitri, he was vexed that his mother had, once again, chosen to ignore his presence. He felt small, invisible and insignificant, when this was supposed to be his moment! His big revelation! She had spoilt everything! At least, Mr Tuckfield didn't treat him that way... He coughed to attract her attention. She looked at him as if he were a mere pet that had strayed in the very room in which he was not allowed.

'Child, I need to speak with your tutor in private. I wish you could leave us now. Go back to your bedroom and keep yourself occupied until I have finished with Mr Tuckfield.'

Dimitri's cheeks and ears were turned bright red by the offence.

'But Mr Tuckfield and I...'

A shadow passed on Sophia's pale face. She left Adam's side to come nearer her son.

'I will not repeat it a third time: could you please go to your room *now*.' She was pointing at the double doors that had been left ajar when she had entered the room. Dimitri's bottom lip protruded in a stubborn pout and he crossed his arms, eyebrows furrowed.

'I don't want to,' he declared firmly.

Before Adam – or Dimitri – could react, Sophia seized her son's arm with surprising speed and strength and dragged him towards the entrance to the ballroom. Dimitri had recoiled, but not quickly enough. He couldn't remember having had any physical contact with his mother before, and this first time felt like the cold claws of a dragon closing on his arm. Shock had made him swallow air the wrong way and he started coughing at first, then began uttering low cries of protest. Adam, still slow to react, didn't know what to do and followed, protesting feebly.

'Lady Chronos, I can assure you that Dimitri was not doing anything wrong!' he finally exclaimed, just as Sophia was pushing her son into the corridor. She pulled the doors shut under the tearful and bewildered eyes of the boy, who had fallen onto the distressed carpet outside the ballroom.

Soon, all the child could see were the two gigantic carved panels that had been closed on him. It took him several minutes before he stood up, went to the doors and applied his ear against the sculpted wood. It was so thick that he just couldn't hear a sound coming from inside. Defeated and befuddled by his mother's new-found strength, he thought it more prudent to walk back to his room and wait for his tutor. Poor Mr Tuckfield! He would have to face his mother alone…

Adam had followed too closely, and had been just behind Sophia when she had pushed Dimitri out and closed the doors. When she turned round, he was so close that he could smell her sweet floral perfume. He understood too late that he had made a mistake.

Sophia Chronos shook her full head of blond curls and smiled a different smile to the one she had adopted earlier. Her whole face suddenly radiated an odd type of satisfaction, as if she were about to achieve something she had longed for for a long time.

'Mr Tuckfield,' she started. Adam was on his guard. The image of Sophia Chronos standing outside the greenhouse came into his mind, and he took a step back. His eyes locked with Sophia's brown… no… *violet* eyes… Violet? Lady Chronos didn't have dark violet eyes, her eyes were *brown*, he was sure of it… Or at least, they *used* to be. He remembered thinking her eyes were surprisingly dark for someone whose whole person was so pale, blonde and transparent. They had been the only things about her that had looked *solid* when he had seen her for the first time. But no, he could see them now, in front of him, looking at him with a feverish gleam in them. They were definitely *violet*.

He took another step back.

'Mr Tuckfield, do not worry yourself. I am not here to admonish you about the time you spend in the company of my son. On the contrary, I am very impressed by your dedication.'

Sophia was trying to keep close to him. He took another step back, she took a step forward. Now she brushed past him, and then she was behind him, circling him like a bird of prey circles its quarry.

'I have been told that you *do* find the time to relax and have your own entertainment.' Her voice was now heavy with meaning; she was close enough to whisper in his ear: 'You have been seen walking to the Guardian's Cottage and back several times over the past few weeks…' As he didn't reply, Sophia came back to stand in front of him. 'I wonder what it is you find at the Guardian's Cottage that we cannot offer you here in the house…' She paused. Her fingers found her dragonfly pendant among the folds of her bodice and she started playing with it dreamily. 'Do you feel lonely, Mr Tuckfield?'

Adam didn't like the way the conversation was going. He was feeling utterly uncomfortable, but somehow didn't have a clue about how to get out of the situation he found himself in. Sophia Chronos carried on talking despite his lack of response.

'I *do* feel lonely. *Every day. Constantly.*'

Suddenly, Sophia grabbed the lapel of his jacket and pulled him towards her, her small pink mouth gluttonously searching his lips. Even though he wanted to get away with all his might, Adam was prevented from doing so by the very vivid image that erupted in his mind and flashed in front of his eyes: that of the woman in the white tunic straddling him on his bed.

Sophia's mouth did not feel like that of a woman starved of love, but that of a greedy succubus with pointy teeth. He put his hands on both sides of her face to try and push her away, his fingers getting entangled in her medusa hair. He could feel himself running out of breath and panicking. If he lost consciousness now, who knows what might happen to him? He clenched his jaws as hard as he could, as if his life depended on it.

After what felt like an eternity, Sophia Chronos's face pulled away from his. Her look scared him: it was full of lust, anger, frustration and triumph. She still had her two hands on his upper arms, clutching at them.

'You are still a young man, Mr Tuckfield. This is an isolated house. Why do you ignore your nature? Why do you deny yourself something I'd only be glad to give you?'

Adam stared at the daylight that was pouring in from the large window behind her. He was desperate to get out there in the cold air, away from the stillness of the ballroom and its vague perfume of decay and decadence; away from the feverish clutches of this woman who, only recently, had been desperately shunning his presence. He tried to shake her off, but she hung on for a few more seconds.

'Mr Tuckfield... Adam... Let go of your fear and embrace me. We are alone here.'

Adam was not entirely sure about that last statement. A few minutes ago, the room had been full of revellers...

'No one will know,' Sophia declared. 'Then every day, I'll welcome you into my bedchamber, and none of us will ever be alone anymore...'

Adam took a large gulp of air and looked at Sophia Chronos in the eyes... In those violet eyes which were not hers, but those of an entirely different creature who was scrutinising him from beyond the grave, a creature so hungry and thirsty that it sowed fear in his heart and mind. What, or who had taken possession of Sophia Chronos? If he had previously admired her cold, haughty beauty, he now found her rather repulsive, with a face distorted by lasciviousness and need.

'I am not alone, Lady Chronos. I have Dimitri, and... I have Maeve.'

The smirk on Sophia Chronos's face melted instantly and a growl started from the bottom of her throat and rose as she tightened her grip on his arms. Instinctively, he lifted both his hands which he clasped around her forearms and yanked them off him. He felt a sharp pain on his left arm. Lady Chronos started walking erratically, throwing thundery looks at him as if they were the sharpest daggers one could find. She hissed:

'Maeve Hayward is a pathetic, vulgar little flapper without a penny to her name who will probably end up in the gutter with child as soon as she's back in London. You are better than that, Mr Tuckfield. You *deserve* better. You deserve ME.'

She stabbed her chest with her fingers as she said it. Then she turned to him, her curly hair escaping all around her face like leaking foam, two red dots burning under her eyes, her chin high in defiance and the huge violet eyes wide open.

'Did you know that I have been on the stage? I was good, you know, very good. I was the new darling of the London theatre scene, playing the best roles… Then I… I…'

A curious thing happened, then. Sophia's body jolted, then the overwhelming energy that had been fuelling her rage and keeping her frame up straight seemed to leave her. Her lithe body slumped forward slightly like a puppet whose master would have abandoned here and there without a second thought. She lifted her hand to her forehead and fell against him. Adam remained there with the weight of Sophia's body against his, his nose tickled by her curls. He could feel a stinging sensation on his arm and his head was filled with fog. *Now what?*

The young man suddenly realised how low the light was in the ballroom, which now looked rather lugubrious, its decaying elegance once again shrouded in silence. Nothing was left of the ball that had taken place only a few moments earlier. He needed to make a decision: he guessed that this part of the house wouldn't have been wired for electricity and therefore, if he didn't make his way back to the occupied part of Whitemoor Hall soon, he would have to blindly find his way out of the South Wing in the dark and burdened with the body of the unconscious Sophia Chronos.

Thankfully, a low moan signalled that the lady of the house was regaining consciousness. She slowly lifted her body to stand up, Adam supporting her by her elbows. She first struggled to open her eyes, only showing the whites; Adam thought she would slump towards him again, but she didn't and managed to focus on him: in those now dark hazel eyes, the young man could read confusion and anguish. She disengaged herself and looked around her.

'Where am I? What am I doing here?'

'We are in the ballroom, Lady Chronos. You followed us here, remember?'

'*Us?* Who else is here?' She asked, her eyes widening and searching anxiously the darkening corners of the room.

'Dimitri was here with us, but you made him understand that his presence was not required and sent him on his way rather, er, vigorously.'

Lady Chronos's face crumpled, and she lifted her right hand to her forehead; she was *trying* to remember. The void in her head was terrifying;

she felt like she was falling into a bottomless pit.

Adam saw the expression on her face go from complete inexpressiveness to recognition. Sophia Chronos's eyes were fixed on the floor and she stabbed the air with her index finger.

'Yes. I can remember coming down the stairs and walking along those unknown corridors. It was just never ending! And so… Dimitri was here,' she lifted her head towards Adam, 'but then… Where is he now?'

'I would have guessed that he is in his bedroom, quietly waiting for us to go back up. We should leave the ballroom as soon as possible, Lady Chronos, otherwise it will be too dark for us to find our way back to the main hall. Shall we?' He indicated the door. As she was about to take a step in the direction indicated, Sophia Chronos was seized by a dizzy fit and her legs gave way under her. Adam caught her just on time and steadied her.

'I'll help you. Use me as a crutch, if you wish,' he proposed, his two hands still firmly holding her tensed arms.

Sophia Chronos hesitated, glanced at his hands on the cream fabric of her overcoat; she was no longer under the influence of the strange cold liquid metal in her veins, although she could feel there was still a foreign consciousness within her, lurking among the folds of her flesh. The thought of this man holding her all the way to her rooms was too much for her to bear. She would have to find the strength to walk unaided. She straightened up as well as she could which, in her weakened state, was not much; she could feel her still numbed muscles protesting under the strain.

'Thank you, Mr Tuckfield, but I think I will be fine.'

And she started slowly towards the doors, remaining as straight as possible and wobbling a little.

They silently walked along the corridors; the light was so low that the walls, the floor and the ceiling would merge together and they could no longer see the worn out patterns on the carpet.

Sophia was painfully aware of her companion, her eyes always discreetly keeping him in check just in case he took her by surprise and seized her arm. She could have sworn she could hear him breathe; she was nervous and anxious, and the effort it took to prevent herself from tripping and falling was having an effect on her own breathing, which was coming in sharp, short gusts.

At last, there was light at the end of the tunnel of dark panelled corridors, and Adam and Sophia found themselves in the Great Hall. The light and the colourful richness of the room hurt their eyes. All the large Gothic wall sconces were lit up around the room and the balconies and were reflected on the shiny oak panelling all around. After the darkness and the desolation of the ballroom, it was a relief to come back to the bosom of the house and find it so welcoming.

To their surprise – and this probably explained the roaring fire in the monumental stone chimney – they found Vangelis Chronos pacing around, talking to himself. A small, round red velvet hat was perched on his white head; his beard was as immaculate as ever, and his crimson cloak made him look like an esoteric – and leaner – version of Father Christmas. He froze when he noticed his stepson's tutor and his wife emerge from under the wooden sculpted arch that led to the South Wing corridor.

He immediately pushed his meditation to one corner of his brain and rushed to the side of his beloved wife, who looked more frail than ever and a little shaken. Sophia Chronos exceptionally accepted her husband's support with relief – it was time, she could feel herself ready to fall to the floor – and leaned against his velvet-clad shoulder.

'Well, well, well, I was not expecting you down here!'

'Neither did we, Lord Chronos!' assured Adam, relieved to be able to entrust his problematic hostess to someone else. Vangelis looked at his wife.

'There, there, my angel, you're going to be alright; have you been feeling unwell?' he asked softly.

Sophia, without lifting her face towards her husband, replied meekly.

'Do not worry yourself. It is nothing. I might have exerted myself too much today. The pain has miraculously been much better lately, and I haven't been very careful, walking far too much and at too fast a pace. I ought to spare myself a little more.'

'Indeed you should,' agreed the scholar, before turning to Adam. 'Thank you very much for your assistance and incredible patience, Mr Tuckfield. The work you are doing in this house is invaluable to us.' He was looking towards the arch from which the tutor and his wife had just emerged; he frowned. 'Dimitri is not accompanying you?'

'He was,' lied Adam, 'but he went ahead to his room as he had... stained his shirt and wished to get it changed immediately. The boy is so particular about his appearance, isn't he?'

Vangelis shook his head sadly.

'I spend so much time in my study that I've never had the leisure to acquaint myself with Dimitri's preferences, I'm afraid.'

Sophia Chronos had recovered her balance and went silently to sit on one of the upholstered benches near the fireplace. For a few seconds, the only audible sound was the cracking of the logs in the chimney, then Sophia's voice startled the two men.

'I am surprised to find you out of your den. What have you been doing down the Great Hall?'

Adam couldn't determine whether her voice sounded genuinely interested or if she was faking this sudden interest in her husband's activities. Vangelis' beard trembled slightly and he explained, with an intensely serious face.

'From time to time, my endeavours become too much for me… I sometimes need to get some breathing space. The splendour of the Great Hall inspires me!' He lifted his arms and face upwards, looking up past the balconies and their galleries, up to the fabulous hammer beam ceiling and large stained glass windows far away above his head. 'I try and absorb the past and history of the building, you see, and nowhere is it so present than in this room. I feel power and inspiration here…'

Adam himself wondered then what kind of scenes the Great Hall had witnessed since the 16th century. He understood what Vangelis Chronos meant about buildings retaining traces and memories of the past… Dimitri himself could actually see the living shadows of the previous inhabitants wandering around the estate, forever haunting the places where they had been alive.

But he also wondered whether the scholar's interest in the atmosphere of the room went further than mere evocation of past times. Was there something more to these walls than just inert construction material? Maybe what Vangelis Chronos was really talking about was something more akin to an energy, a lifeblood running through the building, something he knew to be there and had been looking for since he had arrived at the estate? Maybe his newly discovered ancestor Aloysius Dean had left more than just a laboratory, a few old books and some notes on yellowing paper…

Adam's head was full of strange ideas and it felt ready to explode. He glanced at Sophia Chronos who was still sitting on her bench: her face was a smooth, emotionless blank canvas. She was staring at her hands; her long white fingers were fidgeting on her lap.

Vangelis Chronos had finished his wide-eyed tribute to the vaulted splendour of the Great Hall and readjusted his little hat, his eyes fixed on the glowing embers in the fireplace. He then turned to his wife at the exact moment she was stiffly rising from her bench; they started talking at the same time: Vangelis's 'Shall I have the honour of accompanying you safely to your room?' collided in mid-air with Sophia's 'I think I shall now retire to my room, gentlemen.'

Adam smiled, Lord Chronos beamed and Sophia nervously covered her mouth with her hand, visibly irritated. Vangelis approached his wife and offered his velvet-covered arm, which she took reluctantly. The scholar started talking to his spouse again as if she were a delicate, sensitive child and guided her towards the main staircase. Adam followed the odd couple noiselessly up the stairs. The conversation turned to mundane topics, such as the lack of staff on Sundays, and Vangelis promised to consult Saturnin Bloom on the very subject. Mrs Abbott had threatened to leave if she didn't get any support, he revealed; he then had to reassure Sophia after she had gasped at the news.

Adam took leave of the pair on the first floor of the East Wing and let them proceed up the stairs to the second floor. The relief he felt as he closed the bedroom door behind him was short-lived: he suddenly became aware of the sharp pain on his arm and removed his jacket: his off-white cotton shirt was now sporting a wide dark red stain and the dried blood made the material stick to his skin.

In shock, Adam rushed to the bathroom. There, he soaked the stain in hot water and then removed his shirt to clean the wound: he could clearly see five, surprisingly deep cuts on his skin. The young man remembered Sophia Chronos's hand clasped on his arm. The marks on his flesh looked as if someone had attempted to tear off his inked skin with their bare hands. That didn't make any sense: Lady Chronos hadn't been scratching at his arm like a panther; she had merely grasped his arm a little bit too tightly. She couldn't have made those cuts through the jacket and the shirt, especially as her clear white nails hadn't struck him as particularly claw-like but rather neat, short and round.

He concentrated on the task of bandaging his arm, and then got out of the bathroom with a troubled mind. He felt drained – physically and emotionally. He was desperate to sleep and succumbed to the call of his bed. He slipped between the sheets and the bedspread still wearing his trousers and fell asleep instantly, his unsettled mind finally shutting off for a while.

He didn't hear the knocks or Dimitri's calls coming from the other side of the wall.

*   *   *

In the Guardian's Cottage, Maeve Hayward opened her eyes on a dark lounge that smelled of cooling embers and charred wood. She looked at the small clock adorning the mantelpiece: 5.30pm? But the last time she had looked, it had been 10am! Surely, she couldn't have slept the whole day?

She didn't feel rested but rather sluggish and nauseous. She pushed the flowery rug to one side and slowly stood up. Her short hair was unkempt, her dress rumpled, and she had a stiff neck from the awkward position she had slept in for so long.

The first thing she did was go into her tiny kitchen and make herself some tea; having decided that the air in the cottage was stale and rarefied, she picked up the floral blanket, wrapped it around her shoulders and opened the door. Fresh air rushed in, as if it had been accumulating behind the wooden panel, and surprised her lungs. Smoke was rising from the mug of tea she had in her hand, only to dissolve into the evening air. Beyond the halo of light coming out of the house, the lawn and the fields were pitch-black.

Maeve had grown used to this feeling of the cottage being cut-off at night, like a boat adrift on a sea of darkness. In London, she would go out almost every night; here, she never ventured outside after dark. There was nothing for her to see but the darkness of the countryside; she preferred to leave it to the animals and the elements. She didn't feel welcome in this alternative world of shadows, and she felt safer locked up within the cocoon of the cottage.

To her right, an owl hooted; Maeve inhaled deeply and lifted her face to the sky. That's when she saw it: instead of the black ceiling she had been expecting, her eyes filled with a strange multi-coloured glow that spread above her head, coming from the south-east of the estate. She stood there with her mouth open, fascinated. She turned round and her eyes followed the trail of light that had slightly thickened and morphed into some sort of flowing luminous mist. The coloured vapour was coming from somewhere behind the small coppice, beyond Whitemoor Hall itself, from a place located to the right of the main wood that occupied the east of the estate; she could see its tentacles glide and drift above her head and carry their course further west.

She shivered, her face grave with worry; the best thing to do, she thought, would be to return inside and lock the door against the menace of the outside world.

PART VI

The Eye of Horus

ONE

At last, the Oxford Morris disappeared down the drive. Mr Suleman, who had been standing on the stairs taking Vangelis Chronos's last orders, turned his back rather stiffly on yet another grey and damp day, and disappeared back inside the house.

Adam and Dimitri had been observing the scene from one of the empty upstairs bedrooms in the West Wing. Adam was standing up with his hands deep inside his trouser pockets, and Dimitri was kneeling on a high stool at his side.

'So, they are really gone now, aren't they?' the boy asked. He sounded like he didn't quite believe it.

'Of course, Dimitri, they're really gone. They have to be in London by the end of the day.'

Saturnin Bloom and Vangelis Chronos were attending an important scientific conference at the Science Museum, hosted by the museum's director himself, Colonel Sir Henry George Lyons. The invitation had been one of those that the brilliant scholar couldn't refuse.

They had announced their imminent absence over dinner a few days earlier and had explained that they would be away for a whole four days. As Vangelis Chronos had imparted their plans to his dining companions, a noticeable change of atmosphere had occurred, as if a veil had lifted from above the dinner table. Sophia Chronos's face had become less tense, Dimitri had smiled, Maeve had relaxed slightly and even the usually dejected Gladys had started to walk with something akin to a spring in her step. Only Saturnin Bloom had retained his stern and joyless features. Adam guessed that the assistant might not have been overjoyed at the thought of being away from the estate for so long.

After Vangelis's announcement about the London conference, plotting had been added to the daily curriculum. Since their ghostly encounter in the ballroom, Adam and his pupil had become closer than ever. The boy was relieved to see that Adam was definitively taking him seriously.

Dimitri jumped down the stool, rubbed his knees – the wood of the seat had felt hard against his delicate bones – and exclaimed:

'Let's do it!'

Without a word, the tutor and his pupil cautiously got out of the room and shut the door, then proceeded back to the East Wing. Dimitri nervously patted the folded paper securely placed inside the breast pocket of his blazer. He was about to test the precision of his painstakingly-drawn plans. He could be wrong, of course; but if he were right, what a triumph it would be!

At the precise location where the East Wing and the North Wing met, Dimitri retrieved his map and unfolded it.

'There should be a small recess here, with a narrow access to the service stairs.'

And indeed, almost hidden from view round the corner was a small, discreet door; once opened, it revealed the cold practicality of yet another hidden, narrow service staircase. To their left, a grim little corridor with a low ceiling ran along the whole length of the North Wing. Adam stood on the stairs, looking at the desolate little passage.

'I am not sure I understand the architecture of this place. How can there be a corridor here? Where are the rooms?'

'If you go outside and you look up at the North Wing façade, you'll see that the first floor windows are not aligned with those of the other wings, and are almost on level with the second floor, only slightly lower. That's because this corridor here has been built on an intermediate floor, between the ground floor and the first floor.'

'So there is a whole portion of the North Wing that is… what, hollow?'

Dimitri knocked against the cold wall of the narrow corridor.

'I believe there is a series of empty, windowless rooms there; maybe they were used as stockrooms or extra bedrooms for some servants? I haven't managed to find a way in yet. The double doors that lead to it are locked.'

They walked quietly along the passageway, the bleak grey light of the day only reaching them via small square windows that had been placed too high for anyone to be able to catch a glimpse of the countryside outside, as if on purpose. Finally, they reached yet another stone staircase on the other side of the North Wing. Dimitri didn't hesitate and started down the stairs.

'This is one of my new discoveries,' the boy explained, proudly. 'There is a secret panel at the bottom of the stairs.'

And indeed there was. It didn't look much and wasn't easy to distinguish from the rest of the wall, but there it was indeed. Dimitri crouched next to it.

'We could try and see if it opens,' he proposed.

Both started applying pressure to the bottom of the panel; soon, the piece of painted wood turned on its rusty hinges. The gap was big enough for Dimitri and his tutor to slip through.

They found themselves in a dark, rather oppressive space; when their eyes had managed to accustom themselves to the darkness, they saw that they were standing in a small, basic bathroom: there were some cold terracotta floor tiles, a stained ceramic basin and a toilet bowl. The only source of air and light was a tiny rectangular window located high on the wall above the sink.

In front of them, a door had been left ajar and threw a long, weak streak of light along the tiled floor. Adam pushed it open and realised with incredulity that they had indeed made it: they were inside Vangelis Chronos's crowded study. The two intruders stopped on the threshold. Dimitri opened his eyes wide: he had never been inside his stepfather's sanctuary. How pleased he was with his map! After a speechless few moments, the boy whispered, shaking his large piece of paper in front of him.

'My plan is correct! We are inside the study!'

Pleasure brought some colour to the boy's white cheeks.

In contrast to Dimitri's enthusiasm, Adam now felt racked by unease, if not guilt. He knew they shouldn't have been there; they had been rather reckless to penetrate this usually out-of-bounds realm. He had been crazy to think that they would get away with it, and now, he had a bad feeling about the whole enterprise.

Daylight struggled past the thick curtains that obscured the large study window. Dimitri's eyes devoured his surroundings; he was fascinated by the curious and sometimes gruesome exhibits that occupied the glass cabinets, Vangelis Chronos's very own mini-Cabinet of Curiosities. The place reminded Adam of the Pitt Rivers Museum in Oxford.

But it was not the strange collection of artefacts that attracted the tutor's attention on that occasion; he was looking for clues. He spotted one of Saturnin Bloom's unusual ashtrays: a pair of silver hands holding a cup, full of the brown stubs of the secretary's odorous cigarettes; it was perched on top of a pile of books. On Vangelis Chronos's desk, a dirty plate laid abandoned, together with a fork and knife.

Where was the laboratory, then? They were close. Adam deeply inhaled the stagnant air: it smelt of cold aromatic tobacco and a vaguely sulphurous chemical. It would be logical if there were an access to the laboratory from this very study. There was a locked door at the other end of the room to his left. He walked to it, crouched and applied one eye to the keyhole: he saw a bed and something that looked like one of Vangelis's long velvet coats thrown over the back of an armchair; this was the scholar's room.

He turned away from the door and his eyes ran over the walls, then started searching the floor. He dropped to his knees and began rolling corners of rugs and carpets. Dimitri had abandoned his silent observation of the study and was looking at his tutor with curiosity.

'Mr Tuckfield, what are you doing on the floor?'

Adam dropped the corner of the rug he was about to lift and sat on his heels.

'Can you smell it?' he asked. He lifted his index finger in the air, then touched the tip of his nose. 'It's not the first time I've noticed it. It's always in the air! It smells like someone's let go some fireworks in the room. It's the only clue we have!'

The boy comically started sniffing the air in short, noisy bursts. He made a face as his nose detected the strange acrid smell.

The tutor resumed his search; his pupil silently stood watching over him for a few minutes, his hands crossed behind his back. Then when the boy became tired of being idle, he began wandering around the room again, this time not gawping at the exhibits – even though he would slip a glance or two at some particularly alarming specimens floating in jars of formaldehyde – but looking for some kind of door to an elusive laboratory.

After about fifteen minutes, Adam heard Dimitri gasp behind him. The boy called in a weird high-pitched voice:

'Mr Tuckfield, Mr Tuckfield! Look! There!' he exclaimed, pointing at something on the floor.

Adam jumped to his feet and joined his pupil who was bent over in front of a recess covered in bookshelves. Adam followed the boy's arm and saw a vague shape on the dark rug.

'I think it's a footprint, Mr Tuckfield!' whispered the boy.

They needed more light. The teacher turned a small oil lamp on. He was now able to see what his pupil had found: it was indeed the outline of a footprint, and it was not the only one: two-third of one were imprinted on the floorboard at the bottom of the bookshelves, then there was the one

Dimitri had pointed out, then two more moved away from the shelves and into the room where they disappeared. It looked like someone had stepped into chalk or something similarly white and powdery and hadn't bothered rubbing it off their soles. Both Adam and Dimitri were breathing a little faster now. They looked at each other.

'The footprints are coming out of the wall,' started Adam.

'There is something behind the shelves!' exclaimed Dimitri, panting with excitement. 'We have to see what it is!'

They started examining the shelves meticulously, running their fingers along the edges, moving the books in and out. They finally found a handle concealed behind a row of esoteric encyclopaedias. When pulled, it loosened the corner of a bookshelf; it swung open, revealing a hidden stairwell.

Adam and Dimitri stood at the top of the stairs, hesitating, as if on the edge of a precipice; the smell was stronger now, fuller. The air making its way up the staircase was also hotter than that in the office.

'Shall we go?' enquired Adam.

Dimitri swallowed and nodded. *Yes.*

They started down the rough stone stairs. This was not a recently-built staircase by any means; the steps were irregular and worn out in their centre. There were about twenty of them going down in one single spiral. When they reached the last step, they stopped, taken by surprise.

They found themselves in a large crypt-like space with brick-vaulted ceilings; this was clearly several hundred years older than the house above and possessed that elusive quality of places infused with history. It was also incredibly crowded, crammed with objects from floor to ceiling.

They cautiously moved forward, instinctively sticking together to face whatever challenge would lie ahead. All their senses were on high alert. A very small amount of natural light originated from a long narrow strip of latticed glass running along one side of the room, at the very top of the wall. The laboratory was lit up by a few oil lamps scattered around the place; some were attached to the walls, some had been left on tables, chairs and other pieces of furniture. Only a few of them had been left burning and the light was low, leaving whole sections of the cellar swallowed up by shadows.

The visitors' eyes kept catching wavering patches of light gleaming in various corners of the room. Their ears could distinguish some low bubbling and hissing sounds; betrayed by the acoustics of the room, they couldn't be sure about the provenance of the noises. And the air was full of smells: a mixture of organic, earthy flavours and more artificial, chemical particles. It felt like walking inside the stomach of a giant bilious beast: it was hot, moist and quivering... The whole place felt strangely *alive*.

When their eyes had managed to accustom themselves to the low light and the crowded space, what they saw filled them with anxious awe: there were pots, jars, tins, amphoras, retorts, vases and containers of every shape and size scattered around the place.

Strange antique contraptions were hanging from the ceiling like curious mechanical birds; a collection of antiquated compasses and other measuring instruments occupied two glass cabinets, and ancient maps, framed ephemera and medieval charts showing esoteric images as well as unknown alphabets and symbols covered the walls in no logical order.

A large U-shaped work surface had pride of place in the middle of all the chaos. The gurgling they had heard came mostly from a large, convoluted alembic that had been left to work on a heated plate.

Close by were aligned a series of decanters containing worryingly coloured liquids and metal boxes full to the brim with all kinds of tools essential to scientific experiments: spoons, pipettes and metal thongs, several retort stands, test tubes and swabs, small metal pans and crucibles, mortars, pestles and graters. All looked like they had been recently used, washed and prepared to be picked up again in the near future.

Pinned to a large cork board above the worktop were creased pages covered in complex calculations and equations that had been thrown onto the paper in a fussy, spidery handwriting alongside sketches and illegible notes. Some dirty rags, stiff with dubious dried stains, had been thrown on the floor underneath the tables. Near the work surface stood a blackboard that had recently been wiped with a wet cloth which had left a white smear across it.

As he approached the board, Dimitri felt something crush under his shoe: he had just stepped on a bit of chalk that had rolled onto the hard stone floor; his sole was now covered with the stuff. Either Saturnin or Vangelis had done something similar before going up the stairs and had left those powdery footmarks on the floor of the study, betraying the entrance to the laboratory.

The boy traced a shadowy line across the badly wiped surface with his index finger. He really wanted to scribble something on the blackboard, to feel the satisfaction of the piece of chalk rub against the slate. The first thing that came into his head was a big, round 'HELLO!' He wasn't sure why he was feeling the urge to write this. Maybe it was because he felt observed; it was an uneasy and uncomfortable feeling, because he *knew* there wasn't anyone in the laboratory apart from Mr Tuckfield and himself. He couldn't detect any human aura, and there certainly wasn't any ghost in there. No, it was more the persistent, insistent sensation that something or someone couldn't take their eyes off him and was following his every movement. With a shudder, the boy put down the stick of chalk he had been turning round and round in his fingers and joined his tutor.

A large sculpted oak cupboard was bursting with pots and jars full of mysterious-looking substances. Its contents were spilling out over the nearby mantelpiece upon which yet more containers were closely aligned. Adam was scrutinizing the glass bottles, his face as close as possible. Some contained herbs and powders, others liquids of varying thickness and viscosity. The faded labels on the jars were all written in Latin. As he slowly made his way along the mantelpiece, his nose picked up some pungent, stinging smells and he sneezed several times. Dimitri, who was too short to be at eye level with the bottles, asked in a low voice:

'What are they?'

'I'm not sure... Herbs, powders, roots, maybe?'

'Are they like medicine?'

The boy thought about the small bottles he had often glimpsed in his mother's hands.

'I'm afraid I don't know at all, Dimitri.'

'But if it's not used to cure illnesses, what do you use them for?' insisted Dimitri.

Adam looked around him, still puzzled.

'I'm afraid I do not have the answer to that one.'

Together, they moved further along the room. They discovered a small furnace in one corner and two small simmering alembics in another. Much like Adam's ancestor Aloysius Dean, Vangelis Chronos was not only a respected scientist, but he had also been called to the other side, and had succumbed to the terribly seductive attraction of the occult. This had been Aloysius's laboratory and it had been brought back to life by the present occupant for his own experimentation. So what exactly were an Egyptian god and an alchemist plotting together down here?

'Mr Tuckfield! Look!'

The boy had stopped and was pointing at the back of the cellar. They had almost reached the far end of the room. On the wall was embedded a large sculpted golden disc adorned with hieroglyphics all around its outer edges. And right in its centre was a large eye, not any eye: it was an Egyptian eye, a symbol Adam recognised for having seen it so often. What was it called, again? 'The Eye of Horus', wasn't it? The elongated, kohl-rimmed eye and its elegantly arched eyebrow were supported by a falcon on the left and a cobra on the right. This was an exquisite piece of work indeed, made of faience, lapis lazuli, carnelian and gold. Adam's hair stood on end. This was the real thing, plucked from the obscurity of very ancient times.

Standing motionless in front of the mysterious object, both the boy and his tutor felt oppressed and scrutinised; Dimitri thought that this had probably been the origin of his earlier unease. Could it have been the eye he had felt on his back?

'You are shaking, Dimitri,' said Adam, glancing at the boy's shivering frame. 'What's wrong?'

The boy's wary eyes came back reluctantly to the Eye of Horus.

'I don't know.' Dimitri's voice was choked by extreme anxiety; he was fighting to regain some control over his limbs, whilst the tremors grew more frequent and longer. 'I don't... really... like this thing.' He nodded in the direction of the golden disc.

Both felt at the same time repulsed yet attracted by The Eye. An invisible stream of irresistible power emanated from the ostentatious inanimate object. The glare of the gold gave it a strange, unnatural aura. Adam understood that they were in the presence of some kind of totem; a very ancient, revered symbol whose significance neither him nor his young charge could even begin to grasp.

The young man could see Dimitri's neat little profile at his side and couldn't help being struck by the contrast between his innocent white flesh and the shiny, opulent antiquity of the golden idol. The boy was bewitched by it. Suddenly, his eyes widened and he let a small gasp escape from his lips. The shaking increased at a worrying pace. Adam forgot his own unease, seized the boy's arms and stepped in between him and the bejewelled Eye. Dimitri's head was now thrown back, his eyes rolling in his head.

'Dimitri!' shouted Adam, now in the throes of panic. He turned round and glanced furiously at the impassive Eye of Horus. Adam surprised himself when he hissed:

'You're not having him.'

Adam swiftly lifted the boy off the ground, threw him over his shoulder and made his way to the other side of the room and back up the stairs as quickly as he possibly could, leaving the gurgling laboratory behind him. The child's body didn't weigh a thing, but Adam could feel his shaking limbs through the material of his clothes. Holding onto the boy with one hand, he manoeuvred the bookshelf mechanism with the other and soon, the entrance to the basement was invisible again. The shaking stopped instantly.

Adam deposited his charge in Vangelis Chronos's armchair as carefully as possible, and sat on the edge of the desk, keeping a concerned eye on the boy. After a whole minute, Dimitri slowly came back to his senses and looked around with foggy eyes.

'What happened?' he asked weakly.

Adam jumped down from the desk and crouched in front of the armchair.

'I'm afraid I don't know, Dimitri. You started getting unwell whilst looking at the Eye of Horus downstairs.'

The boy instinctively turned his head towards the entrance of the laboratory, now once again concealed.

'Was it really bad to come here, Mr Tuckfield?'

'What's done is done, Dimitri. Do not worry about it.'

The young man glanced at his pupil's white face. Dimitri's skin was so thin, very much like his mother's; the kind of skin you know would bruise incredibly easily. There was no sign of the grown man he would eventually become: his features were elfin-like. The tutor was overcome by a surge of affection for his young charge, a desire to protect this fragile yet acutely intelligent boy against the world. Where had that come from? He didn't know. He felt like a big brother and an accomplice more than a figure of authority. Maybe Dimitri reminded him of his younger self.

Adam was now on a mission to protect the boy's innocence against the brooding menace whose presence he could feel all over the estate. If that meant exceeding his job description – and by teaming up with Dimitri to break into his employer's office, he had *definitely* gone beyond the call of duty – then so be it. After all, he himself had been tricked into coming to the estate. If his so-called employers had misled his trust, then it was within his rights to retaliate by betraying theirs.

'Are we... Are we going to get punished if we get caught?' enquired the boy.

'But we are *not* going to get caught.'

Adam wondered whether his voice had betrayed his doubts. Somehow, his words had felt heavy on his tongue. At a loss about how to put Dimitri's mind at rest, Adam rested his hand on the boy's shoulder and squeezed it lightly.

Dimitri stretched in the armchair; he was feeling stiff and achy, as if the shaking fit he had suffered from had strained his muscles, joints and nerves. He looked around the room one last time, as if to imprint every detail onto his memory.

'I guess we'd better leave now,' he declared. 'Maybe we could go to the kitchen and ask Mrs Abbott for some tea?'

He then extricated himself from the armchair, stood up and straightened his jacket; he was back to being his calm and composed self. A wave of relief swept over Adam.

Before getting back into the narrow bathroom and retracing their steps to the East Wing, Adam turned round to check that everything had been left as it had been before their visit. The gloomy study was perfectly still. It looked like the sepia photograph of a private museum belonging to an eccentric Victorian aristocrat – airless and lifeless, secretive and macabre. The display cabinets and their ghoulish contents were about to be shrouded in silent and dusty stillness once again.

Adam and Dimitri carefully slotted the bathroom panel into place and retraced their path to the more familiar East Wing. With each step they took further away from the study, they were able to breathe a little bit more comfortably. By the time they reached the classroom, their lungs had managed to flush out the tainted and oppressive air of the laboratory.

TWO

The spicy smoke was potent enough to reach Adam's consciousness deep inside his dreams; as he emerged from his sleep, his eyes flicked open several times, tricked into closing again by the darkness of the moonless night. He felt disorientated at first; surely, this was the middle of the night? And what was that smell that had woken him up? It was a peppery, sweet odour he vaguely recognised, but his sluggish brain refused to identify it. Then it suddenly came, the realisation that this was the heady exudation of Saturnin Bloom's cigarettes.

Just opposite his bed, where he knew the armchair was located, glowed one single incandescent spot. Adam felt the secretary's eyes on him, even though he couldn't make out his visitor at all. He knew Saturnin Bloom could see him through the darkness, and he felt vulnerable with his sleepy brain and stripped cotton pyjamas. He didn't dare move, just in case someone or *something* jumped on him in the dark. He held his breath, waiting for the invisible presence to make a move. After a few seconds, the visitor's unemotional voice erupted from the obscurity.

'I can see you are now awake, Mr Tuckfield. This will make communication much easier, you will admit.'

The orange spot became more intense as he drew on his cigarette and the next invisible cloud of flagrant smoke reached the bed. Then a yellow light grew next to the secretary, who had placed an oil lamp on the table next to him. The glow was just enough to reveal his imposing person to Adam. He was sitting comfortably in the armchair with a small silver ashtray in his lap, his black-clad legs crossed, his face as darkly impenetrable as ever. His inkwell eyes glinted and bored into Adam as if searching for something the tutor would have hidden within his soul.

'When… When did you get back to the house? It feels like it is still the middle of the night.'

'We arrived about an hour ago, and it is indeed the middle of the night, Mr Tuckfield, 3.30am to be precise.'

'What are you doing here? Has anything happened?'

Saturnin Bloom shifted in the armchair; he bent forward, his face as hard as granite, his unblinking eyes full of an almighty thunder.

'Now *you* tell *me*, Mr Tuckfield.'

Adam's heart jumped in his chest. What was the meaning of all this? He rubbed his eyes, trying to clear his head. He then slipped out of bed, feeling that he would be more ready to face the secretary with both feet firmly on the ground.

'I'm afraid I don't quite follow you, Mr Bloom,' admitted Adam, tugging on the right sleeve of his cotton pyjamas.

An impatient sigh, accompanied by yet another cloud of spicy smoke escaped from the hard mouth of the secretary. He stubbed the rest of his cigarette out and placed the silver dish carefully on the small dark wood table to his side. He then crossed his hands on his lap and looked directly at Adam, who felt his skin warm up as if a strong, bright beam was being shone onto it.

'Could you answer *one* question, Mr Tuckfield: whose idea was it to break into the study and violate the sanctuary of Vangelis Chronos's underground laboratory? Dimitri's or yours?'

Adam felt as if the large patterned rug on which he stood was suddenly being pulled from under his feet, and for the fraction of a second, he thought he was about to collapse; then came the unpleasant sensation of his insides turning into liquid and he thought he was going to be sick. He sat at the foot of the bed, passed his hand in front of his face. He realised then that he was scared, and he felt ashamed. He was an adult, he was a teacher. He should have been able to face this with aplomb, and yet, in the presence of the unknown and the supernatural, he felt utterly powerless and baffled, like a child perplexed by the absurdities of the adult world. He closed his eyes to shut out Saturnin Bloom's burning gaze. There was no need to deny anything; his interlocutor *knew*.

'How do you...' he started.

Saturnin Bloom's face displayed a rictus of contempt and pity.

'You seem to forget who I am, Mr Tuckfield. Did you really think that you could fool me? You mortals are so very amusing sometimes...'

An odd flash passed in the secretary's bottomless eyes.

A rising anger had started to seep through Adam's fear. His pride was once again being hurt by the contemptuous Egyptian god. He tightened his fists inside the sleeves of his pyjamas, but he didn't say anything.

'Do you remember seeing a large golden wall ornament with an engraved

Egyptian eye in its centre when you were down in the laboratory? Yes? Well, then. You might know that this was The Eye of Horus, also known as the *All-seeing Eye...* What else is there to add? It has 'seen' you and Dimitri; it has followed every single step you've taken down there and retained it so I could in turn 'see' it myself. The Eye is my remote vision; it 'transmits' everything it 'sees' to me. So there you are.' Satisfied, the secretary uncrossed and crossed his legs again.

Adam could feel his fear and anger intermingling and creating a toxic cocktail that would end up slowly poisoning his senses. Saturnin Bloom looked nothing like a God, but he rather reminded him of a wild mythical creature readying itself to jump on its prey and tear it to pieces. The kind of malaise that pervaded the still air of the bedroom was primeval, overwhelming. The young man thought about fleeing the room and seeking refuge somewhere, anywhere.

'I should punish you, you know, Mr Tuckfield. That's what us gods do when mortals have misbehaved and attempted to defy us.'

He paused for effect, considering the slim human who stood in front of him shivering in his stripped pyjamas, completely at his mercy. He could just reduce him to a small pile of ashes in an instant if he so wished. How incongruous, he thought. He could end their lives in a second and yet, he could no longer give them the gift of eternal life.

'But I forgot, Mr Tuckfield; you didn't even believe in gods before you came here, and I can still sense some kind of resistance to the idea. Nevertheless, you are far from being an ordinary mortal, Mr Tuckfield, and this alone saves your skin.'

The tone was cutting, superior. Adam felt like punching the secretary in the mouth, to stop him from uttering anything else. This thought disturbed him; he had never been a violent man.

'You're too kind,' said Adam, his voice heavy with sarcasm.

'By right, in the future, this house and everything it contains will belong to you. You are therefore the guardian of our legacies: that of your ancestor Aloysius Dean, that of Vangelis Chronos and, to a certain extent, mine. All three are inseparable and contained within the walls of this house. This is where they should remain under your guardianship in the 21st century.'

Adam chuckled nervously.

'But I *come* from the future! I had never heard of Whitemoor Hall in my life before I read that ad in the paper!'

The young man's voice sounded indignant and resentful. Saturnin Bloom's right hand lifted in a rare gesture of appeasement.

'Time is fluid, Mr Tuckfield. Most humans see it as being linear, but it isn't at all. By coming back to 1925, you have changed your future. Not that of your whole family and its past, as you do not have that power, but *your own personal* future.'

'Do I still have one, then? Maeve said...' started Adam.

Saturnin Bloom's eyes flashed once again.

'And what did the lovely Miss Hayward say?' The secretary's voice betrayed his irritation.

'She said... That she... I... That we would never be allowed out of the estate ever again. That we were prisoners and we would never leave. Is that true?'

'You have just arrived, how could you be thinking about leaving already?' teased Mr Bloom. For a few seconds, the strange grimace that passed for some sort of smile appeared again on his inflexible traits, then his jaw clenched again; he took a new cigarette out of his breast pocket and lit it up. As the swirls of smoke danced in front of him, he resumed. 'By the way, you haven't answered my question, Mr Tuckfield...'

'What question?'

'Whose idea was it to get inside the study and find the laboratory?'

Adam sighed.

'I could tell you that I can explain, only I can't. I cannot for the life of me remember how we arrived to the conclusion that we should try and find Vangelis Chronos's laboratory. It probably happened gradually. You see, we have been studying Wilde's 'The Canterville Ghost' and all this must have stirred something in the boy...'

Saturnin Bloom's upper body jerked; ash landed on the lapel of his immaculate suit.

'So he *has* mentioned the ghosts?' he hoarsely inquired.

'I think he decided to unburden himself and he was only too glad to be able to share his experiences with someone. It hasn't been easy for me to admit it to myself, but... yes... I think I can confirm that somehow, Dimitri possesses the power to communicate... at least, to see... I don't know *what* exactly, I guess we could call them ghosts, revenants, apparitions?' At that point, Adam shook his head in disbelief, not quite believing what he was saying. 'He's been telling me that he had always seen them, all the time, everywhere, in the corridors, in the grounds... They have been his only companions in this big house. The living have been neglecting him, and therefore, he's turned to the dead for companionship.' Adam could feel a knot of emotion form in his throat. 'He started reading about them to try and understand what was happening to him. He's had to work it out himself, using the books in the library.'

Adam lifted his head and his eyes met Saturnin Bloom's. Even in the gloom of the bedroom, he couldn't help being struck by the two now fully shiny black orbs.

'So what happens now?' he asked in a shaky voice.

'We have to act swiftly. Failure is not an option, Mr Tuckfield. We need to convince Dimitri to help us get hold of the Book. And I fear we might be running out of time.'

Adam was stunned; how could an immortal ancient god who seemed to be able to manipulate Time itself ever run out of it? How could he, Adam Tuckfield, a simple mortal – and with his all too numerous weaknesses – come to the assistance of such a creature? And why would he anyway? He was only doing it for the boy, wasn't he? To protect him, to prevent him from having to deal with the wrath of an impatient, if diminished, divinity. Or was he being unconsciously motivated by more deeply-rooted desires he wasn't aware of? Was he himself being seduced by the lure of Thoth's power and the faint scent of immortality? And then he wondered: what would happen if they indeed ran out of time? What terrible events would unfold?

His faintly laboured breathing gave him the impression that he was swimming under very murky waters; his lungs felt heavy in his chest. The shadows in the room were closing in on him, the surface illuminated by the feeble side lamp getting smaller and smaller as their conversation proceeded. Something was nagging at Adam, knocking on the door of his consciousness; something he thought was relevant to the conversation he was having with the secretary. Suddenly, he remembered.

'There was a man at the spring,' he said, brows furrowed and finger on his chin, his mind overworking to try and shake the fuzzy sensation in his head. The black orbs of Mr Bloom's eyes shone. 'The man at the Wise Man's Spring, in the woods. Well, not a man... a ghost... Dimitri has told me that just after he had extracted the bag containing the notebook and the jewellery box from their hiding place, a human form had materialised in front of him above the water. He described the apparition as a lithe man with brown skin and a white tunic, who had looked like some kind of priest from a faraway country. Apparently, he is the only ghost whose voice the boy has been able to hear. All the other ones have tried to speak to him but were all mute, or at least, their voices could never reach through to him.'

Saturnin Bloom's expression changed; he looked transfixed, his fists tightened over the arms of the chair.

'Jahi! Jahi's ghost was there! This explains how Dimitri found the journal and the jewels!' The secretary's voice was incredulous. He became more animated than he had ever been. He jumped out of the armchair, his towering frame suddenly filling the whole room.

'This is very significant, Mr Tuckfield, and absolutely unexpected. As I have told you before, Jahi was present when Amunet died. He was the silent witness to her betrayal and he was the one who had consigned the details of her death to the pages of the leather notebook. Now, after his own demise, he can help repair the damage she has caused by restoring the Book to its rightful owner – me – and maybe find some peace along the way. My goal has never been closer.'

The secretary took the leather notebook out of the pocket of his suit and brandished it in Adam's direction.

'Dimitri has to return to the Wise Man's Spring and contact Jahi. He should take the journal with him to facilitate communication. If Jahi was so keen on getting Dimitri to find the jewels and the journal, then he will agree to help him find the Book.' He placed the journal on the table near the armchair.

A sense of doom gripped Adam and he shivered again under the cotton fabric. He had glimpsed a trace of a rather sinister kind of fanaticism in Saturnin Bloom's eyes; a rabid jubilation. For a moment, the secretary even seemed to forget the presence of the young man at his side.

'What are the risks?' inquired Adam.

'The risks?'.

'The risks for the boy, for us, mortals. Surely, if we have to open a door between the world of the living and that of the dead, then there might be some danger of… contamination?'

'*Contamination*… What an interesting idea! Do you see death as an illness, Mr Tuckfield? Do you think that the Book will come out of the Underworld with some kind of lethal spore attached to it? Believe me, there will be no risk to anyone – if everyone involved follows the rules. No, if there were any danger, then it would not come from the Underworld itself, but from that of the living, simply because mortals are so infinitely flawed and weak.'

He paused for a few seconds, his eyes fixed on the complicated pattern of the carpet under his feet.

'Well then, Mr Tuckfield. I believe my short visit is coming to an end. We no longer have any secrets to hide from you, it seems. You have satisfied your human curiosity and seen the laboratory; you have given me the piece of information I required, and I now know for certain that Dimitri possesses the power that will enable him to successfully complete his mission. You should go back to bed, now, Mr Tuckfield. You have lessons to give tomorrow. And pray, remember: we are running out of time. You know what you have to do.'

Saturnin Bloom started in the direction of the door. Adam's whole body felt stiff and heavy; he was unable to move and could only look as the silhouette of the secretary slipped out of the room into the dark landing outside.

When the door closed, Adam expected to feel some kind of relief; it didn't come. He was left on his own in the half-lit room, his pyjama-clad frame now frozen to the bone and his nose slightly irritated by the tobacco spice still permeating the air. He mechanically walked towards the small table and picked up Jahi's journal. His fingers brushed the rough leather of the cover – the skin of an animal which had been slaughtered so many years ago; He wondered about the tales it contained, which he would never be able to understand, stories of deeds and events that his limited 21st century rational mind wouldn't be able to comprehend.

Holding the notebook against his heavy chest, he returned to bed where he buried himself under the covers; he could feel the edges of the journal pressing against the skin of his forearm through the fabric of his pyjama top. He closed his eyes hard, trying to ban from his mind the towering image of Saturnin Bloom. He couldn't help wondering what kind of creature was hiding beneath the skin of his human appearance; what would the god Thoth look like after he had shed his human skin?

For the first time in days, Adam gave in to the acute tornado that had been wreaking havoc in his head; the extraordinary events of the past two months had been gnawing at his sanity and he had fought long and hard not to capitulate. It had come into his mind that the whole thing would probably drive him insane eventually; but excitement, curiosity and a sense of responsibility towards his young charge had ensured that he had managed to keep himself together; now was not the time to flinch.

Wide awake and yet fearing to get out from underneath the layers of blankets, Adam tried to find reassurance in some of his most cherished memories; he attempted to bring up images of his past life: he only drew a blank. He had been shedding his memories, and they were now lying, discarded, all over the house and grounds. He tried again and again to conjure something up, anything, but nothing came; only the big black bottomless well of his decomposing memory. Soon, exhausted by his efforts, he let the darkness lure him into sleep.

THREE

Surrounded by obscurity, Saturnin Bloom stood, silent and still, in front of the door of Sophia Chronos's bedroom. After his confrontation with Adam, he should have walked down all the way back to Vangelis Chronos's office.

Instead, he had turned left and climbed up the stairs leading to the second floor of the East Wing, guided by some kind of instinct he had chosen not to fight against. Because he was a god, his intuition was supposed to be heightened, sharpened. He could sense the vibrations, moods and auras that were invisible to human beings, who only had the mechanics of their brains and guts and their dubious moral codes to guide them.

This divine faculty had been tormenting him these past few weeks, ever since Sophia Chronos had plunged her graceful yet greedy white fingers into the writhing nest of jewels. He had been trying to observe her as much as possible, spying on her every gesture, scrutinising her behaviour. Lady Chronos had always avoided him, but she had recently been even more elusive than ever. They had been playing hide and seek with each other, and he had grown so impatient and frustrated that he had been tempted to storm her rooms in order to put his mind at rest on several occasions. He knew too well how carefully he had to tread. Now that he was tentatively close to retrieving the Book, he couldn't afford to play games anymore. And yet…

At this very moment, he could feel her presence behind the closed door. With clenched fists, he turned away and started pacing up and down the corridor, unable to calm himself down. He knew he had to control his temper, his wrath often resulting in some sudden release of energy that affected the weather system of the estate or created some freakish phenomena.

The appeal of the woman's presence on the other side of the wall kept drawing him back to the wooden door, like some kind of flesh magnet. This was an indication that there was something going on, something even more sinister than he had imagined; something that could potentially endanger the recovery of his powers. At the thought, the god Thoth felt a strong desire to unleash a wrecking storm over the estate and be done with it.

As he paced in the darkness, fulminating against his indecision and making himself mad with rage, the bedroom door opened suddenly, throwing a long triangle of yellow light across the dark red carpet of the corridor; Saturnin Bloom stopped dead in his tracks a few steps away from the threshold; his eyes first caught the silhouette outlined against the light of the room. Then as they adjusted to the contrast, he realised that Sophia Chronos was now standing in front of him, her wild white-blond hair loose over her shoulders, a shimmering nightdress draped around her willowy figure. He couldn't see her face very well, but could only shiver at the luminosity of her ethereal presence. They stayed immobile, facing each other, surrounded by the still nocturnal air. Saturnin Bloom could feel his rage subside; something stirred within him, a mixture of desire, triumph and dread. He was divine and yet, he still wasn't sure about the nature of what or who he was now facing. He had fiercely disliked Sophia Chronos for all her arrogance and self-pity, her spiteful attitude towards him and her all-too-obvious fragile mortality. Now, though…

A flash of silver silk rippled through the air, catching the feeble light coming in from the room behind her; Lady Chronos lifted her right arm towards him in an inviting gesture; her face was still in the shadows, and he couldn't see whether she was smiling.

'So you have finally come to me…' she said in a strange whisper.

His feverish fingers touched hers and her cold alabaster hand closed over his, sending a tremor through his body. Without a word, she pulled him inside the room, which was bathed in a low, warm glow.

She got closer to him, until he could feel the silk of her nightdress brush against the coarser fabric of his suit. She then embraced him with surprising vigour and lifted her face towards his; only then did he see the intense violet eyes.

FOUR

Adam found himself once again standing in front of the door of the Guardian's Cottage. The sound of a typewriter was coming from inside; the satisfying 'click clack' of the keys expeditiously hitting the paper reached him from behind the thick wooden door. He knocked, and the noise stopped immediately, one lone letter suspended in mid-air. The door opened slowly, revealing Maeve: her bobbed locks were unusually unruly, she was wrapped up in a thick woollen shawl and had a pencil pocking out above her right ear. Her brow was furrowed and she looked slightly annoyed at her creative flow being interrupted by an unwelcome intrusion.

Her face softened when she recognised Adam, but she didn't open the door completely and remained on the threshold, leaning against the wooden frame with her arms crossed underneath the shawl.

'Oh gosh, Adam Tuckfield! Nice of you to come and visit me after all this time... I thought you had forgotten I even existed!' Her mouth was set in a sarcastic half-smile, one eyebrow lifted higher than the other. Maeve's face was full of reproach and sadness; she had visibly been hurt by his absence.

'If you thought I had forgotten you, then you are greatly mistaken. All I can do is apologise. A lot of things have been happening at the house.'

'Indeed, and I have to agree that you *do* look exhausted.' Maeve's eyes now betrayed worry. Her features crumpled for a second or two, then she opened the door wide.

'Do come in, but I warn you, the cottage is in an awful mess...'

Adam was thankful to be out of the bitter cold. He spotted the bulky typewriter on the small desk with the sheet of paper waiting for the work to resume, the crumpled balls of the rejects that had joined some well-thumbed magazines and newspapers on the floor. Maeve followed his gaze and tried her best to appear chirpy.

'I am trying to resume my journalistic career, just in case I ever get out of here; it gives me a goal, I guess, otherwise I would just kill myself here and then with boredom. I mean, I've read all the books on the shelves, even the ones I would never have considered picking up! I might have to ask you to do me a favour and to bring me some more from the main library. At the moment, I'm testing my writing skills to see whether they haven't gone dreadfully rusty!'

'Thing is, I'm a jazz journalist and Whitemoor Hall is not exactly a very jazzy place, now, is it? So I've asked Gilbert to arrange for all these,' she pointed at the magazines and newspapers, 'to get delivered here so I can try and keep up-to-date. Easier said than done, if you ask me. I'm no longer in the centre of things.'

She sighed heavily and turned towards Adam, who had let himself fall onto one of the sofas and had closed his eyes. He was sitting still, his legs stretched in front of him, his arms floppy on either side of his body.

'What's happened at the house? Even though it's no more than fifteen minutes away, I often imagine it as being on another planet. I'm wary of it, and on my walks, I make sure I steer clear. I wouldn't want to upset Sophia if she spotted me walking on *her* lawn. And of course, now that I've been useful to them, Vangelis and Saturnin don't really want to know me anymore, so really, I don't speak to anyone whole day.'

She sighed again and joined Adam on the sofa, where she sat with her legs folded under her.

'So, then. What has kept you away for so long?'

Adam glanced sideways, hesitant. He didn't know where or how to start. The young woman was looking expectantly at him, her green eyes slightly reddened but definitely gleaming.

'It's *them*, isn't it?' she exclaimed. 'They've been messing you up as they did me. Sometimes I feel as if this has not been happening to me, but to someone else completely... Everything is so surreal. Do you feel that way too?' She looked away from Adam for a few seconds, her eyes vague with unspeakable fright. 'What have they done to you?' she asked cautiously.

Adam took a deep breath, and started describing all that had happened since he had last seen Maeve: Sophia's behaving completely out of character, as if she had been possessed; the extraordinary experience in the ballroom; the excursion to the very innards of the house, down to the laboratory, and Saturnin Bloom's nocturnal visit only two nights before.

As the young tutor's narrative progressed, Maeve's eyes grew wider and wider; she had placed her hand in front of her mouth as if to stop herself from crying out loud. Her brain was fired up, her heart was racing; she felt terrified and exhilarated all at the same time. Her head tried to make impossible connections and felt about to explode; at some point, she thought that she would just topple over and fall off the sofa, unable to take any more. Adam came to the end of his story, summarising Dimitri's future mission at the Wise Man's Spring, and then he simply stopped talking, as if he had suddenly dried up.

None of them said a word for a whole minute; Adam fixed the tip of his shoes, Maeve looked down at her hands. She cleared her throat before asking in a choked voice:

'And what does Dimitri think about all this?'

Adam looked at her, more miserable than ever.

'I was about to get to this bit. Our little meeting didn't go extraordinarily well. He first looked white with shock, then red with anger. He accused me of having betrayed him by telling Saturnin Bloom and his stepfather about the ghosts; he said that he had told me his secret in all confidence and that I had broken his trust.' Adam shuddered, remembering the boy's distraught features.

'He has been sulking for the past two days now. I think he is disappointed in me, to say the least... I seem to have undone all the work of the past few weeks, you know, trying to win him over...'

The thought of having lost the boy's confidence was hurting Adam more than he could say; it made his heart very heavy indeed.

'Maybe a teacher can never make a good ally for a child, after all; you might have gone too far and become too involved,' ventured Maeve.

'But I was never taken to Whitemoor Hall just to be a regular tutor! This was all part of the plan, that the boy takes a shine to me and confides in me. Saturnin and Vangelis knew what they were doing.'

Maeve looked closely at the young man at the other end of the sofa. He looked overwhelmed, and it gave some kind of fragility to his features.

'You *do* love that kid, don't you?' she asked in a low voice.

Her question made Adam lift his head and look at her; on his face, Maeve read surprise but also relief. He replied with a voice full of incredulity, just as if he didn't trust his own feelings.

'Y...Yes, I suppose I do. He's... He's struck a chord with me, somehow. I can't explain it.'

Maeve cocked her head to the right, a light smile on her red lips, a dreamy vagueness in her eyes.

'Then you have to make sure you two get reconciled and team up to confront whatever is coming.'

Adam interrupted with a self-deprecating smile.

'I've got the impression that it's more *him* protecting *me* than the opposite. I don't understand anything in the world of the Whitemoor estate. I've only ever been comfortable with what I can understand.'

'I'm very much like you on this, Adam. And maybe that's where our weakness lies. That's why we need to help Dimitri and assist him in his mission. It might help us *make sense of it all.*'

'*We?*' Adam frowned.

Maeve straightened up.

'Yes, *we*. From now on, I don't want to be excluded and left out to dry in that cottage whilst you're having your little adventures. Next time you go to the Wise Man's Spring to meet the ghost, I want to be there. I *need* to be there. It would drive me crazy to know what you are doing and all that time to be sitting idly in here.'

She had spoken firmly, authoritatively. Adam knew that nothing would make her change her mind.

Maeve stood up, having suddenly realised that the room had grown colder: she had let the fire die slowly in the hearth. She crouched in front of the blackened heap, poked around, added some logs and coal and waited for the fire to start again. She performed those domestic tasks in silence; Adam started to relax a little; he stretched his weary muscles and allowed them to rest. He was feeling extremely tired, but was infinitely glad to be holed up at the cottage with a kindred spirit.

A knock on the door made them jump; they looked at each other with wide eyes and beating hearts. Maeve stood up, her hands still black with coal.

'Who... Who is that?' she enquired.

'It's me, Dimitri... I want to speak to Mr Tuckfield, please. I know he's in here.' The boy sounded determined but his voice was shaky. Indeed, on the other side of the wooden door, the thin, sensitive skin of his pale face was struggling against the cold which penetrated his double-breasted overcoat.

Adam held his hand up, telling Maeve not to move, then stood up and opened the door.

As if pushed by a sudden gust of wintery wind, Dimitri jolted forward over the threshold and found himself in front of Adam, who closed the door immediately for fear of compromising the warmth of the newly rekindled fire.

Dimitri lifted his face towards Adam and looked him straight in the eye.

'I'll do it. I'll ask Jahi to find the Book for us.'

Adam put a hand on his pupil's shoulder and smiled a thankful, loving and encouraging smile.

'How brave you are, Dimitri. Together, we will restore the Book to its rightful owner and hopefully bring some peace to the estate.'

Maeve moved closer to Adam, slipped her hand in his and squeezed it gently. Dimitri looked at the two adults in turn and a timid smile appeared on his lips. He would never be alone again, ever.

FIVE

The two cloaked silhouettes were standing in front of the iron gates behind which the cold stone stairs descended into the shadows of the Whitemoor vault. Each of them was holding a lamp that threw a vacillating light onto the monument. Under the hoods they had thrown over their heads to protect them as much from the biting cold as from potential prying eyes, their faces were solemn but their eyes betrayed a certain fanatical animation.

If the vegetation had reclaimed the better part of the small cemetery, the entrance to the mausoleum beyond the locked gates had always remained bare, as if weeds had been prevented from growing and creeping over the tomb by an invisible substance. The two figures were studying the papyri that were now flanking each side of the entrance stairs; the stiff, reed-like plants, with their tall stems topped with bright-green feathery clusters of wiry rays looked like soldiers who had been ordered to guard the dead within.

'It's a sign,' said one. 'Look!' he pointed at the ground where the base of the plants joined the ground, 'There is no water whatsoever. Papyrus is an aquatic plant. Observe the way the stems have broken through the stone slabs, as if pushed by an invisible force.'

Indeed, the papyrus plants seemed to have grown from the ground below the slabs, piercing the hard material and cracking its surface in their bid for daylight. They were now close to six foot tall.

'It's high time we went down there and checked what is happening, you know, to make sure,' answered his companion in an urgent, commanding female voice.

The man shook his head slowly.

'No, Sister. We have to follow the rules. If we don't, we might jeopardise Amunet's homecoming. These are perilous times, and we cannot make any mistake. You know that some oppose her return among us? We shouldn't let our impatience interfere with the gods' actions. Besides,' he lifted his face towards the sky and opened his arms, 'can't you *feel it*? It's there, all around us. It's never been so strong. Each time I've come here over the past few weeks, I've felt her, heard her stir within her sarcophagus. The whole of nature around this cemetery has been giving her the strength to awake.

It's a prodigious thing!'

The man's hood had fallen back, revealing his shoulder-length hair and his ravaged face; the left hand-side of his skull – where the hair couldn't grow back – as well as his left cheek were covered in the scars left by the burning German shrapnel that had hit him nine years earlier on a devastated field in France. He couldn't feel the sharpness of the cold autumn night on his mangled skin, but inside, his senses were as acute as ever.

The woman whom he had called 'Sister' winced at the sight of his face. She should have been used to it by now after so many years, but it reminded her so much of what had happened to her darling Alf, who had not been as lucky as Brother Thomas. The latter put his hood back on; her flashback faded.

As they scrutinised the darkness beyond the stairs, the fragrant smoke reached them from the chapel, reminding them of the ritual that would follow. The man put his hand on his fellow worshipper's arm.

'The fire must be ready now, let's go back to the chapel and get started.'

They walked slowly towards the small building, the smell getting stronger with each step. Inside, they were welcomed by the light and heat of the dozen candles and the ceremonial fire they had lit up twenty minutes earlier. Brother Thomas gestured to his companion to close the entrance door, then they both stood in front of the newly-installed altar, a high metallic stand engraved with Egyptian hieroglyphics; the top was curved like a big dish and in the middle of it was now burning a fierce fire. The mixture of wood, spices and dried flowers produced a heady, heavily-scented smoke that rose towards the ceiling then glided over the beams and disappeared between the stones.

Brother Thomas and his assistant stood still in front of the fire and started their incantation. Their voices were low and urgent; the pace of their delivery was similar, down to the second; they pronounced the same words at exactly the same time and they paused in unison, completely, entirely absorbed in their task. The fumes penetrated their system and travelled around their body, putting them in the optimal state for the ritual.

Whilst the small chapel on the edge of the woods filled with strange, exotic words and thick intoxicating smoke, a few metres away, in the desolate cemetery, shadows shifted and the air grew denser. Despite the lack of wind that night, the papyrus plants started to sway gently. A fetid, sulphurous draught rose from the stale darkness of the vault and followed the stairs up to the iron gates, beyond which it mingled with the cold night air, its particles spreading their decay across the cemetery. Soon, the pounding of a heartbeat – slow, deep and sonorous – could be heard shaking the foundations of the mausoleum. The vibrations travelled through the ground and reached the floor of the chapel, where it made the altar rattle and the flames oscillate.

The two hooded individuals fell silent, letting the words of their latest conjuration hang in the air, powerless now that the charm had been broken. They listened attentively and felt the vibrations travel from the beaten earth of the chapel floor up their legs then to their hearts, where they at last felt an instant connection to the former high priestess of The Cult of Thoth.

Brother Thomas felt the skin prickle all over his body as the smoke rising from the altar turned pink, then as deep red as blood. He looked at the woman by his side; he couldn't read her face, but her shiny dark eyes betrayed her true feelings.

'*She* is with us, now…' she whispered, as the sound of the heartbeat resonated within the ancient walls of the chapel and mixed with their own.

*   *   *

Sophia Chronos was sitting at her dressing table, her two elbows firmly pressed against the shiny walnut surface. Bent over, as close to the mirror as possible, her two hands framing her high forehead, she was searching her face for any trace of *the Other*, that alternative version of herself that seemed to have emerged a few weeks previously. She was scrutinising every inch of flawless skin for a clue.

Suddenly, she was distracted by a passing shadow behind her; no, not a shadow, but rather some kind of shimmering red light dancing on the wall. She could see it move in the mirror. As a strange sensation began to rise within her, she stood up, pulled by an invisible force, like a puppet on a string.

She walked to the window, opened the curtain fully and looked outside. There, beyond the Gardener's Cottage and the woods – she knew there was an old abbey but had never really been interested in it – rose a column of bright, red smoke that illuminated the young evening sky. As she remained standing, her eyes fixed on the irresistible phenomenon, a raw, savage kind of joy mixed with triumph seized her from within and surprised her so much that she almost cried out. These, she knew, were not her own feelings and soon, she would be overcome by *the Other* once again.

The now familiar cold liquid flooded her veins, and Sophia Chronos's consciousness was taken over by that being who was slowly taking possession of her, conquering a little bit more of her every day and filling her body and mind with alien, unearthly urges and desires.

A heartbeat started hammering in her ears, and she knew it was not the sound of her own heart but that of another person – a fiercer, stronger, bigger one. It was too loud, and she wanted to run to her bed and bury her head under the pillows to make it stop, but she knew she wouldn't. Her eyes couldn't move away from the flowing cloud of phosphorescent scarlet smoke that lit up the sky like a localised but very raging storm.

Amunet, still buried deep within Sophia Chronos's body, listened to the music of her own beating heart with relish. Not long now… Not long before she could discard that anaemic woman's weak body and finally become alive again. She was tired of borrowing her fey, slender physicality when her own powerful and muscular self wanted to burst out of its host. She contemplated the red skies with jubilation. Not everyone had forgotten her, then, and some members of the community had kept her memory and her legend alive; they were urging her to come back… She would have people to serve her as soon as she was born again. If only she could get rid of this waif of a body now and join them there, in the chapel.

In her enthusiasm, Amunet lifted her two arms and hit the window with both her fists, as if to attract the attention of the flowing river of red clouds on the horizon. She didn't know her own strength, and both her forearms passed through the glass, cutting through the white skin. As the tall glass panel shattered around her with an almighty noise, Amunet retreated, and Sophia Chronos fell to the floor with a cry, like a ragged doll that had fallen out of favour with a capricious child.

SIX

That morning, the estate had woken up under its first serious frost, transforming the landscape by giving it some kind of fairytale appearance: the skies were uniformly, otherworldly grey and everything was covered with a sparkling veil of ice – a sugar-coated fantasy, frozen in time. The air was bitterly cold, and even the noisy crows had decided to stay in bed, their caws absent from the tree tops on the edges of the woods.

Maeve regretted her decision as soon as she stepped outside and breathed in the wintry air. It was her first autumn outside of London and she didn't know how she was going to survive in such bleak surroundings. Oh, to be in a warm tea room or a smoke-filled cinema in the capital!

But one look at Adam and Dimitri, who were standing on the threshold with their grave and expectant faces turned towards her stirred her heart. How could she abandon them? They were so brave and determined, and she used to be just that when it came to covering a story... What had happened to her spirit of adventure? She gave her companions a little smile, straightened up, pulled on her cloche hat, closed and locked the door behind her.

'How is your mother, Dimitri? I've heard that she's had an accident.'

The boy shrugged, his face showing indifference and something akin to annoyance.

'She'll be alright.'

Maeve turned her questioning eyes towards Adam who concurred.

'She should be fine, although some of her cuts are quite deep and it was very bloody; I think it *looked* more serious than it really was, especially as Lady Chronos was wearing her trademark white clothes. But she didn't require any stiches. Ginny has taken good care of her under Vangelis's instructions. Nobody has yet managed to work out how that glass panel has shattered. The windows of the house are incredibly sturdy.'

Once an actress, always an actress, thought Maeve, *she must have loved the drama of it all so much!* She didn't voice her opinion for fear of hurting the boy.

'All right, I guess we'd better go, then?' she exclaimed with exaggerated enthusiasm.

*   *   *

Dimitri, wrapped up in his warmest coat and sporting a winter cap, was showing the way, followed by Maeve – who was almost disappearing in her elegantly oversized woollen coat – and finally, Adam. The frozen grass was making crackling noises under their feet, breaking the silence of the still young day. All three of them were walking purposefully, lost in their thoughts, but also aware that this was a momentous day.

They were making their way to the Wise Man's Spring, where they hoped that Dimitri would be able to convince Jahi to help them in their quest for The Book of Thoth. Of the three, Adam was the most worried and tormented. He wasn't sure that involving Maeve in their mission was entirely a good idea, and he feared for Dimitri's safety. What if the boy simply couldn't make the ghost come back to the place where he had encountered him first time around? And what if Jahi came but refused to help the boy?

During Saturnin's nocturnal visit to his bedroom, Adam had sensed that the secretary's patience had been stretched to its limit. Who knew what would happen if they came back empty-handed? All those questions were swirling around his head and made him feel tense and miserable. He wished someone said something, anything, to release the tension; he felt himself incapable of uttering a word, and he was aware that his two companions were probably in the same state of mind.

They had made their way past the house and were now approaching the gentle hill on which was perched Elliot Mills's cottage. The lights were on – Adam knew that they had probably been on all night; Dimitri had told him about the insomnia that had been plaguing the gardener since he had returned from the war.

Soon, they entered the woods, and as they did so, the spell that had prevented them from talking lifted, and all three opened their mouth at the same time. They stopped and looked at each other; in different circumstances, they probably would have laughed out loud. That morning, they were anxious and paler than usual, the skin on their faces tight and chilled; they only managed a few twisted, apologetic grins.

'Ah, well, it looks like we have all found our tongue again,' said Adam. 'Dimitri, are you all right?'

The boy nodded, conscious of the essential role of guide and messenger he was playing that day.

'I was only going to say that you need to be careful in the woods, it is always very slippery.'

'Well, I'm glad I am wearing appropriate footwear!' exclaimed Maeve, looking down at her sturdy, flat laced-up leather boots. 'It really wouldn't do if I ended up bottom first in a puddle!'

She gave a nervous little laugh; she desperately wanted to be her old devil-may-care self, not this nervous frozen mess.

They carried on walking in the silent woods, passed The Cross where the paths converged.

'What is that cross doing here?' Maeve enquired.

'I think it has something to do with the abbey, which is on this side of the estate, on the edges of the woods,' replied Dimitri, pointing to the right. 'I don't know what it means, only that all the paths in the woods join here, at this central crossroads.'

The boy took the path to the left and soon, he was leading his companions around The Green Rock.

The boy couldn't prevent himself from shivering and his skin from bristling with goose bumps as he caught his first sight of the half-moon pond for the first time in weeks. The Wise Man's Spring looked even more otherworldly than it had done back in September: here and there, the surface of the water was covered with a thin layer of ice; it looked as if a fantastical beast had come and shed some of its scales into the water. A few very small stalactites of ice were hanging precariously from the rock edges, slowly melting away in the morning air. Apart from the liquid sounds of the spring water spurting from between the rocks and flowing into the pond, there was no noise at all, as if all living things preferred to keep their distance.

Dimitri turned to the two adults who had stopped a few feet behind him. They were standing there, looking at the Wise Man's Spring with obvious surprise.

'It's enchanting!' whispered Maeve. She was struck by the aesthetic near-perfection of the place; it was so secluded and peaceful.

'Is that were you found the journal and the jewellery box?' enquired Adam, pointing at the rocky recess to the right of the pond. The boy nodded.

'So what do we do, now?' asked Maeve. She had kept her voice low, almost overwhelmed by the quietness of her surroundings. She and Adam hadn't moved forward and were still at some distance from the pond, as if they were not sure whether their presence would be welcome. The three of them felt they were intruding on a secret world.

Dimitri looked back towards the spring and scrutinised the shiny wet rock surface where Jahi's ghost had disappeared. He was indecisive. The Scribe had materialised because he had had a reason, then: Dimitri had found the objects he had concealed. Now that it had been done, who was to say that he would ever step out into the world of the living again?

'Maybe you should stay away,' declared the boy.

Maeve opened her mouth to protest but Adam was faster. He grabbed his companion's arm.

'Yes, of course, Dimitri. It's a wise decision. Jahi might hesitate to contact you if two strangers stand nearby,' agreed the tutor.

Maeve looked at the tutor with furrowed eyebrows but didn't protest as he led her away from the Wise Man's Spring.

'Look,' he said to Maeve, his mouth close to her ear, 'can you see this large uprooted tree over there? Let's go and stand behind it. From there, we should still have a good view of the spring and we would be able to come quickly to the rescue if needed.' He then turned to the boy: 'We are going now, Dimitri. We won't be far, so if you need anything, call us and we'll come running!'

The boy distractedly nodded without taking his eyes off the pond. He was disappointed not to have found a second lotus flower growing in it, and without the colourful exotic plant, the Wise Man's Spring appeared to him to be grey and ever so slightly gloomy.

Soon, the rustling of leaves and the cracking of twigs under Adam's and Maeve's feet receded then stopped altogether, and the place became eerily quiet again. Dimitri could see the mist of his accelerating breath and feel his heart beating against his ribcage.

He looked around him and chose a rock with a flat top on which to sit on and wait for Jahi. He then took the leather-bound notebook out of the inside pocket of his coat and put it on his lap, with both hands flat on the cover; he then concentrated on spelling out the name 'Jahi' in his head, like a silent call.

The boy was cold and nervous, but also determined. He was fully aware of the importance of his strange mission and he took it very seriously indeed. He was putting his strange power to the test.

*   *   *

Maeve shivered, frozen to the bone. She could have been sitting next to the roaring fire, typing away an article about… Well, about anything, really. She would have found something to write about. Anything rather than standing like an idiot in the middle of a soggy wood with frozen feet and hands, a reddening nose – never a good look – and staring at decaying leaves and naked trees.

She buried her hands deeper in the large pockets of her coat and sighed noisily. It had been thirty minutes since they had left Dimitri by the pond and she was getting bored out of her wits. Adam looked at his companion and distractedly enquired:

'You're all right, Maeve?'

Adam's gaze returned to the pond immediately, worried that he might miss something. The young woman pursed her lips and crossed her arms.

'No, I'm *not* all right. I'm cold and I'm sick and tired of waiting. It was a stupid idea to come here. Nothing's going to happen. How long are we supposed to stay here before we finally admit that *that thing* is not going to show up?'

She had kept her voice down but the sharpness of her tone was unmistakable. Maeve looked at Adam: his face had hardened and his eyes were telling her that her words had hurt him, as if by complaining she had betrayed his trust. She regretted her behaviour immediately and put a gloved hand on his arm.

'Sorry, Adam, sorry… It's my fault, I asked you to become part of it. I haven't got any right to moan. Don't pay attention to my spoilt London girl whinging…'

To her surprise, Adam didn't rebuff her but took her in his arms and held her tight.

'That's all right, Maeve. I'm cold and disappointed too. It's been half an hour and nothing's happened, and like you, I am no longer sure that anything *will* indeed happen.'

Over his companion's head, Adam glanced at the figure of the boy who was still seating on his rock, his eyes fixed on the swirling water of the pond. 'Let's wait for another ten minutes and then we can go to Dimitri and decide what we should do. The boy is going to be disappointed; he is so convinced that he can do something good.'

Their embrace lasted another minute; Maeve had closed her tired eyes and Adam was rocking her gently. They were both warmer that way. Then suddenly, despite the layers of clothes they both wore, she felt the whole of his body stiffen; the rocking motion stopped.

'Adam? What...' She opened her eyes and lifted her face towards him; Adam was staring into the distance, his eyes fixed towards the pond, his features white as a sheet.

'Something's happening,' he murmured.

Maeve turned round, staying as close to her companion as possible.

Dimitri was now standing closer to the edge of the pond, looking tentatively in front of him, holding the leather journal close to his chest. Was it possible that the boy had managed to attract the attention of the Scribe at last?

*   *   *

The water had stopped flowing; the surface of the pond had become immobile and smooth, undisturbed by the clear spurt of liquid coming out from the deepest entrails of the rock: it had all but dried out within seconds.

The boy had jumped out of his rock and was peering at the air above the water where he could now make out the slightest of disturbances. The well-known sensation had returned to the pit of his stomach, and he knew for certain that Jahi had heard his call.

He waited expectantly whilst the air particles in front of him somehow came together to solidify and create a shape. Vague at first, it soon turned into the otherworldly image of Jahi, the Sacred Scribe of The Cult of Thoth. He looked exactly as he had appeared to Dimitri first time around: exotic and lean in his white tunic, yet exuding this immense sense of knowledge and wisdom. The boy panicked. How was he going to start? What was he going to say? There was so much to explain...

'You have come to me, young Dimitri, your heart heavy with questions and dread.'

That voice again... It sent a chill down Dimitri's spine. He swallowed hard, straightened up and tightened his grip on the diary. Then he started his story, encouraged by the ghost's undivided attention.

*   *   *

Huddled behind their tree, Adam and Maeve didn't dare move for fear of interrupting whatever it was that was taking place at the Wise Man's Spring.

From their hiding place, they could see and hear that Dimitri was talking to someone; they couldn't catch even the odd word as they were too far away and the boy was speaking so quietly; and of course, they couldn't see who he was talking to.

And yet, they watched, fascinated by the strange scene that was unravelling in front of their eyes. They wished with all their heart that they too could catch a glimpse of Jahi the Sacred Scribe and hear his voice. And so, their limbs numb with cold and inactivity, and feeling an uncanny sense of anxious anticipation, Adam and Maeve waited some more.

*   *   *

It was over. Jahi had solemnly said his farewell to Dimitri and had gone. As he had done over two months earlier, he had turned round and walked into the wet slab of rock from which the spring gushed out. As soon as he had disappeared, the water had started noisily spurting out again. The boy stayed where he was, feeling faint and nauseous; his conversation with the Egyptian scribe had exhausted him. After a few minutes, he suddenly remembered that he wasn't on his own and looked towards the woods, his eyes searching the undergrowth.

Adam gestured to Maeve and they started towards the boy without uttering a word, even though they both became alarmed as they approached the child: he looked dreadfully white, his skin more translucent than ever, his veins so blue that they could have burst through the surface. His blue eyes had a strange, almost milky quality to them, and all the blood had gone from his thin lips. He was looking straight through them, even though they could have sworn that he was able to hear them; his face was turned in their direction. Being able to see beyond the physical world seemed to have rendered him momentarily blind. A few feet away from his pupil, Adam asked in an anguished voice:

'Dimitri? Is everything all right?'

The sound of the familiar, earthly voice startled the boy. He rubbed his eyes; his irises had gone back to their normal colour and consistency, and he could see again. Maeve crouched next to Dimitri and put a reassuring hand on his shoulder.

'Dimitri. Are you sure you are feeling quite well? You look shaken, poor thing. Don't worry now, we are here!'

She tried to smile. She had never been the maternal type and didn't know what to do. Adam gave the boy a gentle pat on the back.

'It's all right if you don't want to say anything for a while. We can walk back to the cottage, and you will tell us everything once you're on the sofa with a hot drink.'

Even though a hot beverage and a warm blanket were probably the two things Dimitri wanted most in the whole world then, he didn't take his mind off his mission immediately. He opened his mouth to speak, found that it was horribly dry and tried to get some saliva going before he could utter a word. Then he declared in a small yet incredibly serious voice:

'He said to come back in three days. He will have the Book, then.'

SEVEN

Vangelis Chronos had never slept a lot or well, but he now found that his increasingly short hours of rest were haunted by terrible nightmares, and he would wake up covered in an unhealthy, sticky cold sweat. His appearance and body were that of an old man, he knew this too well, but his work was not finished; indeed, he could even declare that it was just only beginning in earnest. His task was so overwhelmingly immense, that a lifetime wouldn't be enough; his ambition was to outlive all his illustrious colleagues and survive their theories. There was still so much to be done, so many mysteries to be discovered and elucidated. His thirst for knowledge had grown as the years had gone by; his feverish scholarly brain had protected him from his human needs and urges, making him almost godlike in the face of his desire for his wife.

Yet sometimes, he was reminded of his all-too-human mortal coil; a strange longing would come over him whilst catching a glimpse of Sophia; occasionally, he would think about what it might have been *if*... Often, he wished his studies hadn't taken control over him and he could let his basic instincts overcome him and allow him to, at last, taste the forbidden fruit he had acquired by cheating and treachery.

In his incredible vanity, in the early years, he had thought that he would be able to make Sophia love him for what he was: a wise, incredibly clever and learned scholar who would give her anything she'd ever wished for. Unfortunately, what she had really wanted had been to be as far away from him as she possibly could within the walls of Whitemoor Hall. She was of the opinion that their marriage had been some kind of contract that had been drawn on equal terms. He had saved her from abject poverty and a life of misery, and she had given her beauty and grace – if not herself – to him, an already ageing man at the twilight of his life. Maybe she had thought that he would die quickly, leaving her free to wander around the estate as she wished, rich, beautiful and wounded.

He had been – secretly – overjoyed when the terrible pain she had been suffering from since Dimitri's birth had disappeared. She had no longer lain in agony during her monthly period, cursing the boy and everyone who dared approach her, lashing out at inanimate objects. Because the intoxicating poison of the laudanum was no longer flowing in her veins, she had been much better company on the extremely rare occasions they had been in the same room since her miraculous recovery. He didn't understand what had happened, but he welcomed the change.

Then of course, there was Thoth, who had denied any involvement with Sophia's improving health. Vangelis considered this state of affairs relatively suspicious and wasn't entirely sure he could trust the constantly scheming Egyptian god.

He held Thoth responsible for his nightmares. Now that after all those years, the god was about the regain his omnipotent powers, the scholar found himself in a terrifying, mind-boggling dilemma: will the divinity reward him with eternal life as he had promised, or will he consider the scientist redundant and eliminate him? Both were keeping him awake at night. If he were granted eternal life, then the possibilities were never-ending, and he would become the greatest scientist and scholar not of one, but of *all* generations; he would turn his secret passion, alchemy, into a revered discipline and allow its influence to spread to all forms of science, art and literature. It would be a triumph.

He would have unlimited access to the god's books and papers *for ever*. Who knows? His research might even find a way in which he could reverse the ageing process and he himself could go back to his most vigorous years and woo his wife properly and not buy her with his money and reputation, as he had done.

But he knew perfectly well that his pact with the Egyptian divinity had corrupted him, and had made him vulnerable and infinitely greedy. He remembered clearly what he had said after Thoth had explained every single detail of the pact he had drafted. Vangelis, horrified at first, had exclaimed: 'But it is the same as selling my soul to the devil!'

Thoth's dark rictus – Vangelis had never seen him smile properly in all those years they had been working together – had changed the features of his previously imperturbable face and he had hissed: 'No, my friend. This is much, much better!'

And Vangelis had signed the papyrus with his blood. In doing so, he had lost his freedom. But what was freedom in the face of such knowledge and insight into unfathomable worlds?

Yet, scenes of terrible slaughter kept coming into his mind since he had heard about the imminent restitution of The Book of Thoth to its owner: his head was flooded with images of the god, reunited with his divine powers and wreacking havoc throughout the estate; in his dreams, Thoth eliminated the humans he had been forced to endure all these years in order to survive, and took possession of Whitemoor Hall, turning it into a massive temple of The Cult of Thoth. He of course was the first to die, because he knew too much.

Vangelis Chronos had started to fear for his sanity, something he had never done before despite all that had happened. Every day, he tried to remain optimistic about the ultimate outcome: he refused to believe that all those years of hard work would be erased in the few seconds it would take the god to put an end to his life. He was too useful to him, because for all his power and swagger, the Egyptian god needed him and his meticulous methods: he could become the archivist and researcher, some kind of High Scribe, and the greatest of them all.

Whenever Vangelis Chronos thought about the role he could be playing in the future reinstatement of Thoth into the pantheon of almighty Egyptian gods, he was able to push his nightmarish visions away. It wouldn't be long, now.

PART VII

The Curse

ONE

Adam, Dimitri and Maeve were sitting in the Guardian's Cottage lounge, still wearing their hats and coats, the cold of the outside world hanging in the air around them despite the warmth generated by both the small wood burner and the steady fire in the hearth.

All three were staring in awe at the ornate iron box they had just brought back from the Wise Man's Spring. It was not the physical object itself that had rendered them speechless, but the mere idea of what it was, where it had come from and, above all, what it *meant*. They could feel the burden of its power on their shoulders. It didn't look anything like a book, though.

Maeve was the first to find her voice again.

'So, this is the fabled Book of Thoth. Is the actual book inside?

She slipped a glance towards Adam, who couldn't take his eyes off the iron casket. He was looking at it with an odd intensity, as if he thought that if he stared at it long and hard enough, he would be able to pierce the metal surface and have a peek inside.

'Has Jahi said anything about the Book? How did he find it?' he enquired.

'He only said that the Book was buried at the feet of a giant sycamore tree somewhere in the Underworld, and that he had to dig for it with his bare hands. He said it had enabled him to do penance for not having stopped Amunet when he could,' replied Dimitri

Maeve let herself slip from the sofa to kneel on the thick rug by the table and look at the box more closely. She passed her fingers over the carvings that adorned it. They represented a crawling, dancing procession of insects and bugs: beetles and flying scarabs, flies and honey bees, butterflies, locusts and centipedes. Their creepy dance had been engraved on each of the four sides of the box; in a mysterious feast of artistry, in contrast to the rather dull metal of the box, the creatures' bodies were iridescent and caught the orange glow of the flames and the yellow light of the lamps. The two handles were moulded in the form of the undulating bodies of two snakes, and a compact sculpted scorpion was guarding the lock. Maeve made a face.

'All those insects… I think I'm going to have nightmares…'

'I believe these all represent creatures that were sacred in ancient Egypt,' suggested Adam. 'Maybe they are displayed here because they were thought to have some form of protective powers?'

They started as the lamps in the room flickered and the fire wavered. Dimitri's face turned paler than ever with exhaustion and surprise. Instinctively, all three turned their heads towards the entrance door.

'There's someone out there,' whispered Adam. It was a strange sensation, the absolute certainty that *someone* or *something* was standing behind the door of the cottage, listening in. The lights were still intermittently going on and off and the fire couldn't settle down again.

'I know. I mean, I *don't know*, really, I just... I can sense it too,' replied Maeve in a low voice. What about you, Dimitri... Do you feel the same?'

The boy nodded.

Maeve felt exhausted and drained. All she wanted to do was to climb the stairs and take refuge in her bed. She could no longer think straight and often felt the taste of hysteria on her lips – it was metallic, slightly bitter.

Adam was about to stand up when the door turned on its hinges and Saturnin Bloom slowly walked into the lounge. His presence filled the room, his tall besuited frame dwarfing the doll's house proportions of the Guardian's Cottage. Dimitri jumped out of his seat and came to stand in front of the table, obscuring the newcomer's view of the metal box. He remained there, erect and silent with his hands behind his back.

'I'll be brief,' started Saturnin Bloom. 'I believe you have something that belongs to me?'

Adam walked towards Dimitri and put a hand on the boy's shoulder.

'Dimitri. Let Mr Bloom see the Book. He's come to take it away, as is his right.'

Reluctantly, the boy took a step aside. Saturnin Bloom's jaw clenched as his eyes fell on the metal box. *The Book, at last!*

The secretary placed his two hands on the handles and lifted the box triumphantly in front of him. In the hearth, the flames jumped up and the fire roared, displacing a huge wave of hot air across the room. The lamps stopped flickering and instead appeared to shine a brighter, clearer light than usual.

Saturnin Bloom was still standing there, his eyes closed, holding the box at arm's length. The handles didn't seem to be made of solid metal anymore: they were the real, scaled, slithering bodies of two live snakes; their cruel, round and glistening eyes had recognised their master. Then the garland of insects started moving, the squirming mass of the creatures seemingly going nowhere but definitely twisting and turning *inside* the metal, their bodies forever part of the object, moulded into it. The butterflies couldn't break free, but you could see their wings flutter under their layer of liquid iron; the scorpion was brandishing its segmented tail, ready to plunge its venomous stinger into anyone whose intention would be to violate the sacred lock. After a minute or two, the secretary opened his eyes – entirely black now – and declared:

'The Book is still in there.'

'Can't you just open the box?' enquired Dimitri, emboldened by his impatience.

'It is protected from any kind of intrusion, human or otherwise. Inside the iron box is a bronze box which contains a wooden box, which contains an ivory and ebony box, which contains a silver box, which contains a golden box. The Sacred Scroll – The Book of Thoth – is inside that last box.'

'And you can't open it?' insisted Dimitri.

'No, I cannot, at least not now. For that, I need the key. Once the first box is open, then I can unlock the others with the same key but a different spell for each one of them.'

'But… Where is the key?' carefully enquired Maeve.

'The key was placed at her request in Amunet's sarcophagus, which lies in the mausoleum by the small chapel.'

'You're going to open the sarcophagus to get the key out?' exclaimed Maeve, horrified.

'DON'T!' shouted Adam.

He froze, three pairs of eyes glaring at him. He didn't know why he had cried out; it had come to him almost violently.

'Adam?' Maeve took a step towards the young man, concerned.

'I… I'm not sure…' Adam swallowed, and sat on the edge of the nearest sofa with his head in his hands. Words and images had started to swim around his mind; he struggled to identify them at first. They felt familiar and yet completely alien. His memories had been sucked out of him within a few days of arriving at the estate; why were those particular ones emerging from the fog of his mind *now*?

He closed his eyes, his hands still held over them, and made an immense effort to concentrate on those bits of flashback he knew were holding something important. After a few seconds during which chaos reigned in his mind, things started to focus and suddenly, it was all clear. He *remembered*. He lifted his head, surprised by the clarity of it all.

'Before I came here, I spent some time doing some research to try and find a little bit more about Whitemoor Hall. I found this crazy website called… Hang on… 'Gates of Delirium', I think, some kind of ghost hunter's website full of weird stories and places. There was a whole section dedicated to the estate on there. It mentioned a book written in the 1970s by some academic who had done some research about this place… And I perfectly remember…' Here, Adam's voice took a coarse, broken turn, 'I perfectly remember that the book mentioned 'an incident'. In November 1925, everyone on the estate was found dead, killed by a mysterious illness… Some kind of plague.'

Adam now lifted his head and looked at his companions with wild eyes:

'It's in there, don't you see? The plague… It's inside the sarcophagus. Don't open it.'

This was a plea to the god Thoth who was standing close to him with his Sacred Book in his hands.

'Like the Curse of Tutankhamun!' murmured Dimitri, fascinated.

Maeve looked at him, concerned that the boy would get scared. Dealing with ghosts was one thing, but being told that you are about to die of a mysterious strand of plague is something else altogether. She herself was fighting a rising panic. This was how it was all going to end, wasn't it? They'd all die in agony, ravaged by an infectious disease coming from the putrefied bowels of an ancient, superstitious civilisation. She would not see the bright lights of London ever again!

She suddenly realised that somehow, she had always known that there was ever going to be only one possible outcome to the riddle being played out on the Whitemoor estate. She tried to steady her trembling voice and asked:

'Is that true? That we are all condemned to die so you can get your precious powers back?' Her eyes were glistening with tears now. She would not allow them to roll on her cheeks, though, oh no!

Saturnin Bloom was still holding the iron box as if it didn't weigh anything. He had listened to Adam's words attentively. The future had warned the tutor about the past which had now become his present. Wasn't Time itself a marvellous concept? he marvelled. Soon he would be its almighty master once again, and then everything would be possible…

He smirked.

'How could I possibly confirm things that have been written fifty to eighty years from now? They haven't happened yet. It is not within my remit.'

Adam jumped out of the sofa and walked towards Saturnin Bloom, stopping only when the secretary's presence overwhelmed him, as if an invisible wall had been erected around his person. The young man scowled.

'Not within your remit? Of course it bloody is! You're a *god*, apparently! You can do what the hell you like, can't you? Including getting your powers back without a thought for the miserable little mortals around you!'

Saturnin Bloom's rictus became darker, more sinister. Mortals losing their patience. Good! It was always great entertainment.

Maeve moved nearer Dimitri, wrapped her arm around his shoulders, and pulled him closer to her.

'What are you staring at?' roared Saturnin Bloom. 'Of course, I will open the sarcophagus and retrieve the key. And I will do this without wasting any more time! You humans think you're just so important, don't you? That you dominate this earth and own everything? Well, let me tell you something: you *don't*. *We* do. Do you think that I will be overwhelmed with compassion and empathy at the thought of your plight? No, I won't.'

Saturnin Bloom then faced Dimitri.

'Dimitri, you have been hiding your unusual skills incredibly well indeed. You *are* very special. Nurture your true nature and your talent will serve you well.'

'What's the point of me being able to communicate with the dead if I'm about to become one myself anyway?' managed to reply a white-faced Dimitri in a small, blanched voice.

'Only Time will tell,' came the answer. The god Thoth, now impatient, turned his back on the three mortals and walked out in the cold, heading towards the small chapel on the edges of the woods.

*　　　　　*　　　　　*

The room was silent and dark around its sleeping occupant. The stillness had spread to the maze of wood panelled corridors outside, penetrating deep inside the very foundations of the house. There was not a murmur, not even the trace of a human breath. It was late morning, and yet the owner of the room was plunged into the deepest dreamless sleep.

Suddenly, the perfect silence was disturbed by some kind of low scratching; soon, it was joined by muffled crackling noises, as if someone were crushing some dry leaves between their fingers, and the unpleasant rasping sounds multiplied and intensified.

On the dressing table, which was covered with a thin layer of white talcum and rice powders, Sophia Chronos's ornate Egyptian jewellery box jolted; each movement disturbed the veil of powder a little further. Something inside wanted to get out and was doing its utmost to find a way to break free.

The strong ancient wood resisted the assaults of the crepitating, invisible force for a while; each jerk of the box inexorably pushed it closer to the edge of the dressing table, tracing a dark path across the dusted polished surface. The noises coming from the casket were becoming louder and more threatening with every second; the container was now being rocked to and fro, the hard wood now hitting the top of the dresser accompanied by some nauseating, unnatural hissing and whistling sounds.

Then the jewellery box tipped over: for half a second, the plump sculpted scarab that adorned the lid looked about to fly away; instead, it plunged towards the floorboards with the rest of the case. That very morning, Ginny had taken the thick rug away to be cleaned and the casket met the cold oak boards at an awkward angle with an odd crack.

The box burst open like an overripe fruit and disgorged its writhing contents: a sticky, shiny jumble of entangled creatures. The butterflies, bees and wasps, stunned, couldn't yet use their folded wings and crawled blindly along the floorboards with the others. Small, greenish snakes glided silently ahead of the moving mass. They spread themselves across the room whilst the case carried on emptying itself of its invertebrate booty. Once the wooden nest was empty, there was no trace of Amunet's dazzling insect jewellery left.

A lone blue dragonfly managed to unfold its crumpled wings and took off woozily. It hovered over the bed for a few seconds before landing gracefully on Sophia Chronos's chest, its thin legs resting on the filigree pendant around her neck. It remained there for a while, hypnotised by its metallic sister. When it attempted to fly off again, it couldn't: its legs were stuck to the metal of the jewel, as if to a particularly strong cobweb.

Slowly, the dragonfly sank a little bit further into the pendant, the frenetic fluttering of its wings useless at freeing it from the devouring trap. Soon, the live insect had disappeared from the surface of the pendant; the aquamarine stone appeared to shine a little brighter in the darkened room.

It was in a bedroom returned to its immobile state that Sophia Chronos woke up abruptly with a rasping gasp, as if she had forgotten to breathe during her sleep. Disorientated and dazed, she brought her hand to her chest and her fingers closed on the dragonfly pendant. For a few seconds, she felt something akin to the fluttering of extremely light wings against her palm, only an eerie, passing sensation.

Her heavy-lidded eyes instinctively searched the room; something wasn't quite right. Then she noticed the absence of the jewellery box on her dressing table. Her eyes followed the path left in the powder to the edge of the varnished surface, then lowered to the floor and widened at the sight of the smashed box.

As she threw the covers to one side and staggered out of bed, she became aware of another consciousness within her, an alien thread of thoughts. She tried to ignore it to make it go away and crouched on the floorboards to pick up the wooden case: the lid was now loose, the clever mechanism that had made it so hard to open now smashed to smithereens by the fall. The large ornamental scarab had lost its lustre and was now slightly chipped.

Tears welled up in Sophia Chronos's eyes as she turned the box around in her hands again and again. Her tearful incomprehension was accompanied by feelings of mounting anger she couldn't control because they were not hers, but Amunet's. When they finally overcame her, she suddenly rose and hurled the box as hard as she could against the wall with an almighty unnatural cry that burnt her throat. Weakened by its earlier fall, the ornate case didn't resist this further assault and landed on the floor in pieces. Only the scarab remained relatively unscathed.

It dawned on Amunet that she might have been too late. The next – and last – phase of her rebirth could only take place on the following full moon, which was a few days away. The sight of the empty jewellery case could only indicate one thing: that somehow, Thoth was about to regain his total powers; and if he did, she knew that his first task would be to make sure she didn't come out of The Underworld, ever. At the moment, he was too weak to be able to stop her. But things were changing and Thoth was about to get his powers back.

No! She couldn't let this happen. She had suffered too much to let him slip through her fingers again without putting up a fight. Would Sophia Chronos's body be strong enough to enable her to weather Thoth's vindictive actions and finally emerge fully-formed, a semi-goddess bringing with her all of Anubis's cunning?

TWO

Saturnin Bloom was walking fast, too fast, even. Adam had to make an enormous effort to keep up. He was a few feet behind the secretary, both of them heading in the direction of the chapel in the woods. Vangelis Chronos's assistant called out to the tutor.

'Are you sure you want to follow me, Mr Tuckfield?'

Adam glanced at the iron box the secretary was carrying under one arm before replying:

'I've never been so sure of anything before.'

'You don't give up, do you?'

'I've been made to give up too many times before, Mr Bloom. I've promised myself that it would never happen again!'

'The 1920s have hardened you, Mr Tuckfield. Good. You are now more worthy of your ancestor, Aloysius Dean.'

'And more worthy of the estate?'

'You could see it like that, yes.'

Saturnin Bloom slowed down and allowed Adam to catch up with him. They carried on walking side by side.

'So you are now feeling a little bit more generous towards a simple mortal?'

Adam couldn't hide the sarcasm in his voice.

'As I have told you before, Mr Tuckfield, you are not just *any* mortal. Even though I have sometimes felt the urge to abandon you to your aimless 21st century life, I couldn't ignore the fact that you had been chosen from birth. The work undertaken by Aloysius Dean, then later by Vangelis Chronos, is inestimable.'

They fell silent for a while. Shreds of morning fog had refused to bulge and were hanging from the trees; the dampness of the air made everything look forlorn.

Adam waved at Elliott Mills who was busy cutting wood near the stables. The gardener nodded, his face as serious as usual but his eyes uneasy. He was probably still reeling from their conversation at the greenhouse, thought Adam. The tutor shivered and glanced at the red-brick building; he remembered what Dimitri had told him about his encounter with the ghost

341

of the young wounded soldier looking for his horse. What would Elliott say if he knew that someone who had died in the war had come back here? Would he be as desperate to take care of him, to reassure him and to soothe him, just as he was to look after his damaged friend in the village? Would he be able to make contact with the ghost because of their shared experience and their common torments?

Just at that moment, neighs were heard inside the building, coming from horses that were definitively alive and well; they startled Adam, who tried to concentrate on his destination. His eyes left the building to look straight ahead at the somewhat muddy path.

As the mausoleum finally came into view, Saturnin and Adam spotted Vangelis Chronos pacing in front of the gates. His head was bent and he appeared to be mumbling to himself; the hands he held behind his back disappeared within the folds of his elaborate garments. He was wearing one of his customary hats – only this one was made of an indefinable dark fur instead of velvet – and he had thrown a rather overdramatic, long flowing winter cape over his usual indoor robes, which had their hems darkened with damp and soiled with mud.

The scholar only became aware of the two men when Adam stepped on a dead branch that emitted an oddly loud crack and disturbed the reverent silence of the place. Vangelis Chronos lifted his head and looked at the newcomers with a fierce, irritated glare.

'Ah! At last… You are very late. I thought you would not turn up at all. I have been freezing here for the past twenty minutes, which I could have used more productively.' He indicated Adam with a nod. 'What is *he* doing here?'

There was no trace of the affable, absent-minded scientist Adam had grown used to. Anxiety, maybe even fear, the tutor surmised, was troubling Vangelis Chronos and made him behave out of character.

'Mr Tuckfield is making sure that his inheritance is not being compromised by an ancient curse,' replied Saturnin.

The scientist frowned, his beard shaking with disapproval. He then sighed and addressed Adam.

'I can't say I approve, but whether I do or not wouldn't sway Mr Bloom's decision. In any case, your presence here might be a necessary evil after all.' The scholar suddenly spotted the box carried by Saturnin Bloom. 'Is that the

Book?' he asked, eyeing the box with a reverential gaze. Adam caught some degree of anguish in the scholar's eyes. Saturnin Bloom ignored the question and turned towards the gates. His face became even more sombre than it already was and his jawline hardened.

'Have you noticed those two papyrus plants growing on each side of the entrance? They indicate regeneration. A new life is awakening in the vault… We cannot wait any longer… Do you have the key?'

From within the multiple folds of his coat and robes, Vangelis Chronos proffered an ancient, slightly rusted and heavy-looking key. Saturnin Bloom snatched it from the scientist's shaking hands – was it cold or fear? – slipped it in the lock and turned it in one sharp movement. A loud clanging noise was heard and the thick chain fell off the iron gates, which protested and refused to bulge at first, sticking to the mixture of mud, dead leaves and stones that had accumulated underneath. Saturnin Bloom pushed the gates with all his might, dislodging one of them from its sturdy hinges, and threw himself down the stairs without waiting for his companions.

Vangelis Chronos took his time to light up an oil torch then pointed at what appeared to be a long leather tool bag.

'Could you please pick this up and carry it down the vault?'

The two men walked down the hard stairs slowly, cautiously. The vault was set much deeper than Adam had anticipated and the air was getting damper and fouler with each step. A distinctive odour of death stuck to the stone; Adam couldn't really define it: it was not the smell of a decomposing body or anything really organic, it was more intangible, something that permeated all five senses: it was in the smell, the taste, the colour, the feel, the everlasting silence; it made you want to flee and at the same time held your attention.

They joined Saturnin Bloom inside the burial chamber. The secretary had deposited the box containing the book on the ground. Lord Chronos placed the torch on a hook and the leather bag on the floor.

The space was completely bare, bar two stone sarcophagi. One was decorated only on one side, with Lord Whitemoor's intricate 'W' sculpted deep into the stone. The other was without a doubt an Egyptian creation: it was made of polished granite and in the shape of a cartouche; the whole surface was covered in hieroglyphics whilst at its foot stood the jackal-headed god Anubis. The lid was flat and smooth, unspoilt.

'What now?' enquired Adam.

Without a word, Saturnin Bloom seized the leather tool bag and extracted three sturdy-looking crowbars. He kept one and threw the other two at the feet of his two companions. Both Vangelis and Adam hesitated; they finally picked up one tool each and waited for more instructions. Saturnin Bloom pointed at one side of the sarcophagus.

'We need to lift the lid all at the same time. Come to this side.'

The three of them took their position besides the tomb and inserted the tip of their crowbars between the lid and the edges of the sarcophagus. Saturnin Bloom kept a close eye on his two companions, who were both reluctant contributors to his task. At his signal, the men pushed on their tools. Adam closed his eyes, readying himself for whatever calamity was lurking within.

Nothing happened for the first few seconds; then a strange noise, very much like an out-of-breath sigh escaped the sarcophagus, and the heavy stone top detached itself from the edges of the tomb. No toxic substance or lethal cloud escaped from it; Adam started breathing again and tried to stem the rising panic and disgust inside him.

Dropping the crowbars, the three men noisily pushed the heavy slab of the sarcophagus, revealing the contents within. They peeked inside: a wooden anthropoid coffin rested upon the bottom of the tomb; it was tall and lean, and richly decorated. It represented a handsome woman in full ceremonial regalia, her eyes heavily made up, her lips full and red and her black locks shiny and abundant. The most unusual feature on the immobile painted face were the immense, almost supernaturally big violet eyes that stared at the intruders from the shadows of the funeral container.

'Amunet...' whispered Saturnin Bloom, one hand resting on top of the wooden box.

For a moment, he remembered the astonishing vitality of his former high priestess; he, more than anyone else, regretted her betrayal. She had turned from ally to enemy; she had chosen her camp and had stolen his Book, condemning him to decades of indignity and powerlessness. Now that she was attempting to come back, he had to punish her once and for all...

Without a word, he lifted the lid; Adam and Vangelis remained wordless, even when they caught a glimpse of the perfect, unspoilt mummy inside. Their attention was immediately attracted by the luxuriant, glossy mane of black hair that cushioned the faceless head and crawled down the rigid shoulders. Each strand seemed to have grown through the layers of linen cloth, pushing its way through the fabric to fill in the restricted space around the top half of Amunet's embalmed body. It looked extraordinary.

Adam thought he had started hallucinating, for he could perceive some kind of vaguely intoxicating effect the air had on his thought processes. He glanced up at Vangelis Chronos, who was staring at the mummy, in shock. On the smooth chest, just above the two joined hands, nestled one single, very ornate skeleton key. Saturnin Bloom stretched a hand towards the bandaged body. First, he passed his fingers over the hair in an almost caressing, tender gesture; then he picked up the key and addressed his two companions.

'Here it is, just as I thought it would be. This is the key that will open the boxes and restore my powers!'

A cry suddenly exploded in the rarefied air of the vault.

'WHAT HAVE YOU DONE?'

It had been more of a roar than a scream.

Standing side by side on the last step of the stairs were two shrouded figures. Even though their faces were hidden by the large hoods of their cloaks, their horror was obvious and made their whole beings shake from head to foot. Saturnin Bloom turned fully towards the new arrivals; he looked almost as surprised as his two companions at this unexpected display of hostility.

'Brother Thomas! Sister Angelina,' uttered the secretary in an even, cold voice. He didn't have time to finish his sentence; the woman he had called Angelina ran across the gloomy space and threw herself over the sarcophagus, hitting her hips and legs against the hard granite. She stretched her arms and banged the lid of the wooden coffin closed as if to protect it against the vilest of degradation. In her effort, her hood had slipped; the deep lines marking her pale face and the unkempt auburn curls betrayed her high state of agitation.

'HOW DARE YOU? How dare you violate Amunet's tomb this way? You will be cursed, cursed, cursed!' She was crying with rage.

In the low light of the vault, the black orbs of Saturnin Bloom's eyes shone with a strange, unnatural glimmer. Adam was observing the confrontation with increased dread, expecting the inevitable, destructive explosion to occur anytime soon. He was desperate to leave this subterranean tomb that stank of death.

Brother Thomas had remained calm despite his indignation. He took a step forward and extended his arm towards his distressed companion.

'Come back to my side, Sister, and do calm yourself.'

The afflicted woman struggled to her feet and went back to stand beside her companion, wiping the mucus under her nose with the sleeve of her cloak. She hissed:

'You will be damned for eternity for your deeds. *She* will punish you once she is among us once again.'

Vangelis Chronos frowned.

'What are you talking about? Who is coming back?' he asked.

Saturnin Bloom gestured to the scholar to be silent.

'So Amunet is coming back, is she?' he started. 'And you have been preparing for her return? So what are the plans? Overthrow The Cult of Thoth and replace it with The Cult of Anubis?'

'You have no right to question us,' replied Brother Thomas cautiously.

He didn't wish to alarm his companion, but he was growing increasingly restless facing the secretary, whose demeanour looked suspiciously confident... too knowing. Something was escaping him, but he couldn't think what. He wondered whether they hadn't made a mistake, interrupting the three men's travails inside the vault. The place was too claustrophobic, oppressive. Maybe they should have waited outside and merely observed.

Saturnin Bloom closed his eyes for a few seconds.

'No right indeed... So who knows about all this at the abbey?'

'At the abbey?' echoed Thomas.

'What do you think would happen if they knew about your betrayal?'

Saturnin Bloom had started to walk towards the two cloaked individuals. Adam could see the back of his head shine under the glow of the torch. The secretary stopped mid-way between the sarcophagi and the newcomers and pointed at the iron box he had left on the floor.

'Do you see that box, there? To you, it looks like a rather ordinary box, a rather ugly one, even. Now, here's a key.' He opened his palm to reveal the item he had just removed from Amunet's coffin. 'This is the key that is going to open that iron box. And after this, it will open a bronze box, then a sycamore box, then a box made of ivory and ebony, then a silver box and finally a golden box...' He paused, satisfied by their widened eyes and bewildered expressions. 'And what will I find in that last golden box? Does that mean anything to you at all?'

Brother Thomas and Sister Angelina obviously knew everything about The Book of Thoth. Everyone at the abbey did.

'Who... Who *are* you?' asked Thomas.

Saturnin Bloom opened his arms in a gesture of both defiance and welcome. Adam and Vangelis Chronos, who had remained close to the sarcophagi, could only see the back of his tall besuited frame, his perfectly smooth cranium reflecting the flame of the only source of light in the vault. They didn't see anything change at all apart from the faces of the two people facing the secretary: they slowly became distorted by a wild, unfathomable terror.

In front of Brother Thomas and Sister Angelina's eyes – but for theirs only – Saturnin Bloom was lifting his mask. For the first time in years, he was dropping the pretence of humanity he had been forced to adopt and was revealing his real self; his body grew even stronger and taller, ripping up the dark suit, splitting the bespoke leather shoes. His whole physiognomy morphed back to the mythical being he really was: the god Thoth, he of the dark-skinned, muscular body and ibis head crowned with blue feathery shoulder-length hair.

No member of the *Makhaut* at the abbey had ever seen him 'in the flesh'. They had revered his image but had never encountered him on this earth. He had appeared briefly in an explosion of 'sacred flames' during certain rituals, but these apparitions had always been heavy with symbolism and drowned in liturgy, with all the members of the congregation overwhelmed by the ceremonial trance.

Thoth opened his mouth – or rather his long, down-curved bill – and disgorged a torrent of ancient Egyptian words; half-incantation and half-curse, it filled the vault with a vortex of strange sounds which became more and more menacing and strident every second, disturbing the fouled air of the vault and forcing Adam and Vangelis Chronos to cover their ears with their hands in a desperate attempt to escape the damning effect of the sacred language.

The last time Adam found the strength to lift his head towards the terrible scene being enacted in front of him, he saw that blood had started trickling down Sister Angelina's nose, mouth and ears. Her companion's hood, still covering his head, was soaking up his blood, the red stain spreading over his shoulders. The pair soon fell to their knees, their faces lifted towards the god Thoth – their features distorted by immeasurable fear and unbearable pain.

Small twinkling silvery stars started dancing in front of Adam's eyes; the poisonous air of the vault finally managed to choke him and he gasped for air before everything went dark.

THREE

Sophia Chronos thought that the best way to avoid fretting about her vanished insect jewellery would be to spend the whole day making crepe paper flowers.

It was some kind of coping mechanism she had turned to again and again over the years: she would cover the small table in her morning room with colourful rolls of paper, scissors, wire, pots of glue, pencils, tissue samples, illustrated botanical books and booklets full of patterns. She would then get to work almost frenetically, head bent and lips tight, her long fingers working rapidly and precisely, her brain trying to banish the negative thoughts that constantly wreaked havoc in her head. It channelled her anguish, kept her panic attacks at bay and focused her mind.

This rather quaint hobby was also an excuse not to interact with any visitors – always intruders to her. She claimed she was too busy to have a conversation with them, whoever they were. And it was something that filled her long, solitary days.

Since the demise of her acting career, she had been looking for something she would be good at and would enjoy – as much as she was capable of enjoying anything. It hadn't worked very well at the beginning, but her perseverance had been worth it, in the end. Against all odds, she had discovered that she was a gifted crafter.

The burning started somewhere near her stomach just as she was in the middle of attaching a strip of paper cut with the fringe of petals to the stamen of her flower. Sophia shifted in her chair, vaguely uncomfortable, and carried on with her work. Soon though, the strange heat intensified and spread, and began to feel more like a vague pain. She froze, erect in her chair, one hand holding the stamen and the other the strip of vivid purple paper. She started to panic, thinking that maybe she was having a heart-attack.

Then the burning became incredibly, horrifyingly real. She felt like someone was holding a flame inside of her, setting fire to her organs. She stood up, dropped her handiwork and clasped both hands on her belly. It was not the agonising pain of her period, it was not the tormenting aches of her damaged hips and groin that were returning to torture her; this was *different*.

She felt her temperature rise and sweat appeared on her forehead, temples and upper lip. She opened her mouth to breathe but could only exhale a gasp of pain; her breath felt so hot she almost expected flames to pour out of her mouth. Her body heat continued to rise and rise, and Sophia began to scream.

Her eyes filled with visions of fierce, devouring flames, and she raised her arms and twisted herself to fight them; she lost control of her limbs and stumbled towards the table, and in one wide sweeping movement, she threw her flower-making material onto the floor.

Her cries of agony soon attracted people who had been in other parts of the house. Ginny burst into the room, followed by Saturnin Bloom and Mr Suleman shortly afterwards. The scene they were confronted with was horrifying: Sophia Chronos was still standing, her blond frothy hair now loose and wild around her head. She was contorting and ripping her clothes off, grasping at the buttons, tugging at the sleeves. She had managed to cast off her delicate blouse and the skin over the lace chemise looked bright red and criss-crossed with the scratches left by her nails.

Ginny started crying, standing away from her mistress, wringing her hands.

'Oh, My lady! Oh, Oh! Mr Bloom, what shall we do?'

Saturnin Bloom was standing slightly ahead of his companions, looking intently at the Lady of the house as she writhed with pain and terror. He raised his arms, as if to prevent Ginny and the estate manager to take a step further towards Sophia Chronos.

'No!' he shouted, stunning the others, 'do not do anything! Do not touch her. It would be the end of you.' And he fell silent, his words hanging in the air.

Suddenly, Sophia Chronos turned round and raised a supplicating arm towards them. Her face and any exposed skin were raw and scarlet.

'Make it stop! Make it stop!' she shrieked, wet curls stuck to her forehead and cheeks, her eyes wild and injected with blood. Her tears didn't roll on her cheeks; they fizzed and evaporated as soon as they came into contact with her burning skin. Saturnin Bloom, stone-faced, still didn't move.

'I beg you, Mr Bloom, we have to do something. She is going to *die*!' bawled Ginny.

'She won't. She is getting rid of the poisonous monster in her, the fire is purifying her, expulsing the alien presence that has slowly been taking over her body.'

He paused, cleared his throat. Then, in a loud, deep, supernatural voice, he roared:

'It is over, Amunet. This is the end. You will not return to this world to play your pathetic power games. I've been stronger and faster than you. Are you surprised? *I* am the god here, and *I* only is worthy of worship. Sophia Chronos is for me, I have won her. Go! Go back to Anubis's lair and find another way to serve him!'

Saturnin Bloom took one step towards Sophia Chronos, seized her right wrist in his large hand and brusquely pulled her to him. In front of Ginny's and Mr Suleman's eyes, the secretary reversed back to his hybrid real self, that of the all-powerful Egyptian god Thoth. Faithful worshippers of The Cult of Thoth, they both fell to their knees but couldn't take their eyes off the scene being enacted in front of them in the once cosy morning room, now turned into some kind of hellish battlefield.

Thoth was now holding Sophia Chronos in his arms; only now, she didn't look like the ethereal lady of the house, but like a high priestess of The Cult of Thoth: the woman who was struggling frantically against him, howling, grunting and roaring was taller, darker, with thick jet-black locks and huge violet eyes. It was a brief vision, as she suddenly burst into flames against the god's body and both were engulfed in a violent inferno.

Ginny and Mr Suleman, prone on the thick carpet, started praying. They prayed for Lady Chronos and for their god; they prayed for themselves, scared of what the consequences would be for witnessing such an event. They prayed for their *Makhaut* back at the abbey... They kept their eyes shut and their faces turned towards the floor, their ears full of the sizzling and hissing of the fire; if they could feel the heat emanating from the flames on their skin, they couldn't smell the burning material and searing of the flesh.

Then it all stopped, as abruptly as it had started. The heat was sucked out of the room, and everything fell silent. Skins cooled in the chilly air. Ginny and her companion slowly lifted their heads: the fire had died out and completely disappeared. The god Thoth had reverted to his human form and was still holding the now unconscious Sophia Chronos in a tight embrace. They were both unscathed by the blaze: Saturnin Bloom was still wearing his dark suit and Lady Chronos's chemise and skirt were still the same creamy colour. No trace of the fire was showing on their bodies or in the room. When he was sure that it was safe to move again, the secretary loosened his grip and summoned his attendants.

'Ginny, Mr Suleman. Please take Lady Chronos to her room. She is safe, now. Come down to the study to inform me when she has woken up.'

*　　　　　*　　　　　*

After Mr Suleman's departure, Ginny was left alone with her mistress, who was now tucked up in bed with some extra blankets. The young maid was still shaking; she lowered herself onto the chair nearest the bed, and put one cold, unsteady hand to her feverish forehead, then looked at the sleeping woman under the feather duvet. Sophia Chronos looked more ethereal, more beautiful and transparent than she had ever been; her hair framed her head like an angelic, furry halo. She looked rested, at peace... And she was smiling in her sleep...

*　　　　　*　　　　　*

Adam woke up sprawled on the dusty floor of the vault, with only the flicker of the weakening torch for company. He coughed briefly, aware of the acrid smell floating in the air. Once he had managed to gather up enough strength to get himself to a seated position, he looked with dread at the sinister funeral space around him: at the exact spot where the two worshippers of The Cult of Thoth had kneeled – and consequently died – there was now a large dark red stain where the two pools of blood had spread and joined up; the blood had trickled down the cracks of the stone floor and had been absorbed by the sand and the dust. Saturnin Bloom and Vangelis Chronos were gone, and so were the iron box, the tools and the leather bag.

He noticed that the air was not entirely clear; it was misty, filled with a thin grey haze. He slowly stood up and instinctively walked to the Egyptian coffin, from which rose thin plumes of smoke. Just as he was about to look inside, a voice called out outside the building.

'Adam? Adam! Are you in there?' It was Maeve's voice.

Confused, at the same time relieved and irritated, he managed to find his voice again.

'I'm in here!' he shouted; his voice echoed all around him. He turned round again and looked over the blackened edges of the stone sarcophagus.

Maeve, holding her primitive torch very tightly in her hand, walked down the stairs, stepped inside the vault and stopped; her horrified eyes hovered on the red stain on the floor. She coughed, fanned her gloved hand in front of her nose to clear the air.

'Adam! Thank goodness you're all right!'

The young man didn't reply. He was standing by the coffin, both hands gripping the edges of the tomb, glaring at its contents.

'They've burnt her! It's all gone!' he exclaimed.

Maeve joined him. The inside of the stone coffin was completely blackened; a thick, irregular layer of black and brownish-grey ashes, peppered with a few charred lumps of unidentifiable nature covered the bottom. Of the richly decorated wooden coffin and the mummy, nothing was left. To have destroyed everything in such a short amount of time, especially the embalmed remains of a carefully prepared mummy, the fire must have been incredibly fierce; and yet, it hadn't spread to the rest of the vault at all.

Maeve and Adam were standing next to each other, their bodies leaning against the cold sculpted stone. Adam was in shock; Maeve respected his silence and remained quiet and still, even though her hands were shaking and her heart was beating too fast.

'It was Amunet's mummy in there,' Adam blurted. 'Saturnin Bloom retrieved the keys; then he killed those poor people – and maybe even your uncle, and set fire to her to prevent her from coming back and… and…' Adam looked at Maeve, anguish all over his features. 'Dimitri! Where's Dimitri? Thoth might try to harm him as well!'

Maeve looked deep inside Adam's eyes, moved her face towards his and kissed him on the lips, then raised her hand to his face and looked straight at him.

'Dimitri is safe at the cottage. One of Saturnin's hooded slaves from the abbey came to tell us where to find you. He was in a hurry and disappeared immediately towards the Hall. I thought it better to leave the boy look after the fire so it's warm when you arrive. He is waiting for you… You look exhausted. Please, do come home with me and leave this awful place behind…'

'But I *need* to know!' protested Adam.

'You need *to rest*. Don't worry, you'll know early enough.'

'We're probably all going to die…' He thought for a moment and took both Maeve's hands in his. 'Maybe we could… Maybe we could escape together?'

'Escape? Where? Didn't I tell you before that it's impossible? That we are stuck here?'

'But maybe we could go back to the 21st century, and therefore, we could be safe from whatever disaster strikes here! You'll be fine, you've been there before.'

Just at that point, he remembered vividly their first encounter in the suffocating, overheated Tube carriage. The vision came and went, and left him vaguely confused; he shook his head to make the doubts go away.

'You are not serious!' exclaimed Maeve with disbelief.

'Yes! I am!' he exclaimed, before lowering his voice again. 'Believe me, I am!'

'And how would we do that?'

'There must be a way we could use the wormhole. The drive is the wormhole, you can enter it in one decade and exit in a different one. Look, Maeve, I…'

The torch on the wall had reached the end of its life and died away, leaving the two friends in near darkness, bar Maeve's small portable lamp. She was relieved, in a way. What was the point of declaring their love to each other if things were about to turn nasty and there was no hope? She waved her torch about.

'Let's go back to the cottage, shall we? This place gives me the creeps.'

At the top of the stairs, Adam lifted his face towards the darkening sky and inhaled deeply. The sharpness of the air made him choke, but he could still smell – and to some degree *taste* – the smoke, the ashes and charred remains he had left behind inside the mausoleum.

Around him, the shadows of the evening were already spreading over the tombs, the not-quite full moon throwing a silvery gleam over the landscape. He couldn't see it, but he could *feel* the presence of the abbey through the darkness; the place was humming with secret activity. He suddenly felt incredibly sad and tightened his grip on Maeve's hand.

FOUR

The night sky was full of glows and noises. Even the inhabitants in nearby Whitemoor couldn't ignore the unusual events unravelling at the abbey. The whole area was filled with unnatural lights and ritualistic rhythms. This was a huge ceremony; the biggest yet.

The villagers had learnt to avoid asking themselves too many questions about the community established within the grounds of the house; they were far too thankful for the steady employment brought to the small village by the estate, and for the fact that they hadn't had to deal with too many of the living casualties of the war: most of the people who had been the most affected had found a haven within the sturdy walls of the abbey, leaving the working folks to get on with their lives. A few were still considering joining the community, but were put off by the un-Christian nature of the religion practiced there; the ones who had lost their faith because of the war were reluctant to fall victim to yet another godly scam. But the promise of a better education, free beds and meals as well as excellent physical and emotional support all sounded incredibly tempting after all the years of struggle.

So the rare individuals who were still in the street attending to their shop, their business or hurrying home for their supper, stopped and turned their faces towards the North-East were the strange lights streaked the sky with velvety brushstrokes of colour. They marvelled at the uncanny phenomenon and at its vaguely hypnotic beauty, but felt the stirring of worry. And then there were the sounds: some kind of low and deep vibration, like the purring of an underground engine; some slow, ritualistic drumming. From time to time, the wind would carry some human voices too, rising and falling like the waves in the ocean.

*　　　　　*　　　　　*

All around Whitemoor Hall, there was a sense of people holding their breath as they watched the horizon.

Sophia Chronos was now strong enough to get out of bed; she made her way to one of her windows and stood immobile behind the new glass panel. Her eyes were wide open and followed the flashes and glows above the top of the trees. She softly pressed her palm against the vibrating glass – the low tremor caused by the ceremony was travelling through the air and made the windows shake slightly. Her skin started prickling all over, but she kept her hand there until it stopped. A little voice in her head was telling her over and over that her fate was being sealed over there, *in absentia*.

And it left her oddly indifferent.

*   *   *

Elliott Mills was probably the person on the estate who was nearest to the abbey building. He was standing on the threshold of his cottage, smoking his pipe, feeling the subterranean vibrations creep up his legs. He had just come back that very same afternoon from a trying visit to Will and his mother.

There had been some changes, some important ones; but he wasn't sure whether he should be crying with joy or screaming with anguish. His friend, who until then had shown very little response to any stimuli and usually sat in a chair, mute and staring at the invisible ghosts of the war, seemed to have woken up from his eight-year silence; but he was angry, *terribly* angry. And all that rancour, which had accumulated inside him for all those years during which he hadn't been able to articulate it, was now bursting the banks of his consciousness and overflowing.

Elliott didn't know what to think. He had been so used to seeing his unresponsive friend not reacting to whatever he would tell him during those hours they had spent together: Elliott talking and talking, and Will staring and staring. The latter's consciousness had suddenly woken up and he had spoken with violence against his fellow men, against the god he no longer believed in, against the whole world. His anger had given him back the energy he had lost all those years ago and he had stood up in the middle of the room, contracting every muscle group in his body, contorting and waving his arms about, raging, raving, ranting, spitting and foaming at the mouth until he had exhausted himself, had collapsed back into his chair and had started sobbing uncontrollably. His poor mother had almost died of fright and happiness.

This regained physical capability might have been a positive sign, but if Will were to become physically violent and dangerous for his mother...

Then maybe, finally, Elliott and the poor woman would have to make the decision to send him to a home, something they had always refused to do, having decided among themselves that they would be able to cope with a Will present in body and absent in mind... So maybe, just maybe, the time had come...

If only this ridiculous circus would cease over there... Those lights and grandiloquent drums prevented him from concentrating and interfered with his thought processes. The gardener shook his head, went back into his house and closed the door behind him; he then allowed himself to hope for the first time in over seven years...

FIVE

Over at the abbey, the power-restoring ceremony was now in full swing and the air was heavy with the smoke of burning incense. In the presence of his congregation, Thoth opened one sacred box after the other, each time pronouncing a specific homily; he then unrolled The Book of Thoth with the help of two carefully chosen members of the community – those individuals had to pay particular attention to not let their eyes wander over the text or it was certain death: no mortal was allowed to read the divine Book.

Once the long roll had been placed flat on the high platform that dominated the vast ceremonial room, the two assistants re-joined the ranks of their *Makhaut*. Thoth kneeled in front of the Book. On the lower ground, the faithful had fallen silent, their eyes fixed expectantly on their god, their senses altered by the fragrant fumes that were swirling inside their lungs.

Thoth carefully placed the palm of his hands at the bottom of the roll, and whispered one unique word only known to himself.

Like a giant boa constrictor, the roll started slowly coiling up Thoth's body as he stood up, the smooth surface of the long ornate papyrus brushing against the god's gleaming brown skin. Soon, his entire body was entrapped within the moving bandage, ready to receive the Book's treasures all over again; he was standing there like a tall, swaying mummy.

The roll tightened around him, whilst the millions of words inscribed on the yellow surface started to sink through his skin, prickling it like minuscule pinheads, injecting every single ounce of power back into Thoth. The god could feel the immense knowledge penetrate him by every pore, infusing him with powers. The papyrus tightened further, pressing against the skin of its willing prisoner, constricting his body more and more as it transferred its science into him. Thoth could feel the pressure and knew it would hurt for a while; he closed his eyes and abandoned himself to the intoxication and pure euphoria of power. As the roll made his physical space narrower and narrower, he could feel himself expand and grow bigger and more powerful inside. He felt the size of a country, of the whole world, of the entire universe… He was regaining his full divine status, and thus in full view of his followers; it would strengthen his influence over them, and when the moment would come when he had to tell them of his plans, then they would follow him without hesitation.

Blue sparks started flying around Thoth. He could feel himself suffocate inside the bandage, his lungs – just like his other organs – tested to the limit. Then the roll loosened its hold, uncoiled and slipped down his body to fall into a knotted, lifeless pile at his feet.

Words couldn't describe the intensity of what Thoth was experiencing at that precise moment. He stood on the wooden platform in all his hybrid splendour, his blue feathered head shining under the heavy candelabras. He opened his arms to the immobile congregation below.

'My friends… Your unwavering faith in me, even at my lowest point, has now been rewarded. The Book of Thoth has been retrieved and I now have regained all the powers that had been robbed from me all those years ago. It is a new dawn for The Cult of Thoth; that of a new beginning… It is time for the *Makhaut* to grow and strengthen away from the damp darkness of England, its unnatural adoptive country. It is now time for us to go back to our natural environment, to the fertile and warm Valleys of the Gods. I am asking you, my faithful friends… Will you follow me to Egypt and help me rebuild my temples?'

A few seconds of stunned silence followed Thoth's short address; then murmurs and whispers started here and there around the room, their volume growing with every second, buzzing like a large swarm of bees. After about two long minutes, it stopped. In the ensuing silence, Mr Suleman, who was sitting at the end of the first row, solemnly stood up to address his god on behalf of all the others.

'The *Makhaut* has spoken.' He paused, still contemplating the implications of the decision that had just been taken, before starting again. 'We will go to Egypt with you.'

Up on his platform, Thoth nodded, satisfied. He had been stuck in England for too long and craved the banks of the Nile. He would go back to the honey-coloured ruins of his temples, which had crumbled hundreds of years ago, and rebuild them bigger and better. He would re-establish himself as a powerful deity with a large following. This was only the beginning… But before he left, he still had a few things to sort out…

*　　　　　*　　　　　*

Vangelis Chronos woke up feeling older and gloomier than ever. The power-restoring ceremony had taken place, he knew as much, but he hadn't been invited. Everyone seemed to have conveniently forgotten his existence. He, who had spent most of the past twelve years in the company of the god Thoth, working on complicated occult experiments, deciphering obscure and esoteric texts, researching and archiving life-changing phenomena, establishing essential scientific – and non-scientific – facts... He hadn't been allowed to attend the most important ritual of them all... He had always refused to be initiated as a member of 'The Family', and this had been his punishment.

The previous day, he had been brought back from the mausoleum and left on his narrow bed, in the bedroom he kept next to his study. He must have been drugged, for he hadn't woken up at all until the following morning.

Now he was standing in the very cold Great Hall, at a loss about what he was supposed to do; he was staring forlornly at the big empty fireplace, which looked like the toothless mouth of some kind of monster ready to feast on him. But where was everyone?

He had wandered around and had found the kitchen and service courtyard deserted; he then had climbed the stairs to the East Wing; there had been nobody in Dimitri's and Adam's bedrooms and the study had been empty as well. He had even attempted to see his wife, but her door had remained stubbornly closed and no one had answered his calls, although she had been in there, he knew it. For the thousandth time, he had been barred from his spouse's bedroom; he had always accepted it, but somehow, that day, after all that had happened, it was affecting him more than he could say. He needed reassurance that all his efforts hadn't been in vain.

How could someone like him fall victim to those feelings of distress and utter dejection? Wasn't he above all this? Wasn't he supposed to be wise? The lure of his studies was too strong to ignore. As always, he would go and find refuge in his research, regaining control of his destiny for a while...

He made his way back to his study, but once in front of the door he paused, and instead of entering his familiar territory, carried on along the corridor that led to a rarely explored corner of the house. The floorboards got creakier and the dust accumulated on the pieces of furniture and picture frames became thicker. Door after door led to ghost rooms that had been locked years ago.

Saturnin Bloom's bedroom was located at the very end of that corridor; Vangelis had never come to that part of the house before and he didn't have the slightest idea about where exactly he was on the ground floor now; he had become completely disorientated after all the twists and turns he had followed. He stopped and fiddled with his beard in front of the half-open door. There was a light inside the room, yet Vangelis knew that the occupant wasn't in. Tentatively, he called out.

'Saturnin? Are you in there?' As expected, there was no answer.

Vangelis knew that he should be turning his back on the door and go back to his study. And yet, he didn't move. There was nothing tangible there, it was more like some strange, irresistible attraction to the room, as if he could *hear* some invisible, inaudible call from beyond the door, or as if he were caught in the magnetic field of something hiding inside the room. His inquisitive scientific mind gave way and he stepped over the threshold.

The room was bare save for a severe-looking wardrobe and a single bed made of a simple iron frame and a mattress covered with a thick linen bedcover. The light came from an oil lamp left on the floor near the bed. Thick, opaque curtains stopped the daylight from coming in. Vangelis Chronos's eyes fell on the dark object on the bed and widened with surprise: for there, carelessly left in the empty room was the iron box containing The Book of Thoth.

At first, the scholar stood away from the bed, recoiling from the sacred object and trying to work out whether he was hallucinating. Was that really The Book of Thoth? Of course, it was: he recognised the garland of Egyptian insects embossed all around the middle section of the iron chest. The metal looked altered in some way: it had lost its shine, taking on a duller greyish metallic shade. This was The Book of Thoth indeed.

When he stepped closer to the bed, he noticed that the lid was open. Before he had time to reflect on the situation, his long-sleeved arm shot out, his fingers slipped under the metal strip and flipped it over. Inside, he could see that the second case – the bronze one – was open too. Vangelis experienced a strange excitement, a sudden surge of adrenalin: he was alone in a room with the fabled Book of Thoth. What had Thoth told him about it? *'The reader of the rolls would know the language of the animals, be able to cast great spells and to enchant the sky and earth themselves.'*

It was the ultimate book; it contained all of Thoth's knowledge and all the secrets of the earth. All the things Vangelis had been working on for all those years to understand, all the answers… they were in this book. All the solutions to all the algorithms, calculations, equations, experiments were there, at the tip of his fingers. His dreams of *owning* the art of alchemy were contained in that box.

If he absorbed all this knowledge, then Thoth would be forced to take him as his associate; he wouldn't doubt or fear anymore. Maybe he could at last make Sophia love and desire him. It was all there for the taking, contained in this series of boxes, laid out in front of him. All he had to do was to open the next box, then the next, and the next…

Vangelis Chronos shivered when his hand at last closed on the tight papyrus roll covered in tiny writing – part Demotic, part hieroglyphics. He could feel the age of the document and its potential power under his fingers.

The hands and the roll disappeared within the folds of the scholar's velvet cloak. He swiftly made his way back along the dark corridor, looking like a scheming ghost sliding over the grubby carpet. Confronted with The Book of Thoth, the scientist had severed his ties with reason, ditched his wisdom and embraced some kind of illuminated folly.

He burst into his study, holding the sacred roll in both hands as if it were a fragile kitten. He crossed his office to his bedroom and, once in there, walked to a tall double door. He paused for breath, before turning the handle and stepping inside a narrow, claustrophobic room. In his head, he could still hear Thoth's words: *'The reader of the rolls would know the language of the animals, be able to cast great spells and to enchant the sky and earth themselves…'*

He couldn't wait any longer. He unrolled a short section of the document, and started reading.

At this exact instant, the god Thoth, who had been sitting next to a small window in one of the abbey buildings, turned his face towards the house. He shook his head in disapproval and briefly despaired at human weakness. He gave them a choice, and they always chose the road to their own self-destruction…

SIX

A dam was shaken into consciousness by a small hand on his arm. His eyes flicked open: the lounge was still plunged in obscurity, with only the weak rays of moonlight peeking through the curtains. The small house seemed to be huddled against the cold outside. He could vaguely make up the small frame crouched next to the sofa on which he had uncomfortably been sleeping.

'Dimitri? What's wrong? It's the middle of the night!'

The boy's face was very close to Adam's, and the young man could feel his pupil's breath on his cheek as he whispered in his ear.

'I've just seen Vangelis.'

The voice had an unfamiliar tremolo to it, and a short sniffing noise confirmed that the child had been crying. Adam froze under the woollen cover.

'Vangelis?' Adam adopted the boy's hushed tones, so as to not wake up Maeve who was asleep upstairs in her room. He was still in the same position, his head against the flattened pillow, his face turned upwards towards the ceiling he couldn't see for lack of light. It was an intimate situation, during which Adam felt something pass between the two of them: a bond of secrecy and trust.

'In the room... He was in the room where I was sleeping,' whispered the boy.

Adam could hear how fast the child's breathing was. Another sniffling sound...

'It's impossible, Dimitri. Vangelis doesn't break into people's rooms... Besides, he would have needed to enter by the door down here. It would have woken me up.'

'Ghosts don't need any door.'

'What do you mean?' Adam sat up, startled.

'I saw Vangelis's *ghost* in the room,' he explained, still whispering. 'He was standing at the feet of my bed, looking at me while I was sleeping. When I opened my eyes, he mouthed something... I think... I think it was 'Say goodbye to your mother for me'. He looked sad and very old, older than I remember.'

Even if he couldn't see properly, Adam knew that some fresh tears were rolling on the boy's cheeks at that very instant.

'But… but… It would mean that…'

'Yes. I think Vangelis is *dead*,' declared Dimitri, in a serious yet wistful voice.

For a moment, they stayed immobile in the dark: the adult was sitting with one hand over his mouth, looking at the blackness straight ahead; the boy was on the floor, stooped like a rag doll and weeping quietly whilst mourning the passing of his stepfather.

Adam reached for the lamp on the side table, then for the watch in his pocket: 6am. He stood up and put on his shirt and trousers, keeping an eye on the now silent boy on the floor. He went to the kitchen to splash his face with cold water, came back to the lounge and crouched in front of the boy, putting a hand on his shoulder.

'I am running to the house now. I would like you to stay here and explain everything to Maeve when she wakes up.'

'I want to come with you!' protested the boy.

'No, Dimitri, sorry, not this time. I want you to stay safe here and make sure Maeve remains within the walls of the cottage as well. Do not get out of here until I return, and do not open the door to anyone, understood? I am going to try and see if I can find out what's happening.'

'But we know, don't we? Vangelis is dead… I wouldn't have seen him if he hadn't been.'

'I trust you, Dimitri. I do not deny that you saw your stepfather earlier, and that's what worries me so. There may be danger…'

'Are we all going to die, then?' There was an odd air of resignation on the boy's face; Adam looked at him, disconcerted by the child's question.

'I don't know …' He was lost for words.

Dimitri looked gravely at his tutor.

'You'll be careful, won't you?'

Adam smiled feebly.

'I will, Dimitri, I promise. Now, watch over Maeve while I'm away, please.'

'Do you love her?' enquired Dimitri, innocently.

Taken by surprise by this unexpected question, Adam didn't see any reason to lie to the boy.

'Well, yes, I do, Dimitri… I do…'

The tutor put on his winter coat and struggled for a while to light up the torch before walking out of the cottage in the direction of Whitemoor Hall. Dimitri, standing on the threshold, saw Vangelis Chronos's white, ghostly form emerge from the darkness on the other side of the low wooden gate; the ghost's empty eyes followed the light of Adam's torch that was slowly fading into the distance. This time, the spectre didn't acknowledge the boy and soon, he dissolved into the cold air of the night.

Dimitri closed the door behind him; he took Adam's place on the sofa, covered his legs with the thick blanket and closed his eyes to better concentrate. He listened to Nature slowly waking up from its chilly night. Since Jahi had brought The Book of Thoth back from the Underworld, he had started to hear too many spectral voices in his head and to see too many passing shadows everywhere he went. He wondered whether some cracks had appeared in the usually safely sealed up door that separated the Kingdom of the Dead and that of the living.

He didn't find any companionship in the presence of the ghosts anymore; he had started to feel threatened. These new apparitions were a different type of spectres, rather remote from the silent, slightly tragic ones he used to encounter; they were more menacing and deformed, with grimacing faces and shrieking voices from beyond the grave; it was all getting too much and for the first time, the boy wished it would stop, once and for all…

*   *   *

Adam reached the main entrance to the house at the same time as Saturnin Bloom, who was coming from the direction of the abbey.

'Mr Tuckfield…'

'Mr Bloom… I see that you have retained your human appearance.'

Saturnin Bloom patted his chest.

'I have grown strangely fond of it. It is much easier to go about my business looking like one of you. I keep my real appearance for the grandiloquence of the ceremonies during which it is always good to impress the masses… But tell me, what are you doing coming up to the house at this early hour, whilst it is still mostly dark? It sounds like you've made yourself a cosy little nest at the Guardian's Cottage… Is Dimitri still there?'

'He is… He's seen something at the cottage that requires further investigation.'

Saturnin Bloom crossed his arms.

'I wonder what that could be?'

Adam sensed that Saturnin Bloom was mocking him, once again; the secretary perfectly knew the reason for his presence at the house.

'Dimitri thinks that he's seen Vangelis Chronos's ghost in his bedroom,' he explained, 'and that his stepfather is dead. I wanted to check whether that was the case.'

The secretary stayed silent for a few seconds.

'Let's get inside, Mr Tuckfield. There is not enough light out here,' he finally said. Once in the house, he declared: 'I am afraid the boy might be right, Mr Tuckfield.'

'What's happened? Did you kill him down the vault, as you did the other two?'

'Oh no, Mr Tuckfield! Not at all…'

The strange rictus Adam had seen so many times on the secretary's face was back, twisting his cruel mouth, creasing the corners of his dark eyes without compromising the smooth, stone-like texture of his face. He started walking, waving his companion to follow him.

'The two members of 'The Family' you saw in the vault were traitors to me and to the community that had welcomed them in their midst, so I destroyed them. Vangelis Chronos has betrayed himself, and in so doing precipitated his own destruction.'

Adam realised that they had reached the scientist's study. Saturnin Bloom stood next to the open door, showing him in.

'After you, Mr Tuckfield. I think you'll find the answers to your questions in there.'

Adam stepped inside the study, which looked even more sinister than he remembered, although the lights had been left on. The display cabinets and shelves looked undisturbed and the desk was still heavy with the tools of scholarly research. He then noticed that the door to the scholar's bedroom had been left ajar. He looked at Saturnin Bloom, whose immobile face didn't betray any emotion as per usual. He had to see for himself.

He entered the bedroom cautiously, dreading what he would find there. He didn't see anything untoward at first, until his eye fell on a fragment of dark velvet fabric on the floor, peeking out from behind double doors. He took a step closer.

There was yet another room behind that door, but its entrance was blocked by Vangelis Chronos's slumped body. He seemed to have been struck whilst standing up and had fallen back against the wall and slipped down to the floor. Adam felt bile rise in his throat; it was a terrible sight.

The scholar was indeed dead, but it was obviously not the fall that had put an end to his life. His body had been altered by a disease that had acted terrifyingly swiftly; his face was set in an expression of abominable pain. His eyes were wide open and rimmed with red and purple shadows. Blood had been trickling down his nose, mouth and ears and had stained his white hair as well as his beard and his clothes. Every inch of exposed flesh – his face, neck and hands – looked terribly bruised and covered with a red and black patchy rash. The tip of his nose and that of all his fingers were black with gangrene. There was a thick roll of what looked like paper close to his right hand, the dead scientist's arm seemingly extended towards it in a last, desperate effort: it was The Book of Thoth.

Saturnin Bloom stepped behind Adam and declared coldly:

'Septicemic plague. Do not touch him or the roll, Mr Tuckfield.'

The secretary stepped forward and picked up the sacred manuscript. Feeling increasingly nauseous, Adam was then reluctantly distracted by the décor of the room where Vangelis Chronos had met his death; he just couldn't believe his eyes: the small compact room, some kind of glorified cupboard or walk-in wardrobe, looked like the lair of a deranged fan.

The walls were covered in colourful theatrical posters and postcards of all shapes and sizes – Adam recognised the names of classic plays by Oscar Wilde and William Shakespeare, and that of some West End theatres. Magazine covers and articles, most of them taken from the influential *The Play*, all represented the same thespian beauty; they had been carefully cut up, glued to sheets of cardboard and pinned to the walls – more had been archived in scrapbooks now stacked up high on shelves.

One name kept catching Adam's eye: 'Miss Sophia Augarde'. The actress was either pausing for the camera in her best clothes or 'in character'; the pictures were black and white or hand-coloured. Her image was repeated again and again on every surface: a younger, healthier and visibly happier Lady Sophia Chronos.

The already claustrophobic space was crowded with theatrical props: annotated scripts, tiaras, hats, feathers, flower crowns, musical instruments and artificial flowers. A few costumes were hanging on a narrow rail, some recognisable from the pictures on the wall.

Adam couldn't move, shocked by the clash between a lonely death and a glamorous, thrilling life on the stage. As he looked around the room, Sophia Chronos's gaze kept coming from all four corners of it; her eyes followed him and made him feel paranoid. He was desperate to turn his back on this stuffy overcrowded space, now also tainted by the scent of death, but he just couldn't take his eyes off it. He turned to Saturnin Bloom with his questions written all over his face.

'Ah! Sophia Chronos!' exclaimed the secretary. 'Worthy of such a devoted worship, don't you think?'

The secretary grabbed Adam's arm and pulled him away.

'Come, come, Mr Tuckfield, let's get away from this place, you look close to collapsing.'

'But…' The young man *was* feeling faint, there was no doubt about that.

'I'll explain once we're out of here.'

Once the bedroom door had been slammed, Mr Bloom let go of Adam's arm. The tutor readjusted his shirt and jacket and tried to regain his dignity.

'What about him?' he enquired, pointing at the bedroom.

'I knew Vangelis Chronos was dead before I came here, Mr Tuckfield. Some people from the abbey are on their way now. They will dispose of the body.'

Adam couldn't help looking at the closed bedroom door, his eyes still full of the grim scene he had come across inside.

Just at this moment, as if on cue, two cloaked figures emerged from the shadowy corridor and stood on the threshold of the study without uttering a single word. One was tall and broad but slightly slouched, whereas the other appeared smaller and slight under the thick white material and was afflicted by a nervous, fidgety demeanour. They had their hoods up over their heads and Adam couldn't make out their faces – if they had any at all. He also wondered about their hands and feet, which remained invisible, covered by their garments.

The tall man was carrying a stretcher, and the other a folded canvas sheet. They looked like two awkward ghosts who were new to the business of haunting and did not know exactly how to conduct themselves.

'Oh good, you're here!' exclaimed Saturnin Bloom without looking at them. 'He is in there, in the bedroom.' He gestured towards the door and the two men shuffled past Adam and Saturnin before entering the room.

The tutor avoided looking at the secretary and kept his gaze on one of the bookshelves, counting the volumes there as a distraction. The silence in the study was barely troubled by the sounds of the two men moving the scholar's body in the next room.

Finally, after a few minutes, they came out carrying the scientist's corpse, which they had covered with the sheet. As they walked past Adam, the young man's heart jumped as he snatched a glimpse of the men's personal tragedies: the effort of arranging the body on the stretcher had disturbed the tall man's hood; one of the lamps caught his torn nose and ravaged mouth: he *almost* didn't have any face after all. Then the tutor's eyes stopped on the smaller man's hands which were tightly holding the handles of the stretcher: the skin on both was terribly mangled and colourless with some fingers missing. His gaze followed the sad procession until it had exited the study and disappeared.

Adam swallowed, troubled by the sight of the men's injuries and the grimness of their task. He heard the clicking noise of Saturnin Bloom's lighter, followed by a waft of the now familiar aromatic tobacco.

'Do not trouble yourself with the physical and psychological well-being of those two men, Mr Tuckfield. They will be fine. My 'Family' has taken good care of them since they arrived at the abbey. That's why the Cult has been so prosperous, you see: human tragedy ensures its success, and the war that ended seven years ago was one on an epic scale!'

Adam frowned and shuddered at Saturnin Bloom's visible glee, but didn't interrupt the secretary, who began to sound like a university professor lecturing a student whilst pointing at some strange life form he had been studying.

'Those two men, for example, were stretcher-bearers during the war and had to endure unimaginable duress; they have witnessed indescribable scenes of carnage and suffered terribly in their own flesh. But we have given them a new lease of life, we have dressed their wounds and offered them solace. Oh, of course, they will never again be the happy-go-lucky young lads they were before the whole thing kicked off, but they have found a purpose.'

'Yeah, to serve *you*,' sneered Adam, letting himself drop heavily on the nearby armchair. He felt stricken and afflicted by it all. Saturnin Bloom blew – almost spat – a huge cloud of smoke.

'Indeed, Mr Tuckfield, and they are forever grateful.'

The tone of voice was haughty, cutting and final. Adam almost heard the god roar with annoyance underneath the unemotional voice and the human skin. Saturnin Bloom walked around the desk to Vangelis Chronos's chair, sat down and fixed his blacker than black gaze on the mortal across the polished surface.

'What happened to Vangelis Chronos?' asked Adam finally.

'He disobeyed and gave in to greed, Mr Tuckfield, it's that simple. So far, so mortal. He knew that no human was allowed to read The Book of Thoth. It's a sacred volume for divine eyes only. But you see, Vangelis Chronos was a scientist and a scholar, and his thirst for knowledge was never satiated; he did deserve the respect the scientific community gave him: he was very highly thought off and rightly so. He was obstinate, rigorous and resilient in his studies.'

'But he had two *very* serious weaknesses: he was an alchemist and he was obsessed with his wife. This led to a terrible imbalance and left him vulnerable and corruptible. Contrary to his 'straighter' colleagues, he believed in the occult and in the way it goes beyond the rational thinking of normal, accepted science. He considered the understanding of science and of the physical world to be the gateway to something *bigger*. And when we met, he was given the undeniable proof he needed to validate his esoteric beliefs.'

'And then, there was Sophia... Vangelis had been obsessed with her since he had seen her on stage in London early in her career. But he was out of the country a lot at the time, doing some research in Greece and Egypt and lecturing around Europe. But he would go to her plays each and every time he was back in the country. He was extremely busy, much older than her, and socially awkward. He had never been married and, to my knowledge, had never had any room in his heart or diary for what you'd call *romance*. He admired her from afar, and was collecting memorabilia connected to her performances. Don't ask me how he managed to obtain all these; I guess he was persuasive enough and money has never been an issue for him...'

'When he purchased Whitemoor Hall in 1913, I had been in residence for several decades and mostly on my own since the death of Lady Whitemoor

– Amunet – in 1867. I immediately made myself known to Vangelis and we sealed a pact to help each other achieve our respective goals. *I* wanted to regain my powers and needed an assistant and archivist; *he* needed someone to guide him through the nebulous mass of esoteric knowledge left by your ancestor Aloysius Dean in the underground laboratory. We agreed on the charade you've seen yourself: I would become the secretary and assistant to his distinguished scientist. It was a great plan, Mr Tuckfield. Vangelis grew increasingly confident in the powers held by the occult and understood that it could help him obtain something he had always wanted: the actress Sophia Augarde. He knew that she would never agree to marry him because of his age and because she was about to become Mrs Henry Emery – have you ever heard of the great actor Henry Emery, Mr Tuckfield?'

'I... think the name is familiar, yes...'

'The star of his era... A great personality, fabulous talent, great presence, you know...'

The name jogged Adam's memory.

'That's it! Maeve said something about him... He died suddenly, didn't he? From a mysterious illness?'

Saturnin Bloom's eyes filled with that black void Adam had seen so many times.

'Septicemic plague.'

Adam stared at Saturnin Bloom.

'Do you mean...?'

'It was part of the deal, Mr Tuckfield. Vangelis wanted Sophia, whom by that time had found that she was expecting Henry's child out of wedlock. If those two married, it would then be impossible to do anything, and he was *desperate*. I have rarely seen a man so *obsessed* with a woman. Henry and Sophia had brought the wedding date forward to try and cover up the blunder. We had to act swiftly.'

'You've killed him!' exclaimed Adam, stunned.

'Well, he got ill with that terribly messy plague... He took it rather badly; it wasn't a pretty sight *at all*.'

Silence fell on the stuffy study. Adam tried to imagine the suffering endured by the actor but simply couldn't find it in him. Saturnin carried on with a fresh cigarette in his hand.

'With Emery dead, things unfolded quickly. Sophia was thrown out of the production she had been working on when it had become obvious that she was with child; some jealous lesser actresses thought it good for their own career advancement to have the rising star out of the way and worked hard on destroying her reputation once and for all. Her pregnancy was a difficult one and she could barely stand for most of it anyway. In the end, everyone deserted her. To make matters worse, she had been profligate with her money, and therefore lost her comfortable apartment and most of her possessions in a relatively short amount of time.'

'By the time she gave birth – and you probably know how *that* went, although you might not know that only *my* divine intervention prevented her from dying – the situation was desperate. And then, 'miraculously', one of her oldest fans – who had been waiting in the wings for the right moment – appeared out of nowhere, pretending to have looked for her everywhere; he offered her marriage as well as wealth and security for both herself and her child and whisked her away to a country retreat without further ado.'

'A real 'fairytale', then,' said Adam sarcastically. He was feeling sick from the smoke, the lack of air and Saturnin Bloom's story.

'I am telling you this story because it is your legacy, Mr Tuckfield, you're the one who will have to deal with the repercussions of Vangelis Chronos's behaviour.'

'And those repercussions, what will they be? Lord Chronos is dead, and then what?'

'The next phase is in your hands. By going against the will of the gods and reading the roll, Vangelis Chronos has released a curse that is at this very moment spreading across the estate and is ready to strike again.'

Adam jumped out of his armchair.

'This is it! This is the disease that killed everyone! It was not hidden in the sarcophagus down the vault, it was *in the Book*!'

'In a way it was. The disease was not present in the boxes, it didn't exist in the physical world until Vangelis Chronos chose to break the rules and cast his eyes on the Sacred Book. The plague is now stalking everyone on the estate and will infect people at random.'

'What do we need to do to stop it? There *is* a way, isn't there?'

Saturnin Bloom looked at the mortal in front of him, vaguely amused by his earnestness and rising panic. He rose slowly from his chair.

'Of course, Mr Tuckfield, there is *always* a way.'

SEVEN

The Oxford Morris that had brought Adam to Whitemoor Hall was parked in front of the entrance underneath the *porte-cochère*. It was still early in the day but the light had started to decline already; the grey skies had turned heavy and threatening, and the sturdy walls of the house had gone one or two shades darker. The tower was looming over the small group of people like a malevolent totem.

On the stairs stood Sophia Chronos, as bright and straight as a column of light; everything about her person seemed to glow: the mass of white-blond hair piled up high on her head, the pale porcelain skin, the lace and silk garments... She was perfectly immobile, her chin slightly lifted, looking haughty and supernatural: the perfect embodiment of her newly-acquired status. Only the pink glow spread across her cheekbones and the new vivacity in her brown eyes betrayed the sweeping emotional upheaval she was experiencing.

She had been liberated from the shackles of the uneventful, painful and miserable existence she had been leading for the past eleven years; she had been buried alive from the moment she had set foot on the estate, she could see that, now. But fate had worked in her favour and had relieved her of her husband's stifling attention. She hadn't even felt sorry for the scholar when she had heard of the circumstances of his death; she had known all along that his morbid curiosity would be his downfall.

She was now the concubine of a god and their wedding ceremony would take place the following day in the Main Hall of the abbey; then soon, they would leave the loathed Whitemoor Hall and travel to Egypt, where her new companion already had palaces and temples waiting for them. Her imagination wasn't wild enough to even try to imagine what this would look and feel like. It was simply overwhelming.

Her god had even promised that she wouldn't have to put up with that child of hers anymore. With the boy out of her sight, she could start a new life all over again... Even her body was now healed, and any trace left in her flesh by Dimitri's birth had disappeared. She could now pretend to the world and to herself that he had never been born, that she was whole again. She felt lighter, taller. There, on the damp stairs of the entrance porch, under the shadow of the tower, she smiled, her eyes set on the broad back of her divine saviour.

Saturnin Bloom could sense Sophia's gaze on him: it burnt through the fabric of his suit, sent ripples through his skin and travelled down his spine; he felt a jolt of lust, but remained focused on the task at hand.

His estate manager and high priest, Mr Suleman, was already at the wheel of the car, ready to go. His instructions were rather straightforward: take the car along the drive to the entrance gates and get out onto the road outside, let Adam out and then execute a U-turn and come back to the house. Everything would probably take less than twenty minutes at most. An easy task, really, all things considered...

Adam Tuckfield had a knot in his throat. He was trying to keep it all together, but he was close to tears. He knew he had better not be over-demonstrative about his distress, because he had been given the biggest challenge of his life: he was about to receive the keys to Whitemoor Hall, as its legitimate guardian. He would have the exclusive task of securing the future of the estate and its legacy as a centre of excellence for science and alchemy.

Word would spread fast once he had gone back to the 21st century, Saturnin Bloom had explained. Secret societies, occult groups, academics and intellectuals interested in the mysteries of the unknown and the powers of the esoteric would hear about Whitemoor Hall and seek its bottomless fountain of knowledge. He, Adam, would be the one they would ask for and he would guide them and make sure the house's secrets remain within its walls. He would be the CEO of the Whitemoor estate and would bring it up to date into the 21st century. Everything had been arranged and thought through carefully: funding, bank accounts, official papers; lists of trusted people to contact – accountants, lawyers, security agencies, even building and service companies... Adam would only have to walk in and take the helm of the whole thing. An Egyptian god had set up the equivalent of a corporation which didn't trade in money but scientific and esoteric knowledge.

The young man was acutely aware of his intimate, ancestral link with the house, but still questioned the wisdom of leaving everything to him. Had he proven himself? Not really. He doubted that he was fit for the task.

He had loved the slow, hushed existence he had had at Whitemoor Hall most days. He would miss his teaching post: no more lessons in the little study upstairs, no more walks around the estate listening to Dimitri's tales of discovery. The boy hadn't shown up yet, and Adam was wondering whether he was still at the cottage, waiting for a sign from his tutor.

Adam was only half-listening to Saturnin Bloom's last instructions now, his head full of Dimitri and Maeve... Maeve, his guardian angel! He just couldn't leave without saying goodbye. But then seeing her might just rip his heart apart...

He didn't want to leave, but he didn't have any choice, and Thoth had left him with his back against the wall: the god would counteract the curse only if Adam agreed to his side of the bargain and left the 1920s Whitemoor Hall immediately to return to the era he had come from. This and only this would save lives and prevent the catastrophe described in Dr Winston-Dunst book.

The bargain had now been done; everything had to be completed by the end of the day; afterwards, the curse would have been active for too long for it to be stopped, and it would have claimed its first victims after Vangelis Chronos. Things had to move quickly, as the floating miasma of diseased spores was loose around the estate and was hunting for a living form in which to bury itself. Adam had to go *now*.

The young man had required assurances; Thoth had only been able to give his divine word, which was not to be doubted. Once the promise had been made, he couldn't go back on it, he had claimed; his words were as good as sacred, and the estate would be spared the assault of septicemic plague at his command. Adam could step into the future – and his present – knowing that the past had been set right.

The set of keys changed hands – their heavy, metallic bulk pressed against the skin of Adam's palm; they carried the weight of the history of the house which was now made more real than ever to the tutor: he could *touch it*. His head filled with Maeve's heart-shaped face, and then, her clear, throaty voice rang in his ears.

'Adam! We're here, Adam!'

Sophia Chronos pursed her lips whilst Saturnin Bloom sighed at the necessary evil of the brief reunion – he had sent for the woman and child in a rare demonstration of compassion towards Adam.

The tutor turned round: he saw three figures advance along the path that meandered to the small coppice and the Guardian's Cottage: Ginny was walking in front, her face deprived of any emotion and looking straight ahead, her task accomplished; behind her followed Maeve and Dimitri, hand in hand. The set anguish on their faces was temporarily disturbed when they saw Adam. The tutor walked around the car to greet them feverishly; they were all fighting contradictory emotions.

'Oh, Adam, are you all right? Dimitri's told me about uncle Vange… I still cannot believe it, the silly old fool!'

Her gloved hand rose to his cheek, only to retreat before the tip of her fingers had touched his skin. She had remembered that they were not alone. Dimitri let go of her hand and seized his teacher's arm.

'Ginny said you were leaving… Take me with you, please!' implored the child, his pale face lifted towards Adam.

'You cannot leave us like this, Adam… It's too cruel!' Maeve whispered, trying not to dissolve in the sea of her own distress.

'I have no other choice, Maeve. Nothing is under my control anymore… if it has ever been.'

He had whispered the acknowledgement of his powerlessness in her ear, his cheek brushing hers, his lips almost in contact with the velvety lobe of her ear where one minuscule silver earring shone like a drop of morning dew. He inhaled deeply, trying to take in as much of her rich powdery scent as possible, to take with him into the 21st century.

'Please Mr Tuckfield, take me with you…' Dimitri was now weeping silently. He was scared to be on his own again, left with his ghosts to wander around the house and grounds of Whitemoor Hall, for how many more years? Instinctively, he took Maeve's hand again.

Saturnin Bloom had silently approached the small group.

'Come, come, Miss Hayward, Dimitri… It is time Mr Tuckfield went. He now has a much superior calling. By leaving now, he is saving your lives.'

Maeve's perfectly made-up features froze into a stunned expression. She searched Adam's face for answers.

'Adam? What does he mean?'

Saturnin Bloom stepped forward, determined to put an end to this long preamble.

'Your uncle has broken a sacred rule by reading the words of The Book of Thoth, Miss Hayward. He has been punished for his actions, but has also condemned every mortal on the estate to death. The curse is gathering strength as we speak. By going back to the 21st century to preside over the revival of Whitemoor Hall, Mr Tuckfield is giving all of you a new lease of life. The curse will be lifted as soon as he emerges on the other side of the wormhole that links our two eras. I have promised.'

'But what about *us?*' Maeve lifted her arm towards Saturnin and Adam, her hand still holding Dimitri's cold fingers. 'We want to be with you, Adam. We love you. You can't disappear like that from our lives!'

The young woman didn't want to go into hysterics; she had always loathed women who used whining, moaning and screaming to try and win something or someone back. She had dignity, she was strong! Maybe if she could go back to London and throw herself into her work and her social life, then maybe she could *forget*... But she perfectly knew she wouldn't. And now there was Dimitri...

She tightened her grip on the boy's hand. He responded to the squeeze by looking at her and they exchanged a gaze that sealed their understanding. Maeve nodded, the child blinked and sighed. They walked past Saturnin and Adam, and took their place besides Sophia Chronos and Ginny on the steps, their faces twisted by their efforts not to give in to their emotions. For a few seconds no one moved, and the only perceptible sound was that of the raindrops falling on the ground with an increasing intensity and hitting the dark stone of the house.

Adam looked at the group; his heart was swollen and ready to burst. His whole being felt like he was about to break into a thousand pieces that would scatter across the ground there on the gravel and lawn of the estate. Then his vision went blurry and people's faces started swimming in front of his eyes; he clenched his jaw, turned round and climbed inside the car, pulling the door as hard as he could. The honourable vehicle shook and jerked, and he was on his way.

Just as the car emerged from under the *porte-cochère*, it stalled. While Mr Suleman attempted to restart the vehicle, Adam turned and looked through the small round window above the back seat: something made him lift his eyes towards the tower; and that's when he saw her...

There, standing at one of the narrow windows on the second floor, was the face of a sad little girl; she was almost a shadow, but he could still make out the tangled hair and the bottomless eyes Dimitri had described to him when they had visited the tower together. She waved at him in a sorrowful goodbye gesture. Adam was surprised by the sudden movement of the car and banged his head against the glass before turning back, stunned.

As the Oxford Morris turned into the long drive that led to the entrance gates, Adam shook off his lethargy. His skin started prickling as the vortex of the wormhole began materialising, shaping itself to fit the width of the alley. 'Beech Avenue' – as the drive had been christened because of the almost military regularity of the rows of beech trees on each side of the road – started to look slightly blurry all around the car.

Adam, now aware of a strange torpor spreading through his body, rubbed his eyes before obeying a small voice in his head – he thought he had recognised Dimitri's clear tone – and once again turned round to look at the drive through the back window. He couldn't help gasping: along the section of road the car had just past through, dozens of ghostly figures had begun emerging from behind the trees; they were there and not quite there, holding themselves very straight, and moving in slow motion. They were coming from the darkness in between the trunks, their almost transparent features turned towards the car; both groups joined into one sluggish column in the middle of the road, intently starring at the vehicle as if to will it to stop.

The further the car moved along the drive, the more ghosts – for that's what they were – stepped out of the shadows in ungainly and hopeless pursuit. The effect was chilling. What would happen if for any reason the car stalled again? What would they do to him? Why was he able to see them now, and not before?

The same physical reactions as on the day of his arrival started to manifest themselves: the raised pulse, the cold sweats, the dizziness, the explosion of light and colour as the car accelerated and raced through the wormhole, shaking off its ghostly pursuers, leaving the past behind whilst rushing towards the present...

By the time the Oxford Morris reached the gates and its grinning solar and lunar guardians, Adam had lost consciousness.

EIGHT

Adam was woken up by the high-pitched tremolo of a curious blue tit perched in a nearby tree and the weak warmth of a clement autumn sun. The sky above him was pure blue. The rumbling of the engine of a plane preceded the appearance of the shiny white object with a long cloudy tail that came next in his field of vision. *The rumbling of a plane...*

Adam scrambled to his feet, his heart pounding in his ears, and stood there on the grassy verge. He looked around him groggily, trying hard to concentrate: one single narrow road, fields; the cast iron gates of the entrance to Whitemoor Hall, complete with their sinister metallic sun and moon which were shining intensely under the sun – with the high, looming wall stretching on either side. Beyond the gates, Adam could see the ribbon of the drive and its beech sentinels. The rest was hidden by the high, expanding trees of the estate.

His foot almost got caught on one of his three travel bags. One had been used as a pillow, and the soft leather still sported the imprint of his head. Was he back? Yes, he was! There were clues scattered everywhere in the landscape: the line of electric pylons cutting through the fields to his left, the half-dozen wind turbines slowly rotating in the autumn air straight ahead. Then the planes: there were several of them now, the smoke from their engines criss-crossing the sky before dissolving into the infinite blue mass.

Another engine sound started then grew louder, until he spotted a car coming along his way. He froze. *Look busy*, he urged himself. He really wasn't ready just yet to confront anybody; what would they think of his 1920s clothes?

His cheeks burning, he crouched and unzipped the bag but lifted his head just as the car went past him. It was one of those brand new, shiny vehicles, and he could have sworn that his eyes had caught the glow of a sat-nav screen and that the passenger had been on her phone. Welcome back to the 21st century.

He fished out his own mobile from the first bag and turned it on. It flashed:

Tuesday, 30th September 2014

Impossible. Now it was as if the last two months had never happened!

He was back to square one!

He idly looked at the phone which seemed to have recharged its batteries between 1925 and the present: his inbox was nagging him, with several unopened messages clamouring for his attention. He didn't feel like reconnecting immediately. He hit the 'off' key and threw the phone back onto the pile of clothes, picked up his bags and walked to the entrance.

The heavy chains were gone. He pushed one of the gates – it was heavy, squeaky and quite rusty, but hadn't lost any of its majesty. The young man hesitated as his eyes travelled along the drive until the point where it turned sharply to the right towards the house. The rows of beech trees were higher and stouter than he remembered and were still hanging on to their russet-coloured autumn leaves. The grass was incredibly high and full of weeds, anarchic edges and bushes had grown erratically. Nature had woven a cocoon around the estate to better hide and protect it from the dangers of the outside world.

Adam felt the cold finger of fear along his spine: would the ghosts suddenly appear from behind the trees as they had done on his way out? Would they swarm around him and drag him to the Underworld? He was alone, on foot, and felt incredibly vulnerable. He tried to fight his anguish and called upon his resolve. He had to return to Whitemoor Hall. He was its guardian, now. He had some work to do.

Carefully balancing the bulk of each bag, he started walking in the middle of the track: his shoes were instantly covered in white dust; it hadn't rained for ages… He sometimes kicked a random stone with the tip of his shoe, and the small lump would jump into the air, ricochet off the track several times before rolling and pausing further along the drive. Nothing stirred apart from the birds in the trees.

It took a long time to reach the point where the track changed direction to lead directly to the house. Adam slowed down just before that point and his breathing and heartbeat accelerated. No one from the outside world had been able to catch a glimpse of the house after the 1925 disaster, Dr Winston-Dunst had written. When the short enquiry had ended without neither conclusive nor satisfactory results, the various gates had been locked and no one seemed to have been able to remember who had kept the keys and where. Would Whitemoor Hall be beyond repair? Had Saturnin Bloom played a game with him? He turned the corner.

No, no game had been played at his expense: Whitemoor Hall was still there, as high and proud as it had been in 1925, if looking a little forlorn and in need of affection. Adam's eyes glided over the building, taking in the roof, the windows, the overgrown lawn, the invading ivy creeping up the walls. He started walking again, coming closer and closer, and noticing a few more details: rusty gutters, rotten window frames, curtains visibly heavy with dust...

He felt a jolt of optimism: the house was in much better condition than he had feared. If there hadn't been too many leaks, it wouldn't take that long to put it on its own two feet again and turn it into the centre of excellence it had been earmarked to become.

What would he do with the abbey now that 'The Family' had decamped to Egypt?

He followed the drive up to the *porte-cochère*: leaves, twigs and mud had accumulated against the bottom of the double entrance door and moss had invaded the stairs on which Sophia Chronos, Maeve and Dimitri had been standing the last time he had set eyes on them. His heart sank; he realised that he would never see them again. What had become of them after his departure? Had Maeve been allowed to go back to London and pursue her journalistic career? And little Dimitri: had he been able to fulfil his wishes and become an explorer? Had he managed to finish his ambitious map of the house?

He walked beyond the south corner of the building, having a peek around the service yard. He could now see the shape of the Gardener's Cottage at the top of the hill further to the east. He was thinking about walking to the abbey to make sure...

Maybe he'd get inside the house instead. Instinctively, he shook the smallest bag he was carrying: the reassuring jingle of the bunch of keys settled his worry. He couldn't really carry those bags any longer, he thought, they were cutting through the material of his clothes and rubbing against his skin; he would drop them in a sheltered corner of the service yard. He was pretty sure that nobody would turn up to steal them.

There, standing at the south-west corner of the house, his arms crossed over his chest, Adam Tuckfield breathed the air of the Somerset autumn. He was back home, in his ancestor's house. He turned round to take in the vast expanse of the estate and the wild richness of Nature. The place didn't look sinister or foreboding anymore; maybe its ghosts had left at the same time as the ancient Egyptian god Thoth had decamped for the hotter climes of the banks of the Nile. Adam then looked to the west.

That's when his heart missed a beat, then lurched, pumping blood to his face. He dropped his bags on the ground. There, further along the path, was the Guardian's coppice, and it was above the top of those trees that he saw the rising smoke... He closed his eyes, opened them again. No, he was not mistaken: there was a gentle, lazy column of white-grey smoke ascending in the clear sky. A mad hope seized Adam. He began to run in the direction of the coppice. Behind him, his mobile phone started ringing, providing a rhythm to his race.

He reached the corner of the small wood; he could smell the logs burning in the chimney! Yes, the cottage was there, in exactly the same state as it had been eighty-nine years earlier... The thatched roof, the wisteria growing in an arch over the entrance...

That's when he heard it: the 'click-clack' of the typewriter coming from inside. His legs almost gave way, then. He opened the wooden gate and put his trembling hand on the handle; his heart was beating so fast that he wasn't sure whether it would cope. He turned the brass knob and pushed the door; a mixture of vanilla, tea and burning wood reached his nose and brought tears to his eyes. They were there, the two of them, exactly as he had left them back in 1925.

At the exact moment he stumbled inside the familiar lounge, Maeve stopped typing and looked his way; Dimitri, surrounded by large sheets of paper, pencils and crayons, was amending his map of the house to fit in a new area he had recently discovered; he lifted his head, and at the sight of his tutor, he smiled widely.

Maeve shook her shiny head, stood up and, with tears of relief in her bright green eyes and a smile on her red lips, opened her arms to him.

'At last! We've been waiting for you...'

THE END

THE RIGHT PLACE

by Carya Gish

Publication: Winter 2017

Catherine 'Kat' Moorhouse is a quiet, mature 14-year-old girl interested in history and nature. She was only a baby when her mother, a musicologist from New Zealand, died in a car crash while on a research trip. Since then, she has lived on and off with her journalist father, Simon.

After a vicious bullying campaign that has left her seriously shaken and heart-broken, Kat is relieved when her father decides to move to Dorset for an indefinite period of time.

The girl feels at ease in her new environment and falls in love with the county's ancestral landscape. She is particularly drawn to St Catherine's chapel in Abbotsbury, with which she shares her name. One evening, on Chapel Hill, she meets a mysterious woman, also called Catherine, who works for a local and reclusive elderly aristocrat, Ronald Sinclair. The origins of Lord Sinclair's family are rather dubious and are the stuff of legend in the area.

As her relationship with Catherine develops, Kat finds herself at the same time fascinated and repulsed by her new friend and understands that nothing is what it seems in this idyllic part of England...

The Right Place is inspired by the Dorset landscape and history and by PJ Harvey's song 'The Wind' which is about St Catherine's chapel.

For more information about *The Right Place* and to read a free extract, go to:
www.missgish.com/the-right-place